LONG
TRAIN
HOME

LONG
TRAIN
HOME

A Novel

Jeff Houlahan

LEVEL
BEST BOOKS

First edition

ISBN: 978-1-68512-120-4

Cover art by Level Best Designs

This book was professionally typeset on Reedsy.
Find out more at reedsy.com

For Kim. Always.

Prologue

He watched from the shadows as she walked away from the Lost House. She was young and pretty and tired. From where he stood, shrouded and still, one long stride into the alley, he could see the dark circles under her eyes. It was time. Her sin would become his. His hand went under his coat and felt for the long blade strapped into the lining.

Chapter One

"You can't fly? Are you fucking kidding me?"

I can hit and I can hit with power and I can run and I can field and I can throw. I'm what the scouts call 'a five-tool' player. I can take one low and outside and turn it into two if the right-fielder jakes the play. I can jack a mistake, back-row bleachers and cherry-pop quick. I can smother a short hop like an unwanted puppy and nail a jackrabbit from shallow leftfield. But I won't get on a plane.

They can live with it if you crave the occasional long line or forget to ask for ID, and they might even overlook taking it up the ass if you can put it over the fence. But if you won't fly, you better be able to hit .400, knock in one hundred and fifty runs and never chase the high cheese.

"What the fuck does that mean? What are you telling me? You can't get on a fucking plane?"

Kevin McCarthy slammed his fist on his desk. McCarthy was the Montreal GM. My boss. He looked like an IBM executive. No, hungrier than that—like the CEO of a California start up that was going to hit it big but hadn't yet.

"Yessir."

"Have you ever flown?"

"Just once."

He stared at me for a second.

"What did you do in college?"

"I only played one year and we didn't fly much, mostly buses. When the team flew, I would drive with George."

1

"Who's George?

"Team mascot."

"What the fuck was his problem?"

"Sir?"

"George, the mascot. What was his problem?"

"He was deathly afraid, wouldn't even go near an airport. His daughter ended up becoming a flight attendant. He disowned her."

Kevin paused.

"Are you fucking with me, Ryan?"

"Yessir. About the daughter. Not about the rest."

"What was he?"

"Excuse me?"

" What the fuck was he? What kind of mascot?"

"An armadillo, sir."

"You have got to be fucking kidding me. The guy dressed up every week in an armadillo costume and he was afraid to fly? I'd be praying the fucking plane went down."

McCarthy spun his chair so he was looking out the window across the St. Lawrence, then spun it back.

"Have you seen anybody?"

"Sir?"

"You know what the fuck I mean. A psychiatrist, psychologist, whatever."

"No sir."

He reached for the phone and buzzed his assistant.

"Lara? Do you have Dr. Benedikt's number handy?"

He listened for a second.

"Right then, talk to Freddy. He'll be able to track down the number. Set up an appointment for Ryan Spencer. We'll be down there in a second and Ryan can give you some times and dates that work for him…"

He looked at me for confirmation. I shook my head. Kevin clicked the mute button but kept the phone where it was.

"What's the problem, Ryan?"

"No problem, Mr. McCarthy. I just don't need to see a psychiatrist."

"It's nothing to be embarrassed about, Ryan, I can't give you names but there are seven guys on the team seeing Dr. Benedikt for one thing or another. And your thing is just fear of flying. If I told you what a couple of those guys were…"

He paused then waved his hand.

"Never mind. Just understand that this is no big deal and nobody will know about it unless you choose to talk."

"I don't have any problem with psychiatrists, Mr. McCarthy, but it's not a psychological problem. I'm not afraid to get on a plane. I just won't."

I might have saved some time if I had got to this earlier.

The GM looked at me for a second then flicked off the mute button.

" Never mind Dr. Benedikt's number, Lara."

He hung up the receiver.

"What are you doing, Ryan? I thought we were all happy with the deal—3.4 a year for three years is a lot of money for a guy that's never put a ball in play in a professional league."

I flushed and shook my head.

"I'm happy with the deal, Mr. McCarthy. To be honest I'm not sure how I'm going to spend the money you're paying me now. In fact, I thought we could just arrange for the team to dock my salary for the games I'll miss."

He had been leaning over the table and now he settled back in his chair and looked at me.

"You'll give us money back?"

"Yes sir."

He looked at me for a long time before speaking.

"Keep the money. It's not the fucking money. I just don't like getting dicked around"

"I wouldn't do that, sir."

He continued to look at me for several seconds. He might have been waiting for me but I had nothing.

"You know what? I don't think you would. Okay then, why can't you fly?"

"Won't, sir. And it's personal."

"Won't. Can't. What's the fucking difference?"

"I'm not sure sir, I…"

"Then quit wasting our time. The Montreal Expos are on the hook for more than ten million dollars so I'm not sure how much of a personal life you get to hang on to. Why won't you fly?"

I shook my head.

"I'm sorry, Mr. McCarthy but it's personal. All I can tell you is that I made a promise."

"A promise?"

I nodded.

"To who?"

I didn't answer so he pushed forward and leaned across the desk. It was a big desk so he wasn't able to get very close.

"Ryan, you realize that this is the kind of thing that would probably allow us to void your contract, don't you? We don't have any specific clauses about flying but I expect that most judges would see a willingness to fly as an implicit expectation when you sign a contract to play one hundred and sixty-two games of baseball per summer."

"You don't need a judge, Mr. McCarthy. I'll sign anything you want. I know it's not right to spring this on you after we've signed a contract. I want to play for Montreal but if you don't want me under the circumstances, I understand."

McCarthy was mad. He thought he had wedged a titanium crowbar up my ass and would just lever hard until I popped. Instead, he was standing there with his limp dick in his hand and only one of us was going to get hurt if he leaned on that. He sat back in his chair and swung it away so that I was looking at his back. He was balding at the crown. Face-to-face, he didn't look like a guy who was losing his hair.

We sat there for thirty or forty seconds until I began to wonder if he was expecting me to leave. I shifted in my seat and the leg stand creaked. I'm not sure if he had been waiting for a sound but he immediately swung his chair back around.

"We like you a lot, Ryan. We think you're going to be a very good player. We wouldn't have invested all that money in you if we didn't think so. "

I nodded.

"But we try and avoid paying big money to high maintenance players – you get the concept of high maintenance, Ryan?"

I nodded again.

"There are lots of reasons to avoid high maintenance players, they are a lot of extra work, they tend to be streaky players, they say and do things that make me want to kick them in the face until there's brain snot coming out of one eye..."

He paused to let that sink in.

"...but the biggest deal is that of fairness. If it goes too far the other players on the team see it as favoritism and then the room goes sour and once the room goes sour it doesn't matter how much talent you have, you don't win. You understand what I'm saying?"

I was still trying to shake the image of the GM kicking me repeatedly in the head. He was going to have to catch me lying down.

"I think so, sir."

"So, I want you to tell the team that you can't fly, that you freak out, need a straitjacket, it's a terrible burden you have to carry and you're seeking psychiatric help. It's a disease that we're treating. You understand? I'll explain to Mr. Brassard. He won't want the money back. It would make him look like a tightwad and that he's punishing a player with an illness. But he's not going to be happy. The best thing you can do is start hitting on the first day and don't stop until the last game of the World Series."

The Expos had finished fifth in the East Division the season before and needed two quality starters, a good set-up man, and help up the middle if they were going to contend—I could bat 1.000 and they would probably still finish no better than third. I nodded and stood up. I stuck out my hand and there was an awkward moment while he stared at me before taking it.

"I was a lot happier the last time we did this, Ryan."

" I understand, sir. And I'm sorry to cause you more trouble than you already have."

His face softened a little.

"Part of the business, Ryan. You fucking ballplayers are all crazy. No offense."

"None taken, sir."

"Okay, that's it then. Thanks for coming by, Ryan."

It was several steps from his desk to the door and he stopped me as I pushed on the handle.

"How are you getting to Florida for spring training?"

I turned around but he was facing out the window looking across the city.

"I was going to drive, sir."

"Not a fucking chance. Take the train."

"Yessir."

I waited for more but he was finished. I think. So, I left.

Chapter Two

"**M**ove it, jelly-bean."

I was looking at a pale, hairy gut, pooching over the waistband of wrinkled Bermudas and through an unbuttoned Hawaiian shirt. I tilted my head back, careful my chin didn't rub against the front of his shorts. It was a long way up. His skull was shaved but not maintained and it matched the messy goatee around the sneer.

"What's that?"

"Sorry, bud...my locker."

I looked to both sides. There were dozens of empty lockers scattered around the room. A couple of guys looked up from what they were doing but most of the room pretended not to notice.

"This is the locker I was assigned."

He made a face.

"Carlos could fuck up a two-car parade. He should know by now this is my locker. Close to the showers, can't see it from Ballsie's office, not in Clay's line of fire if things don't go well. Plus, with the money you're making you should be able to build yourself a nice little clubhouse of your own."

Somebody snickered across the room. Other than the showers and the money I wasn't sure what the hell he was talking about but I hadn't taken my gear out of my bag yet so I just pushed my stuff down the bench to the next locker and stood up. He had to step back. Standing close he was still a couple of inches taller than me. And fifty pounds heavier. I sat down at the next locker. He waited until I was settled.

7

"Not trying to be a prick, man, but that's mine too. I need my space."

I had seen all the movies. Now I was supposed to get up in his grill and we would throw some punches and wrestle around the dressing room until the manager came in and broke it up. He would have grudging respect for me for fighting back and we would end up best buddies and leading the team to the championship. I picked up my gear and moved across the room to a stall against the far wall. He watched me, still grinning. I could feel my face going red and kept my head down. I don't know if anybody was watching.

* * *

There were only a half dozen guys out on the field, most of them, like me, in shorts and tees. It was April in Vero Beach so the thermometer was heading towards ninety, but there were still a couple of players in full uniform. The guys who knew each other had paired up and were long tossing waiting for the drills to start. I had been through this before—it was a lot like the first day at a new school—so I watched the clubhouse door. Two of the Hispanic players came out talking in Spanish and walked by me without looking but just after them, a tall blond kid with almost translucent skin and red cheeks ducked out the door. He stood looking around and almost got hit when it pushed open hard behind him. It was the big guy who had moved me with one of the guys who had been sitting nearby. They stepped around the kid and headed to an empty spot on the grass. He stood at the door looking uncertain and I went over.

"Wanna throw?"

"Sure."

We headed out to a spot in the field at the end of the line of tossing players. There were balls scattered around the field and I scooped one up as we walked. He spoke first.

"I'm Benjamin Fraser."

"Ryan Spencer."

"I know who you are."

"Yeah. It made the papers, I guess."

8

"I'll say. "

"What about you?"

He turned to me.

"What are you saying? You've never heard of me?"

"Sorry, I don't follow baseball much."

"Just kidding. They took me in the twenty-first round. I got an eight thousand dollar bonus. You wouldn't have heard of me unless you read the really small type. What do you mean you don't follow baseball much? "

I shrugged.

"I've never followed sports much."

He looked at me.

"You're a ballplayer, what do you mean you've never followed sports much?"

I shrugged again.

"It's kind of boring, no? "

"Are you kidding me? So, what do you do when you're not playing?"

"Read. Write. Play a little guitar."

"Read and write? Oh man, this is going to be good. Ballsie's going to love you."

"Ballsie?"

"Dave Balducci. The manager. You don't know who the manager of the team is?".

"Sure, I know Dave Balducci. I just didn't know that was Ballsie."

"Yeah, hard to connect those dots."

We threw the ball for about ten minutes before one of the coaches came out and gathered all the players on the infield and Balducci strolled out from the dugout to address the players. He walked into the middle of the pack and the players moved away so that there was a thin strip of empty ballfield around him.

"Well, gentlemen, it is the start of a new season."

There were a few murmurs from the players.

"Some of you have million-dollar bonus checks in your back pocket and some of you had to hitchhike from Bumfuck, Montana just to get here."

There were a couple of chuckles. Apparently bumfuck could still get a laugh. Or maybe it was Montana.

"None of that matters to me. As far as I'm concerned you are all starting from the same point. I don't care if you won twenty games for us last year or if you are coming off a twenty-loss season in A-ball, the spots on this team will be filled by the players that give us the best chance of winning."

He paused for a second and the guy who had taken my locker farted and tried to keep a straight face while he looked at the manager.

"I can see you didn't do anything about your Asperger's over the winter, McKay."

McKay turned and looked back at the speaker, a lean dark guy with thick eyebrows and a smirk.

"Fuck you and your assburger, Gionnas."

Gionnas rolled his eyes.

"You are one ignorant fuck, McKay. It's Aspergers, you 'gotta have another donut', piece of shit."

"Yeah, you just keep working on your abs, Gionnas. Do enough crunches you might be able to catch up to the gas once in a while. "

"Enough."

The manager's voice was harsh and loud.

"I'll do the talking. Gionnas. When I want to hear from you, I'll ask. And, McKay, stop acting like a jackass. This isn't grade school and we don't need a class clown. And I don't need our ace getting into it with our number one catcher."

Balducci stared down both players. Gionnas nodded and looked at the ground. McKay smirked at the guy beside him but kept his mouth shut. The manager let the silence hang for several seconds until McKay stopped smiling. Balducci returned to the rest of the players.

"So, this is a chance for all of you to show what you can do. Starting from here everybody's got the same shot at a spot on this team. Any questions?"

I looked around but nobody moved so I put up my hand. One of the guys on the other side of the circle, a big man who had a locker close to McKay's, rolled his eyes. Fuck him. Balducci stared at me for several seconds, giving me an opportunity to reconsider, then nodded.

"Mr. Balducci, I'm just curious. If we're all starting from the same spot and we all have the same shot at a spot on the team, how do you know who your ace and your starting catcher are going to be already?"

The manager's face went flat. There was a long pause. Nobody spoke. I could hear the distant whine of a truck gearing up in the parking lot. I kind of wished I was in it. Actually under it might not have been so bad.

"What's your name, son?"

He said the word 'son' like he wished he could blow the letters up to the size of his fist, sharpen all the edges and then shove them up my ass.

"Spencer, sir. Ryan Spencer."

The manager started to speak and then stopped. His mouth pursed. He started again.

"I may have spoken out of turn, son. If you've won twenty games in the big leagues—in fact, if you've won one game you probably have an edge over somebody who's never thrown a pitch to a major league hitter. Same goes if you've hit thirty home runs in the show. In fact, if you've ever stepped in against a big-league pitcher with fifty thousand fans waiting to piss on you if you strike out and managed to put one in play then you probably have an edge. But if you've had a bunch of suits chase you around like a pack of horny hounds dogging a bitch in heat and let them stroke your dick while they stuffed money in your pocket—that won't get you an edge. And being a smartass won't help much either."

I had an urge to point out where his simile/metaphor had gone awry but thought better of it. Out of the corner of my eye, I noticed Benjamin slide a step to his right.

"Yessir."

"Any more questions, Spencer? No? Anybody else? Alright, let's get started"

Balducci never took his eyes off me even as the coaches organized us into groups. They split us up by position, infielders, outfielders, pitchers, and catchers. Fraser went over with the pitchers. I should have guessed somebody that tall and spindly had to be a pitcher. I lined up with the infielders. It felt good to be handling the ball again. The first couple of sharp grounders felt awkward. I dropped one and had to scoop it up bare-handed to make the play, but it only took a couple before I started to feel the rhythm. There were four of us at third and we would each take five groundballs then step to the side to let the next guy in. The first guy stepped in without even looking at the three of us. He was Hispanic, about an inch shorter than my six foot one, ten or fifteen pounds heavier, a bit thick in the middle and heavy-legged. His face was round and soft under the chin and there were lines starting to show around his eyes, but the ball seemed to dive into his glove and he had a quick first step, reading the angle where bat would meet ball and making small adjustments before the ball was on the ground. The next two guys weren't nearly as slick and one of them, the older guy who had come out of the clubhouse talking to McKay, had stone hands and slow feet. I wasn't as smooth as the first guy, but I was pretty sure I was better than the other two. In my last set, the coach hit a sharp grounder well to my right. I took a quick step and laid out, catching the ball in the tip of the webbing so just the top half of the ball showed above the glove, pushed myself to my feet before I had stopped sliding and swiveled towards first as if to throw. I would have had the runner. The young guy whistled. The Hispanic guy and the older guy with stone hands looked at me and kept looking until I turned back to take the next grounder. The looks hadn't been friendly.

I took my last couple of easy grounders and then they called us in for some BP. A half dozen of the outfielders stayed out to shag balls and the rest of us gathered around the batting cage. The coach that had been hitting to us, an older guy who didn't talk much and who the veterans treated like a ballboy, went out behind the protective cage at the mound and started tossing. Batting practice wasn't first come, first serve. The older guys, the big-league regulars picked up bats and pushed through the crowd of players milling around the on-deck circle. They had seen the script and the rest of us hadn't.

The first player to the plate was a tall broad-shouldered guy I had seen taking grounders with the shortstops. He stood out because he was six-two and Anglo. He had soft hands and good technique but there were some balls he just couldn't get to. Now, it was easy to see why he was a big leaguer. He took the first five pitches to right field with an inside-outside swing. Four line drives, three of which dropped out of reach of the right fielder and the fifth pitch, a deep, high fly that fell into the stands about eight rows deep. Three kids waiting in the stands chased after the ball as it clattered around among the aluminum seats. The next five he hit to centerfield, putting two over the fence. Then he made a small adjustment to his stance and pulled five balls hard to left field. Only one stayed on the grass side of the wall. He finished off by spraying five balls around the infield and laying down three bunts. He walked away from the plate without speaking to anybody.

The second player up was an enormous redhead who had been taking balls with the first basemen and who started talking as soon as he got in the box.

"Get that weak shit off the mound, Charlie. Bring on one of the big dawgs."

Charlie ignored him and soft-tossed a ball over the plate that the big man smashed back up the middle just inside the guard fence missing Charlie by a few inches.

"It's your call, Charlie, but I'm going to be coming after you if you don't bring in a real arm."

Charlie threw and again the ball came up the middle and if he hadn't stepped to his left behind the fence he would have been hit. Charlie scowled and stared in at the redhead.

"Stop with the fucking hairy eyeball, Charlie. I warned you. Get me somebody that can throw the fucking ball. That rag-arm shit you throw messes with my swing."

The old coach looked in at the redhead for a second and then turned to the spot along the right-field line where pitchers were throwing. A couple of pitchers were already standing watching. Charlie raised his right arm. One of the pitchers slipped off his warm-up jacket and trotted across the field to the mound. I didn't recognize him. He took the mound and waved his hand for the redhead to step out of the way so he could throw a couple of pitches then waved him back in. He wasn't throwing full out but it was

13

still a completely different game. The ball snapped like a wet towel on cement. But we didn't get to hear that sound after the first couple of pitches because the big man teed off on everything. Every ball was pulled into the stands or popped up. One of the coaches, a pot-bellied, redfaced guy with pockmarked skin, standing along the third base line called out.

"Go the other way, Toner."

The redhead didn't even look over his shoulder.

"I don't go 'the other way,' Coach."

He stretched 'coach' like taffy on a July afternoon so that the contempt hung in the air.

The coach muttered something I couldn't hear.

"Have another beer, Billy, let me handle the hitting."

Toner popped up three in a row, getting madder and madder with each swing, before catching the last pitch clean and pulling it over the stands into the parking lot. It was a minor league park but it was still four hundred and twenty feet in the air to get over the back wall.

"Eat that, suckers."

He flipped his bat against the fence almost hitting one of the rookies and stripped off his shirt as he walked through the crowd of players heading for the dressing room.

It took more than an hour to work through the regulars and when I got to the plate, Ben Fraser was waiting to throw. I gave him a quick nod but he either didn't see it or ignored it and started into his wind-up. I had never thought much about BP, just taken my cuts and got out of the way, but I liked what I had seen the shortstop do. He looked like a pro, like he knew what he was doing. I started with an inside-out swing to right field, catching the ball weakly on the end of the bat and skittering it down the first-base line.

"Same again."

He put it in the same spot but I caught it flush this time and lined it into right field. It wasn't as clean as the drives the shortstop had hit but it was solid. I followed the flight of the ball for a second trying to sort out what I needed to do to catch it cleaner, probably shift my fe... The ball hit me

14

in the ribs and I went down hard. I lay on the ground for a second trying to catch my breath. The first couple hurt like hell and I was just trying to breathe without crying. The guy waiting to hit next was a black guy that I had heard somebody call Clayton. I looked up from the dirt at him and he stared back without expression. I looked towards the mound and saw McKay. He must have stepped in while I was admiring my line drive.

"Sorry, son. I thought you were ready."

The catcher, the guy who had gotten into it with McKay earlier, hadn't moved out of his crouch and now he looked over at the line of guys behind the cage.

"Who's up next?"

I was still on the ground but I put up my hand.

"I'm good. Just a bruise."

I wasn't sure that was true but no reason not to be hopeful. I stood up and the pain doubled me over.

"You sure?"

I looked back at him.

"Gimme a couple more."

He shrugged and settled in to take the next pitch. It was already coming when I turned back to the mound and I had to jump back to avoid getting hit in the same spot. I almost screamed. It might be more than a bruise. I stood at the plate with the bat on my shoulder staring at the mound. McKay threw another pitch that caught the inside corner. He was throwing at least his B stuff. I stood two feet off the plate with the bat on my shoulder as he threw a couple more pitches in the same spot. I just watched, not taking my eyes off him, not even thinking about swinging. The catcher spoke quietly so only I could hear.

"Hit or sit down, jelly bean."

McKay had got cocky and wasn't stepping behind the screen. I held the same pose as if I was just going to watch another ball go by but as he rocked forward I cocked the bat and committed. He put the pitch in the sweet spot and I turned my wrists over quickly so that the ball would stay low coming off the bat. I hit it flush and the ball took him high on the pitching shoulder.

I wanted to hit him. I was trying to hit him. I prayed to God to let me hit him. In that moment, if you had told me the ball would crush his face and skull to leave him diapered and spoon-fed by strangers, and that my nights would be a looping slideshow of every unforgiving revolution of the ball and my days would be shrouded in remorse, lit only by the long fuse of unquenchable regret, I still wouldn't have been able to check that sweet stroke. But it took him high on the shoulder and he dropped like pants off a hanger. It was luck. Make no mistake, I got lucky. There's no way I could be sure I was going to hit him. In fact, I wasn't positive I could get it close enough to really scare him. But I was trying. I lay the bat against the fence and went into the dressing room without waiting to see how he was.

* * *

Everybody flew out of Florida the next day and I got on the train.

Chapter Three

I woke up shouting. The train ground to a stop and I managed to get my arms up in time to avoid my head bouncing off the seat in front. Packages and suitcases tumbled from the overhead racks and there were screams as passengers were thrown forward or hit by flying luggage. I heard a woman cry out in the seat behind me but I couldn't make out what she said above the squeal of the train wheels and the voices tumbling over one another like tossed dice. I pushed up on one knee and looked behind me but in the dim light I could only make out shadows. There were shapes in the aisle that could have been packages or people. The lights came up suddenly and I had to shade my eyes. It took a second for my eyes to adjust and then I could see that it was mostly luggage between the seats but there was a man on one knee beside a woman who was sprawled face down on the floor. She wasn't moving and he had his hand on her arm. He pulled her hair away from her face and leaned forward, speaking quietly into her ear and she turned her head when he spoke. He spoke for several seconds and then she nodded and he was able to help her to her feet. There was something familiar about the man. He was ordinary looking, on the short side, a little thick in the middle, dark, receding hair, and a round friendly, intelligent face. But calm. All around him people were talking and crying and shouting and he stood speaking quietly to the woman, his face placid and composed. The woman looked dazed. Her husband pushed a lock of hair away from her eyes, kissed her on the forehead and then settled her back into her seat by the window, one hand on her arm and the other around her waist.

I sat back in my seat. Something had changed while I was sleeping. I had sat down in a seat covered in cheap blue cloth that was now thick plum velvet. The windows were smaller and the ceiling higher, with luggage racks running the length of the car and the lights were fixtures that hung from the train ceiling at three or four foot intervals rather than recessed into the walls and ceiling. The passengers were dressed differently than I remembered, most of the women wearing dresses or skirts with waist jackets and wearing or holding hats. The men were also holding hats or trying to find them scattered around the train car and almost all of them wore suits and ties. I looked down at my clothes and they were not what I was wearing when I stepped on the train. I had dressed in worn jeans, a red work shirt, and creased black dress shoes with no socks. The train had been full of people wearing a similar uniform, jeans or chinos and work shirts or t-shirts under thin sweaters. Now I was wearing brown wool pants, a tweed jacket over a thick linen white shirt, and an untied bowtie. Something had changed. Or I was dreaming.

"Ladies and gentleman!"

The voice came from the front of the car and I recognized the speaker as a porter because he was dressed like something out of the old movies that I flipped past on TV. He was wearing a charcoal grey jacket over matching pants and the white collar of his shirt stood starched and tight against his throat. His pants and jacket were rumpled and the sleeves of his suit were a little short like it had been washed at too high a temperature or perhaps didn't originally belong to him. His peaked hat sat snug and low on his head so that his eyes were shaded but I could see that they moved constantly, not resting for more than fraction of a second on anybody's face and often focused on a spot behind and over the heads of the passengers. He waited a moment before speaking again.

"Ladies and gentlemen!"

His face was blank and composed like he had no thoughts but those pertaining to luggage and correct seating and directions to the bar car. That his own life took up no space, that it was dimensionless and without coordinates. All that moved were his eyes and his lips when he spoke. He waited now for the car to quiet and it did. Then he spoke again.

18

"I'm sorry for the disturbance. We have made an emergency stop because of a tree down on the track. If anybody has injuries that require treatment we have a nurse on board who will be able to see to you. If any of your belongings have been damaged, please speak with me or one of the other porters and we will fill out the necessary forms for you to receive compensation. "

His voice, strong and assured with a trace of southern states, belied his eyes.

Several people spoke at once. He stood waiting, not trying to control the situation, just watching, expressionless, until the voices subsided again. When it was quiet he spoke once more.

"I or one of the other porters will be coming from seat to seat to discuss any of your concerns. There was no damage to the train and we will be moving again as soon as the tree is removed from the track. We will be attempting to make up the time lost over the next several hours and we expect to still arrive in St. Louis on schedule. Again, we apologize for the inconvenience and will be around to address your personal concerns shortly."

Voices rose again with questions but he walked down the aisle and pushed through the doors to the next car without looking at anybody. The seat next to me was still empty as it had been when the train left Montreal heading for Saint Louis. Part of me just wanted to fall back asleep and wake up in Saint Louis wearing jeans and red work shirt but I wasn't tired and if this was a dream I might as well enjoy it. I stepped into the aisle. There were a couple of men still wrestling suitcases out of the aisle and back into the overhead racks. I picked up a small gray satchel that had slid almost under the aisle seat beside mine and the man who I had been watching, the one who had helped his wife back into her seat, met my eye, nodded at the purse, and then to his wife. Her eyes were closed and her head lay against his shoulder. I took the couple of steps to his seat and handed him the purse. He mouthed thank you and winked like we were part of a shared joke. I nodded, not sure how to respond. I stood for a second but he had returned to writing in a small pad in his lap. I turned and left to find the bar car.

It was several cars away and by the time I found it the train was moving again and there were no seats available. Several men were standing along the bar and I pushed into a small space and waved at the bartender, darker than the porter, almost delicate with a narrow face and a spare slightly-hooked nose but the knuckles on the hand that settled on the bar were thick with scar tissue and there was at least one fresh scab. He had shed his jacket and cap but was wearing a grey vest over his white shirt.

"Yessir?"

I started to order and then realized I wasn't even sure I had money. I held up a finger to stall the bartender for a second but before I could order I heard a voice behind me.

"I'll have a Bock's, bartender and get this gentleman anything he wants."

I looked over my shoulder and the man from my car stood behind me. He spoke with an accent. I found a wallet in my pocket. I never carried a wallet but here it was, a polished worn leather billfold. I held it up.

"It's fine. I have money."

The man smiled.

"I never doubted that, young man, I would just like to buy you a drink."

I flushed.

"Right. Sorry. Sure."

There was a pause while we looked at each other and then he made a little nod towards the bar over my shoulder. I turned around and the bartender was still looking at me.

"Oh. Right. What do I want? I'll just have a Sprite."

The bartender's expression didn't change but he pulled his hands from the bar.

"Excuse me, sir?"

"Sprite? No? How about 7-Up?"

"Yessir."

The bartender leaned down and pulled a squat stubby beer with a yellow label from below the bar, wiped the crushed ice off the outside, and flipped the cap off with a quick motion. The bottle cap caught for a second on the edge of the bottle and instead of flipping back over his shoulder onto the floor, it shot forward across the bar, and without thinking I reached out and caught it before it hit a red-faced man who looked like he had been in the bar car since the trip began. I caught it just at his ear and stuffed it in my pocket. He must have felt the breeze of my hand or maybe I had grazed his ear so he turned and looked at me. I looked straight ahead pretending I didn't notice. The bartender looked at me until the man turned back to his conversation and then he gave me a small nod and a flash of a smile, like a schoolboy nudged out of line who steps quickly back into place. He emptied the beer into a tall glass and leaned across the bar to hand it to my new friend. He reached further to his left and pulled another bottle from under the bar—then took a glass from the rack above but I put my hand on his before he could pour.

"That's a 7-Up?"

"Yessir. Isn't that what you ordered?"

I pulled the bottle across the bar. It was a miniature version of the bottle that the beer had come in, stubby, brown glass but instead of a paper label, it had a white painted label '7-Up' with a woman in an old-fashioned one-piece bathing suit standing to one side of the logo. I turned the bottle around and read the slogan 'A fresh-up drink. For the stomach's sake do not stir or shake. You like it, it likes you.'

"No, that's fine. I'll just drink from the bottle."

"You'll need it opened first, sir."

"Right."

I handed it back to the bartender and he flipped the cap off and handed it back before looking over my shoulder.

"That will be $1.10, sir."

A buck and ten for a beer and a soft drink—I was dreaming or had ended up on some nostalgia tourist train ride by accident.

"Cheers." The man had his glass raised and I raised my bottle and tapped it.

Even saying that single word I could hear the strong Italian accent

"Thanks very much, mister."

I stuck out my free hand.

"Ryan Spencer."

The man gave a small bow and took my hand.

"A pleasure to meet you, Ryan Spencer. My name is Rico Fermi."

It took me a second but now I knew where I had seen him, in Physics class on the first day when the professor had talked about and shown pictures of the great men of science.

"Enrico Fermi? The Enrico Fermi? "

He smiled.

"The Enrico Fermi? That's lovely and very kind but all that I am very sure of is that I am an Enrico Fermi."

"The Enrico Fermi who won the Nobel Prize for Physics?"

The man looked at me still amused.

"Hmmm. A young man who reads the back pages of the newspaper. How unusual."

"And the history books."

The man looked at me for a long second and I realized later he was probably checking to see if I was making fun.

"Time will tell. It's only been three months since I first held the medallion."

"Three months? What year is this supposed to be?"

"What year is it *supposed* to be? The year is 1939."

He looked at me closely again.

"Are you all right, Mr. Spencer? Did you bang your head when we stopped so suddenly? Should we perhaps sit down?"

I was about to ask if he was playing a part, if we were riding on a travelling re-creation like the Civil War re-enactments but I stopped myself. It was him. My physics professor had been obsessive about the history of physics, our final exam had included photographs of 'the giants', whom we had to identify. This was not an actor playing a part. This was Enrico Fermi. I had recognized him when I had first seen him and the only thing that had prevented me from knowing it was Fermi was that it couldn't be. But it was. He was staring at me, waiting. So, I was dreaming. But even in a dream who squanders the opportunity to talk to Enrico Fermi?

"No, No, Mr. or is it Doctor….? Or Herr Professor? I.."

"Rico, is fine Mr. Spencer. If you were in one of my classes perhaps Dr. Fermi but here…" He waved his arm around the smoke-filled bar car. He shrugged.

"Sure. Rico. Right ." I looked at him for a second.

"This may be difficult for me, Dr. Fermi…talking to one of the greatest minds of the twentieth century and calling him Rico. I played Pony League ball with a guy named Rico and he was never sure how many people were in the Three Stooges."

"I'm not familiar with the Three Stooges, Mr. Spencer, but my guess would be three."

"Please. Call me Ryan. Larry, Curly, and Moe? "

I slapped my forehead fast with both hands several times and then pretended to poke him in the eyes with two fingers.

He stared at me. I was losing him. I could wake up any minute and I would have used my five minutes with Enrico Fermi trying to explain the Three Stooges. I waved my hands, trying to wipe away the last couple of minutes.

"I'm very sorry, sir. Rico. I'm just a bit nervous talking to you. Could we find a place to sit down? I would love to talk about your work, neutrinos, weak interaction theory, the Manhattan Project."

"You have read my work?"

"Well, not much of the primary literature, mostly, from textbooks."

"Textbooks? My work is in textbooks? "

Oh yeah. 1939. Fermi had only published his work on neutrinos in the last several years and his weak interaction theory was even more recent. And the Manhattan Project hadn't really begun yet. I was going to have to be careful.

"Well no, not textbooks exactly. My professor was very current. He read the latest works and would create his own course notes. He was very taken with your work."

"Indeed, What was his name? Perhaps I know him."

Shit.

"Baldacci. David Baldacci."

23

"Italian?"

Fuck.

"Uh, yes. I guess he must have been but I think he was born in the US. I believe his family had been here for many years."

"Hmmm. Still. It's unusual that I don't know that name. I thought I knew most of the academics in this field."

"Oh. He didn't do much research. I don't think he published at all. He was a teacher."

Fermi shrugged.

"Well, we need teachers. And he sounds like a good one."

Two men had just stood up from their bench seat and moved to the bar and I made a gesture towards the empty seats. Fermi nodded.

"After you, young Ryan."

I think he didn't want to get trapped against the window.

"So, how are you enjoying America?"

He smiled again.

"It's an interesting country. I admire its energy but I worry for its naivete."

"Sir?"

He waved his own comments away.

"I've only been here a few months, I should not be commenting on your country."

"I'm a Canadian."

"Ahh. I have a cousin in Toronto. Are you from there?"

"No. But not far. I'm from a small town just outside of Ottawa. Do you know Ottawa?"

"Yes, Ryan. I know the capital of Canada. What are you doing here?"

"I play baseball, sir."

His face lit up.

"Ah, the baseball game. It is an extraordinary game. Physics in slow motion. Masses, forces, velocities, accelerations, and trajectories, it is a game made for the observant physicist. I wish I had played. For me, it was only football. Or rather soccer."

"You played, sir?"

He smiled again.

"All Italians play football …or they are not Italians. Even clumsy, short-legged bookish boys."

"I'm sure you're being modest." He couldn't have been more than forty and he looked fit and strong.

He laughed out loud.

"Well, there's no way for you to check so as far as you need to know I ran like a wild horse. But those days are done."

"Are you just visiting America, sir?"

"I am working in New York City. At Columbia University."

"Working on what?"

He looked away over my shoulder. I knew that Fermi had been one of the first to understand the implications of Einstein's work on nuclear fission. I knew also that Fermi had begun working with several other scientists on how to release and control the energy stored in atomic nuclei, work that would develop into the Manhattan Project and ultimately Hiroshima and Nagasaki. He looked away for a long time then back to me.

"It wouldn't interest you."

"Are you sure?"

He looked at me hard then, his close-set eyes narrowing a little.

"You are a curious young man. Why would you not believe me when I say that it wouldn't interest you?"

"Well, your work has always fascinated me, I can't imagine this would be any different."

"What of my work?"

"Well, weak interaction theory."

"Excuse me?"

"Weak interactions? Beta decay?"

"Ah, beta decay." He looked away again.

"And weak interactions. We did discuss the weakness of the interactions although I don't think we ever talked of 'weak interaction theory'. Where did you find this term?"

"I'm not sure. I must have read it somewhere."

He smiled slightly.

"Perhaps your professor coined it."

"Maybe."

There was a short pause.

"Do you understand my thoughts on beta decay, Ryan?"

"Not completely, sir. I know is has something to do with how non-charged particles interact – interactions that aren't related to electromagnetic forces..."

He sighed.

"Yes. Those damn ghosts."

"Ghosts?"

"The elusive neutrino. It all makes sense if the neutrino exists."

"Oh, it exists. The neutrino exists. Reines and Cowan discovered it..."

"Who?"

Shit. I had forgotten the timelines. It would be decades before they would confirm the existence of the neutrino. I looked at him unable to think of a way to answer. There was a long pause before he prompted.

"Reines and Cowan?"

" I misspoke. I was thinking of the neutron, not the neutrino."

"He tilted his head and looked at me for a long second and then shrugged.

"Fine. You misspoke."

He returned the hat he had been holding on his knee to his head.

"I should be returning to my seat. My wife will be wondering..."

I put my hand on his arm

"Enrico, can I ask you what may seem like an odd question?"

He smiled and nodded.

"I think I have been well prepared for such a question these last several minutes."

"You know Einstein's work well?"

"I have read all of his work and most of it several times. Is that enough to say I know it well...?"

He shrugged.

"I would always like to know it better."

"But you know it well?"

"As well as any physicist and probably better than most."

"Does his work really suggest that travel through time is possible?"

He looked at me for a long time.

"Why this question?"

I forced myself not to look away.

"Time travel. It's a fascinating idea."

He paused again.

"You begin by asking me what year it is. You appear not to recognize the drink you ordered. Then you tell me with great certainty that neutrinos exist and mention the surname of a young student from New York University who recently attended a lecture I gave at Columbia. A young man who appears promising but has barely begun in physics. And then you ask me about time travel because 'it's a fascinating idea'. "

He stopped and looked at me. I stared back. Finally, he shrugged.

"Alright. It is true that the general theory suggests that under unusual circumstances one could travel across time. It is difficult to conceptualize without practice but the theory suggests that if you could move faster than the speed of light then you could move backward in time. But, of course, that is in reference to another specific observer. That is one way. Although there is great disagreement over whether faster than light speeds can be reached and what the consequences would be if they could. The general theory also suggests that closed time loops could be created. That is, all time past and future is connected on a long loop so that the future eventually curls around and connects to the past. In theory, this would allow travel from the future to the past but this is all speculation. There is no evidence that under realistic conditions closed time-loops are formed. Einstein's theory also implies that theoretical tunnels could exist in space-time that would have properties whereby if one end of the tunnel was moved at close to the speed of light away from its starting point and then back to the starting point while the other end remained stationary the moving end would have aged less than the stationary one to an external observer but inside the tunnel, time would stay synchronized despite the motion. Thus, somebody who entered at the accelerated end and travelled through the tunnel to the stationary end would exit 'in the past.'"

He had looked away while he was describing these options but now he looked back.

"But all of these are theoretical and if you are asking me do I think they are realistically possible I would answer, no."

He could see the question coming and held up his finger.

"For one simple reason. For the same reason that I am skeptical of life elsewhere in the universe. If man can travel through time why have we not met even one time-traveler? Where are the tourists from other eras? I have not met a man from the thirty-fifth century for the same reason I have not met a man from another planet. They do not exist."

He looked at me for several seconds.

"Although I have less confidence in my argument than I had when I stepped on this train."

He put his hat on his head then and stood up.

"I must see to my wife now. It has been a pleasure talking with you, Ryan."

* * *

I sat for several minutes and the bar car thinned out as men headed back to their seats. The train was slowing a little and I looked at my watch—not the watch I had been wearing when the train had pulled out at one PM, it had a heavy silver bezel, a silver link band, and a dust cover that I flipped open—it was 8:40 and we weren't due into Penn Station until after midnight. This must be Albany.

When I returned to my car, Fermi was sitting beside his wife. Both of them were awake but not talking. Fermi was reading and making occasional notes in his small pad. He didn't look up, either he didn't notice me or he wanted to avoid further conversation. I started to slide into my seat and stopped. I had been in the window seat and the aisle seat had been empty but now my window seat was taken. It looked like somebody had dumped dirty laundry in a haphazard pile but when I looked a little closer I realized

28

there was a body inside the tangle of shirts, sweater, and pant legs. I sat down and then nudged the kid's shoulder, but he didn't move. I nudged him again.

"Quit pretending, kid, I saw your eyes open already."

He opened one eye again and looked at me. But he didn't speak.

"That's my seat."

He didn't answer.

"You have a fight with your folks and run off?"

Still no answer.

"Look you can't just sit here for the rest of the trip. Your parents are bound to be looking for you."

Not to mention now that I was sitting beside him I could smell him. And he didn't smell good.

But still no answer.

"Okay, then you just hang tight for a second, kid. I'm going to go find the porter and we'll get you back to your proper seat. He'll know where you belong."

"No."

He sat up then. He wasn't very old, maybe twelve or thirteen. He wore coarse jeans, what I always thought of when I heard the word dungarees—although I wasn't exactly sure what dungarees were—which he had rolled up at the cuff several times. He had on two shirts, I could see both collars, and a sweater tied by the arms around his waist, and a small tight knitted hat that looked a little like a watchman's cap but was homemade and not very well. Every piece looked like it could use a day off. I was already out of my seat when he spoke. I looked down at him. He was trying to keep his face strong and defiant, but I could see the small shake around his lip and the reddening around his eyes.

"I don't have a ticket."

I sat back down.

"How did you get on the train without a ticket?"

I could see his jaw clench and he shook his head.

"Look kid, we aren't negotiating here. You tell me how you got on this train and why or I'm going to go talk to the porter. You've got no stick."

"Shit. Fucker."

He turned away to the window. In the reflection, I could see his eyes fierce but wet staring out into the night.

"You're call, kid." I stood up.

"I got on when the train was stopped. Back there when the train stopped for the tree."

"That was in the middle of nowhere. What were you doi...oh."

The kid kept staring out the window.

"How did you get the tree across the track."

"I had a little axe. It ain't hard to cut a tree down. I left it in the bush back there. Figgered if I got caught sneaking on a train with an axe it might go pretty bad."

"But you had to get the tree across the tracks."

"Weren't so hard. I'm stronger than I look."

"Then what?"

"Easy as shit then. Them porters stand outside smoking. They're supposed to keep an eye out but they're more interested in smoking and talking than watching. I just stay down in the long grass until they aren't watching and then hop the train."

"Where you headed?"

He turned then and looked at me like I was stupid.

"Same place you are, Mister."

"What's waiting for you in New York?"

His jaw clenched again and he shrugged.

"Nothing much."

I decided to take another tack.

"How old are you?"

"Sixteen."

"Try again, kid."

He scowled and turned back to the window.

"Talk to me or meet the porter."

"Fourteen." Without turning around.

"You sure?"

"I'm small for my age."

'And stronger than you look."

"That's right, mister. You laughing at me?"

I was. Kind of. But I shook my head.

"Okay, fourteen years old and sneaking on a train. What are you doing?"

"My folks died in a car accident and I'm trying to get to my uncle's place In Iowa."

It sounded like bullshit to me but I left it.

"Okay here's what we're going to do kid. When the porter comes around, you pretend you're asleep. I'll tell him you got on in Albany and you must have had a ticket because they let you on but now you're sleeping. If he makes me wake you up, you look for your ticket and pretend you lost it. I'd say you were with me but I'm pretty sure he's going to remember that this seat was empty from Montreal to Albany."

The kid nodded. Within a few minutes, he was asleep or pretending to be. I closed my eyes but couldn't sleep. Can you fall asleep in a dream? And then dream again. Was it like the Russian dolls, a dream inside a dream inside a dream? One reality and a thousand, a million, a billion illusions? One real man and a thousand, a million, a billion imagined shadows populating a desert that extends from ocean to distant ocean?

The boy slipped past me. Even awake, I almost missed it. It was only the edge of his sweater brushing my knee that caught my attention. I opened my eyes but only to narrow slits. I could see his legs and he stood in the aisle for several seconds. I couldn't tell without turning my head but I was sure he was watching me. I kept my head and my breathing even and he moved away down the aisle. The lights had dimmed again and the passengers were sleeping or staring out the window into the darkness. There were almost no sounds in the car beyond the rustling and coughing of people moving in their sleep. I twisted my head around the side of my seat and watched the kid disappear into the car behind us. We were near the end of the train so he didn't have very far he could go in that direction. I stood up and followed him. Fermi had his eyes closed and his wife's head rested on his shoulder.

31

I couldn't figure out what the kid was doing. Why move around the train and risk drawing attention to yourself if you were just trying to get to New York and then on to Iowa? I stood at the glass door leading into the neighboring car and watched him push through the next set of doors. I followed him, stumbling over a foot stuck into the aisle and had to catch my balance. The man cursed but I kept moving. By the time I recovered, the kid had moved into the space between the cars but not into the next car, so that now he was only inches away from me, separated by a pane of glass. I couldn't see what he was looking at but his posture was rigid, his arms directly down at his sides and his fists clenched and unclenched again and again. He stood for a minute or more without moving except for his hands. Finally, he reached out and his fingers rested on the door handle for a second. His hand jerked and spasmed as if he has grabbed a downed power line and then he turned back the way he had come pushing at the accordion doors separating us. I twisted to the side and fell into an empty seat but he was seeing nothing when he walked past. His head was up but tears streamed down his face and he bumped against the sides of seats several times on his way down the aisle.

I stood up and moved through to the swaying platform between the cars. The kid had been looking into a car that was used by the crew. The window of the door was curtained but the curtains were parted so that there was a four or five inch space through which I could see into the room. There was only one man in the room although there were playing cards and a couple of glasses sitting on a table to one side of the bunks. The man was asleep on the lower berth of a bunk. He slept on his back with one hand behind his head and the other resting across his stomach. My eyes were drawn to the hand I could see, stained with black grease and with a fresh scrape along one knuckle. It was the hand of a working man, scarred and calloused with thick square nails, one black and peeling and ready to come away from the skin, and the tip of the pinky tilted away at an odd angle like it had been broken and not healed properly.

He was a big man although it was hard to tell how big lying down. His face was pale and sagged a little at the cheeks and chin. His hand jerked like

32

it will sometimes when we're sleeping but when I looked back to his face his eyes were open and looking directly at me. His expression didn't change and he didn't look away. I could have imagined that he wasn't really seeing me—that he had been snatched from sleep and was still seeing the dream he had been in, spinning out like ribbon from a rolling spool except that his eyes were cold and clear and knowing. I was struck still for a second but then nodded. His face was unflinching and impassive. He just watched me. I turned away and went back to my seat. When I got there the boy was asleep or feigning it.

I must have slept too because I was awoken by a porter, a different porter than had announced the tree on the track.

"Excuse me, sir, do you mind waking the passenger next to you. I must see his ticket."

He spoke softly but the car was quieter even than it had been and his voice sounded loud.

"Do you think we could leave him? He's my nephew. He boarded at Albany and I was coming from Montreal and agreed to meet him and bring him to my sister's in New York. He definitely had his ticket in his hand when he came aboard. "

The porter was unconvinced.

"Your nephew?"

He looked from my well-cut clothes to the rags that the kid was wearing. I nodded.

"My sister and her husband are separated and the boy's father drinks too much and has trouble holding a job but will only let my sister have him for the summers."

The porter still wasn't entirely convinced but wasn't able to see what my angle might be.

"That's fine, sir, but I will need to see his ticket when he awakens."

"Certainly."

The porter walked away but the boy still didn't stir. I fell asleep beside him. When I awoke we were pulling into Grand Central and it was 2010 and the boy was not beside me nor were Enrico Fermi and his wife sitting across and two rows back from me.

Chapter Four

It was a close call. Even million-dollar bonus babies can hear the sound of splintering ice when they put a twenty-game winner on the DL for two months. The only thing that saved me was that nobody was really sure that I had done it on purpose. Look, they were a little bit right. You could strap McKay to a cross and plant him sixty feet and six inches from the plate and I could pound balls off a tee and be lucky to hit him ten times in a hundred swings and probably never hit him in the pitching shoulder... but I would have been happy to try.

So, if Lee Harvey couldn't shoot straight does that mean that JFK died by accident?

McCarthy called me into his office and Balducci called me into his, but what could they say? I was just trying to get good wood on the ball. But things went south with the team.

The clubhouse had its neighborhoods. The Latinos hung out together in the lockers by the entrance. They spoke Spanish and played loud dance music, heavy on the bass and autotuned but often with accordion out front. There was a crew of older guys with wives and kids who had lockers in the far corner away from the showers and Balducci's office. The young guys vying for spots had ended up in a line along the wall. The three black guys had a set of lockers about four down from my locker. The rednecks had staked out their territory in the corner by the shower entrance and MacKay was sheriff. The exceptions were, Nick Fagan, the big shortstop I had seen on the first day. And me. We sat alone. Nobody spoke to me unless they had to. I wasn't sure what Nick's story was.

I had this fleeting thought that dropping McKay would earn me a fist bump or two. The guy was a prick, anybody could see it. If he hadn't had a ninety-five mph fastball he would have been the guy handling the bolt gun in a slaughterhouse…because he liked the sounds and smells… and the cows didn't make him feel stupid…most days. Instead, he threw filthy smoke and thought he was clever because every time he opened his mouth somebody nodded. I had figured his posse—a crew of deep-fried peckerwoods who played third person shooter and listened to country or heavy-metal—would be pissed. But the Hispanics hated me too because I was after one of their guy's jobs …and I had DL'ed their best pitcher. The rookies hated me because we were battling for jobs and I had a juicy contract and a leg up on a roster spot…and I had DL'ed their best pitcher. The black guys kept to themselves… and I had DL'ed their best pitcher. Everybody else was pissed because I had put a twenty-game winner on the shelf.

The first day after they stretchered McKay off the field I showed up forty-five minutes before we were due on the field. I could hear the clubhouse as soon as I stepped into the hallway—Latin music and loud voices. I came around the corner into the room and the talking stopped—the music kept pulsing but nobody spoke. Most guys looked away, but Tom Akins, one of McKay's boys, a quiet brooding guy who made even his friends a little nervous, stared until I was by him. I shoved my gym bag into the cubby, stuffed my book into the top shelf, and sat down. Akins and two more of McKay's boys, Hank Stoltz and Blee Fanteaux, watched me from across the room. I looked over and then looked away.

"What are you reading?"

It was Fagan—his locker was further along the wall. I reached up behind me to pull down the book and turned the cover so he could see—*A Confederacy of Dunces*. He smiled small.

"Sounds about right. You like New Orleans?"

"Never been."

"Nice town."

He went back to taping his ankles. Things went like that for a couple of weeks – an occasional word from Nick but that was it. Who knows – maybe if I had made it through spring training without anything else happening, things might have come around. But that's not how it went.

One of Mackay's crew, Riley Cooper, had dragged in a set of antlers and hung them over his locker. He was a good-looking kid who had made a bet that he could sleep with ten different women during training camp and the rules were that he had to have photographic evidence. The antlers were from an eleven-point buck and he was hanging printouts of his successes off each point. I'm not sure whether it took Nick two weeks to notice or two weeks to do something about it but he was watching as Cooper hung the fourth photograph. Riley made a big production out of pulling the picture out of his back pocket, unfolding it and flattening it carefully on the wooden seat of his locker then threading it onto one of the points so that the white-grey nub poked out between the girl's naked legs. She couldn't have been more than eighteen years old. It was like Fagan had been waiting and as soon as Riley spiked the picture on the antler Nick stood up and walked across the room. He didn't say anything or even look at the guys scattered around the locker, just pulled the pictures off the rack one at a time, not ripping them but pulling them off so he didn't do any more damage than had already been done by the horns.

There were five guys sitting in a semi-circle, MacKay, Cooper, two of our starters Hank Stolz and Blee Fanteaux, and Akins, but none of them moved. Nick's face was expressionless but we could all feel it. Fagan was vibrating. Once he had removed all four sheets of paper he placed them face down in a neat pile on an empty locker seat. Then he reached up and grabbed the base of each antler, testing them gently before bracing himself and ripping the antlers from the wall, tearing a chunk of drywall out and exposing the wood framing beneath. Chips of paint and chalk dust flew down from the wall and Cooper, Mackay and Akins had to scramble out of the way so as not to get hit by the rack as it swung down off the wall.

The weight almost pulled Fagan over but he caught himself. He set the trophy down on the floor and I think they thought it was over. They weren't feeling it. Nick walked over to where Enny Ramirez was sitting by his locker. He had been working on one of his bats but now he slid out of the way and

Fagan reached around behind him to get one of the two bats waiting to be sanded. Nick walked back over to the antlers and started swinging. The rest of MacKay's crew had stood up when Nick came back and Riley started to speak but then realized they were only getting up to move away and he shut up and moved with them. Nick swung hard and methodically and it went on for what seemed like several minutes but was probably no more than forty-five seconds. Of course, forty-five seconds is a lot of time to beat on a set of antlers. Balducci came as far as the door of his office and watched. Nick was breathing hard when he was done but his expression hadn't changed. He stared down at the pile of dust and bits on the floor for several seconds and then turned and walked back to Ramirez. The bat was still in one piece but there were several dents in the meat of the bat and I could see a place where a long splinter had come loose.

"Sorry, Enny"

"S'okay, Nick."

Fagan turned and started back to his locker but then turned around—none of us were sure what would happen next and all five guys took a step away from him but he just bent down, picked up the pictures, crumpled them in his hand, and threw them into the garbage can beside the shower door.

I began to clap loud and slow from where I sat and then stood and continued to clap for a minute or more. Nobody joined me. Yeah, I'm pretty sure that didn't help.

* * *

Managers don't like rookies. Rookies are all about potential and potential gets managers fired. The last thing that a manager wants is a talented team that isn't ready to win—you put a bunch of first-round draft choices in a lineup and they finish sixth? You better have your resume up to date. And rookies are almost never ready to win. What do you think Willie Mays hit in his first full major league season? .274 with twenty home runs and sixty-eight RBI's. Not bad but if he's your cleanup hitter, you're in last place. If he bats seventh, you win the pennant. How about Hank Aaron? .280, thirteen home runs, and sixty-nine RBI's. The 1954 Milwaukee Braves placed third because Aaron spent too much time in the heart of the lineup. Barry Bonds? He batted .223 with sixteen home runs and forty-eight RBIs. If he bats eighth you finish first, if he bats third you finish last…Pittsburgh finished last. Management wanted me batting third or fourth.

But I was hitting the ball hard. There's only one way to get good at bats against quality pitching and that's to wait for your pitch. I was always working the count—with three balls and no strikes, my 'swing zone' wasn't much bigger than a grapefruit. The pitcher had to put it right in my wheelhouse, in a spot where it was going to be off or over the wall. At oh and two I was using the whole strike zone and slapping the ball around like a pale Rod Carew. Never saw the man play except on tape—he retired well before I was born—but I had watched lots of tape. I have never seen a player that hit quite like Carew. All art, no muscle. It was a feminine game—he would hate that, but I admired it. It wasn't about getting all jacked up, veins bulging and jaw muscles knotted…huffing, puffing, and then swinging to bring down the house. It was precise, surgical, tidy, and shone a light on the guy crossing the plate not the guy standing at first base adjusting his socks. The only guy I ever saw who reminded me of Carew was Ichiro—the same single-minded discipline, the same commitment to placing the ball exactly where he wanted it. I've been around the game long enough to know that a player's character on and off the field don't necessarily match up—I knew a guy in college—bases loaded, tie game in the bottom of the ninth, three and oh count—would swing for the fences. But he couldn't pass a homeless guy in the street without handing over his last ten dollars. And his roommate? Always moved the runner over but would steal the last nickel out of a blind man's cup. So, was Carew a saint or sinner, who knows? But he played a monk's game. Sparse, humble and offered to a greater god than a Saturday afternoon baseball crowd. He walked the path of forgotten angels to wherever it led and he couldn't be bought for a twenty-five dollar ticket no matter how many times it got paid.

Yeah. So, Balducci didn't talk to me…at first. He got friendlier as training camp wore on. He watched me whack it and rack it for about two weeks before deigning to speak. That third week he stood behind the cage and watched. After the fourth consecutive rope to right field he said,"Nice stroke, son, might want to bring the back foot in a little."

I looked back at him and nodded. But I didn't move my feet. The fucker only had 117 at-bats in the majors and he hit .207—I could hit .207 wearing a live badger as a hat. But it was nice to get a civil word. After that, he stopped by the batting cage once in a while. He usually dropped a couple of pearls of wisdom. I paid no attention to his advice but he didn't seem to notice and never gave the same advice twice. He even stopped by my locker a couple of times. The conversation usually went something like,

"How you feeling, son?"

"Fine, sir."

"Everybody treating you fine? Your apartment okay?"

"Yessir, everything's fine."

"You let me know if you have any problems…if anything comes up that's causing you trouble."

"Yessir. I will, sir."

"Okay then. You keep it up, son. You're doing just fine."

"Yessir."

One time he looked down at the book on the bench and then back up at me.

What the fuck's a garp?"

"It's just a name, sir."

He looked at the book again.

"Go easy on the reading. Hard on the eyes."

"Yessir."

He looked like he wanted to say a little more but then turned and walked away. I stopped reading in the clubhouse for a couple of weeks.

We had a decent spring, winning more than we lost. I batted .312 with eight home runs, eighteen RBIs and twenty-one walks in twenty-seven games. Half the time I was hitting off A or AA pitching but that's still pretty good hitting. The big redhead, Barton Toner, crushed thirteen home runs in twenty-four games and struck out twenty-nine times and Fagan hit .379

with nine home runs and a bunch of walks. The regular third baseman, Jaime 'Jimmie' Munoz, had a tough training camp and that wasn't making me more popular. Munoz was having trouble getting the ball out of the infield and every time I cranked one out of the park the team made a point of not gathering to congratulate me. Even the other rookies got the word. It's a long trip around the bases when even the guy on the on-deck circle won't look at you.

My sixth home run was a walk off tenth inning shot and as I came around third base I saw that most of the guys were picking up their gloves and heading for the clubhouse. A couple had already disappeared into the tunnel. Balducci stood with one leg up on the dugout looking out at the field, he was shaking his head but wouldn't look at me. I think he was embarrassed. I know I was. Spring training was big business these days and there were more than ten thousand fans in the stadium, and they were all standing on their feet cheering and wondering why there was nobody at home plate to greet me.

I'm not sure where it came from but I started yelling and jumping up and down as I moved down the third base line towards home plate. Screaming and laughing like a maniac. Guys looked up in the dugout from where they were gathering their stuff but I just kept shouting and laughing and acting like I was trying to avoid getting mobbed so that I could make sure I touched home plate. About ten feet short of home plate, I fell to the ground as if I had been brought down by the weight of players jumping on me and hugging me. The crowd had gone silent and the players from the other team who had started heading for their dugout stopped now and watched me. My teammates stopped moving toward the tunnel and Stoltz dragged McKay back out of the tunnel and they pushed to the rail to get a look. I squirmed in the dust as if I was trying to get out from underneath a pile and pushed myself along the dirt on my back with one foot, reaching out with one hand for the plate but still falling far short of touching it. Balducci had moved off the steps and I could just see the top of his hat behind the line of players at the rail as he moved the length of the dugout and into the tunnel.

"Enough guys, enough! I have to touch the base or the run doesn't count.

Let me get some air!"

I just kept laughing and pushing with the one leg inching closer to the plate. This went on for ten or fifteen more seconds, me laughing and inching through the dust pushed along by one foot. Ten or fifteen seconds can seem like a very long time…in front of ten thousand stunned, standing, silent fans. The home plate umpire spoke quietly.

"Just touch home plate, son. Everybody gets the point."

I stopped pushing myself through the dirt and looked up at him.

"You think?"

He nodded.

"Too much?"

He shrugged.

I stood up and brushed myself off. I made a pretty good production out of it, slapping out every bit of dirt I could find and then jumping on home plate with both feet before walking down into the dugout, pushing past the players, eyeballing every last one of them as I went by. Nick Fagan was sitting where he always sat and he didn't look at me but he was smiling. I didn't mind him. He didn't stand up for anybody's home runs.

You're probably thinking that everything changed after that? Not a chance. Nothing changed. Nobody came out to greet me after home runs. Nobody spoke in the locker room. The only difference was that nobody left the dugout before they had a chance to see if I would go crazy again. I didn't. Timing is everything.

* * *

There was one last bit of strangeness before we broke camp. A travelling carnival landed in town. It was about ten days before the end of training camp and most of the cuts had been made. I already knew I had a job—they don't pay you a guaranteed 3.4 million and then send you to the minors. And I was tattooing the ball. We had practiced in the morning and then been given the rest of the day off so I decided to go to the fair. I'm not exactly sure why, I've never been a big fan of carnival rides. And I wasn't about to go on one alone. Is there anything sadder than a guy stepping all alone onto a Ferris wheel? How about that guy stepping off one? I always figured they were failed suicide attempts. They sat there swaying at the top as the carny let couples off below and just couldn't get up the nerve to stand up and step off. It's bad enough to be alone in the world but to be alone and have no finish had to be a bitch. So, I didn't go for the rides. Maybe, it was the food. I've always been a sucker for deep-fried and sauced. Doesn't really matter what…chicken wings, pork balls, egg rolls, tacos, pierogies. Even onion rings. I draw the line at zucchini, the ratio of chlorophyll to hydrogenated carbons was just too high. And then follow the greasefest up with cotton candy and half a pound of fudge and I was balanced on the narrow picket fence between shame and bliss. Who knew they were neighbors? They are.

Or maybe it was the girls. I don't chase girls. It's not like I haven't had chances although not as many as you might think. I'm just waiting for the right girl. But that doesn't mean I don't like to look. And girls dress for looking at the fair. It might have been gingham dresses and bonnets in the old days but it's tight tees and Daisy Dukes these days and I'm okay with that.

It could be the games. I can throw and I can't stay away from the milk bottles and the baseballs. None of the scouts had really noticed because they always showed up to watch me hit but I could get my fastball up over ninety if I was pushed. I didn't have the freakish ninety-eight, ninety-nine, one hundred mile per hour velocity but with work, I could have got it up around ninety-four or ninety-five. And even ninety or ninety-one is major league if you have another pitch or two and you can locate the ball a little bit. And I could locate the ball. And I could make the ball move.

When I was a kid we would call it 'double-jointed' when somebody could do something weird with their body—put their foot behind their head while they were standing up, lie on their stomach and pull their feet up around their ears—but double-jointed is the kind of bullshit that nine-year-olds make-up. Turns out that the real term is hypermobility and there is something about our tendons, ligaments, connective tissue that gives us a wider range of mobility. I was pretty flexible but there was actually something weird about my wrists. I could rotate them in either direction way further than most people could—if I put my hand out palm down and twisted it counterclockwise I could turn it almost three hundred and sixty degrees so that I was looking at the back of my hand again. There is a much tighter range of motion in the clockwise direction but I could still turn my hand almost 180 degrees so that my palm pointed to the sky. And I had big hands. Way bigger than you would expect for my size. I had been able to palm a basketball since I was fourteen. I'm not sure if what they say about big hands is true—I've never had an independent appraisal. It's not like I need to buy special pants.

Anyway, it meant that when I threw the ball I could get it to do some strange stuff. In fact, I couldn't throw the ball straight. It always ended up tailing one way or the other but I knew exactly how and how much it would tail. So, I had a decent fastball and then I had about three or four other pitches that just differed based on how I held the ball and how I snapped my wrist. My curveball dropped like a dead man down a well—if it was waist high twenty feet from the plate it was going to end up in the dirt. My slider was brutal because I threw it almost as hard as my fastball but it slid left like a car losing traction on a wet curve. Most of the rotation from a slider comes from the grip—you grip the ball off-center with two fingers and when you release the ball it slides off the index finger so that there is some clockwise spin—but I got so much rotation on my wrist that I was able to grip the ball a little closer to center and hang on to more velocity. I could throw a splitter too. Big hands help with the splitter because you can bury the ball in the notch between index and middle finger but still get lots of rotation and velocity. But my favorite pitch was the 'screwgy.' Not many pitchers had made their living throwing the screwball, Carl Hubbell, Mike Marshall, Mike Cuellar, ¼ of arguably the greatest rotation in baseball history, because it's so hard on the arm. You had to come over the top and then torque the arm counter-clockwise and it created a bunch of unnatural strain on the elbow. There were half a dozen guys who had blown up promising careers trying to add 'the screw' to their repertoire. It wasn't a big problem for me, though because I got almost all the inward torque from rotating my wrist rather than elbow and shoulder. I was able to get the ball to 'hop' inside on a right-handed hitter and it looked a lot like the motion on my fastball and didn't seem to cause much wear on my arm. All that to say, that I could knock down milk bottles like Jon Bon Jovi knocks down soccer moms.

And so I had worked my way through all the chintzy prizes, the key chains, the plastic change purses, the foot-long green and yellow stuffed snake, the knock-off smurfs, tweety birds, and kermits, until I was holding the four foot white tiger. You might think that carnies are pissed when you win the big prize but they aren't. By the time I was done I had spent eleven bucks and the tiger probably didn't cost much more than that wholesale. Plus, once somebody gets on a roll the word spreads and by the time I was down to the last set of milk bottles, there was a big crowd around the booth. And I'd just made it look easy—he was going to have a bunch of spaghetti arms throwing for the next hour or two and it wouldn't cost him more than a few key chains.

It turns out there is something sadder than a young man rocking gently in the breeze as the Ferris wheel inches to the bottom like the last clacking Heart in a giant Crown and Anchor game—it's him pushing his way through moms and dads and sugar-smeared toddlers and pre-teen Beyonce's wearing cutoff shorts and hand-drawn mascara teardrops, cradling a four foot high stuffed animal in his arms. So, there I was—just me, the white tiger and the hanging question—what kind of guy sets out to win a four-foot tall stuffed animal without having somebody to give it to? Where was a sixty-foot drop from a carnival ride when you needed it? That's when I spotted Jimmie Munoz and his family. I didn't even know he had a family but I shouldn't have been surprised, Munoz was probably thirty-two or thirty-three years old and it turned out most of the older guys had families. A couple of them were already on their second.

I had my head down, walking fast and looking to dump the tiger as quick as I could but I happened to look up and Jimmie was watching me. He smiled and nodded. He had his arm around his wife and was holding the hand of a little dark-haired brown-skinned girl maybe six or seven years old. Jimmie's wife was pretty but tired. And she was showing. Not enough that I would have said anything but enough that I was pretty sure she was pregnant. The little girl looked tired too but happy, a thin spray of ketchup on one cheek and a thin blue blanket in the hand that wasn't being held by her father. I think what probably happened is that he recognized me as somebody he knew but wasn't sure from where. I've had that happen, where you see somebody outside of context and, for a second, you just know you know them but have no idea from where. And so he smiled and nodded. And that was enough for me. I walked over and stuck out my hand, tucking the animal up under my left arm but still having to turn a little to the side so that it wasn't in his face.

"Hi, Jimmie."

He had figured out who I was by the time I got to him and the smile disappeared. He didn't put his hand out at first but I left mine hanging, pale and white in the harsh uncertain glow of the carnival lighting. He had started this. He looked to his right at his wife and she was smiling uncertainly looking from his face to mine. He looked down at his daughter. She was staring at the tiger. Jimmie's face was softer than I remembered from the dressing room, like there were muscles that he only used in the clubhouse and on the field. Muscles that pulled his brow a little lower, and hooded his eyes so that they recessed deeper into their sockets, and muscles that pulled the skin tighter across his cheeks and his lips into a shallow crevice. Jimmie's wife said something softly in Spanish and he looked at her then nodded and took my hand.

"Hey."

"Hi, Jimmie."

We stood for a second.

"You and the family been here all day?"

He nodded but didn't speak.

His wife spoke to him again in Spanish. He looked at her for a second and then back to me.

"This is my wife, Adelina."

She smiled and took my hand. Hers was small and warm and the smile moved out from her lips like a wave, reaching to her hairline and the place where her ears pressed flat and neat against her head and to where her throat moved gently as she swallowed.

"It is a pleasure to meet you. But..." She placed her far hand on her husband's shoulder,

"Jaime is not so very good with names." It was a question.

Her English was lightly accented but very good.

"Ryan, ma'am. Ryan Spencer."

Her face shifted slightly but the smile remained.

"Ahh, the new player. The third baseman."

"Yes ma'am."

I almost apologized. She turned with her hand still on her husband and nodded at her daughter who was still staring at the tiger.

"This is our daughter, Ariadna. Ariadna, say hello to Mr. Spencer."

Her eyes slipped from the tiger for a second and she looked at me and ducked her head but I saw Jimmie give her hand a gentle tug and she looked back up.

"Hello." And then her eyes went back to the tiger.

"Hello, Ariadna. It's nice to meet you."

I turned back to Jimmie.

"You have a beautiful family, Jimmie."

He hadn't been looking at me, gazing over my shoulder at the lights whirling in the dark and losing himself in the jumble of a dozen different songs rolling and tumbling from a dozen different rides. He pulled his eyes back to my face.

"Thanks, man."

I stood for a second not sure what to add. Jimmie started to speak.

"Well, man, we've got to..."

I crouched down in front of the little girl and pulled the tiger in front of me. I nodded at the stuffed animal.

"Ariadna, do you like him?"

Her eyes couldn't leave its face now that it was right in front of her. She nodded but once she started it was like she couldn't stop, her head just nodding and nodding.

"Would you like him?"

For a second she nodded harder but I saw her father's hand tighten around her small hand and she stopped. She still couldn't take her eyes off the stuffed animal but her face had changed, her eyes filling, like she was watching something she loved disappear into the horizon. I stood up. Jimmie's face had hardened. I looked only at Jimmie but I could see that his wife was watching us although I couldn't tell what her expression was and I felt that looking at her would end everything. I spoke quietly.

"You would be doing me a favor, Jimmie. I'm not taking this to my car. If Ariadna doesn't take it I'm going to find a place to dump it and whoever can carry it is going to own it. Really. "

He just stared at me. I spoke even more quietly. I wasn't sure even his wife could hear.

"I'm not expecting anything, Jimmie. I know this doesn't change anything. This has got nothing to do with you and me—it's just a piece of shit stuffed toy you could buy for her a dozen times. Could you let this one go?"

He looked at me for several long seconds, then looked down at his daughter. She wasn't watching the animal anymore, she was watching her father and when he looked at her the hard lines fell out of his face like tent poles collapsing in the wind and he gave a little nod at the animal still resting on the ground. She threw her arms around the tiger's neck and hugged it to her body and I took my hand from the top of its head where I had been keeping it from tipping over into the dirt. Jimmie took his arm from around his wife's waist, bent down, and scooped his daughter up in his arms. She clutched the animal to her chest. The tiger's white striped head fell over her shoulder and its paws flopped down well below her feet dangling against her father's hip.

"Thanks, man."

He was looking over my shoulder again. His wife spoke then.

"You are very kind, Mr. Spencer."

"No problem, Mrs. Munoz."

"Call me, Adele…and thank you again."

She turned back to her husband.

"Let's get our happy, tired girl home, Jaime."

I think she meant it to be a small kindness.

Chapter Five

O pening day. The pitch came in high and inside. It would have hit me if I hadn't shaved that morning. I got up out of the dirt and dusted myself off, dug in hard with my back foot, looked out to the pitcher and he put the next one in the same spot. I looked up from the ground at the umpire and he just stared back over the catcher's shoulder without changing expression. The catcher sniffed the air.

"What's that smell, Jerry?"

The umpire smiled but didn't answer him.

"That's going to leave a stain, rook."

I was leaning on the next pitch. It wasn't like I dropped my foot into the bucket or flinched, nothing so obvious. I just didn't commit to the swing the way I needed to if I was going to make solid contact. You have to start the weight shift before you know where the ball is going and then rely on your athletic skills to hold up if it's not in your wheelhouse. But you have to commit to the swing. You can't have even a small piece of your mind preparing to drop on your ass. And the curveball froze me. If I had been committed I would have been able to stroke it. I knew when it left his hand that it was a curveball. It spins a little different and the release point isn't quite the same. But I wasn't completely committed. And so it froze me and then dropped over the plate. It hadn't even been that good of a pitch, dead nuts in the heart of the plate and if I hadn't been a little twitchy I would have stroked it. Instead, I watched it. It may be subtle to a fan but their catcher saw it.

"No shame there, son."

Which wasn't what he meant at all.

The pitcher was already getting ready to go into his windup and I dropped one foot out of the batter's box and raised a hand to the ump without taking my eyes off the pitcher. The umpire stepped out from behind the catcher, waved both arms and the pitcher stepped off the rubber. I pulled the other foot out of the box reached down to adjust both socks and then stood up and pulled at the shoulders of my uniform. I closed my eyes and reminded myself that there were a few things worse than getting hit in the head with a baseball. Every batter knows that the guy on the mound can kill him. And we just give it up to God.

He couldn't afford to waste another one at my head. And he wouldn't have liked the pitch he just threw, it had been too good. He knew that six times out of ten I would have taken that off the wall. So, he was going to be thinking that he could throw the same pitch but better. Don't start it quite as high and inside so that when it broke it would catch the outside of the plate a little above knee high. Location is the key for pitchers. If they can hit their spots, most times they are going to be successful. But if I know the spot then it's just sweet meat, baby. And he didn't know it yet but I was a lowball hitter. The ump stepped back into his crouch behind the catcher.

"Play ball."

I'm not sure how I got out of the way. I was committed. I knew that ball was going to be low and outside and here it came, filling my eye like an eclipse. I swear the pitcher gradually disappeared around the edges of the ball until all I could see was his right foot falling forward on his follow through. And I knew it was going to hit me.

But it didn't.

I got out of the way. Somehow. I ended up on my back with my right leg straight out in front of me and my left leg tucked under me. I lay there for a second stunned by the force with which I had hit the ground. The umpire stepped out in front of the plate and bent over with his back to me to sweep the dirt off the plate and then went back behind the catcher. I got up, dusted off my pants, and stood watching him until he was crouched behind the catcher.

"Play Ball."

I didn't step back in. I continued to stand looking at him while he stared out at the pitcher. He spoke without looking away from the mound.

"Get in the fucking box, kid."

I looked at him for another second and then stepped back in. The count was three and one. He really couldn't afford to come too far inside. He threw a fastball that caught the inside corner. It was a good location. If I had been holding a couple of strikes I would have tried to foul it off but I could afford to let it go. And pretend to flinch. You don't have to do much. A shadow of a shoulder turn that says you're more concerned about getting out of the way than making contact.

I stepped out of the box and knocked dirt out of my cleats. I undid the snap on my glove, adjusted the glove, and then did the snap up again. I pulled at both shoulders of my uniform again. They were sure I was done. He was going to call for the curveball again. But this time it wouldn't be a mistake. He was going to call for it to drop right through the sweet spot. In his mind, I was done. For this at bat, for this game, probably forever. And they weren't going to just bury me, they were going to piss on me first. Put the ball right in my wheelhouse, freeze me in front of thirty thousand people and my teammates and then smile as the umpire swept my balls off the plate.

It was the curveball and it started just inside and off the plate about ribcage high. I had timed my slidestep forward perfectly and I could see the ball rotating and imagine where it was going to be when it got to the plate. It was a little higher than the first big curve so it was going to end up about belt high. I heard the catcher say "Shit." He knew as soon as the ball left the pitcher's hand that I wasn't frozen. Everything felt perfect but I ended up just under the ball. A tiny fraction of a millimeter makes such a difference. I sent the right-fielder to the wall. I was almost at second base before he leapt and caught it just over the fence. I trotted slowly back across the diamond from second base. The catcher had stepped out in front of the plate watching the flight of the ball all the way and then continued to stand there watching me. When I got close, I nodded. He just stared at me, his mouth tight and grim.

I skipped down the steps into the dugout. Nobody looked at me except Balducci.

"Nice at bat, Spence."

"Thanks, skipper."

I grabbed my glove and went out to third base. There are a lot of unwritten rules in baseball but one of the sacred ones is that when one of your guys gets knocked down, one of theirs takes it in the ribs. McKay's buddy, Jackson Jones, was pitching for us—they were all cut from the same physical mold, big ass, thick thighs, the beginnings of a gut. He was a big man but he didn't throw hard. He topped out about ninety and he had a sneaky change that looked a lot like his fastball even after he let go of the ball and he could mix in a decent slider. The first batter got two sliders just outside and then hit a fastball over second for a single. The next batter reached for a change over the outside of the plate and popped it up to short. Ramirez—Fagan had been given the day off—walked the ball to the mound and I followed him. They both looked at me as the three of us stood at the mound.

"Nothing inside, Jonesy?"

He just looked at me, flat-eyed. I looked over at Ramirez and he looked back without changing expression. By now, the umpire had started out to the plate to break us up but I held up my hand and called out,

"No worries, Jerry, we're done.

He stopped but didn't turn around, waiting for us to drift back to our positions. I looked at Jones and Ramirez.

"Really? Nothing? I'm on my own?"

They just looked at me.

"Okay, I get it. My problem. I'll take care of it. Not like that weak-ass shit you throw was going to raise a welt anyway, Jones."

"Fuck you, Spencer."

The umpire had started forward again and I let him get within about ten feet before I turned and walked back to my spot. When I turned back the three of them were standing at the mound and the umpire was staring at me red-faced. I gestured at where I was standing as if to say "What? I'm where I'm supposed to be." He raised a warning finger and then turned back to the plate.

* * *

My chance came in the eighth inning. We were down four-zero. I had one of our three hits, a double off the left-field wall. They had thrown at my head again but when I put the next ball off the wall they must have realized they couldn't afford to waste any more pitches. The third time up I had hit a hard liner that the centerfielder had tracked down. But I was still burning. We were on our third pitcher and nobody had even come hard inside on a single batter. Balducci was stewing, too. You never had to say it, the manager just looked at you and you went out to the mound and bruised somebody. Now, nobody was looking at him or me.

But their pitcher was throwing a three-hitter with a four-run lead and had only thrown seventy-seven pitches so they let him bat for himself in the eighth. The guy leading off the inning had hit a single and then stole second, the second guy up had grounded out to the right side of the infield and moved the runner to third. Sorenson, our mop-up guy, ends up walking the pitcher, usually unforgivable but with a man on third and one out it wasn't so bad. It set up the double play. But we would have to turn it slick because their lead-off guy was quick out of the box and up the line. He hit exactly the ball we needed. I was playing in tight on the edge of the grass and he rapped a sharp one hopper right to me. It was an easy play—I throw a hard strike to second and the second baseman flips to first to beat the runner by a couple of strides. Hiltz wouldn't even have to avoid the slide because the pitcher's a fat fuck who's barely halfway down the base line and he isn't going to slide anyway because god forbid he do anything that could jeopardize that precious arm.

I didn't even look at Hiltz. I think it probably would have taken their pitcher high on the cheek and busted up his face but he got his hand up in time and so it broke his wrist instead. The ball bounded into centerfield and the guy flopped to the ground, writhing like a fish on the dock. Their manager was out of the dugout like a man running for the lake after waking up on fire. The umpire came out from the plate, whipped off his mask, pointed at me, and then pointed to the stands. I was out of the game. In the confusion, the runner on third trotted across the plate.

Left wrist. Non-pitching arm. Too bad.

* * *

Fagan caught me coming out of the shower.

"What the fuck was that, Spencer?"

He was standing between me and my locker so I stepped around him. I took off my towel tossed it in one of the laundry bins scattered around the room and pulled my boxers down off the shelf of my locker. When I turned around he was standing in front of me again.

"I asked you a question."

I looked at him.

"I have to get dressed, Nick."

"What the fuck was that about out there?"

I motioned down at my naked body.

"Do you mind, Nick?"

He looked down and then back up without changing expression. Most guys might have flushed a little. Not Nick.

"Fine. You dress. Then we talk."

He stepped back a couple of paces. I took my time, getting my belt cinched just right and making sure that my tie was knotted tight and symmetrical. I left the suit jacket hanging – the room was air-conditioned but it was still a little warm and humid. My guess is that the home dressing room was probably a little dryer and cooler. I sat down in front of my locker.

"Okay, Nick. What's on your mind?" Fagan had been standing there the whole time like a soldier at parade rest, hands behind his back, feet shoulder-width apart. The guy was intimidating but I was trying not to let him know it.

"You cost us two runs."

"One."

"The pinch runner for Eisenberg scored."

It took me a second. The pitcher's name must have been Eisenberg.

"Jewish?"

Fagan's face clouded.

"What?"

"Never mind. What's the big deal—we were down four to zero."

"You know what the score is now, smart guy?"

It didn't take a genius to figure we must have come back. I shook my head.

"Six to three. We've got a man on second."

I looked at him for a long second.

"You better get back out there. They might need you."

I didn't look down but I could still see his fists clench and unclench at his sides. It took him a second to speak.

"You never fuck the team, Spencer."

"Are you kidding me, Nick? The team? You sit there in your little bubble and don't say boo to anybody but the skipper and Hiltz. And you only talk to Hiltz about positioning. Since when did you become a team guy?"

He took a deep breath.

"That's what you think? If I don't play grab-ass and tell fuck stories I'm not a team guy? I don't have to like them and they don't have to like me but we're a team."

"Right. Sell that shit somewhere else, Nick, I'm not buying. That fucker put me down twice in one at bat. That second one, I don't know how it missed me. I'm going to be seeing that in my sleep for a long time. Then he came after me again in the fourth. And nobody did a fucking thing. Nobody has to shake my hand after I win a game for us but if I'm getting hung out like that, it's every man for himself. Nobody's running me out of this game. Nobody on their team and nobody on mine."

He looked away. Then spoke quietly

"Give it time."

"Fuck you."

"If it happens again I'm kicking your ass."

"It's going to happen again so dig in, old man."

I was shaking mad. I could feel my back tightening up. It always did when I got mad. Fagan was calm like he was asking directions from a stranger.

"And it wouldn't hurt you to fly with the team."

He turned and walked away.

Chapter Six

They brought my Dad into the morgue on a morning I was working. The guys rolling the gurney had to stop because we had laundry piled in the middle of the floor and they couldn't get through to the doublewide stainless steel doors. This was unusual, it was a small military hospital—people died there but not often. And this guy was in a body bag. Usually, it was somebody who had died in the hospital and they didn't get bagged until they got to the morgue. When they arrived in a bag it usually meant a car accident.

Me and Jimmy, the kid I worked with, cleared the laundry stacks out of the way so the gurney could get by and then stepped back to let them wheel it through. This was the first time I had seen a body while we were working—it would only happen twice more in the two years I worked there. We stared at the bag. Jimmy always had something to say.

" Geez. What happened. Car wreck?"

The smaller of the two guys shook his head.

"Nope. One of the flyboys went down."

Jimmy looked over at me right away. He knew my dad was a pilot. The guys wheeling the gurney didn't notice. I stood where I was for what seemed like a long time. Everything slowed down and I could feel the air drift to a stop in my lungs even as my heart beat faster and harder... but my brain was still working. I couldn't remember how many planes we had at the base but it had to be at least thirty or forty and almost as many pilots. What were the chances that this was my dad? It seemed like a long time but it couldn't have been too long because the guys had only got to the door when I asked.

"Do you know which one?"

The smaller guy grabbed the tag and looked at it.

"Guy named Spencer."

He said it without turning around. I slumped down onto the laundry. I remember that Jimmy ran out of the room.

* * *

Dad didn't get me started playing ball. But he was a good athlete. Most of the pilots were – eye-hand coordination and reflexes were a big part of being a good pilot but you had to be able to process a lot of information at once and make decisions quickly so most of them were pretty bright too. Dad was smarter than most. He had an aeronautical engineering degree and had started flying while he was at school. The flying bug bit hard and he had headed to the Canadian Air Force recruiting center on the same day he had written his last exam. He missed his graduation because he was in Manitoba at training school.

My dad was an odd combination—he took up more than his share of most any room he walked into but he was a bit of a ghost in our house. He just wasn't home that much and when he was he didn't have much to say. Women loved my dad—he was a big smiling guy and Gregory Peck handsome. It was the military so the hair was supposed to be cut high and tight but the flyboys always wore it a little longer and everybody looked the other way and Dad pushed that even harder than most. I had watched them together at parties and Dad would end up with a crowd of people around him while he told stories. Flying stories, sports stories, women stories, stories about one of the guys standing in the circle around him, a story that made the guy sound funny or brave or stand-up. Men loved him, too. Mom would stand beside him for a while smiling quietly and nodding when he looked down at her for confirmation and it seemed to me that both the men and women were envious of her standing there under his arm. Dad would eventually lift his arm from around her shoulders as he was gesturing his way through a story and she would slide away as if to get a refill and then just not come back. Nobody ever noticed. Mom would often stand alone then and it didn't seem to bother her. She would just stand with her drink looking around the room. Sometimes somebody would come over and she would talk but not so much that they would stay long.

Everything was different at home. Mom filled the house. She was always cooking or cleaning or working on some big project, wallpapering or painting the bedrooms. And she usually sang while she worked. And she could sing. Mostly blues and old country, Etta James. Patsy Cline and George Jones. She worked part-time, twice a week, as a teacher's aide but she was usually home before me so I was hardly aware of it. When Dad was home he would be asleep in the La-Z-Boy or following Mom around the house. When he followed her she would talk to him, telling him her plans for the house or about things the neighbors were doing or how things were going for me at school. Dad wouldn't say much, just following her from room to room grinning and nodding. And even as a kid, I noticed that he didn't seem able to stop touching her. She would walk by him on her way to another room and he would stop her to push a strand of hair off her forehead or just put his arm around her waist and pull her close to him. She would lean in for a second but then give him a quick kiss and wriggle free.

But he wasn't around a lot. He played every sport, baseball in the summer, football in the fall, and hockey in the winter. And when it wasn't sports he was out with the other pilots or the aircrew. As a kid, you're not aware of these things but I realize now he just didn't like being alone. And we didn't participate in that part of Dad's life. I don't remember seeing any of Dad's games and the only time I saw Dad's friends were when they came by to get him. Except for the official events when Mom would stand beside Dad while he told stories. Mom decided everything. I can't remember ever asking Dad for permission to do anything. He just wasn't the guy for that. And if he was home while I was getting in trouble—bad marks or missing school—I would look over and he might give me a small shrug...or he just wouldn't look at all. We both knew there was no help there.

I can't remember how I ended up playing baseball but my guess is that Mom signed me up, Dad just wouldn't have thought of it. But I do remember

Dad showing up early in the year for one of our practices and watching us fumbling around in the infield while one of the kid's dads slapped grounders at us. He watched from the stands for a few minutes and then came down out of the stands and stood along the first base line. When the coach came down the line chasing a ball that he had squibbed down the line my Dad stopped him and they had a short quiet conversation that I couldn't hear. The guy nodded toward the end of the conversation and my dad went back to our car popped the trunk and pulled out his cleats and glove.

He sat on the bottom bench of the bleachers and I watched as he laced up his cleats with quick practiced motions and then picked up his glove in his right hand and strolled out to where we were standing, half a dozen seven-year olds scratching at bugs in the dirt while we waited for our chance to catch a ball. I'm not sure where he had been coming from because he was wearing grey pleated pants and a charcoal dress shirt and it could have looked odd with the cleats and the glove except that he owned the field. If you had never seen a baseball game before you would have assumed that this was what players wore. I don't remember him speaking to us although he must have. I just remember him in the shallow crouch and his arms slightly bent and forward from his body and his eyes focused on the batter and then as the bat came around raising up on his toes and moving before the bat hit the ball but never moving in the wrong direction. If the ball was within a couple of feet on either side of him he was always square and set and the ball disappeared like a rabbit down a hole. I knew that he was going to the ball but it felt like he was calling the ball to him. That's all that I can say. It felt like a dance and dad was leading not following. I had never seen him more still than in those fractions of second before the ball was hit, poised like a drop of water on a hat brim, and then the release as potential turned kinetic and the lines intersected in space and time in a way that seemed inevitable.

Of course, the kids still stumbled around flailing at grounders like kittens trying to catch a housefly or looking up just in time to take a ball in the chest or shin. Dad worked with us for a few minutes but I think he had expected that once he had shown us how to do it we would all be able to do it. I don't think he was aware that it was magic, that his brain and his eyes and his muscles were connected in a way that, by accident or selection, allowed him to do things few men could do. He gave up then, shrugging at the coach hitting grounders, and kissing me on the head before strolling off the field. We watched him as he walked across the base lines and then back up into the bleachers and continued to watch until he had settled into his seat with his shoes and glove beside him on the wooden slats. I don't remember him ever coming back to a practice. But I might just be forgetting.

And then he was dead.

* * *

People came running down the hallway and into the laundry room, nurses, and admin staff, there might have even been a doctor in the group, I don't remember. They gave me something, a pill, and had me lie down in a private room. They must have called mom because when I woke up she was in a chair beside my bed looking out the window. She didn't speak to me even when she realized I was awake. And that's how it went from there. The house felt empty even when we were both there. Dad was gone and Mom shrank to almost nothing. In my memory, she was always at the kitchen table looking out the window at nothing as the ash grew long grey, and cold. She must have moved—I just don't remember it.

I stayed for two years to finish high school and then left. We hardly spoke in those two years. The only extended conversation I remember well is the one where she made me promise not to fly.

Chapter Seven

"How are you doing, kid?"

I had started slow. I was hitting the ball hard but they just weren't dropping for me. I must have left a dozen balls on the warning track and had another dozen line shots that ended up right at somebody. By the end of April, I was hitting .217 with one dinger and seven RBIs. Baldy was still putting me out there most days but it was worrying him.

"Fine, sir."

"You're taking some good cuts, Ryan. Don't worry about it. They're going to start dropping."

"Sure, skipper."

He patted my shoulder and then stood looking at me for a second. I looked up at him, waiting. He wanted to say something more but then just nodded and turned away. It would have been a lot more reassuring if he hadn't been sweating so much. I was going to have to start hitting.

"Are you alright, kid? Anything I can do for you? A towel? A neck rub? How about I rub your balls and lick your asshole?"

McKay was back. I ignored him and the laughter from his cronies. He hadn't been cleared to pitch but he was only a few days away from getting his spot back in the rotation. We needed him. We were six and fifteen heading into May, the starters were getting shellacked and only a couple of guys were hitting. Fagan was batting .310 with an OBP over .400 and Jerome Walford, the right fielder, had put eight balls over the fence and knocked in seventeen runs. Nobody else was batting over .250 or had more than two home runs. Our middle and late inning relief had been good but it hadn't mattered because we were usually down four or five runs by the sixth inning.

"Spencer?"

I ignored him.

"Spencer? I know your blind but you can't fucking be deaf too. You hear me, asshole?"

I just kept putting on my shoes but I knew it wasn't going to end there. I heard the bench scrape as he stood up and came across the floor to stand in front of me.

"Spencer? You deaf?"

I didn't look up from my shoes.

"I hear you, McKay."

"Good. Now, don't you think this fucking experiment has gone on long enough?"

I answered without looking up.

"What experiment is that?"

"The third baseman experiment, asshole."

"I don't fill out the lineup card, McKay."

"That's right but all you need to do is let Baldy know you're not up for it. You've tweaked something and need a couple of days off."

"I feel fine, McKay."

He leaned in closer but didn't lower his voice.

"Stop feeling fine, Spencer."

I didn't say anything. My shoes were on and tied but I stayed bent over them.

"This is a strange game eh, Spencer? Anything can happen out there. Balls can get away from you. Bats too. I've seen some pretty strange injuries even in the pre-game warm-up."

"Go sit down, McKay."

McKay looked over his shoulder to where Fagan was standing with his back turned, pulling his shirt from his locker.

"This doesn't concern you, Nick."

64

"Sit the fuck down, McKay, before I break your other collarbone."

The big pitcher straightened up.

"What are you doing, Fagan? You want this punk playing third base for us? He's killing us, batting in the middle of the order, and not doing the job. Munoz might not be fucking Mike Schmidt but he'll put more balls in play than this asshole does."

Fagan still hadn't turned around.

"I'm not kidding McKay. You sit down or get ready to go back on the DL."

McKay stood there for several seconds, opening his mouth a couple of times to speak and then thinking better of it. He finally turned and stomped back to his locker.

"I don't need a babysitter, Nick."

He didn't speak for several seconds.

"You're holding the bat a tad higher when you set for the pitch than you were in spring training, Ryan. And then you're overcompensating when you drop the barrel on the ball. Have a look at the tape."

I had a look at the tape. He was right.

* * *

The first game in May was the last game of a four-game series against the Padres. Hank Stoltz was starting for us. Stoltz was another one of McKay's crew although I hardly ever heard him speak, he just snickered along with the other guys. He was a left-hander with a fastball that topped out at eighty-nine miles per hour, a big looping curve, and pretty good control. He was twenty-eight years old and almost at the end of his string as a starter. If he dropped another mile or two off his velocity he was going to be a late inning specialist who came in just to get the occasional left-handed batter. But today he was on. He was painting the corners and not walking anybody. We were up two-nothing in the sixth and I had been in on both runs. I had been hit by a pitch in my first at-bat—pitchers we're still coming after me without repercussion but as long as they stayed away from my head I would put up with it—and had scored on a Hiltz double. Then in the fifth I had knocked Fagan in with a sharp single over second. In between, I struck out on a great slider. I started the season batting third but Balducci had dropped me to sixth in the order.

Stoltz got into trouble in the seventh, another guy who wouldn't stay in shape and tired late in games. He got the first batter to chase an outside curve that the guy tapped weakly down the third base line. I scooped it easily and the ball beat him by three or four steps but popped out of Toner's glove and the runner was safe.

"Where the fuck's Munoz when we need him?"

I recognized McKay's voice. Toner rubbed at his glove but didn't look over. Stoltz kicked at the dirt around the mound and then glared at me from underneath the bill of his cap. The throw had been right where it should have been and it went up on the board as E-3. The next guy walked and we got lucky when the next batter hit a rocket down the first base line but Toner had been trying to keep the runner close to avoid the double steal and was in position to catch it and step on first for the double play. We were one batter away from being out of it. Then Stoltz laid an eighty-seven mph fastball over the heart of the plate and their number eight hitter made it two-two. The way the guy skipped around the bases you would have thought he had never hit a ball that far. He probably hadn't. Couldn't weigh more than one hundred sixty-five pounds in a raccoon coat and Stoltz gives him something he could hit 390 feet. Balducci had a righty and a lefty up in the bullpen after the walk and he called for the righty as he walked out to the mound. Stoltz made a show of kicking at the dirt and slamming the ball in Balducci's hand but he wanted out of the game. He knew he was out of gas. Friburg came in and got the pinch hitter on a tap back to the mound.

I was up second in the eighth inning. Walford struck out on three straight pitches none of which would have been a called strike. That was his problem, whenever he came up in a tight game he wanted to be a hero and he forgot what made him a good hitter, pitch selection. The funny thing about Walford is that there were pretty good chunks of the strike zone where he just couldn't get around on the ball. But he could stick around the league a long time hitting mistakes. You could tell when Walford was in a good streak because he would walk a lot and get called out on strikes a lot. It seemed like everything else would be over the wall or off it. He was in trouble if he was striking out swinging or hitting weak grounders. His last nine at-bats had been swinging strikeouts or groundball outs. Somebody had to tell him to stop swinging at pitches he couldn't hit but it wasn't going to be me.

I tapped my cleats one last time and stepped in. The first pitch was right in my wheelhouse but I got under it and fouled it back behind the screen. I stepped out, adjusted my gloves, and started to step back into the box but caught a motion from the dugout from the corner of my eye and stepped back to look over. Nick was standing at the rail. He never left his seat during our at bats except to hit. He was leaning with his forearms on the rail and when he saw me look over he straightened up, held his hands up as if he were holding a bat, and then slowly dropped his hands about an inch. I nodded. He was right. I had forgotten about lowering my hands. I stepped back in and the guy made the exact same mistake. I swear I watched the ball flatten against the barrel the way a speeding car collapses against a concrete wall in slow motion but instead of smoke, steam, and sheared metal it was followed by clean sweet decompression. The fans watched the ball flight and so did the umpires and maybe the catcher because he was looking that way anyway. I didn't bother and neither did the pitcher. I just put my head down, started my trot and he kicked at the dirt waiting to see whether he was going to get the chance to throw another pitch. Balducci met me at the top of the stairs and bumped fists but the rest of the guys ignored me. Except Fagan. He was back at his spot on the bench but he gave me a short nod and a small smile. That was it for us, we didn't manage another runner over the last five at-bats but Friberg and Guiterrez came in and shut the Padres down. We were seven and fifteen.

Chapter Eight

There was somebody in the room with me. It was too dark to see but I could hear him breathing and occasionally he would shift and the blankets would crease and rustle. The train had stopped so it was still and quiet, the usual wobble and clatter paused. I lay with my eyes closed and listened to the short, shallow panting from the end of the bed. Whoever it was sat near my feet. I could feel where the mattress was depressed slightly. There was a sudden roar of sound and the air pressure in the room shifted as the train rocked and rattled past. The noise filled the room like rushing water and seemed to go on for hours and I concentrated on the weight of the body at the foot of the bed waiting for the subtle change that would precede hands at my neck or the blade to my ribs or throat. My breath caught in my chest like tiny shards of inhaled glass, snagged and bound and filling my trachea until it was packed and blocked and not even a trickle of oxygen was slipping by to the alveoli of my lungs. The passing train was gone then and the room was silent except for the faint receding vibrations, so faint that I wasn't sure if it was just the memory of a noise like the phantom pain in an amputated limb. There was a second where it was possible that I had imagined the sound of his breathing and the rustle of linen and the weight at my feet but then he shifted and the room filled and shrank and closed around me like cellophane. I could feel the skin pull tight across my cheekbones and the heat suck deep into my core so that my hands and feet felt thick and cold and useless and I closed my eyes in the darkness and ignored the dancing lights and tried to breathe slowly and quietly but heard the air molecules tumble loud and shuddering like glass bottles tossed down a laundry chute.

"I know you're awake, mister."

The voice was young. Not a child, but an adolescent.

"I ain't gonna hurt you."

"Turn on the light. The switch is beside the door."

My voice shook a little but not as bad as I had expected.

I heard some rustling for several seconds.

"I can't find a switch, Mister. I think there's a lamp beside you."

There had been a switch when I had come into the room. I reached out to the side of the bed and almost immediately felt a marble lamp base. I felt around until I found the switch. I had to shade my eyes and it took me several seconds to get a clear look at the young man sitting at the end of my bed.

It was the same kid. The kid I had met on the train the first time. But the room was different than when I had fallen asleep. The walls of the berth papered rather than painted and the mattress thicker and softer, the light muted. And the kid wasn't exactly the same either. There was no question it was the same person but he was older. He was taller and although still skinny he had put on a little muscle. The kid stood now, in the narrow space between the bed and the door. I pushed myself up on my elbows.

"How did you get in here?"

He waved his hand.

"They might as well not put locks on the doors."

I looked at him for a second then nodded.

"Okay. Why did you come in here?"

He slumped back down on the bed then, facing away from me.

"I need a place. And I remembered you from a couple of years ago. You seemed alright. Like maybe you wouldn't turn me in."

"A couple of years ago?"

He didn't look at me but his hands that had been rubbing at his pants went still.

"You don't remember?"

"What should I remember from a couple of years ago?"

69

"Train had an emergency stop? You found me in the seat beside you and helped me not to get caught out? You don't remember?"

The last question came out tired and quiet.

"I remember. But it wasn't two years ago."

He looked over his shoulder at me.

"Actually a touch more than two years ago, mister. Maybe it don't seem like it but time's funny that way. I remember because that was the first time I found him. And it was almost four years to the day from when Pauly died."

It was happening again. But I couldn't keep up with him.

"Saw who? And who's Pauly?"

His face closed down and he shook his head. I tried again.

"What's your name?"

"Georgie Abbott."

"What's the date, Georgie?"

"May second."

"What year?"

He looked back at me again.

"What year?"

"What year."

"This some kind of test, mister? You think maybe I'm crazy? Don't know what year it is?"

I had no answer so I just looked at him. He shrugged.

"1941. Satisfied?"

I nodded. 1941. One of us was crazy. This was 1941. What was I doing in 1941?

"Did you hear me, mister?"

I looked up. He had asked me something.

Georgie was looking at me.

"Are you okay, mister?"

I gave my head a quick shake.

"I'm fine, Georgie. And call me Ryan."

"Sure."

He hesitated for a second and his eyes drifted closed and he swayed to one side before catching himself. His eyes came open slowly and he spoke quietly without looking at me.

"Is it okay if I stay for a bit, Mr. Ryan?"

"It's just Ryan. Ryan Spencer."

"Ryan? What kind of name is Ryan? For a first name? I never heard of it."

"Yeah, well Georgie isn't so great either."

He looked over and his face darkened and he straightened a little.

"My daddy named me after the Babe. It's not so bad. "

"Where are your parents, Georgie?"

"What's it matter, mist...Ryan?"

"Well, you're sixteen and on your own. Seems a little young."

"They're dead, like I said."

"Who looks after you?"

"Nobody. I look after myself."

I looked him up and down—the torn, dirty pants held up by an old shoelace knotted at the front, the wool sweater with holes in both elbows, fraying and loose at the waist and neck, and a worn short-billed chore cap. I couldn't see his feet but I didn't imagine the shoes would be much better.

"How's that working out for you?"

"Fine."

"Yeah. Who's Pauly?"

He shook his head.

"Never mind. This was a bad idea. You rich fucks are all alike."

He stood up but then stumbled sidewise and slumped onto the bed again. He cursed and pushed himself to his feet and stood with his eyes closed sucking in air trying to maintain his balance.

"Alright, Alright. Relax, Georgie. You take some time in here but we're going to talk when you wake up and I want to hear the whole story."

He didn't even nod, just slumped back on the bed and crawled up in the corner as far as he could get from me and closed his eyes.

There was no way I was getting back to sleep. I dressed and left, locking the door behind me.

The bar car was towards the back of the train. It was late and I was pretty sure that I would be able to find a seat. There were only four men in the bar car, three men in rolled-up shirtsleeves, their suit jackets piled in the corner of one seat, playing cards at a table, and a big, light-skinned black man with white, thinning hair standing at the bar talking to the bartender. He wore a dark conservative suit with a patterned tie and had a brown soft leather briefcase at his feet. I nodded to him and he nodded back. I looked at the bartender.

"Root Beer, please."

He pushed a bottle and a glass across the bar to me.

I pushed the glass back towards the bartender and raised the bottle to the man at the bar.

"To cold beer."

He smiled faintly and raised his glass.

"What's a jig know about good beer?"

I turned towards the table of men playing cards. I could see out of the corner of my eye that the black man had not turned away from the bar. It had been an odd, short night and I was tired. I looked at the speaker. He was a medium-sized guy with a red flush around his eyes that suggested he had been drinking for a while. But there was no slur in his words that I could detect.

"Since when does a white man have to drink in the same bar car as one of them?"

He looked over my shoulder at the black man as if I wasn't there.

The man at the bar spoke without turning around.

"Since four days ago, my friend. The Supreme Court ruled on April twenty-eighth that black passengers have the right to the same accommodations and treatments as white passengers."

There was a short pause.

"Mitchell v. The United States. You can look it up."

He still hadn't turned away from the bar. The bartender was polishing a glass and he held it up to the light to look for spots.

The man at the table sneered.

"You can put on a white man's suit—you're still a circus act."

The other men at the table laughed as if he had said something funny. The man at the bar didn't speak just took a sip from his beer. The speaker leaned in and talked quietly to the other two men at the table and then the three of them started to stand up. I felt the familiar tightening in my lower back and the twitch in my hands. I had been leaning with my back on the bar facing them since the first guy had spoken.

"Just so you boys know, I'm with…" I hesitated and turned to him and stuck out my hand.

"Ryan Spencer. Pleased to meet you."

He took my hand.

"Arthur Mitchell, son. Nice to meet you as well."

He nodded his head at the bartender,

"This is James Rollins."

The bartender nodded at me but didn't move from where he was standing, now with his hands below the bar. I turned back to the men at the table.

"I'm with Arthur and if there's going to be trouble, I'm in."

The man looked incredulous.

"You siding with this'n?"

"I'm with Arthur."

He stood for a second staring at me but then slowly sat back down and the other two men sat back down too. Arthur and I finished our beers without talking.

"Ryan, I'm going to have another beer in my seat, would you care to join me? Usually I travel with my wife but something came up at the last minute and she couldn't accompany me on this trip. I couldn't sleep and perhaps another drink and some pleasant conversation might ameliorate that."

"That sounds good, sir. That first one went down pretty smooth."

The bartender put a root beer and another beer on the bar and I reached for my pocket but Arthur raised his hand.

"It would be my privilege to get these."

"I appreciate that, sir."

"Please, Ryan. Arthur."

I followed him forward to an almost full section of the train. He slid into the seat by the window and gestured to the aisle seat beside him.

"You bought an extra seat? Or couldn't get a refund for your wife's seat?"

He smiled gently.

"No Ryan, the gentleman who had paid for this first-class seat decided that he would be more comfortable sitting in coach. Don't worry, nobody will be fighting you for it."

I sat down beside him.

"Is it true what you said back there?"

"About blacks having equal rights on trains for the last four days?"

I nodded.

"Yes. In theory. The Supreme Court ruled exactly as I described. However, the Interstate Commerce Commission is responsible for the railroads and they have refused to prohibit segregation in interstate trains or buses. I'm optimistic it will happen soon but the truth is that if the train personnel had refused me entrance to the bar car I would have had little recourse."

"You're the Mitchell in Mitchell v. The United States?"

The man smiled and raised his glass of beer.

"Arthur Mitchell, congressman for the south side Chicago district in the great state of Illinois, the first Democratic congressman of color in the one hundred and sixty-five-year history of this grand experiment we call the United States, a contributing architect of the New Deal, a proud supporter of the greatest leader in the recorded history of mankind, Franklin Delano Roosevelt, and as recently as 1937 unworthy to ride in a fully paid first-class railcar seat while traveling through Arkansas."

I raised an eyebrow.

"What was that last bit?"

He lowered his glass.

"I was traveling from Chicago to Hot Springs several years ago with my wife and a gentleman got on the train at a stop in Jonesboro, Arkansas. He was clearly shocked when he saw my wife and I occupying seats in first class. He had the gall to ask me if I was sure I hadn't made a mistake when I boarded the train but I showed him our tickets. I thought that would be the end of it but he complained loudly to the conductor that he had assumed a first-class ticket came with a guarantee that he wouldn't have to 'share a car with a couple of darkies'. There was some vocal support for that position among the other passengers and ultimately the conductor forced us to move back to the car designated for blacks only—what they called the 'trash bin.' The coach was partitioned into three sections all with toilets but only one which still flushed. It was hot and overcrowded and stank of cheap liquor, body odor, and human excrement. "

He was a calm and dignified man but even four years later he couldn't completely disguise his shame and rage.

"I'm a congressman for God's sake."

"So, you took it to court?"

He nodded.

"First, to the International Commerce Commission and then to the district court but they both dismissed the case. Thankfully several of my colleagues in Congress, mostly black of course and all Republican, agreed to support me in bringing the issue to the Supreme Court. The decision came down four days ago. And here we are, you and I."

"That's a great story, Arthur. And a happy ending."

"We'll see."

"Sir?"

He spoke more quietly looking down at his hands.

"There's always a cost, son. My wife has not and will not travel again. She thought that by marrying a congressman she had risen above the possibility of that kind of public humiliation, that Jim Crow was a thing of the past at least for the privileged people of color. To discover that she could still be pulled from that train and pushed and prodded down the tracks onto a stinking, fetid sewer on wheels has changed her. I think she felt that the days when a black woman could be scorned, humiliated, and worse without fear of reprisal were behind her. Her, at least, if not all black women. To find that between her and humiliation was a shadow-thin membrane that could be torn by a single harsh word has changed her, has made her fearful and angry and unforgiving.

And I'm done. My party was not happy with the suit. The company that we brought the suit against is from Chicago and they are not happy with the results and have made dramatic reductions in their financial contributions to the Democratic party and have threatened to discontinue all contributions if I run again. And so, in theory, I can ride in all sections of the trains but my wife hates me and my career is uncertain. And if a white stranger had not stepped forward tonight I would have been humiliated, beaten, or worse, without threat of reprisal. So, Ryan, a great story? A happy ending? Time will tell."

We sat for a while longer in silence. Then he patted my leg.

"I think I could sleep now. Thanks for your help and your company."

I stood up and we shook hands and he turned away, his head to the window as if to sleep, but I could see his eyes open and unblinking in the reflection of the glass.

Georgie was still asleep curled up in the top corner of the bed when I got back to my coach. I had only been gone a couple of hours and he had looked tired enough to sleep around the clock. I lay down on the far side of the bed lowering myself gently so as not to wake him and was asleep in seconds.

When I awoke there was a sliver of light across my face where sunlight knifed through a narrow gap in the curtains. I had a moment where I didn't know where I was and then I remembered. I looked to my right and could make out the shape of the boy in the grey gloom of the room. It looked like he hadn't moved at all from the position he had fallen asleep in.

"You awake, mister?"

Now I noticed the faint wet gleam of his eyes. I reached over and pushed the curtains open and he shaded his eyes against the light.

"You up for some breakfast, Georgie?"

"Nah, I'm alright."

I pushed myself up and leaned back against the window feeling the gentle rumble of train over track.

"When did you eat last?"

He shrugged.

"You don't look like you should be watching your weight, Georgie. A couple of eggs and a pile of pancakes will do you some good. My treat."

He shook his head.

"If you don't mind, Mister, can I just stay here 'til we get to California?"

"It's almost another two days to San Diego, Georgie – you can't stay here until then. And, what, you're not going to eat until we get to San Diego?"

He picked at the blanket bunched against the wall beside him. He spoke without looking at me and his voice trembled a little.

"How long will you let me stay here?"

I looked at him for several seconds but he wouldn't look up at me.

"Okay Georgie, story time. What's this about?"

He looked up then. He was pale and there were still dark rings under his eyes but his jaw was set and the shake in his voice was gone.

"You'll let me stay if I tell you?"

I'm made a circular motion with my hand – just tell the story. He dropped his head again.

"Fuck you."

He pushed himself down to the end of the bed and reached over to pick up his shoes. They were thick coarse work boots with no laces and he lifted one foot up onto his knee and jerked the boot on. He bent over and started to pull on the other boot but the tongue got pushed down into the bottom and he couldn't get his foot in. He cursed again and yanked hard on the back of the boot but the boot was too small to start with and with the tongue jammed into the toe there was no way he was getting it on. I watched as he tore off the boot again and started ripping and pulling at the tongue but then he caught himself and took a breath and calmly worked the tongue free and slipped the boot on. He stood up and started to open the door. A second ago he wouldn't leave to get breakfast but now he was willing to walk out the door.

"Close the door, Georgie. Tell me your story and you can stay."

He stood with the door open a couple of inches and then shut it quietly and sat back down on the bed. The tension drained from his body and he looked small and deflated hunched at the end of the bed. I waited. Several moments passed and I was about to say something when he started.

"Jack McKillops killed my sister six years ago. Pauline was seventeen. He killed her with a long-bladed knife that he carries in the inside pocket of his long coat. He grabbed her from behind and stuck it in her side, and the blood came right away like somebody had turned on a faucet, running in three thin streams through his knuckles and onto the ground. She kicked and bucked but he was too big and strong and he just kept pushing the blade against her with the one hand and pulling back on her head with the other. It didn't take long. There was too much blood. She tried but nobody can lose that much blood and keep fighting. He held her hard against him until she wasn't moving at all and then he laid her on the ground, wiped his hand and the knife on Pauly's dress, put the knife back inside his jacket, and walked out of the alley. "

I stared at him but he looked at his hands.

"How do you know this?"

"I was watching. "

He looked over then and for a second his face twisted and crumpled like discarded foolscap but then he composed himself again.

"Pauly was pregnant. She had a boyfriend, a boy from school, the son of one of Pa's friends. I know that now but I didn't know it then. I just knew that her and Pa had fought about something and she had left crying. I followed her. She walked for more than an hour but she had to stop several times. We ended up down near the railyard, a rundown house on a side street one block over from the tracks. There weren't any signs outside but Pauly seemed to know where she was going and she walked right up to the front door and knocked. I was across the street watching and it was a woman that came to the door. She looked like somebody's grandmother. She smiled when she saw Pauly and she took her by the arm to bring her in the house. I sat on the stoop of a house across the street and waited. I'm not sure how long I waited but it must have been a while. I dozed a couple of times and once I heard somebody clattering down the stairs and jumped up in time to be out of the way when the door opened and a man came out. I didn't notice McKillops standing across the street until just before Pauly came out but he must have been there at least part of the time…else how would he have known Pauly was there?"

I nodded.

Anyway, Pauly come out the door and she didn't look so good. The same woman was at the door and she hugged Pauly and then closed the door behind her. Pauly walked slow away from the house. Like she was sore. I didn't know then that she had got rid of the baby but I could tell she was hurting. I'm not sure why I didn't go to her. There was something in her face. Something sad and lonely. She was always happy to see me but I wasn't sure she would be that day so I just followed her. And so did McKillops. And she went down that alley. I guess it was a shortcut and she wanted to make the walk as short as she could. And he caught up to her and grabbed her and killed her. And I watched from the end of the alley. And when he walked out of the alley I was behind some boxes and he didn't see me, just walked out into the street, turned right, and walked away as if he was out for a Sunday stroll. I don't remember much of the rest. I stayed with her and eventually somebody came by and found us and took us to the police station. They called Pa and he came down and got me. He was never any good after that. He already drank pretty good but he really started then. He died when I was twelve. I been on my own since then.'

"What about your mother?"

"She died when I was born."

"And you've been on your own since you were twelve?"

He nodded.

"How? What do you do for money?"

"I can work. Pa was a printer. He showed me how. And every town has a newspaper and they're almost always looking for somebody to work the night shifts. And I'm good. And I'm young so they don't have to pay me as much. And if there's no printin' jobs I can sell papers. I'm good at it. "

"Okay, so why are you here? In my room? Afraid to leave?"

His face darkened.

"Cause McKillops is on the train."

"This train?"

Georgie nodded.

"Okay. Keep talking."

"I sat outside that house every Saturday after that for two years—I couldn't go on schooldays and they wasn't open on Sundays. I saw McKillops twice. Once, just walking by. I don't know if he just happened to be passing by or whether he was watching but that day he just walked by. The second time was like with Pauly. He watched the girl go in and then he left for a couple of hours—I guess he knew the schedule. Then he came back and watched the door and when the girl came out he followed her. But she walked one block to the corner and then got picked up by an older man in a car. McKillops stood at the corner watching where the car had gone way after he couldn't see it anymore. I followed him then and he went over to the railyard and hopped onto the crew car of a train that left in the next half hour."

"He works for the railway?"

"Yeah. Master mechanic. They actually send him all around the country to troubleshoot the tough jobs. He lives in Boston but hardly ever stays there. He's got two sons but hires a woman to take care of them when he's gone. He goes through sitters like cheddar through a grater. There's not too many that like him but everybody's a little scared of him."

"How do you know all this?"

"Once Pa died I quit school. I started talking to the train crews. Some of them will talk to you even young as I was. If I have a little money I'll bring a flask and that will usually get some of them talkin'. And I found his place in Boston. He must make pretty good money – it's a nice enough place."

"Why are you doing this?" I was pretty sure I knew the answer.

"I'm gonna kill him."

I remembered the man I had seen staring at me from the bunk.

"That seems like a tall order."

He looked at me then.

"I'm gonna kill him."

"She's gone, Georgie. Nothing brings her back. Why don't you just tell the police."

He snorted.

"The cops. Think they're going to listen to a kid about something that happened six years ago? And he knows all the train bulls. Plays poker with them on the long trips. They're his kind, mean and rough, most of 'em. And they're all tight with the local cops in every railroad town. And Pauly ain't it. He got another four I know about. Two of them near the spot where Pauly died. Same story, knifed in an alley. One about a year after Pauly and the other about two years ago, both were in the papers although nobody was saying they were connected. It was him though. Young girls with a knife. The other two I read about in the papers while I been traveling. One in Chi-town and the other in Newark. I just heard about them ones because I had tracked him there and read the papers. Always the same story, young girls, near the tracks. That's often where the doctors set up shop—nobody wants them in the nice part of town."

"So, he targets women that have had abortions?"

Georgie nodded.

"Yeah, he's a righteous man. Doing God's work."

"How does he get away with it?"

Georgie snorted.

"He's got the perfect set-up. He's always on the road and he picks places where he's got a short stopover, usually hours, so that there would barely be a record that he was in the town where the girls died. Like this trip—he's headed to San Diego to work on a job and so as far as anybody knows he's just en route from Boston to San Diego. But he's got a plan. He'll be taking a few hour layover somewhere along the way, probably San Fran, and looking to leave a body. I know about those five girls but the number has to be way higher."

"And he's figured out that you're watching him?"

Georgie nodded.

"How?"

He shrugged.

"He's seen me too much. It's been three years I been following him and I keep showing up where he's at. I think he's known since the trip I met you. For the last year or two, he's been asking about me. Who the kid is that rides the trains alone? Where's he's going? He knows that I've been asking after him. He doesn't know who I am but he don't need to."

He looked at me.

"Nobody does except you. But he knows something ain't right. And he's a cautious man. He's figgered out that I know something and he's gonna' take care of me soon as he can."

"How can you know that?"

He smiled then but it barely made it to the surface.

"You remember the last train ride?"

I nodded.

"He saw me that time. He found where I was sitting. With you. You were sleeping and I was pretending to. It was late and the coach was dark, most everybody was asleep. He stood over us for a long time. Wearing his long coat. Warm cozy train like that and him with that long coat. He never put his hand into the longcoat, just stood there with his arms hanging at his sides looking down at us. Don't know if he was looking at just me or the both of us. But the conductor came into the car then and he moved off."

"And this ride?"

"He saw me. I got no ticket again and so I been sliding from car to car. It's better if I can just stay in one spot on the train and not attract attention but I had to move to stay ahead of the conductors. He spotted me again. And he won't wait now."

"So what's your plan?"

He shrugged.

"I don't know yet. Just follow him south. Maybe get some work for awhile. One of these times I'll get the chance I need and then I'll kill him."

"Not much of a plan, Georgie."

He shrugged again.

"It's coming together."

I nodded.

"I think the police is the best idea, Georgie."

He nodded.

"We'll see. It might be that's a way I can go."

"Anyway, you held up your end. Sit tight. I'll get us some breakfast."

I arranged for eggs, bacon, pancakes, juice, and coffee to be delivered to my cabin. I met the porter in the hallway of the car to take the food and tip him. He thought I was trying to be discreet about a young lady companion. I should be so lucky. It had clearly been a long time since Georgie had eaten. He ate most of the pancakes and more than his share of the bacon.

The train wouldn't be into San Francisco until early the next morning. The schedule had us getting into San Francisco around five AM with a two-hour stopover and then the last ten-hour stretch to San Diego. Georgie stayed in the cabin all day and I brought him lunch and supper. We had arranged the bed back into facing seats and I had convinced the porters that they didn't need to make up my cabin. After that first burst of talking Georgie didn't have much to say and spent his time staring out the window at the passing scenery. I spent much of the day wandering the train with occasional stops in the bar car.

I ran into two of the guys that had been playing cards the night before but they pretended not to recognize me. I walked by Arthur Mitchell's seat but it was empty. I was certain he had said he was going right through to California but it was possible he had decided to get a berth. I didn't see Jack McKillops anywhere. I made up the bed early and rolled into my blankets while it was just barely dark. Georgie and I had hardly spoken since before breakfast. He only grunted when I said goodnight. I slept without waking until we pulled into the San Francisco railyard. It was the stillness of the train that woke me. I hadn't pulled the curtains the night before and the lights of the station platform shone in through the window. I was alone in the room. I hadn't undressed the night before and was wearing the same wrinkled khaki pants and white linen shirt that I had been wearing for the last two days. I looked out the window and saw that there was a thin scattering of people leaving the train and heading for the stairs down into the railway terminal.

Georgie was standing in the shadow of a large pillar looking down the track. I watched him as he leaned out around the pillar looking down the length of the train. I couldn't see what he was looking at but it had to be the crew cars. I pushed myself to the edge of the bed and put on my shoes and leaned across the bed to look out the window again. Georgie was still standing by the pillar. I left my room and turned left. I had to walk through several cars before arriving at one where passengers were disembarking. I got caught behind a couple wrestling with three large pieces of luggage and it took me several minutes to make it to the platform. Georgie was no longer standing by the pillar. I looked down the track and saw his skinny frame flattened against the side of the building. He took a quick look up the tracks towards where I was standing but it was several hundred feet away and there were a few people milling about and I don't think he noticed me. Then he took a look around the corner of the building and he must have been reassured by what he saw because he jumped down from the platform and was gone behind the edge of the building.

I ran up to the corner where he had been standing. Light was beginning to show on the horizon so it wasn't full dark but it was still difficult to see. There was a long stretch of open space, maybe two or three hundred yards in front of me, crisscrossed with tracks. I could just make out a tall man in a long coat who was almost at the narrow guardhouse next to the small employee gate that was set into the chainlink fence separating the railyard from the city. Georgie was about one hundred yards behind McKillops.

I hopped down and moved to the edge of the brick terminal building. The fence extended about two hundred feet to my right to the public entrance of the terminal. McKillops pushed through the employee gate without stopping. The sound of the gate rasping open carried across the open yard and I heard no voices. Either the guardhouse was empty or McKillops wasn't a man to exchange pleasantries. But the way that Georgie walked in a diagonal line away from the gate until he got to the fence told me that somebody must be in the guardhouse. The guard would be more worried about people trying to sneak into the terminal but a young boy leaving by the employee entrance was still likely to arouse questions.

I started across the open area, tripped over some baling wire tangled on the ground and sprawled headfirst, just getting my arms down in front of me in time to avoid banging my chin off a rusted chunk of discarded track. My hand came down on the twisted edge of the track and I felt it tear into my palm. I cursed and either the sound of my voice or the clatter of me stumbling around must have caught Georgie's attention. I saw his face turn, pale in the dim light coming from the roadside streetlights and then he quickly turned, got down on his belly and squirmed under a gap in the fence. His shadow popped up quickly on the other side of the fence and then he was gone behind the shrubs and bushes that had grown up along the fence. I hurried across the tracks but could feel the warm flow of blood across my hand and wrist and the gash was starting to burn. The guard looked up when I got to the gate saw me holding my bleeding hand started up out of his seat but I pushed through the gate and quickly up the path leading to the street that ran in front of the terminal. He must have given up almost right away because when I looked back at the guardhouse the door didn't open.

Georgie loped across the street that ran in front of the train station and disappeared around the corner into a narrow side street. When I got to the corner he was walking about a block ahead of me and another block beyond him, McKillops. We were hemmed in by an odd jumble of long low factory buildings, pulled in tight along the street like a grey battered honor guard with only a narrow curb so that all three of us walked in the street. There was nobody else about. I had to walk quickly to keep up. Neither man turned to look back. McKillops was moving with long, easy strides and Georgie scampered along behind almost breaking into a trot at times. I checked my pocket watch, the train would be pulling out again in forty minutes and I couldn't miss it if I was going to make the game tonight. We had walked for three or four blocks and Georgie had narrowed the gap between him and McKillops to about ninety feet when headlights shone up ahead in the gloom. Mckillops had to step to the side to let the white panel truck rumble by and then Georgie and I, in turn, stepped back onto the curb and the three of us stood like men waiting for a bus and the red taillights bumped down the street towards the harbor. The driver, an older man with thick white hair turned to look at me without changing expression.

"What do you want, boy?"

McKillops spoke at a normal volume but the narrow street funneled the words clearly down to where I stood. He sounded calm. Georgie didn't speak. He just started walking to where McKillops stood. It was light enough now to see that he had a revolver hanging loosely from his hand as if carrying a lunch pail. I hadn't seen it when he had been in my room. He must have had it hidden on the train. I wasn't sure if McKillops had seen it yet but then,

"That's a big shooter for such a thin sliver of shit stain."

His voice sounded steady and unconcerned. Georgie kept walking without speaking until he was within ten feet of McKillops and then raised his arm. McKillops' eyes widened. The first trigger pull dropped the hammer on an empty chamber, Georgie must have been keeping one chamber empty for safety, and McKillops took a step towards Georgie, maybe thinking to grab him but there was ten feet between them and Georgie just kept pulling. The first bullet hit Mckillops high on the right shoulder and spun him to the left and the second bullet missed him.

I couldn't hear if McKillops or Georgie made a sound because the blast of the gun reverberated through the alley. Georgie realigned without moving from where he stood and shot twice more. At least, one of those shots hit McKillops because I saw his body shudder with the impact and he fell. Georgie walked three strides forward to where McKillops lay and shot him in the head from a foot away. Just like that. Stepped up, put the gun against McKillop's forehead and pulled the trigger.

For a second it was still. McKillops body was sprawled on the ground, and Georgie and I stood, twenty-five feet apart, in the brightening gloom of dawn with the dull blast of five shots dissipating like late morning fog. The black shadow grew under McKillop's head and started to leak down the street. Georgie turned to me then. He didn't say anything. He just shook his head. I'm not sure what it meant, whether it was regret or a warning or advice. Then he dropped the gun and ran. Up the street and away from the station, around the corner and gone. I turned back the way I had come and walked back to the train.

I didn't hear the sirens until I was almost at the station doors. The train was only a few minutes from pulling out when I got to the platform and the porters were at the car doors helping passengers back aboard. Georgie had left nothing in my room and taken nothing but there were still the rumpled blankets and sheets where he had slept and the faint sour smell of unwashed clothes. The train pulled out for San Diego. I would have been three days on the train by the time I arrived and would have missed the first two games of the four-game series.

I was going to have to hurry to the ballpark to make it for the 7:30 PM start time.

Chapter Nine

I started to heat up in San Diego. The train had got in on time but the traffic had been bad getting to the stadium and I hadn't made it until the top of the second. Munoz had started but had struck out, popped out to first and ground into a double play in the seventh and now we were down a run with two on, none out and Jimmie in the hole. He sat on the bench staring between his feet—he knew he wasn't getting out of the dugout. Balducci tapped my shoulder

"You're up if Tuquet and Hilz can manage to stay out of the double play, Spence."

I nodded.

Clayton Tuquet, our leftfielder, pulled the ball deep and hard down the third baseline and the team gathered at the rail to see if it was going to stay fair but the cheers of the crowd and the slumped shoulders made it clear that the ball had hooked foul. I looked down the bench and Fagan was the only other player still sitting. He stared impassively ahead. Most of the players stayed at the rail to see the next pitch and Tuquet was way ahead of a change-up and popped up to the catcher just out in front of home plate. The players moved away from the rail and scattered to the corners. Tuquet was a hothead and you had to keep your head down after a tough out. We had already gone through eight water coolers and Tuquet had been responsible for six of them. This time though it looked like he had settled for breaking his bat over his knee because he came in the dugout holding the barrel half in his right hand. As soon, he got to the bottom of the dugout steps he fired it off the concrete dugout wall. It caromed back and our utility infielder

Ramon Gonzalez had to skip out of the way to avoid getting hit. It bounced off the opposite wall, rolled along the dugout floor, and nudged against my shoe. Gonzalez didn't look at Tuquet, just moved to the end of the dugout and sat down. I picked up the bat and walked down to where Tuquet was standing glaring out at the field and tapped him with the splintered end.

"Here Clayton, if you're looking for the other half it's probably up in the stands right next to your jockstrap."

Fucking baby. Balducci and the coaches had to hold him back. The cameras actually caught Tuquet dragging three or four bodies up the dugout still flailing away with the broken bat stump as I headed out to the on-deck circle.

Hilz hit into a fielder's choice moving the runner on second to third while the Padres took the easy out at second. The first pitch was a hanging curve that I put thirty rows deep in left center. Nobody was at the plate when I got there. On the bright side, Tuquet didn't come after me in the dugout. They had calmed him down enough that he just gave me the long, blowtorch glare. Yeah, right, my time would come. Whatever. Brad Minton, a closer we had picked up from Cincinnati in the off-season, got the last three outs in a row and we won the game four to two. Minton had been up-and-down as a starter for most of his career, never winning more than twelve games and one year going eight-seventeen, but at twenty-eight years old, he had decided he was willing to move to the bullpen and had switched from straight over the top to three-quarters. He had lost a couple of mph's off the fastball but now it hopped and darted like a spastic dragonfly and he had been nearly unhittable when we could hand him a lead in the ninth, which hadn't been often. We were eight and fifteen.

"Baldy wants to see you when you're dressed, Spencer."

"Right, Schmitty."

Teddy Schmitt was Balducci's bench coach and one of the few coaches who spoke to me. Most of the rest of the coaches worried more about cozying up to the players than pleasing Balducci but Schmitt and Balducci went back a long way.

"What's he want?"

He made a face.

"He didn't say but we can probably guess, no?"

I shrugged and finished dressing. I was usually one of the first ones dressed and out of the locker room. I grabbed my book from the bottom shelf on my locker and moved down the row of players still changing. Nobody even looked up. Balducci's door was closed so I knocked.

"C'mon in."

He was still wearing his baseball uniform, smooth, unwrinkled, and dry. He waved at the chair across from his desk.

"Nice poke, Spencer. Were you waiting on the curve?"

"Yeah, he was starting most hitters off with it."

He leaned forward with his elbows on his desk and steepled his fingers under his nose. He spoke through his hands.

"What was that all about with Tuquet?"

"He's a child. He almost took Ramon's foot off. Four-year-olds throw tantrums when they don't get what they want, not grown men."

"So, then you make him look like an asshole?"

"I didn't make him look like an asshole."

Balducci sat for several seconds.

"So, you've given up?"

"Given up what, sir?"

"Fitting in?"

"Fitting in? I'm not sure a lobotomy and six months of twenty-four-hour-a-day online porn could get me there, skipper."

Balducci ran a hand over his face and looked at the door I had left open.

"Could you keep it down, Spencer?"

I stood up.

"Anything else?"

He didn't look up from his desk.

"Stop messing with the bull, Spencer."

I didn't answer.

* * *

90

We won the next night's game 9-1 and I had two singles, a triple, and scored three runs. We ended up with nine wins and two losses on the West Coast swing and got back to Montreal one game under .500. I had played every game but one, gone thirteen for thirty-one with nine walks, eight runs, seven RBIs, and three home runs. Munoz had played one game, we had lost five to one and he had gone oh and four with two strikeouts. We had come back through San Francisco at the end of the road trip and I had spent an afternoon at the library going through the newspaper archives.

It hadn't taken me long to find the article because I knew the year and the date, although the story had shown up three days after McKillop's death and was short on details.

An unidentified man was shot to death near Waverly Street on Wednesday morning. The killer had not been identified. Chief Charles Dullea said, "We are confident that the assailant will soon be captured and brought to justice."

It would have been nice to have a name but if McKillops had been looking for another victim it's unlikely he would have carried identification, And what were the chances of another murder on that morning, on that street? It had to be him. A search through the rest of the year's stories suggested that Dullea's confidence had been misplaced. The headlines were mostly filled with war stories as the US got pulled closer and closer to war but even in the back pages nothing about McKillop's death showed up. No announcement that a killer had been captured. On a hunch, I scrolled back through past archives of the *San Francisco Examiner and Chronicle* and found two murders of young women that occurred within a mile of the train station. One was a twenty-three-year-old nurse in 1936 and the other a nineteen-year-old nanny in 1939. Neither of the stories mentioned pregnancy but it was unlikely they would have known or if they had that they would have written about it. If this was some wild hallucination or psychotic episode I was getting a lot of the details right.

There had been no more overnighters on the West Coast trip but right after the last night game in San Francisco, I headed to the train station. The rest of the team would be flying out in the morning and getting into

Montreal late Wednesday afternoon with the first game of a four-game series against Philadelphia going Thursday night. My train wouldn't get into Montreal until early Friday morning. Balducci wasn't happy that I was going to miss the Thursday night game.

Chapter Ten

Nippy Jones bumped me in the aisle.

"Sorry, buddy."

But he barely looked at me. He was still three cars from the bar car and this was no time to get slowed down. I had imagined that now, with Jack McKillops dead I would stay in my own time. Nope. I was standing outside my berth, stretching when the ballplayer went by. I didn't know then that he was a St. Louis Cardinal or even a ballplayer—just a young dark-haired guy with the early flush of booze in his cheeks and a burning concern that fun might be happening without him.

I hadn't fallen asleep until Denver, around noon on Wednesday. By then I had been awake for almost twenty-four hours. Every time I closed my eyes I had been back in the street watching Georgie pull the trigger, shake his head at me and run up the street.

And now the young man I had seen get on the train in St. Louis wasn't helping me get back to sleep. McKillops had been a big man. A couple of inches taller than me so six foot four at least and had carried a lot of weight. But easy, like it had been tailored for him. The man I had seen get on the train in St. Louis hadn't been quite as big as McKillops but he had the same slightly oversized head, sharp-angled nose, thin pale lips, high broad forehead with a black widow's peak that fell across his forehead, the peak just starting. His face was smoother than McKillop's, not as timeworn yet. But in twenty years he was going to look just like the guy who had looked back at me from the bunk. You could have called him handsome except for the eyes. They were sunk deep and shadowed, as if he had evolved somewhere different than the rest of us. Someplace where what was in your eyes could get you killed. I sat in my seat for several minutes.

He was sitting in the second car from the end. He sat straight but relaxed, his hands folded in his lap. He had the same big knuckled hands as his father but they were softer, paler and well-manicured. His dad's hands had been nicked and chipped like a country road sign, smeared with fresh grease and stained with old dirt and grime that couldn't be scrubbed loose. They had been the hands of a man who knew hard toil and who expected work to hurt. This man didn't work with gears and pistons and searing steam. But the eyes that watched me pass in the aisle were the same, flat and blank like the eyes of a big cat shadowed in a tree deciding when and what to eat. My gaze rested for a second on his face but then I let it slide lazily along to the seats beyond his. He looked at me, dismissed me and then for a second came back, some vestigial neurons buried deep in the folds of his brain triggering, trying to send a message to his conscious mind but the signal fading like a thin trail of rainwater soaking into the ground and leaving only a faint dark line that disappeared quickly in the heat of the sun. The porter came in behind me and distracted him.

I kept walking back into the last passenger car. There was an open seat there. I sat down in it and the older woman in the window seat looked at me but she didn't speak. I sat there for what seemed like a long time but was probably more like ten or fifteen minutes and then got up and walked back out the way I had come. He didn't turn around to look as I walked up from behind but as I walked by his seat it felt like his eyes locked on the back of my head and followed me all the way out of the car. I have no idea whether I was just imagining it.

Back in my seat I worried at it like a deep hangnail—but you can't stay awake forever. When I awoke I was even less sure what I thought about the man that had boarded the train in Missouri. But I was thirsty too so I followed Jones through the train to the bar car. The bar was three deep with mostly young fit men although there was a sprinkling of young ladies and older men. I leaned over to one of the guys at the back of the group around the bar.

"Who do you guys play with."

He had a beer bottle in one hand and the lopsided grin he gave me suggested that it wasn't his first. He nodded with his chin over to a man standing against the wall signing autographs.

"You telling me you don't recognize that guy, bud?"

The man against the wall had an open farmer's face with a strong hooked nose and a grin wider on one side than the other that he flashed only occasionally. He looked vaguely familiar but no name came to mind.

"Sorry."

The guy's eyes widened.

"You should be sorry, pal. That's Stan The Man. Best player in baseball, bar none."

Stan Musial. I knew he had been a great player but I couldn't even remember what team he had played for.

"Who's he play for?"

"Are you messing with me, buddy. You don't know who Stan Musial plays for?"

He looked at the book in my hand.

"There's your problem. Get your nose out of the book and take a look around. Jesus H."

He turned away to tap one of his buddies on the shoulder to tell him the story of the guy who didn't know what baseball team Stan Musial played for and I moved through the crowd. I spotted a guy a little to the side not talking to anybody. He was dressed in the same travelling uniform as the rest of the players, suit jacket, pressed dress pants, white shirt and tie but unlike most of the players his jacket was still on and his tie was high and tight against his collar. He held a beer in one hand but only took an occasional sip. I leaned in.

"What team do you play for?"

"The Cards."

"Where you headed?"

"Boston. We've got a three-gamer there this weekend. One on Saturday and a Sunday doubleheader."

I stuck out my hand.

"Ryan Spencer."

He reached for my hand and had to tilt a little to the left to do it and winced when he did.

"Whitey Kurowski."

I nodded at his arm.

"Bum shoulder?"

He shook his head but didn't add any details.

"What do you do, Mr. Spencer?"

"Call me, Ryan. I'm a ballplayer." It just came out without thinking.

He smiled without parting his lips.

"Who do you play for?"

Shit. I didn't even know if there was a Montreal baseball team in whatever year we were in.

"I play up in Canada. You ever play up there?"

He shook his head.

"Closest I ever got was Rochester. Where in Canada?"

Oh well, here goes nothing.

"Montreal."

He made a little face.

"How you like it?"

"I like it. Montreal's a nice city."

"I don't mean the city. I mean playing with the colored fellas."

I knew Jackie Robinson had played in Montreal but I wasn't sure when and I hadn't known there had been more than one. If I remembered right he had played one season in Montreal the year before he joined Brooklyn and I knew he had played his first year for Brooklyn in '47.

"It's been fine."

He nodded as if he wasn't sure.

"They say he might play in the bigs next year, is that right?"

I shrugged. I was in way over my head. I wasn't sure Robinson had even had a good year in Montreal. Although he must have to make it to the Dodgers the next year.

"He's good enough." Well, at least, I knew that was true.

Whitey looked doubtful.

"There's going to be guys don't want to play against them let alone with 'em."

"Yeah, well, that's their problem."

Kurowski shrugged.

"I guess you're right. I don't mind one way or another. If he's good enough to play, that's good enough for me. It's just that not everybody thinks that way."

I nodded.

"Well, nice talking to you Mr. Kurowski. I think I'll get a pop and head back to my seat."

I turned away.

"Ryan?"

I turned back at his voice.

"We've got a ninety-minute wait in Chicago. A few of the boys were going to try and find an empty ballfield and get in a little practice. We might be short a player or two, you want to come along?"

"No thanks, I've..." I stopped. I had a chance to play pickup ball with the 1946 Cardinals...and maybe Musial would come out.

"Actually, that sounds good. I could use the workout. Thanks."

He nodded.

"The train will get into Chicago in around twenty minutes—we'll be gathering on the platform."

* * *

"You kids want to play some ball?"

The only way I would have known it was a ball-field is that there were three kids playing catch when we walked up. The three boys had been tossing the ball lazily back and forth occasionally rolling easy grounders that they scooped and looped casually to each other. I guess it was why they called it sandlot ball. It was an empty lot beside a stock pen that wasn't being used and looked like it hadn't in a while. Flimsy wooden planks nailed to crooked fenceposts, some barely anchored into the ground, were all that would have held the livestock in and it didn't look like it could have held up to a strong breeze let alone a rumbling, shamble of hard-muscled cattle. One hinge on the big swinging door had rusted through and the door hung precariously by the bottom hinge with the bottom corner of the door buried in the ground.

Where the boys were playing was just an uneven expanse of hardscrabble dirt with the occasional tuft of grass or weed poking out of the ground. This would have been where the cattle milled around as they were funneled into the stock pen and if it rained the ground would have been churned into a stew of mud and piss and shit and when the rain stopped and the sun came out it would have been baked into the rough cracked hardpan that the boys were playing on. I had been looking for a backstop and a short chainlink fence separating the field from the stands and the benches and red dirt basepaths in a grass infield with the lines chalked white like the last thin ribbon of snow in spring before the sun turns it into a damp dark shadow and then it's gone. But those are baseball fields in 2010, not 1946. In 1946, ballfields are anywhere you can hit a ball three hundred feet without breaking a window or losing the ball.

The boys only had two gloves between them, frayed orphans the color and shape of chewed tobacco, but they caught the ball easily and threw with practiced indifference. Even the little guy without a glove plucked the ball easily out of the air or as it skidded along the ground. They had seen us coming but ignored us, maybe thinking we were older guys coming to bully them off their field. But now they looked over and the short guy's eyes widened. He turned and said something I couldn't hear to the other two guys and the three of them stopped throwing the ball then stood and watched us without speaking. Schoendienst spoke again.

"We're just looking to loosen up before tomorrow's games, boys, do you want to play a little."

It took them a second to answer and it seemed like the Cardinals had been through this before because they just stood and waited. Finally the kid without the glove called over.

"Are you Red Schoendiest?"

"That I am, son."

"And is that Harry The Hat?"

Schoendienst looked to his left at the tall, slim man with the long preacher's face and the lazy grin.

He nodded.

"Sure is.

He turned and said something to the other guys that I couldn't hear then turned back.

"And you're asking if we want to play ball?"

Schoendienst nodded.

"That's right, boys."

"Shit, yeah."

"Come on in here then. Here's how we'll do it."

Schoendienst looked around, then nodded his head at a slight, quiet guy with sunken cheeks and big ears.

"You wanna throw, Cat?"

He shook his head.

Schoendienst turned back to the three boys.

"Can any of you three throw a little?"

One of the kids was tall and dark-haired and wore frayed grey pants that were a couple of inches too short and showed a thick strip of bare skin, not sock and the other two boys looked at him. The shorter guy spoke first.

"Andy can pitch a little. He's the best from around here."

The tall kid blushed but didn't speak.

"Okay then, Andy. You're our boy. Nothing too nasty eh, we don't want to look bad."

The kid nodded seriously and Red smiled.

"Just kidding, kid, throw everything you've got. Here's how it's going to work, there's …"

Red stopped and counted.

"…fifteen guys. We'll put nine in the field and the other six guys will hit.

As soon as you make an out you go to the field. Andy, you pitch until it's your turn to hit and we'll decide who throws then."

Andy went to the mound and the kid without a glove whose name was Danny went to short and Herb the blonde stocky kid ended up in left field. Schoendiest was hitting first and got to the plate and looked out, saw that Danny didn't have a glove and held up his hand to stop Andy from going into his windup.

"Kid, where's your glove?"

"It's okay, Mr. Schoendiest I don't need one."

Red looked over to where Whitey and I were standing and nodded at his glove where it lay on the ground.

"Whitey toss the fucking kid my glove, would you."

I was closer and grabbed it and walked it out to the kid. I held it out and he just looked at it and then at me. We stood there for a second without Danny reaching for the glove. He nodded at it.

"Is that Red's glove?"

I nodded.

"I don't think I can wear Red Schoendiest's glove."

"He wants you to."

He looked in at the plate where Schoendiest was staring out impatiently.

"Take the fucking glove, kid. Let's get this show on the road."

He looked back at me and I held the glove out a little further and he finally reached out and took it. He rolled it around in his hands several times and finally Schoendiest shouted at him.

"It's a fucking glove, kid, not your sister's hoo-ha—you can put your fingers in."

A couple of the players laughed and the kid blushed but carried the glove back to his spot.

Schoendiest let the first pitch go by just to see what the kid had. Andy was okay, but not close to major league and Schoendiest turned hard on the next pitch and sent a screaming liner over short and rounded first looking for the ball to see if he could take another base, whether it would get between the outfielders and give him a chance to keep running...but the outfielders weren't moving. Danny had taken one step to his left, jumped and stretched and the ball had buried in his glove. The kid had some crazy hops and soft hands. It was a play Schoendiest himself might not have made. It took him a second to realize what had happened and the other guys were laughing now. Marty Marion who was at second so Danny could play short strolled over from second base and grabbed the kids arm and raised it to show Red the ball.

"Fuck off, Slats."

The guys laughed even harder and Danny flushed pink again and tried not to smile. Schoendienst kicked at the ground.

"Should have let the little fucker use his bare hands."

The guys laughed even harder. Schoendienst trotted out to third base and I tossed him the glove I was using. That was just the beginning though. The kid caught everything. And nothing bounced true on this field. He seemed to have an otherworldly anticipation for when the ball was going to make an unexpected carom and his hands would flash to the spot. Always two-handed so that ball seemed to be on its way to first before it had time to settle in the glove. He had the pro's ability to make the 'catch and throw' seem like one smooth unhinged movement. I could see Kurowski and Schoendiest and Marion exchanging glances—this kid was already a major-league infielder...using a borrowed glove...on a dirtshit field. Maybe there was one in every town.

A small crowd gathered, mostly young kids and mothers although there were a couple of men standing to the side, either shift workers or guys that couldn't or wouldn't find work. The game settled into an easy rhythm, players chattering and laughing and moving from the field to the batting line-up. Joe Garagiola, the catcher, was the cut-up, swinging wildly at a pitch way over his head as if he didn't know better and then lining the next ball over second for a clean single but going hard for second even though the throw had him beat by twenty feet. Then making Marion chase him around second base and out into shallow right field before flopping in the dirt in feigned exhaustion and Marion slapping the tag on his ear.

I ended up in line behind a short, stocky guy who stared intently at Andy.

He noticed me watching him.

"The kid tips off his curve."

I watched him for a bit and didn't see it at first but then it jumped out at me – when he was throwing a fastball he went right into his windup but when he was throwing a curve he held his glove in front of his face and arranged his grip in the glove.

"Wouldn't last a day in the bigs even if he could pitch."

I shrugged.

"Pickup ball. We're just having a little fun."

He shot me a look and made a sour face.

"Whatever you say, bush league."

The hitter in front of him, a young guy with a sturdy build, lined the ball over first base. I hadn't got either of their names. The stocky guy who had called me bush-league stepped into the batter's box pulled his cap down tight on his head and peered out from under the bill at Andy. Andy took some time to adjust the ball in his glove and threw a big looping curve that the guy ripped over Danny's head and into the gap. He ran hard with his head down just catching the inside corner of first base with his outside foot. By the time he rounded second base he had almost caught up with the guy who had been on first and was loping easily around the bases. The first runner pulled into third base standing up and the guy who had lined the ball over short passed him nudging him with his shoulder as he went by and sending him stumbling off the bag. Schoendienst at third took the relay, tagged the first runner and fired the ball to Garagiola standing blocking the plate. Garagiola had the runner by several steps but the guy just kept coming and took him high in the chest with his shoulder, knocking him hard to the dirt. Garagiola hung onto the ball but lay for a second on the ground, clearly winded, before struggling to his feet.

"Geez, Country, can't you lay off just this once."

"Sorry, Joe."

He didn't look sorry. He walked by me to the back of the line and gave me a flat stare as he went by.

"Go get'em, bush league."

I stepped in with the bases empty. Andy went right to his windup and threw me a seventy-five mile an hour fastball, he might as well have set it on a T. I've hit plenty of balls sweet and flush but I had never hit a ball that clean and I don't think I ever will again. A baseball swing is all about timing, the feet, the hips, the hands and there is only one absolutely sweet spot where all the pieces fit together exactly like they're supposed to and you can go your whole life and never put all the pieces together absolutely perfectly. But when it happens you don't feel it anywhere but your balls. Nobody moved except to turn and watch. The ball was gray and spongy and not absolutely round but I still hit it four hundred and fifty feet. It was fifty feet in the air when it went over The Hat's head and a hundred feet past the deepest outfielder when it hit the ground and rolled up against a rusted overturned barrel. There was silence for a second and then everybody started hooting and hollering. The blonde kid looked around at the other fielders and then shrugged and trotted after it. I put my head down and jogged around the bases and the first baseman nodded at me as I went by.

"Helluva ball, kid."

I nodded. Marion slapped me on the shoulder and Schoendienst just shook his head in semi-mock wonderment.

The guy called Country looked at me as I came away from home plate and I stared back.

"Beat that, big league."

Sometimes it's hard to resist.

Making Danny hit wasn't the worst thing that happened that day but it felt like the first domino. I get it though. The kid was too good. We had to see if he could hit. He had avoided coming to the plate for over an hour. A couple of guys tried to give him a shot but he just shook his head and they moved on because there was always somebody else who was happy to get their cuts in. If Danny hadn't been so good nobody probably would have noticed that he hadn't batted. But you couldn't watch a guy pick'em like that without wanting to see him swing a bat. Schoendienst flied out on his third time through the line-up and went right out to where Danny was standing at short and held his hand out for his glove.

103

"Let's see what you can do, kid."

Danny looked over Red's shoulder at Andy who was staring back at him and then down to his feet.

"If you don't mind Mr. Schoendienst, I'll just field."

"What do you mean? You're going to hit just like everybody else. If you can hit half as good as you can field, son, you're a ballplayer."

"I ain't much of a hitter, Mr. Schoendienst. Never have been."

"Yeah, well, none of us could hit much when we started. Get in there and take a few cuts."

"If it's all the same to you, Mr. Schoendienst, I think I'll just play in the field somewhere."

I could see Red was getting annoyed but I could also tell there was something going on that we were missing. Schoendienst reached out and pulled his glove off Danny's hand.

"Hit or fuck off, kid. I don't have time for this."

Danny looked at Andy standing to the side of the mound and the only word I could find for the expression on his face was desperate. Andy shrugged, so small I almost didn't see it. Everybody in the field and around the plate had stopped and was looking. The small crowd knew something was going on but couldn't figure out what.

Danny stood for a second and then started walking slowly toward the plate. He had never looked slighter. Nippy had been about to hit but stepped back and held out his bat and Danny took it from him without looking up from the ground. He stepped into the box that had been scratched in the dirt with somebody's boot heel. Garagiola stood behind the plate his ballcap backwards on his head, holding his heavy iron mask in his hand looking at the kid but not dropping into his crouch. The bat hung loosely from Danny's hand, the barrel dragging along the ground and he stared down at the ragged piece of splintered wood that we were using for home plate then reached out and tapped it once, pulled the bat up over his shoulder and looked out at Andy. Garagiola squatted behind the plate. Andy held out his hands as if to say 'What do you want me to do?' but Danny just looked at him impassively, his face fishbelly white and damp except around his eyes where the skin glowed fever red like the evening sun through the greasy smoke of a tire fire. Andy stood for a few seconds longer but then shrugged and threw the ball and Danny swung and missed.

We all saw it. We were ballplayers. Danny couldn't keep his back foot in. As Andy let the ball go Danny's foot dropped. He tried to keep his face impassive but you could see his eyes widen and his shoulders tighten as the ball left Andy's hand. Danny swung weakly at the pitch, bent at the waist with his lower body shifting away from the plate and his upper body trying to lean into the swing. Andy kept the ball on the outside of the plate but that made it worse. Danny couldn't cover the outside half of the plate because he was pulling away and so he took three weak swings, didn't come close to making contact with the ball, dropped the bat on the plate then turned and walked through the players waiting to hit and then through the thin crowd of mothers and their children gather at the edge of the lot and then up the street to the corner, his shoulders curled into his chest, broken wings around a still-beating heart. Nobody spoke except Red.

"Kid."

But Danny didn't look back. He turned at the first corner and disappeared.

Nippy moved forward and picked up the bat and stood uncertainly at the plate but the sun felt hard instead of warm and the guys drifted in from the field. The game was over.

* * *

They would have found her body even if Red hadn't made Danny hit, but somehow they still seemed connected.

The police cars were pulled up against the curb and the ambulance had pulled onto the sidewalk next to an overgrown lot behind a small brick factory building. The cops were leaning against their cars and one of them had taken off his hat and laid it on the rooftop. An unmarked car pulled up just as we got to where the police cars were parked and a short, spare man wearing a grey short-brimmed fedora with the brim turned up got out of the driver's side and a tall, bareheaded man running to fat got out of the passenger's side. The short man moved with quick determined steps without looking at us. I could tell the bigger man recognized some of the players because his step faltered for a second but then he moved after his partner who was already talking to the cops. I couldn't hear what they were saying, but after a couple of words the cop reached behind without looking and grabbed his cap pulled it down tight over his forehead, and then led the detectives across the gravel and a few feet into the grass and weeds. They stood in a semi-circle looking down at something in the grass. The cop's partner stayed at the car. He hadn't even looked over when the detectives had shown up and he still stood staring down between his feet. I walked across the street, past the police car, and over to the edge of the grass.

She was young. It was hard to know how young. Probably under twenty. Her dress had been a scoop throat so I could see the deep, wide gash beneath her chin. The blood had pooled and started to congeal beneath her head and her hair lay in thick sodden ropes around her face. Her skin was blue-white and smooth like polished beach stone except for a thick oil paint ridge of blood on her cheek.

"What the f…."

The detective had noticed me. He turned to the cop.

"Could you at least keep the gawking assholes from trodding all over the scene, Laughlin? For fuck's sake."

He turned back to the body without looking at me again. The cop grabbed my arm and led me away.

"Let's go, buddy. Across the street."

I let him lead me away.

"Do you know her, officer?"

"Look pal, just get back on the other side of the street and out of the way." He gave me a little nudge on the shoulder to keep me moving and turned back.

The Cardinals were still in a small cluster on the sidewalk and a crowd of locals had started to gather around them. I turned back expecting the cop to have started back towards the body but he stood against his vehicle looking away from the scene.

"Officer Laughlin?"

He cut his eyes back towards me and lifted his chin a little.

"Is there anybody around here who does abortions?"

He looked at me for several long seconds and then turned and walked over to where the detectives were crouched next to the body. I stood in the road for a moment and then headed up the street toward the train. Red called out like he had for Danny.

"Ryan?"

"The train leaves soon Red and I don't want to miss it."

I looked back from half a block away and the team was following. The cop and both detectives were standing straight and looking in our direction. I couldn't tell for sure that they were looking at me but it seemed like it.

* * *

I expected the detectives to show up before the train left the station but they didn't. The good feeling that the sun and the game had carried was gone and the players drifted off, a few to the bar car but most to their berths. I walked through the car looking for the young man with the hard mouth and the barren eyes. He wasn't where I had seen him sitting and there was nothing on his seat. I walked the length of the train but didn't see him. He was gone. He had stepped off the train in Chicago and he was gone now. Faded into the city. He would take another train out in the next day or two, to wherever he was from. And wait.

On the way back to my seat I stepped to the side for an older gentleman coming out of one of the bathrooms. I didn't get a good look at him because his head was down as he adjusted his jacket and I was past him when I heard his voice and felt his hand on my arm.

"Time is treating you well, young man."

I turned and looked at an older, worn, rumpled version of the man I had met weeks ago in my life but seven years ago in his. He had looked his age in 1939 but now he looked much older than his forty-five years.

"Dr. Fermi. It's a pleasure to see you. You're returning to New York?"

107

He shook his head.

"No, visiting New York. I teach now at the University of Chicago."

"Right, I knew that."

I knew that shortly after our first meeting Fermi had moved his laboratory from Columbia to Chicago and begun working on the Manhattan Project in earnest. Fermi gave a puzzled smile.

"You've been following my career, my friend?"

"It's Ryan, Dr. Fermi, Ryan Spencer."

He smiled, a little embarrassed.

"You saw through my 'young mans' and 'my friends.'"

I shrugged.

"My wife is not with me on this trip, would you care to sit with me and we can talk. Of time. And how it seems to have passed you without leaving a trace."

"I don't want to impose, sir, I'm sure you have important things you are working on. I couldn't…"

He took me by the elbow.

"I'm alone and I've had enough of my own thoughts. They're boring even me."

His seat was in the middle of the car and the seat beside him was empty even though the rest of the car was full. I pointed at the seat.

"Are you expecting them back?"

He leaned over and spoke softly.

"It's the one perk of position I take advantage of. I have bought both seats so that I can work in peace if I so desire."

He shrugged and patted the seat.

"It is yours."

We settled in.

"So, you still play baseball, Mr. Spencer?"

"Yes sir."

"You have followed my career and I must confess I have tried to follow yours. With little success. I'm bad with names."

"It wouldn't have mattered, Dr. Fermi, I'm not a major leaguer. I'm still trying to make the big leagues."

He looked at me closely.

"I suspected that must be it. That you were playing in the bushes."

"The bush leagues."

He waved his hand.

"But it's been seven years since I've seen you and although you are still a young man you can't be as young as you appear and that is a long time to play for little money or acclaim."

"Yes, it is."

"I'm sorry, Ryan, I don't mean to pry."

"I guess dreams die hard, Dr. Fermi."

He nodded.

"Please, call me Rico. Yes, they do, Ryan."

"And your work, sir, it goes well?

He looked at me again.

"You know about the project I was working on?"

"Yes sir."

He looked down at his hands in his lap.

"It has gone very well. Better than I ever could have expected and worse than I could ever have imagined."

"They say it shortened the war by several months and saved many lives."

He smiled softly. He didn't speak for a long time, just staring down at his hands, and when he finally spoke again he didn't look up.

"They always say something, don't they? It's always for the best, no? But one hundred thousand people were here, talking, singing, a mother holding her child's hand as they walked to school, perhaps a young man and his girl were kissing for the very first time…"

He stopped and I thought he might be done but he wasn't.

"…and then the final wind. It would have been on them without warning, stripping the skin from flesh and then the flesh from bones and then bone to dust, returning them to their elemental form."

It was late afternoon and the sun filtered through the window and backlit the dust motes floating around Fermi's head.

"Are you sorry?"

He shrugged.

"That I worked on it? What is to be sorry about? The bomb would happen with me or without me. And it was an enormously stimulating project. These are brilliant men. And we are the same, these men and me. It is a puzzle and once we have seen the puzzle the rest is inevitable. We cannot stop thinking of it. I remember the day we tested the bomb. The power is difficult to imagine. We were a dozen kilometers away and I had torn a napkin into tiny pieces and held it in my hand and the force of that blast sent those pieces fluttering away like muttered words. I knew then we had moved past the imaginable and arrived at a place where so very, very few could understand and only those of us who could live inside the mathematics. Only those of us for whom the abstract symbols drew a hidden world, a world of curling waves and shifting shapes that appeared at the edges of our vision and was lost when you tried to look direct upon it but beneath it all a terrible, terrible energy tethered by silken webs fine as angel's hair. "

He looked over then and shrugged.

"But it is lonely."

"Lonely?"

He looked away and his eyes were even more deeply shadowed than I had first thought and now his lip trembled slightly and he spoke as if to himself.

"Sometimes I wish I could be like the rest."

He waved his hand to take in everyone in the car.

"There are so few of us who understand. And when we are together the comprehension is too terrible for words but the knowledge stretches from horizon to horizon so that we can speak of nothing else and we are drawn together by what we share and thrust apart by what we fear and I'm only sorry that I know too much. That we have set the great stone in motion and it is only a matter of time before we all are crushed like delicately painted eggshells and that when the stone finally comes to rest it will be in a dark, and smoking place, a torn and blasted landscape where symmetry of form and elegance of function will be whispers in the wind for a thousand, million years."

"That's the only way?"

He had been talking to himself and I startled him when I spoke but he recovered and shrugged.

"It's the way it always goes. It begins as a miracle and then a natural wonder and then an expensive luxury and then a universal necessity and finally an afterthought. Think of the domesticated horse, the knife, the gun, the steam engine, electric lights, the radio, motion pictures, the automobile, the airplane…have you seen the television?"

I nodded.

"Yes, a pleasant diversion, the television. Why should the power of the atom be any different? First, the most powerful country in the world owns it. But when Britain? When Russia? And then it will be any country that wants it. And then it will be corporations. Coca-Cola or General Motors. And then it will be groups and clubs with their own marginal interests and imagined slights. And then it will be private citizens, hobbyists in their basements, all of us with unimaginable power available like soda pop and ketchup."

He stopped.

"I shouldn't be talking to you of this. It is my burden."

"You're not a religious man, Rico?"

"I was, you know. I am Italian. I know the sacred and the sorrowful and the blessed mysteries and the Way of the Cross and the holy words of Luke and John and James and Paul and the transfiguration of simple bread and wine to flesh and bone and that my sins are too much to bear but not too great for the Son of God. "

"But…?"

He shrugged.

"You grow up. It's a silly story for children. It has no place for thoughtful men."

"It might be a comfort now."

"I have no doubt of that. I wish for God. I pray for God. I beg for God like Prometheus must have begged for death. I dream of God when I sleep and God holds a golden cage that contains a two-headed eagle that he feeds

111

wine-soaked dates and mice drunk on sweetened milk, and the raptor's eyes blaze like liquid flame but what is all that but a child's cartoon, the inchoate creations of an infant bereft of imagination, the crayon scrawl of a spastic hand governed by a witless mind—against the unimaginable wonders of the natural world."

He stopped then for several seconds and I thought he was finished but he wasn't.

"When each of us is greater than the gods we could imagine, then who will judge us?"

We sat and talked after that. He apologized many times for speaking as he had. That he was a self-indulgent and deluded man and that I should pay no mind to the ravings of a shabby academic. And we moved on to speak of other things, of baseball and the war and movies he had seen but I had not, of FDR and Billie Holiday, who he loved and Charlie Parker, who he didn't understand although he wished he did. But behind his eyes was darkness…and oily smoke and twisted earth. Eventually, there was little left to say except goodbye. He stood in the aisle to shake my hand. He would be dead in eight years at the age of fifty-three and I was sure I wouldn't see him again. I went back to my berth and when I awoke we were in Montreal. And it was 2010.

Chapter Eleven

Her name was Julie Drouin, the girl lying in the long grass with her head resting in her own blood. She was nineteen years old and had left her family in Joliet in the fall of 1945 to attend the Secretaries Training Institute in Chicago. That was all I knew of her because it was all they wrote.

Most of the national papers were available through the Montreal library and the Sun, the Times, the Tribune and the Daily News had all covered the story. The city was still searching for the Lipstick Killer in the spring of 1946 and all four stories on Julie mentioned the Killer without stating that he had struck again. By then, there had been three deaths attributed to the Lipstick Killer, two women in their thirties or forties and a six-year-old girl who had been dismembered and scattered through the Chicago sewers. All three had been killed in or taken from their apartments. William Heiren, a seventeen-year-old college student, was arrested a few weeks after Drouin died and convicted of the three murders and was still, sixty-four years later, sitting in a jail cell in Dixon, Illinois. There was never a mention of the Drouin killing in any of the stories about Heirens—the police had figured out early that Julie's death wasn't connected to Heirens.

There were dozens of murders of young women every year in Chicago but I only found one more around the stockyards. In 1953, seven years after Julie had been killed, Betsy Firnelle, a twenty-year-old nursing student, her throat cut and her body left in the long grass to be discovered by some kids cutting across the abandoned field behind one of the small factory buildings. I searched the archives up until 1956 but there were no more murders of young women in the area around the station and no word that anybody was ever arrested for the Drouin or Firnelle murders. But, if this was McKillops, the killings weren't going to be confined to Chicago.

In every major city from Baltimore to Los Angeles, I could find one or two more stories about young women who had died between 1946 and 1955 in areas close to railway stations. Some newspapers were willing to supply the grisly details and I found eleven stories about dead young women whose throats had been cut. Stories that took up space but had no bottom... stories written in chalk just before the rains came. Stories that caught your eye for a moment and then were forgotten as you moved on to more important things, the movies, the corner store for milk and bologna, late for work, and the bus already pulling away. Eleven lives passing unnoticed beneath the skin thin layer of recorded history and then, one from a fading trail of bubbles breaks the surface and for a split second heads turn, steps falter and eyes are drawn, as by an unexpected flicker of color or a small movement that doesn't fit, but it's just a moment barely discernible and quickly forgotten in a million similar moments and they turn back to look ahead and find their pace again and it is as if they never slowed and the bubble never burst.

And I didn't know, was it McKillops the younger doing them all, or were there men in every city and town waiting for the opportunity?

* * *

We won nine in a row at home. I was hitting and so was everybody else. On those rare days when we could only scrape together a couple of runs, our pitchers shut the other team down. We were eight games over .500, twenty-five and seventeen, going into the last game of the homestand. McKay started. He had won four straight with one no decision since coming off the DL and had started twice during our streak, a one–hit complete game shutout against Cincinnati and a seven–two shellacking of the Mets. The guy was a prick, but he could pitch.

But McKay wasn't good that day. He got into trouble in the first inning, walking the first two batters before getting the number three hitter to ground out to first, moving the runners up a base. Richards, the Pirates clean-up guy, already had fourteen home runs and was on a pace to hit more than fifty. There were still whispers about steroids but if this guy was juicing, he wasn't very good at it. He was six foot two and whippet sleek at one hundred and eighty-five pounds. He didn't muscle balls out of the park, it was all timing and quick-twitch fibers. With first base open, McKay pitched pretty carefully and ended up walking him. Richards had worked the count to full and then McKay threw a tight hook that just missed the outside corner. McKay stood and stared down the umpire as Richards jogged to first. The umpire stared back until McKay turned and stalked back to the mound slamming the ball furiously into his glove. He made a mistake with the next batter, leaving the ball high over the center of the plate but Velasquez missed by just a little, sending the ball to the warning track and knocking in the runner from third. Mckay threw four straight balls to the next batter loading the bases again and the Pirates' seventh-place hitter smashed a sinking line drive off a sweet ninety mph fastball that I backhanded just off the ground. I rolled the ball towards the umpire at home plate and jogged off the field without looking at McKay. We were down one run, but it could have been worse.

McKay stormed into the dugout and fired his glove off the back wall nearly hitting our pitching coach.

"Motherfucker! Where do we get these fuckers? Cocksucker! I'm busting my ass and he can't see the fucking corners?! They've got one fucking job to do, see where the fucking ball crosses the plate and this fucker can't keep his fucking eyes open?! For fuck's sake! I'm the one painting the fucking corners, all that motherfucker has to do is see it!"

"It missed."

I should have kept my mouth shut but it made me sick to listen to him. Not just that he was wrong but that he was going to throw the game away. He couldn't pull himself back. Now, he would try and throw everything hard, his location would go and he would get smacked around the park. It was bad enough that he was full of shit, but now he was going to cost us the game. He froze when I spoke. Nobody had been speaking except McKay and now he was silent and the dugout was quiet except for the muted sounds of the crowd. When he turned, he came right at me. I got my arms up in time to stop him from getting his hands around my throat but the force of the rush sent me stumbling back and I fell, cracking my head off the concrete dugout wall. I had my hands up around my face to stop the blows although I was dazed. The players just stood around in a tight half-circle while Baldy, the coach, and Nick dragged him back. I lay there on the hard, cold concrete feeling the chill against my legs and back but the spreading warmth behind my head. A couple of the coaches helped me to the dressing room with one of them pressing a towel to the back of my head to stop the bleeding. Brady Turnstine, the third base coach, stayed with me while I sat in the training room with the towel pressed against the back of my head waiting for the doctor to come out of the stands.

"You know what your problem is, Spencer?"

I didn't even look up.

"You can't keep your big college mouth shut."

I hadn't said fifty words in the locker room over the last month. I looked up then.

"Yeah, Turnstine, I'm the problem. And college. Me and college are the two big problems."

He didn't say anything and I spoke again.

"You know what's coming eh? It's going to be six or seven nothing within the next few innings because McKay can't keep his shit together. He's going to walk three or four batters and then he's going to groove one to the middle of their order and we'll be lucky if the ball stays inside the stadium. And then we'll all get to hear about how the ump missed the call and we would still be on a streak if the ump hadn't missed one. And you'll just smile and nod, Brady. But just because you eat it with a spoon doesn't mean it's not bullshit."

He didn't speak although his face had tightened. I waited for a second.

"I'm fine to wait for the doctor. No need to keep me company."

He stood up and left without speaking.

The doc finished with me and I was back on the bench by the fourth inning. It had been worse than I expected—it was nine-one and McKay had been pulled in the third. Now, we clawed our way back and had the score at ten to eight with two on in the ninth but Nick struck out on a ninety-three mile-per-hour cut fastball. The streak was over. We were twenty-five and eighteen.

* * *

The crowds at the player's entrance after games had grown since the streak started and there were usually hundreds of fans waiting, mostly kids but a few of the autograph sharks who do it for the cash. I was out early because I had already showered and I worked my way through the crowd, signing as I went. The team had recently added a couple of security guards to keep a corridor open for the players to get to their cars but it still took fifteen to twenty minutes to move the one hundred and fifty feet from the player's entrance to the parking lot. I tended to ignore the older guys that weren't there with kids although I knew that lots of the autograph sharks brought nieces or nephews or borrowed friend's kids just because they knew it gave them a better chance of getting an autograph.

McKay came out behind me with three of his pitching buddies and they pushed past without stopping to sign. I had noticed a guy waiting at the edge of the crowd with what looked like his son, a little guy maybe six years old scanning the players coming out of the door and then looking past as soon as he realized we weren't who he was looking for. When McKay came out the kid's face changed and he tugged hard on his Dad's arm and they moved forward. It took a minute and McKay was already past them by the time they got close and the father, a young guy with long dark hair, maybe in his mid-twenties, wearing faded jeans, an Alouettes sweatshirt, and a ball cap on backwards, reached out and tugged on McKay's shirt. McKay stopped and looked down at his sleeve without looking at the guy. He pulled the sleeve out away from his arm and looked at it closely. Even from where I stood I could see the faint smudge of the guy's thumbprint.

"I'm sorry, Mr. McKay, but my son is just a huge fan of yours..." His voice quavered a little, and trailed off as McKay's eyes slowly moved from sleeve to face. They stood like that for a second just looking at each other, the little boy also looking, his eyes not leaving McKay. The other three guys had stopped and they stood, grinning. McKay brought his sleeve up into the guy's face.

"Do you see this, asshole?"

His son continued to look up but now his eyes flicked from McKay to his father trying to sort out what was happening.

The father nodded.

"I'm sorry, Mr. McKay, it's just we've been waiting for almost an hour and my son just loves you. He has your—"

"Do you know how much this shirt costs, asshole?"

The father took a quick helpless look down at his son and then back up to McKay.

"No, Mr. McKay, I don't but we were—"

"That's right, buddy, you don't. How much do you make a week? Four hundred? Five hundred dollars?"

The guy didn't even try.

"A week's pay. You would have to work for a week to pay for this fucking shirt. And you just reach out with those greasy, filthy, fucking hands and grab it. Like it's a paper towel in a public shitter."

The guy looked down at his son and it was enough to make him try one more time.

"I'm sorry, Mr. McKay, it's just that my son would give anything for your autograph. I can pay for any drycleaning or—"

McKay reached out and stuck his finger hard into the guy's chest.

"This is not about money, pal, it's about manners. And maybe this will be a lesson to you and your kid..."

McKay didn't even look down at the boy when he said it.

"...to have some fucking manners next time."

McKay turned away with his crew. He made a point of stopping to sign a couple of autographs but worked quickly through the crowd to his Hummer.

The crowd had gone quiet for a second while it was happening but as soon it was over they had started calling out for autographs again. I stepped forward as quickly as I could but the guy and his son had melted back into the crowd. I looked over the heads of the people still calling for autographs and saw them walking away across the parking lot tarmac. The man had his arm resting over his son's shoulder and kept looking down at him but the boy walked beside him his arms hanging loose and slack at his sides looking out to the side across the nearly empty parking lot to the houses and highway in the distance.

"He is not a nice man, Mr. Spencer."

I hadn't seen her in several weeks but I recognized Jimmy Munoz's wife right away. She had been standing to the side waiting for her husband to come out.

"Hello, Mrs. Munoz. No, he's not."

She smiled.

"Are you being overly polite or have you forgotten my first name."

I flushed.

"I remember your name, ma'am. Adelina."

"It's nice to know that it is not so easily forgettable."

"It's a beautiful name. Almost as beautiful as Ariadne."

She smiled again.

"So, you remember very well."

She looked across the parking lot to where the Hummer was turning on to the stadium access road.

"My husband does not care for Mr. McKay."

"No offense, ma'am, but he doesn't care much for me either—I'm hoping he's not a very good judge of character."

I had expected this comment to sour the conversation but instead, she laughed and her thin delicate face opened like a sundew in the morning.

"Jimmie doesn't like that you are a good third baseman and a very, very good hitter."

Her face became serious.

"He knows that he is getting older and slower and a little softer and it hurts him to see the end approaching. And you are young and strong and better than he was even when he was a very fine player."

She paused again.

"I think he admires you. Not just that you are a good player...although all of you silly boys admire very much this ability to catch and throw and hit and run. More than you should. It is a child's game played by children with beards but even a man like McKay, you will tolerate and more just because he can throw a baseball very quickly. So, yes he admires your ability. But he has told me stories. Of things you say to McKay and how you hurt the pitcher who tried to hurt you and how you say little but try very hard."

She paused.

"But you are taking his job. That makes it hard to like you very much."

She shrugged and I heard the door scrape open behind me and I could tell by Adelina's expression that it was Jimmie. Most of the fans had left while Adelina and I stood talking so Jimmie was able to move quickly towards the parking lot. I thought that she would move away from me towards her husband but she didn't and Jimmie walked up to us. He kissed his wife on the cheek and she pulled him close and said something to him in Spanish. He turned to me and nodded without speaking. Adelina laughed again looking back and forth between the two of us.

"It is nice to see teammates share such a strong bond."

She looked at us for several seconds and even her husband showed a shadow of a smile, then she laughed once more and took her husband's arm.

"C'mon, mi amore, we must get home. If I let you get talking to your dear friend Mr. Spencer, we will be here half the night. Mr. Spencer, it was a pleasure talking with you. I hope we have a chance to talk again in the future."

She looked at her husband.

"Say goodbye to the nice man, Jaime."

He narrowed his eyes at her as if he was angry but his lips still hinted at a smile and he leaned in and kissed her on the forehead. He turned back to me.

"See you, Spencer."

He hadn't spoken directly to me since the day at the fair.

"You too, Jimmie."

They turned and walked away and she took his hand. I watched them walk almost all the way to their car and then turned away before they could see that I was watching.

Chapter Twelve

I had already seen her that day—in a coffee shop on Callowhill Street on the way to the Free Library in Philadelphia. The line-up was too long so I spun around to leave and bumped into her, almost knocking her over. She would have fallen down if I hadn't grabbed her arm and held her up. I apologized but she had kept her head down and pulled away and walked past me without speaking. I turned and watched her as she hurried away, past the people lined up at the counter, and stood in front of the cash looking up at the menu over the wall. She was slim with dark curls that fell to her shoulders and, in profile, her face was pale, delicate, and fine. She wore jeans that tapered down to her ankles and black loafers and a thick wool sweater that fell almost to her hips. She appeared to concentrate hard on the menu and never looked my way. That would have been it, a strange girl in a coffee shop in Philly. Except here she was sitting three tables away pretending to leaf through a stack of books while I worked my way through the newspaper archives. Maybe Baldy had hired somebody to follow me. He was worried—I wasn't hitting and we had dropped three of the first four games of an eleven game East Coast swing.

Balducci had his coaches working the hotel lobbies making sure that the guys weren't partying too hard—we had a couple of guys who would have burned a votive candle at both ends. Everybody knew it and the watchdogs weren't hard to evade if you were really committed. They had gone to a few extra lengths with me. Twice, Balducci had shown up at my door after midnight under the pretext of running the next day's line-up card past me. And twice more I had heard somebody pause outside my door for several seconds before walking away. When I heard them I helped out by playing with the volume on the TV or getting up and moving around loudly so they wouldn't have to wait around long. I wasn't going out, but I was barely sleeping. At least eleven women had died so far and McKillops was loping through the 1940s while I was playing hit and catch in Pittsburgh. Time was travelling on two parallel tracks—here it was inching but back there it was ripping up track like a runaway locomotive, leaving behind charred ties, twisted metal, and dead bodies. It made sleeping tough.

And now I was sitting at a table in the Philadelphia Free library sneaking looks at a gamin-faced young woman who pretended not to notice. I was trolling for stories about young women murdered in the '40s and '50s and any mention of the name McKillops, but couldn't keep my mind on the work. I finally gave it up, got up from my table, walked over, and stood beside her chair. She tried to ignore me for a few seconds but I just stood staring down at her and she eventually tilted her head to look up at me.

"Yes?"

She had obviously regained her composure or she was a good actress. There was nothing tentative about the way she spoke.

"Did you find what you wanted?"

"Excuse me?"

"At the coffee shop?"

She pushed her chair away so that she could look up at me more easily and it scraped along the hard concrete floor causing the few other patrons to look up. Most of them continued to watch us.

"I'm afraid I don't understand?"

"You don't understand my question? What's not to understand about 'Did you find what you wanted'?

"I understand the question I just don't understand why you're standing over me asking it."

I stepped back but tried to keep pressing.

" I didn't mean to upset you, but you ran into me in the door of the coffee place and I wanted to..."

"You aren't upsetting me. I'm afraid I didn't recognize you from our little collision. I was preoccupied with other matters and barely noticed, to be honest."

I could feel the blood rising into my face.

"Oh."

I was beginning to feel foolish.

"Okay. But it just seemed odd to see you here as well as to run into you there. Like it might have been more than a coincidence...that maybe...and it seemed to me that you were...that just now, you were...."

She sat looking up at me without speaking and without expression, waiting for me to finish. I trailed off without completing the sentence. She just continued to look at me. She was good at this.

"Well, okay then. My mistake. I guess. So, as long as you're fine..."

She continued to look at me without responding. I turned around and went back to my table gathered up the stacks of Newspaper Indexes and returned them to the Newspaper and Microfilm Center. I had to walk by her table to leave but she didn't look up from her reading and I took a quick look over my shoulder at the top of the stairs. She was still looking down. I might have been losing my mind.

* * *

Things didn't get any better on the rest of the road trip. I couldn't commit to a swing and I was late on everything. I hadn't lost my patience though and managed to work the Philly staff for five walks and hit a seeing eye single through the right side of the infield in Game three but that was it, I was three for thirty-three for the road trip by the time we left Philly, batting an even .300 and the team was twenty-seven and twenty-five. Baldy sat me down for the first game against the Mets. It made sense but the only games I had missed so far were because I was on a train and it hurt to be sitting in the dugout watching Jimmy take balls at third. He had a good game, going two for three with a walk, a double, and two RBIs. Baldy didn't have much choice but to start him the next night. He came out of his office as I was looking at the posted lineup card. He looked at me but didn't speak, just shrugged. I knew what he meant but it still hurt a little. McKay hooted when he saw the lineup and made a point of going over and slapping Munoz on the back and shouting that "it looks like we have our starting third baseman back." He looked at me when he said it but I kept my head down lacing up my cleats. I looked over after McKay left Munoz's locker and Jimmy was looking at me. I nodded and he nodded back and gave a little shrug as if to say "Who knows?"

Not playing left me jangly and enervated. It was after midnight when I snuck out of the employee entrance of our hotel near Penn Station but this was New York City so there were still people around. It had rained just after the game so the streets were damp but it was warm enough for shirt sleeves. I walked past Penn Station and up Seventh Avenue into the garment district. It didn't feel like a place where a young woman could get an abortion or end up dead because of it. I kept walking, north into Hell's Kitchen. It may have been a tough neighborhood once but now it just looked like a hip downtown spot that hadn't priced itself out of the range of twenty-something university students and struggling musicians. I ended up on Ninth Avenue after one AM, hungry and thirsty, and stopped in at a little place called Zemi's. The hours on the window said they closed at midnight but the room was ¾'s full and the waitress met me at the door and seated me at the bar. I noticed Nick right away. That's how it is when you end up in a bar on your own, you check out the room. He was sitting at a table in the corner with a guy I had never seen before. And their hands were on the table. Touching. Not holding hands but each man with a hand on the table the way any two guys might let their arms drape across a table. But they were touching. My first impulse was to leave. I felt like I had walked in on something private, something I wasn't supposed to see.

"Sir? A menu?"

Too late.

"Yes, please. And I'll start with a Sprite."

"Seven-up alright?"

"Fine."

The bar put my back to Nick and his friend so I couldn't see them unless

I swiveled around in my chair. I wanted to turn and look, to see if I was mistaken. Maybe they were just two guys in a bar, old friends from high school who got together when Nick was in New York. But it hadn't looked like that.

I ordered Pad Thai and watched the TV over the bar that was showing a West Coast game, Dodgers and the Padres. The Padres mop-up guy was getting smacked around and looked like he might let the Dodgers back in the game but the Dodgers third baseman hit a low screaming line drive with the bases loaded. The shortstop leapt, snagged it, and then doubled the guy off second to get the Padres out of the inning. Nobody in the restaurant was watching or reacted, but I imagined Nick's eyes on the screen. From where he was sitting he would have to look right over my head to see the game. And he would look. It was baseball.

I'm not sure Nick loved baseball. He played like he practiced, with an ascetic's precision and discipline. Clean. Spare. No excess adrenalin. Nothing left for fist pumps or chest bumps. Everything was measured. He would take five quick, even strokes standing in the batter's box and when he was done he would stand with the bat hanging loose from his right hand watching the at bat in front of him. Most players have a routine just before they step into the box, stretches, bat whirls, glove tugs but not Nick. He just walked to the plate stepped into the box, set himself in his wide, slightly pigeon-toed stance, and waited. If the pitcher took more than eight seconds to go into his wind-up he would signal the ump and step out. I had noticed early in the season that he always stepped out at about the same time and I had started counting it off and it was always eight seconds.

His swing was short and his hands stayed close to his body so he could decide to turn hard on a ball or stroke it clean and neat to the opposite field. He didn't step into the pitch, just an economic hip turn that generated bat speed without giving up control. His first step out of the batter's box after he made contact was always with the bat in his hand and the second without, the bat falling to the ground beside the plate. I don't know if he practiced it or if it just happened but it was always the same. He wasn't the fastest guy on the team although he was fast enough for a big man…but he

126

was the best baserunner. On a ball into the outfield, we all curled outside the basepath to get a better angle at the turn but Nick always started his curl four strides out of the box and if you had tracked his path it might have varied by a couple of centimeters at most. I had seen him out before games repeating that run a dozen times, checking to see where his feet would land, making sure that the dirt was flat and solid and he wouldn't stumble or slip. Then always the same stride around first. The first long and powerful and if he saw an opening, a chance to take a base, the second shorter as he dug in hard and then lengthening a little over the next few strides until he was at top speed. If there wasn't an opening, then two short strides to pull up but always watching to make sure the fielder didn't bobble or throw to the wrong bag. And through it all, the same flat expression. Most guys will chat at first base. Not Nick. Not a word. Guys would talk to him but he wouldn't even acknowledge they were speaking. Eventually, most guys stopped talking to him but a couple never quit. I think they thought they could throw him off his game but he never even noticed.

I don't know if Nick loved baseball but he wore it like skin. He was watching the game and I was sitting underneath the TV. I didn't turn around through my Pad Thai. It was good, with hints of lime and cilantro but not too strong. But the thought of Nick behind me watching the game was ruining my dinner. The bartender came and cleared my plate and I ordered a coffee and risked a look over my shoulder. Nick was sitting alone at the table watching the game and his eyes drifted over to mine. He gave a short nod and I flushed as if I had been caught peeping through a window before nodding and turning quickly back to the bar.

My coffee was almost done and the bartender had slipped the bill under the saucer when Nick came over.

"Ryan."

I turned. They were both there. The other guy looked a little older than Nick, maybe forty, dark hair, short and neat and dressed Wall Street casual, a lightweight grey-green suit with narrow lapels over a dress shirt, no tie, and the edge of a white T showing at the neck.

"Hey, Nick."

I avoided looking at the other guy. Nick stepped a little to the side.

"I'd like you to meet a good friend of mine, Mick Farrar. Mick, Ryan Spencer."

I looked over then. He nodded at me.

"Nice to meet you, Ryan."

"You too." Nick and Mick. Cute.

I was twisted a little awkwardly in my chair so that I could see both of them and we stayed like that for a few seconds without speaking.

"You okay, Ryan?"

"Sure, Nick."

We didn't speak for another second or two.

"Is this a story, Ryan?"

"Not for me."

He looked at me for a second then nodded again.

"Well, enjoy your dinner."

I nodded.

"Nice meeting you, Ryan."

"You too, Mick."

They left then and I gave them a five-minute headstart before paying my bill and walking back to the hotel. The only person in the lobby except staff was Smitty and he scowled when he saw me but didn't say anything.

Chapter Thirteen

"Hey Pablo, throw me a towel."

Akins had come out of the shower naked, dripping, and spotted the stack of towels over by the five Latino players sitting in a circle talking quietly in Spanish. None of them were named Pablo. One of them, Alberto Guitterez, our set-up man, looked over and muttered something out of the side of his mouth to Diego Martinez who had just been called up. All five of the guys laughed.

"What did you say, Pablo?"

Guitterez looked over.

"I said my name ain't Pablo."

"Pablo, Juan. Whatever. Just pass me a fucking towel."

That quieted the room. Even his boys knew Akins had stepped over the line.

Guiterrez looked at him now, up and down, stopping for a long second at his groin then back up to his face.

"Chupa me huevos, maricon."

Akins flushed and stepped forward.

"What did you say?"

Jimmy leaned over and grabbed a towel off the top of the pile and tossed it across the room.

"Never mind, Akins, there's your towel."

Akins grabbed the towel and slipped it around his waist but kept coming. Guiterrez stood up.

"What did you say to me, asshole?"

Guiterrez didn't answer. He just stood, his long arms hanging loosely at his sides, waiting to see what was going to happen.

"I asked you a question, asshole. What did you just say?"

One of Akins's buddies called out. "Hey Tommy, relax, it's no big deal."

"Keep the fuck out of this, Riley. Me and fucking Pablo here, we're gonna get to the bottom of this. What did you say, pal?"

"Lick my balls."

Everybody looked over. Usually, Nick was the last man out of the locker room, slowly and silently stripping down in front of his locker. By the time he was down to a towel, everybody else would have showered and he would have the room to himself. So, now he was sitting in full uniform except for the jersey that was lying beside him on the bench. And acting as a Spanish-English translator.

Akins swung his head back and forth a couple of times between Guiterrez and Nick before finally settling on Nick.

"What the fuck, Nick?"

Nick had leaned over to start unlacing his spikes and spoke down to the floor.

"He said 'lick my balls.'"

It took a second for Akins to sort it out but as soon as he did he jumped at Guiterrez but Alberto had been ready from the first time Akins had asked the question and he threw a hard right that took Akins just under the left eye and almost dropped him where he stood. Akins caught himself and it looked like he was going to stay up but his foot slid into the growing puddle of water around him and he went down. Riley Cooper and Stoltz grabbed Guiterrez but Jimmy and Diego came across the bench and dragged them off. Fanteaux moved in, backhanded Martinez and Diego slugged him in the back of the head sending him to the floor. Jackson Jones grabbed Ramirez by the throat, pushed him up against the wall, and slapped him with an open hand—he was about to slap him again when Ramon Gonzalez hit him from behind with a bat. Jones dropped Ramirez, staggered to his left, and tripped over the towel cart before slipping to the floor. By the time Baldy was out of the office, there were seven or eight guys grappling and throwing punches and a couple of guys trying to pull themselves up off the wet floor.

He looked like a farmer who had stumbled in on his mom, wife, and daughter all doing the same door-to-door salesman—it was hard to tell if he was going to spit, cry or throw up. He looked wildly around the room then started screaming names, waving coaches and players in to pull players off the pile. Me and Nick were the only ones who didn't move. Nick didn't even look up. I had put my book down but didn't move from where I was sitting, I was pretty sure they didn't need me in there.

Nick sat leaning forward with his elbows resting on his thighs looking down at the floor between his feet as if he wasn't even hearing the commotion. Two of the coaches had wrestled Guitterez off of Riley Cooper and McKay had let himself be pulled away by Balducci. Eventually, they got the two groups on opposite sides of the room but I couldn't stop watching Nick. It was like he was alone in the room. Nick didn't look up even when Brady Turnstine, the first base coach, stumbled away from the pack after taking an elbow over the eye nearly slamming into Nick as he pinwheeled into the back wall.

Nick deliberately undressed until he was naked, stood up, wrapped a towel around his waist, and walked to the shower through the players gathered in clumps around the room. They didn't notice when he walked through to the shower but by the time he came out things had calmed down and a disheveled still overwrought Dave Balducci was giving a speech. He had gathered the team in a circle. He was trying to play the calm leader role, but he looked like a trombone player who had been asked to audition in a phone booth.

"I don't know what the hell was going on here tonight and I don't want to fucking know."

He glared around the room and then swiped at a drop of sweat that had rolled into his eye. His semi-combover was disheveled and his jersey was pulled out of his pants on one side. A couple of the guys had to hide their smiles behind their hands. Balducci didn't notice.

"We're a team! Through the bad times and the good times, we're a team! Nothing's bigger than that. Nothing!"

He looked around the room again. His voice was a little shaky.

"We can have these fights in here. Sometimes the emotions run high and things happen that shouldn't happen but that's okay as long as when we step out of this clubhouse we stand back-to-back against the world. We may fight each other but only until somebody tries to hurt one of our own. I know…"

The team was standing massed around the door to the shower listening to Balducci. Nick had finished showering and now worked his way through the group. He didn't acknowledge the manager or anyone else, just walked through the mass of players who had to step to the side or back up to let him get by. A small path through the players opened up and all the players looked away from Balducci to watch Nick wind through them and then continued to watch him as he walked to his locker and started dressing in his street clothes. Balducci looked at the players' heads turned away from him and then at his coaches but they were watching Nick as well. Balducci watched for a couple of seconds then,

"Ah, Fuck it."

And slumped back into his office. The players stood for a second watching Nick but then the trance seemed to break and they started drifting off towards their lockers. The tension had drained from the room. There wasn't going to be any shaking hands and making up but the fight was over for that night.

Chapter Fourteen

I couldn't find Georgie. I had been through the cars twice and he wasn't on board. There was a chance he had a berth but Georgie didn't seem like the kind of guy who would be able to afford a berth. And McKillop's son was on the train. He was older, harder, more polished. He had been well-dressed when I had seen him the first time but not like this. His suit looked hand-tailored, he had an expensive brushed felt broad-brimmed fedora on his lap, and he wore a heavy gold watch. Almost nobody wore a watch, but he did even though he never checked it. He was in the same car but in a different seat. He had an older businessman in the seat next to him, clearly a stranger. I walked by once and he didn't look up. He seemed more relaxed than when I had seen him first, not watching the aisles with the same vigilance but it didn't feel like sloppiness or complacency. It felt like he knew when to relax, when to conserve energy and when to be poised to act.

Where was Georgie? It hadn't occurred to me that I would end up here on my own. Georgie was supposed to know what was going on. He had to have been watching, had to know there was still somebody out there. I had expected Georgie to be here and following the hard-eyed man in the fine-tailored suit. I hadn't thought through what would happen next because that would be Georgie's job. Now, it was just me and all I knew for sure was that McKillops was going to have to walk through my car to get off the train. And we were still four hours from our first stop, New York City.

I must have napped because the train was slowing and it felt like just minutes before, that I had walked by McKillops in his seat. But there was a chance he had already slipped by while I was sleeping. I stood up and went to look through the glass doors separating the two cars. He was sitting in his seat. Around him, people were starting to gather their belongings, but he sat still and calm, reading a newspaper. I returned to my seat. The train had left Montreal just before midnight and now the bright morning sun poured through the train windows. The train rolled into Penn Station and people started to thread down the aisle past my seat. We only had forty-five minutes in New York and it was almost ten AM—I didn't expect this to be where McKillops got off the train but you never knew. He had killed in daylight in Chicago.

A family pushed past, a young man and his even younger wife with three kids all under three. The man had the youngest in the crook of his arm and was trying to shepherd two young boys, one of them crying, ahead of him with the hand holding a suitcase. His wife was behind struggling with a slightly smaller suitcase and trying to peer up over her husband's shoulder to see where the boys were. In the commotion, I almost didn't notice McKillops go by. He wasn't carrying anything, not even the newspaper, and he slipped by the family when the smallest of the two boys tripped and fell and they all stopped to scoop him up. I scrambled out of my seat but couldn't get around the family, who had started moving again. It took me a few seconds to get to the door and when I did McKillops was striding towards the stairs. I had no idea what I should do. This was Georgie territory. McKillops was just a guy on a train and I had a ballgame to make. What was I going to do, follow him all over New York? It was ten in the morning. It's unlikely he was heading off on a killing spree, and, in fact, how did I even know he was a killer? I stood on the platform just outside the door as McKillops went up the stairs two at a time and his head, his upper body then his legs disappeared up past the low ceiling. I watched long after he had gone. I let him walk away. I let him slip the leash without threat or prayer or promise, without mark or scar or burn, without the sense or scent of danger when he walked among the lambs. Regret and shame caught in my throat like a sharpened stone. McKillops was gone and I had another two days until I got to the West Coast. I turned and went back to my seat.

I sat down and slid over to the window seat and looked out the window onto the tracks. I felt somebody sit down beside me but didn't turn to look.

"You okay, mister?"

I'm not sure what I expected when I turned to the speaker but it wasn't what I saw. It had been a man's voice and there's no doubt that this was a man. But he was wearing a pale blue skirt and jacket with a white blouse and a pale blue pillbox hat. And he wasn't wearing makeup or a wig—from what I could see his hair was cut tight to his head and it looked like it had been at least twenty-four hours since he had shaved. I just stared until he spoke again.

"Sir?"

I shook my head.

"I'm fine. How are you doing?"

"Fine, sir."

"You sure?" I nodded at the outfit. He looked down at himself.

"You think this is odd?"

"You don't?"

"I've seen odder."

There didn't seem to be much more to say about that.

"Where you headed?"

"Pittsburgh. I've got family there. You?"

"LA. I'm playing ball out there."

"No shit? I should have guessed. You look like a ballplayer. Pacific Coast League?"

"Yeah."

"Who you play for?"

"LA."

It seemed like my best bet.

"Right. The Angels. You guys are on a tear. Looks like you might win the whole thing."

"You're a big fan?"

He shrugged.

"My sister's husband played some ball out west. He played for Portland and then San Fran but he was never quite good enough. Threw hard but he realized he was never going to get a chance in the bigs so he packed it in and came home."

I leaned over and stuck out my hand. He shook it.

"Ryan Spencer."

"Nice to meet you, Ryan. Name's Tommy Naylor."

"What do you do, Tommy?"

"I'm a cop. "

I raised an eyebrow.

"Cop?"

"Yep. Second black patrolman hired in the 80th precinct"

"Sounds like a story."

He laughed.

"I don't make you nervous, do I, Ryan?"

"Why should you? Black man in a dress? It's a little odd but not scary."

"Black man? Who says 'black man'?"

We sat for a second before I spoke again.

"So, why the outfit?"

"Long story."

"I guess I've got until Pittsburgh."

He looked away for a long time, long enough that I thought maybe he had forgotten or decided not to tell me but then he started.

"I fought in the war. With the 92nd Infantry. Me and my brother joined up in '42. I was assigned to the 92nd and spent two years at Fort Huachuca in Arizona. My brother ended up on the West Coast. He was a good kid but a hothead and he got in a couple of scrapes and ended up loading munitions at Port Chicago. You know the story?"

I shook my head.

"Really? Only twelve years and nobody remembers. Port Chicago is where they sent the Negroes that they thought couldn't cut it. Either too stupid or too erratic or troublemakers. And my brother ended up there. Mostly they were responsible for loading munitions on ships headed for the Pacific. But nobody really knew what they were doing. The white officers had no experience and the black soldiers didn't have any either. I used to get letters from Kenny telling me stories. These guys were loading one-thousand-pound bombs by the dozens and the officers in charge had set up races and were betting on which of the divisions could load faster. The guys would slow down when the white officers weren't around, they knew it wasn't safe. But when the officers were around they would get pushed hard. In his last letter, Kenny told me that they were loading almost ten short tons per hour. They were using winches with faulty brakes and he had seen half a dozen munitions hit the deck from two or three feet high. He figured it was just a matter of time. He was right."

He stopped for a couple of seconds and then started again.

"They were loading two ships, the SS E. A. Bryan and the SS Quinault Victory. Nobody knows exactly what happened but the E.A. Bryan was holding almost a million liters of heavy fuel oil and the Quinalt Victory was holding fuel too. They hadn't started loading munitions onto the Quinalt Victory yet but the E.A. Bryan was half loaded with thousand-pound bombs, forty millimetre shells, and six-hundred-pound incendiary devices. They think something got dropped and exploded. The fireball was three miles in diameter. Every man on duty at the pier died in the explosion. Three hundred and twenty men. Including my brother."

I shook my head.

"Shit. I'm sorry."

He looked over.

"In some ways, it gets worse. They moved a bunch of men to Mare Island Navy Yard three weeks later under the same officers and conditions. Two hundred and fifty-eight men refused to load munitions. They were arrested and eventually fifty of them stood trial for mutiny and the other two hundred and eight were convicted of disobeying orders. The trial lasted six weeks and it took the military panel eighty minutes to find all fifty men guilty and sentenced them to fifteen years at hard labor. It was probably better Kenny died.

"Anyway, that's Kenny's story. I went to Italy in 1944 and was there until the end of the war. We faced some pretty heavy fighting. I never got hit, not even a scratch. But I saw some guys go down. By the end, you thought it was just a matter of time. But we ended up holding a small town in Italy for the last couple of months of the war and then we got word it was over. In a week we were home."

He looked over.

"I was excited. The GI Bill was passed and it was going to be a chance to go to college. I didn't know a single black man," he grinned at me, "...who had graduated college. I knew they were out there but I had never met one. Now I was going to be one. I couldn't get a bank loan to supplement the GI Bill money but the church in our neighborhood collected money for three Sundays and raised almost fifteen hundred dollars. But the DVA..."

He looked at me and I shook my head.

"Department of Veterans Affairs. They turned down my application. Flat. I had been busted back to corporal in my last six months in Arizona for striking an officer. Guy jumped me in a bar and I didn't find out until later that he was an off-duty captain. Didn't matter. I was good enough to go to Italy and fight the Germans but not good enough to send me to college when I got home. I appealed but the fix was in. It was an office full of fat old white men and they figured they were wasting money on one of us."

I winced but he just stared at me without changing expression.

"I sat around my folks' house for six months. Drank too much and slept too little. Met Elizabeth at a church dinner my parents dragged me to. She wasn't that much to look at but she carried herself like she knew something I didn't."

He looked over at me.

"I know we're all supposed to talk about our wives like they're the most beautiful woman we've ever seen. Like we have perfect vision everywhere but when we look at our wives."

He paused.

"But I can see. I know what my wife looks like and I've seen lots of better-looking women. Seen several on this train. I just don't want to be married to them. I'm with the woman I want to be with. Don't tell me that ain't romantic."

He paused again.

"Anyway, we got on pretty good. And I kept going out to the church dinners just to see her. Used to drink all week but sober up on Sunday. And then I asked her out and she told me she wouldn't date a man who didn't have a job. She wasn't mean about it. Just said it flat out. My Lizzie, she wears her skin tight and trim, like she spent her whole life working on it so it fits just right. And I knew she was right. Why would she? Just like the rest of us, she had carried too much weight. She wasn't going to add to the load.

That Monday I went down to City Hall and put in an application to be a city police officer. I knew they had hired a couple of Negro patrolmen and were looking to hire some more and they gave preference to vets. Heard back in two weeks and started within a month. It was pretty bad. I was only the second Negro police officer in the 80th precinct and Clifton got transferred out to the 30th, Hamilton Heights, three weeks after I started. I guess two Negros in the 80th at the same time was pushing the boundaries of good taste. I'm not sure what I expected but I sure didn't get it. Nobody wanted me there. Still don't. Blacks are starting to move over from Bed Stuy but it's mostly Italians and Jews and Irish...a couple of Greek neighborhoods. I guess the brass think they need a black face in the neighborhood but they're the only ones. I've been there almost seven years and they've never assigned me a locker."

He looked over at me.

"Every single officer in the precinct has a locker. New guys assigned to the precinct have a locker from day one. They have lockers standing open that haven't been used in months but when I asked about a locker the lieutenant told me there were none.

"I started off wearing my uniform to work on the subway. But then I would get chewed out for looking sloppy, wrinkled jacket, scuffed shoes. Plus, I felt like a circus freak. People would look at me like I was a horse that could count. So, I tried bringing my uniform to work in a garment bag and changing in the washroom but, the first day, when I got back from my shift I found my civilian clothes smoldering in a trashcan outside the looie's office door and a bunch of guys not looking at me but smirking. I tried again the next day, figuring maybe they had had their joke and we could just move on. But when I got back my clothes were balled up in the corner. Somebody had pissed on them and put dog shit in the pants pockets. Classic cop move. Crude but effective.

"I was pretty near the end of my rope. It looked like the only way that I was going to be able to do this was to go back to wearing my uniform to work and that felt like a defeat I couldn't tolerate. In some ways, it felt like the last straw. I couldn't walk back into that station house in my wrinkled blues the next morning and stand next to Zobel and Driscoll while Mooney chewed me out in front of everybody and Lieutenant Giamatti sat behind the glass window in his office and looked out at us. And the stupid grinning O'Connell brothers standing there, looking like they had been out most of the night and then slept in their uniforms.

"I was sitting at the kitchen table trying to decide if I was going in to work. Lizzie and me had been married about six months then. Had a little apartment east of 80th near Fulton Street. Bainbridge Street. I forget the number. She was sitting with me at the kitchen table, both of us drinking coffee. She was in her uniform. She worked at a nursing home on Staten Island. We weren't saying much. We had said pretty much all we had to say and so we just sat. But she had brought a bunch of clothes down that she had decided to take into the church. Lizzie had never been small, she was almost six feet tall and big-boned but she had dropped a little weight from the nursing home work and was donating some clothes. Lizzie offered something about 'Too bad you can't wear those.' And then she left. I sat there looking at the pile of clothes. I was mad and I was done. I was certain I couldn't be a police officer anymore, but I had one more day in me. I put on a plain beige linen dress that fell to just above my knee. I was about an inch taller than Lizzie and though I was bigger through the shoulders, not a lot bigger and the dress fit okay, a little tight but not bad. I added nylons and a pair of gardening sneakers that I only used on the weekend.

"I took the subway dressed like that, carrying my blues in the garment bag. Didn't look away from one single person. And I got a few that stared.

140

Nobody said anything. At least, not so as I could hear.

"And I walked the three blocks from the subway like that and up the steps to the station house and into the roll call hall. There were a couple of guys hanging out there shooting the bull but I ignored them. I pulled a chair into the center of the room with the dress swirling around my knees as I walked and they straightened up from where they were slouching against the wall to watch me. I took my uniform out of my garment bag and laid it over the back of a chair and pulled my cap and shoes from the bottom of the bag and placed them on the chair seat. The dress zipped up at the back and I had to reach back over my shoulder and push the zipper down as far as I could and then curl my arm up between my shoulder blades to pull the zipper the rest of the way down. I could barely catch the zipper between my fore and middle finger and it took me a couple of tries to get a grip on it and pull it the rest of the way down. I pulled the dress off my shoulders and it fell to the floor around my feet. I stepped out of it and picked it up from the floor, folded it, and put it in the garment bag. I took off my sneakers and rolled the nylons down over my boxers. I had to move the cap and shoes from the chair so that I could sit down to pull the nylons off. I didn't take my time but I didn't hurry.

By the time I was down to my boxers the word had spread and the room had started to fill up. There were probably twenty-five cops in the station house, some just getting off duty and others like me coming on, and most of them were in the roll call room by the time I stepped into my uniform pants. They had scattered around the outside of the room against the walls. They watched in silence. I buttoned up my shirt, cinched the tie up tight, and shrugged into the jacket. Then the belt. Last, the cap pulled down low and snug. Nobody said a word. Not to me. Not to each other. And I didn't give a shit. For the last bit, the lieutenant showed up and stood in the door but even he didn't speak. I rolled up the nylons and stuck them in the garment bag with the dress and the sneakers and hung it on a coat rack at the back of the room. And I left. I had to go by the lieutenant to leave the room and I threw him a hard salute. We never saluted except at funerals or award ceremonies but it just seemed like the thing to do. He stepped out of the doorway but wouldn't look at me.

"I figured I was finished but I didn't care. It had felt good not to care what they were thinking. I had spent every day for two months trying to figure out what they wanted me to be and to just let that go had felt real good. That was my best day on the job. I thought it was my last day and I was going to do it right. I spoke to everybody I saw in the street that day, most of them white. Some wouldn't speak to me but most of them did. One of the Greek deli owners had a window broken the night before. Nothing stolen, probably just kids horsing around and I helped him clean it up and took his statement. He shook my hand before I left.

"I spent the whole day expecting a police car to pull up and bring me back to the station house to meet with the lieutenant but it didn't happen. Then I figured it just wasn't a big enough deal and they would call me in and fire me at the end of my shift. But when I got back to the station house nobody wanted to speak to me. Just like always. But the dress and nylons were still in the garment bag and the garment bag was still on the coat rack. And I changed back into my dress in the middle of the roll call room again and guys came in again to watch but not as many. And I took the subway home and people stared at me but they didn't speak. And Lizzie was at the door when I got home and she was never a woman that was big on a sense of humor, but this made her smile. She understood even before I did…that if you just got to a place where you didn't care what they thought, what they said behind their hands, then you could find your own place in the world. You could find a little path that you could walk that could make some sense to you. But you had to go all the way. You couldn't pretend not to care. You had to go the whole way. And that dress got me all the way. And it still gets me all the way. "

"How is it now?"

"Still not good. We have a few more colored at the station and they've given us our own locker room. Lots of the boys still don't want to change with us. There's a couple that are okay, but they don't step too far out of line. But I got my people on my walk, colored and white, and I look after them the best I can. And after almost seven years I think I'm just a cop to them. And they think of me whatever they think of cops. And that's okay. But I don't think I'll ever stop wearing the dress. Reminds me not to care."

I nodded. There wasn't much else to say and we sat in silence. I leaned my head back against the window and closed my eyes but I couldn't sleep.

The train had started moving again and I hadn't seen McKillops get back on the train. There was a chance he had walked away and I had let him. Now, it was a two-day trip to the West Coast and another ten days before I was coming back. Time enough for a lot of women to die. I had been counting on Georgie being on the train and having a plan. It had never occurred to me that I would get back here and it would be just me and McKillops.

My eyes were closed but I sensed the shadow fall across my face. I let my eyes open slightly and could make out a silhouette standing in the aisle looking down at me. He had one hand buried in the pocket of his overcoat and he stood for a long time. I couldn't risk opening my eyes any further and I couldn't see him clearly. He stood for a very long time and I could sense him looking down at Naylor and then back to me and I had almost decided to sit up and confront him when he turned quickly and walked back towards his car. Tommy sat up.

"That's a bad fella, Ryan. You know him?"

I had thought Naylor was asleep. I straightened up in my seat and looked over at him.

"No."

"Well, he thinks he knows you."

"Maybe that was all. Maybe he thought he knew me."

"He was carrying something in that pocket. Not a gift. I've seen the look before. I think if I hadn't been in this seat he might have slid in beside you and I think if he had sat beside you, you wouldn't have stood up from your seat. "

I tried to smile.

"I think your imagination is getting the best of you, Tom. I'm sure he just mistook me for somebody else, trying to place me."

He smiled gently.

"I'm not prone to flights of wild fancy, Ryan. And I know bad men. That man is trouble. He's trouble for you and anybody in his path who catches his attention. With a man like that you keep your head down and you hope he doesn't notice you. But he's noticed you already. So, you look behind you and you watch in front of you wherever you go. And you hope that somebody else catches his attention and he forgets about you. Because if he doesn't you will have to deal with him sooner or later."

I nodded and he nodded back.

"Good. At least, you're not pretending anymore. Now, we're eight hours from Pittsburgh. Get some sleep, I'll take the first watch."

I looked over at him and he grinned back.

"Just kidding. I think he's decided to wait."

But I don't believe Tom slept. I woke twice and both times he was awake and reading. We pulled into Pittsburgh between seven and eight PM, not quite dark but the shadow of the train station stretched long and distorted across the tracks. Tom was already standing looking back down the aisle to the neighboring car. He spoke quietly so that only I could hear from where he was standing.

"I think he will be getting off here, Ryan. He's standing and gathering his things. But you should think twice about taking on this guy. He's in another league."

I looked back but didn't answer.

He sighed.

"Okay then. But keep your head up and your eyes circling. "

"I will."

"Okay then, Ryan."

He stuck out his hand and I took it.

We both seemed like we would speak but then neither did. He stepped off the train and I watched him walk up the platform ignoring the swiveling heads, walking easy in low pumps and his tight blue skirt.

I heard the door between our cars slide open and I kept my head turned toward the window. I could see a reflection of the inside the coach behind me and watched the aisle behind me. He paused for a second. I couldn't

144

make out his face because the light in the car was low and the reflection was blurred and indistinct but his shadow fell like a black gash across my seat. The muscles in my neck and shoulders tightened involuntarily but I forced myself not to turn and look at him. I thought he might speak and I wasn't sure what I would do if he did. But he didn't. He walked away up the aisle and out the door onto the platform. Over his suit, he wore a long black coat that fell almost to his ankles and he moved quickly across the platform and into the Pittsburgh train station. I got up and started to move after him but then turned back to my seat to get my jacket and cap. McKillops had seen what I was wearing but not the jacket so it might keep him from recognizing me.

I pushed through the doors and got lucky. McKillops had stopped at a newspaper stand, ostensibly to buy cigarettes, but scanning the room, his eyes breaking the station into quadrats and working methodically around the interior of the station. He never looked at the boy working the stand as he took the cigarettes and handed over the coins. But he was distracted for a second by a stray that had somehow made its way into the station and was now barking and growling at a young woman and her small daughter. The woman and child stood frozen in the middle of the floor and in seconds one of the ticket sellers was out from behind his counter and two men that had been standing talking jumped forward. One of the men kicked at the dog, a medium-sized mutt, with matted yellow and black fur, and caught it hard in the ribs and it yelped loudly but didn't run away. The men continued to kick at the dog as it snapped and growled at them but McKillops had only looked away for a second and had then turned his gaze back to the room. But it had been enough for me to slide behind a pillar before his gaze would have fallen on the spot where I had been standing.

I counted to ten and then stepped out from behind the pillar as if heading towards an exit door at the far end of the station. I snuck a quick look over my shoulder and saw him walking across the floor to an exit on the other side of the building. There were several men dealing with the dog now. McKillops had to almost brush against the men as he went by but he didn't even turn his head to watch what they were doing. He was a man with plans.

145

I turned and went after him.

It was only a few blocks to the riverfront through a tough blue-collar neighborhood butted up against a commercial and warehouse district. McKillops crossed the narrow road in front of the station. And then down a darkened street under the raised tracks that crisscrossed the area. I followed him. It was dark and shadowed under the tracks and although I could hear his footsteps echoing faintly ahead I had to stop and let my eyes adjust to the darkness. After a second I could make out the shapes of boxes and piled debris hunched along the brick abutments that supported the overhead rails. I couldn't see the girders and support beams above my head but they felt low and close.

I started walking again following the fading sound of McKillops's footsteps but stopped almost at once. My breath caught in my chest and my eyes open wide and strained into the dark. Something had moved against the wall. Nothing that I could make out clearly, just the sense that the subtle differences in darkness had shifted, like a ripple on the black, oily surface of water you wouldn't dare to drink. The darkness shifted again. The grey of cunning wolves crouching against the charcoal black of hunchbacked, watchful carrion birds under the dark slate of storm clouds pregnant with a thousand, thousand ashen spiders covered in hairs as thick and coarse as steel wool.

"Bum a cig, buddy?"

The voice was thick and hoarse but weak and indistinct like it was rarely used. It came from my left and low and he shifted again and I could make out the tangled shelter of blanket scraps and torn boxes piled against the concrete wall. I exhaled in a long ragged stream that sounded loud in my ears and I kept walking. I heard him speak again but I was too far away to make out the words. The smell of urine and excrement was almost overwhelming and now I could make out other bodies shifting and twitching beneath scraps and debris. A man stepped out of the shadows almost directly into my path, but I stepped around him and although he reached out with one hand for my arm his eyes were clouded and unfocused and it seemed like the response of a dim, cave creature who was no longer conscious of their movements and

146

for whom those responses no longer conferred any advantage but were the vestigial remnants of some ancient and now inexplicable, indecipherable adaptation. I turned and looked but the man stood facing into the shadows from where I had come. There was no sign that he was aware that I had passed.

I stepped out from beneath the overpass into the glow of the streetlights and my shoe caught a short length of twisted rebar and sent it skittering and clattering over the gravel and stone. Far ahead, I saw McKillops slow but not turn. He knew somebody was there. I pulled my cap down tighter over my eyes and zipped up my jacket. He knew somebody else was walking the streets but he couldn't know it was me. The street had widened, with abandoned lots to my left that bordered more tracks, and ramshackle narrow brick buildings to my right. Up ahead McKillops turned onto a narrow side street. I hurried forward but then stopped. He knew somebody was behind him and he wouldn't ignore that. I crossed over the street away from the alley. I looked ahead to where McKillops had disappeared around the corner and then back the way I had come. Piled against the cement abutment of the overpass were scraps of discarded metal and wood. I could see a three-foot piece of rusted iron pipe sticking out at an angle from the scraps. I walked back and pulled it out. The pipe was thicker than a bat handle but the weight and length was right. I swung it a couple of times and although the swing felt a little awkward the pipe hissed as it knifed through the night air. I walked by the side street down which McKillops had turned, the pipe dangling from my left hand, letting my eyes drift casually to my right. He had stopped just around the corner and was pretending to struggle to get a cigarette lit. I kept walking away up the street and I could feel his eyes on my back. I walked about a hundred feet along the street and then stopped as if trying to get my bearings and looked around. He stood out in the street under a streetlamp in the full glow of the light, watching me. There was no point in pretending now. I stood and looked back.

"Why are you following me, boy?"

He didn't yell but his voice carried easily up the street. I had no ready answer. I hadn't expected to be standing here in an empty street with this man who killed as easily as he spoke.

"Did you hear me, boy?"

"Not tonight, McKillops."

He was far enough away that even though he stood in the light I couldn't make out his facial expression. He didn't speak for several seconds. His voice was gentler when he spoke again.

"I'm just a man who can't sleep taking an evening walk, son. What's your worry?"

"Then you won't mind some company?"

He was quiet again for several seconds. Then,

"I'm a lonesome man, son, I would appreciate the company. Let's walk and talk together."

"I don't think so, McKillops. You do your walking and I'll be here. Behind you."

He shook his head and his oiled hair flashed and glinted beneath the street lamp, like heat lightning on the distant horizon.

"Be sensible, son."

He stepped out of the circle of light and started taking slow steps towards where I stood.

"I'll not be a dog on a leash I can't see and neither will you. Let's walk together like men and tell our stories. I think you misunderstand mine and I'm sure I don't know yours."

He took measured steps as he spoke. His right hand was buried deep in his coat pocket. I let him continue walking without answering until he was about twenty-five feet away and then let the pipe slide out from behind my leg. I was sure he must have seen it while I was walking away but the way he pulled up and his eyes widened when he saw the pipe told me that he hadn't. So, he did miss things.

"What do you think you're going to do with that, boy?"

"Crush your skull if it's necessary, Mr. McKillops."

He had been looking at the pipe but now his eyes came quickly to my face. The first time hadn't registered but this time it did.

"How do you know my name?"

148

"You're your father's son, McKillops."

"What do you know about my father?"

"I know that the world would have been a better place if he had died on the birthing table blue and angry. And the same goes for you."

His face darkened for a second but then he laughed.

"I can't argue with you on the first. My father was an angry and violent man. We often felt his fists."

He took a step forward as he spoke and I raised the pipe to my shoulder. His eyes went to the pipe.

"Are you sure that will be enough, son?"

I snapped my hips and the pipe scythed through the air with a thin whistle and then I had it back on my shoulder.

"I'll take my chances."

Without looking away from my face he nodded towards the hand buried in his pocket.

"This could be a gun."

"If it was a gun I would be dead already, Mr. McKillops. And you never use a gun. I think I know what you have there."

He stared at me for several seconds and then turned away and started walking. I walked after him.

We were a strange parade for several hours that night but we didn't speak again. He led me across the Liberty Bridge and into the Flats on the south side of the river. We crossed fourth and fifth and sixth and he tried to lose me and he tried to trap me. But when he turned corners I approached cautiously and kept away from doors or alleys that he could jump from. Twice, I came around a corner and couldn't see him on the street but was sure he hadn't had time to reach the next corner. I moved from one side of the street to the other avoiding deep doorways and hiding places and both times discovered him waiting across the street from where I stood in the shadows of an alley. Both times he just stepped out from where he was hiding and continued walking, once back the way we had come and once in the direction he had been heading.

McKillops stopped for a coffee and a plate of pierogies at an all-night diner and I found a Formica-covered table across the room from him. We were the only two in the diner except for the cook. The cook took my order and a long look at the pipe that I had leaned against the wall beside me but didn't say anything. McKillops took his time and a refill and smoked another of his cigarettes before getting up suddenly and walking out. He didn't look at me when he left the diner and I threw a couple of bucks on the table and followed him out the door into the night. Because I had to be cautious I did lose him twice, and the second time I wasn't able to find him. But by then it was almost light and people were about. I looked for him for the next hour, frantic that I had left him a window but hoping that I had been able to distract him long enough.

By 6:30 AM I still hadn't found him and I had to be back at the train before it pulled out. I wasn't sure exactly where I was but I could see the steel cables of the bridge from where I stood and I worked my way to the river. It ended up being a different bridge than I had crossed the evening before and I had to ask directions a couple of times before I found my way back to the station. It was after 7:30 AM and I was tired and hungry. The train would be pulling out in less than an hour. I stopped at a little cafeteria in the station and ordered breakfast, wolfing it down quickly. Back on the train, I walked past my seat and to the door that separated my seat from where McKillops had been sitting. He was in his seat. His long coat was folded neatly on the seat beside him but his hair had lost some of its sheen and a piece of hair flopped down onto his forehead. His face was flushed and he stared down at his hands and I could see the muscles in his jaw working. He didn't notice me at first but then he finally looked up. He didn't change expression but his eyes held mine until I turned away and went back to my seat. I had another two days to Los Angeles and I knew I couldn't fall asleep in my seat.

I was going to have to stay awake for another fifty-two hours or find a place to sleep.

* * *

I had fallen asleep. An electric rush straightened me in my seat. I turned to my left certain that he would be there but the seat was empty. I pushed up on the back of my seat to stand and looked around the car but people were reading or talking or napping. A couple of passengers looked up at me but then went back to what they were doing. My heart pounded hard against my shirt and my lower back muscles tightened and clenched so that I had to sink back into my seat. It took me a second to get my breathing under control and then I stood and walked to the door separating my car from McKillop's. He was still in his seat and his eyes were closed but as I looked at him they opened and he looked straight at me. There was no momentary hesitation. It was as if he had been wide awake and watching me through his eyelids. Then he grinned. I turned and went back to my seat. I had to get some sleep.

I cornered one of the porters just outside the bar car.

"I'm afraid there are no empty berths, sir."

"Nothing? You don't keep anything back for you guys or unexpected VIPs?"

"I'm afraid not, sir."

He started to pull away but I put my hand on his arm. The hand had a twenty in it. He looked at it.

"This is urgent, friend."

He looked at the twenty ruefully.

"There's nothing, sir. But I can get you more pillows for your seat."

I shook my head.

"Can't sleep sitting up. C'mon, you must have an idea."

He looked at me.

"Sometimes people will rent their berths. We don't allow it but it happens sometimes."

I looked at him.

"Do you know anybody that might want to rent their berth?"

"I might be able to broker something, sir."

"How much?"

"Hundred for them. Fifty for me."

I pulled another one hundred and eighty dollars out of my pocket.

"Tell you what, you keep this just between you and me and I'll give you two hundred. You get whatever doesn't get spent to rent the berth."

He nodded.

"This may take a little time. Where will I find you, sir?"

I told him my car and seat number.

"I'll be there or in the bar car."

He nodded again and started to turn away. I put my hand on his arm.

"I'm serious about keeping this between you and me. You may have somebody asking about me and I don't want you telling anybody where I am."

He looked at me for several seconds.

"Is there something I should know, sir?"

"It's nothing that will come back to you. There may be somebody looking for me who I don't want to find me."

I stayed in the bar car nursing a 7-Up and watching the small towns and farmlands flash by. He was back in less than forty-five minutes. He didn't come into the bar car, but gestured from the door for me to follow him. I followed him down through the train to one of the cars near the front. There were six berths in the car and mine was a small single berth at the front. The porter pushed open the door. The bed was already turned down.

He held out his hand and I gave him the money.

"You have twelve hours."

"Twelve hours?"

He raised his eyebrows.

"I told you there were no empty berths. The gentleman who paid for this berth is sitting in your seat. He won't want to sit there for the next two days."

I hadn't really considered how long I would have the cabin for, but it made sense that I wouldn't have it for the rest of the trip.

"Right. Twelve hours. You may have to wake me."

He didn't answer and started to walk away. I asked the question to his back.

"How much extra did the guy pay for his berth?"

He answered without turning.

"Ninety dollars."

I went into the room and shut the door behind me. It had a slide lock that wouldn't have kept out a small child if they got a running start but I had to count on McKillops not knowing where I was.

It was dark when I awoke and the train wasn't moving. We must be in St. Louis. It had been around noon when I had fallen asleep so I must have been sleeping for at least nine or ten hours. I lay for a few minutes, coming completely awake then let myself out of the room. There was nobody in the hallway of my car and I worked my way back through the bar car, which was empty as well. As I approached my car, a crowd started to build and I had to push my way through to get to my seat. Three of the porters, one of them the guy that had arranged the berth for me, had cleared a space around my seat and a cop was sitting in the aisle seat talking to a gentleman in his mid-forties. I tried to catch the eye of the porter who had arranged for my berth but he avoided my gaze. I moved past a porter standing with his arms out holding back the onlookers. He made a grab at me but I shook him off and moved across beside the porter.

"What happened?"

He didn't look at me and I thought he wasn't going to answer but he did.

"Just after the train stopped, he woke up with a guy beside him holding a knife against his side. When he looked over the guy got up and left. Just walked off the train. By the time we got here the guy was long gone. "

"His name's McKillops."

"Nope. Hanrahan."

He kept his arms out and facing straight ahead. I was standing right behind his shoulder, talking almost into his ear

"I mean the guy with the knife."

"You said this wouldn't come back on me."

He talked softly almost without moving his lips.

"I didn't expect this. I didn't think he would try this."

"Yeah, right."

I stepped away, a little closer to where the cop was interviewing the man.

"Did you recognize your assailant, sir?"

The man shook his head but didn't speak. His face was damp and pale and he held his hands in his lap. I could see them shaking from where I stood.

"Did he speak to you?"

The man shook his head again.

"He didn't ask you for anything? Your wallet? Your watch?"

The man shook his head again.

"Do you think he meant you harm?"

The man looked over at the officer then.

"He had a knife against my side. I wasn't asleep when he sat down beside me although my eyes were closed. I looked over as soon as I felt the weight settle into the seat. The tip was already against my skin when I saw his face. I know that he meant to put that blade into me. To slide it in like a needle through cloth. But when he looked at me he stopped. Something in my face made him stop but he sat looking at me, deciding. We sat like that for several seconds, it felt like minutes but it was probably seconds. And then he pulled the knife away, stood up, and walked away. Off the train and into the crowd. I watched him until I couldn't see him anymore.

The cop was quiet for a second.

"Do you think you can stand now sir?"

The man nodded.

"I think so."

"Well then maybe we can continue the interview at the station."

The cop stood up and he and his partner helped the man to his feet. He staggered a little but they caught and steadied him. They led him through the growing crowd, pushing people out of the way, and got him to the door and down onto the platform. He stopped for a second and spoke to them but I couldn't hear what he said. The officer who had been speaking to the man in his seat said something and it seemed to reassure the man and they kept walking towards the stairs leading up into the main terminal.

The porters talked quietly with the crowd that had gathered and got them moving away from the seat. In a few minutes, the car was empty other than the regular passengers. A couple of them looked at me curiously, standing alongside the seat. Maybe, making the connection that I had been in the seat earlier but that a different man had been assaulted there. I walked to the end of the car and looked through the window at McKillop's seat. It was empty. No coat, no newspaper, nothing. I walked back through the train looking for the porter that had found me the berth. I found him delivering a meal to a berth three cars away from where I had slept. He put his hand up before I could speak.

"Don't talk to me. You're going to get me fired."

"Where should I go. Should I—"

"I don't care what the fuck you do, man, just stay away from me. You're bad news."

I started past him to head towards the sleeping car.

"And stay the fuck away from that berth. The cops are bound to be along to have a look. And if not the cops, our guys. Just keep you're fucking head down."

He was right. They were going to be looking at Hanrahan's berth and my seat and if I was found in either, there were going to be questions. And questions might not be a bad idea but I didn't know how to explain who I was and where I was from.

Chapter Fifteen

She was sitting behind the dugout in San Diego, the same woman I had seen in Philly. She had cut her hair and added sunglasses but it was her. I saw her again in San Francisco. Twice. She had probably been in LA too.

She always left her seat before the ninth inning. After the first time in San Fran, I tried catching her in the parking lot but with no luck. The second time in San Fran I drew a walk in the first inning and spotted her sitting five rows back of the Giant dugout just to the outfield side. I trotted down to first and took a big lead. The pitcher tossed over and I had to slide back into first headfirst. I jumped up and raised one hand.

"Jimmy, can I have a T here?

"Time out!"

The ump waved his arms and stepped over onto the foul side of the first baseline. I think he thought I was just going to dust off but I walked over and stood in front of the woman. I stared up at her but she looked away over my head as if she hadn't noticed.

"Nice to see you again, ma'am."

I talked quietly but it carried. People turned in their seats to see who I was talking to. She looked down at me and then looked around as if to see who I was talking to. But she knew.

"This is the third game I've seen you at—it can't be a coincidence. Something you want to say to me?"

The new haircut suited her. I couldn't see her eyes behind the glasses but I still remembered them. Crystalline green, steady and unblinking like a wild animal.

"Play ball!"

I stood for a second longer but the first base ump came over.

"What the hell you doin', Spencer? Scouting 'em while the games on? We don't have time for this shit. Let's go. Get back on the bag or I'm calling you out."

I took a last look and went back to first. The spell broke and people turned their attention back to the field and the noise started to pick up again. Nick was up next and lined a double to right-center. I got a late start and ran through the stop sign at third base. I would have been out by ten feet on a good throw but it was about twenty feet up the third baseline. I looked over as I crossed the plate but she was gone. I was sure she wouldn't be back and she wasn't. I didn't bother dressing quickly after that game.

The next series against the Dodgers was uneventful. Except for the fight. We swept the series and I went seven for fifteen with two doubles, two home runs, and four walks. I'm not sure what the difference was. I was seeing the ball better. Even when I was making outs, I was hitting the ball hard. And we were all hitting. Except for Nick. Nothing seemed different. He prepared the same way he always had, arriving early, stripping down to his jockey boxers, taping both ankles, and then dressing slowly before heading out to the field and walking and jogging the basepaths. He still spent almost a half-hour inspecting the area between second and third, smoothing out any wrinkles or divots. He still took his cuts at BP and sprayed the ball all over the field with several over the fence. But it didn't seem to translate to the field. His strength was having the patience to wait for a mistake, and with Nick, there were a lot of spots that were mistakes. But now he was chasing good pitches. And for the first time, it was starting to show.

In San Diego, he hit a weak tapper towards first with two out and a man on third to end the game. But when the pitcher came over to cover first they got tangled up and both went down. Nick was up cat-quick and stood over the downed pitcher. The guy tried to get up but Nick leaned over and shoved him back to the ground and got into his face. I couldn't hear what he said from the dugout but it didn't last long before their guys were on

Nick, grabbing him by the arms and pulling him away. Nick wrenched himself free but meanwhile, the pitcher was on his feet and Nick got up in his grill again and the guy stuck his glove in Nick's face, Nick popped him and the guy went down. Their first baseman grabbed Nick in a headlock and players streamed from both dugouts. Within seconds there were forty guys scuffling all over the field. I stayed in the dugout and watched. Nick had ended up at the bottom of one pile but pulled himself free, moved to the edges of the melee, and stood watching for a second before catching sight of me in the dugout, He walked across the field and sat down beside me, nodding his head at the chaos.

"Not going out there?"

"Once I figure out who I'm rooting for."

We sat for a second. It looked like the umps were starting to get things back under control.

"Have you spotted anything?"

I looked at him, surprised.

"Are you asking me for advice?"

He shrugged.

"Can't seem to work my way out of it."

"You're chasing balls I've never seen you swing at."

He grimaced.

"I know. I just can't seem to lay off them."

"You've spent your whole career laying off those pitches and now you can't?"

I shrugged.

"Doesn't make sense."

The fighting had stopped and guys started straggling into the dugout.

"Who's the girl?"

"What?"

"The lady in the stands in San Francisco."

"I don't know – I just keep seeing her around. It feels like she's following me."

"Watch out for those."

McKay walked by and glared at me. He had a mouse under his left eye and a scrape on his chin.

"Didn't see you out there, pussy."

"I was too busy watching that one hundred fifty pound shortstop kick your fat ass, McKay."

He pointed his finger at me but kept walking.

Nick and I sat without talking for a second.

"Wouldn't have hurt you to find a dance partner. Might have gone a little ways toward fitting in."

"Fitting in? Are you kidding me, Nick? These guys don't get off the bench when I hit a walk off. And they've been throwing at me all year. Because they know they can. Because there's not one fucker on this team who's going to do a thing about it. But I should go running out on the field and toss mitts with guys I don't even know. Fat fucking chance."

It caught me by surprise how angry I was.

"What do you think would have happened if that had been me out there? If I had gone after him and their guys had jumped me? Every last one of them would have been my problem. I would have had to take them on one at a time while these assholes hooted in the dugout. And you. You're one candid photo away from having to fight every one of those guys yourself, too. Don't think any different. Right now you're one of theirs. A bit of an oddball, but one of theirs. If they ever find out what you really are, dig in buddy, you'll be on your own."

I had gone too far. He looked at me for a couple of seconds then got up and walked into the locker room. I sat where I was until they started to shut the lights down in the stadium. I got up and went down the darkened tunnel to the locker room. It was empty except for Balducci and Smitty.

* * *

Things got worse after the brawl. I kept hitting but guys were actually going out of their way to hurt me. I got thrown out stealing twice in San Diego because guys 'missed' the sacrifice sign and I looked like a jackass

159

on a suicide squeeze when the guy took the pitch and stepped out of the box. It wasn't even close enough to slide. But I went seven for nine with six walks in a three-game series against San Diego and we won all three. Balducci tore up the room after the last game in San Diego. He knew what was going on.

I cooled off a little in San Fran but we still took three out of four and headed into the All-Star break with forty-one wins and thirty-six losses. I had been in the running for the All-Star roster early in the season but then cooled off and they picked the Cincinnati third baseman. I was okay with it.

Chapter Sixteen

Georgie didn't look at me when I sat down. He just kept toying with his beer, turning it in small circles that left moist rings on the table. He was still lean, almost gaunt. He must have been approaching forty but he looked older, the vertical lines furrowing both sides of his mouth, permanent creases that didn't disappear completely even when his face was still and relaxed. His hair had receded a little but not much and it was still dark although now that I was sitting this close I could see a few grey strands.

"Have you seen him?"

"No."

"He probably won't get on until Denver. We get into Chicago late and there's a six-hour stopover. That's where it's going to happen."

We sat for a few minutes without speaking.

"How did you figure it out?"

"Reading the papers."

I nodded. His face twisted for a second and the lines deepened around his mouth and his eyes almost shut.

"Took me way too long. I just didn't want to admit it to myself. I was reading the out-of-town papers when I could get them and the bodies were showing up. I convinced myself it wasn't our guy."

We sat again for a minute.

"How many?"

"Seven. That I'm certain of. Could be more."

I winced.

"I wasn't sure."

"You were sure. Just as sure as I was."

It was eleven AM and we were the only ones in the bar car. He picked the cigarette up from the ashtray and drew hard so that the tip glowed red and hot. Georgie sucked the smoke deep into his lungs and held it there before releasing it in a slow, steady stream.

"There's two of them. Identical twins. One's a dentist and the other does odd jobs. The dentist looks like a regular guy, married, three kids, two daughters and a son, churchgoers, living in a Phillie suburb. The other guy is a little dodgier. Doesn't work much. Looks like his brother pays the rent and helps him out. He's our guy. Word is that he disappears for weeks at a time. Nobody knows where he goes. I've followed him twice and both times he ended up on the train. Both times he stopped at his brother's place first, probably to get money."

"What's the plan?"

He still hadn't looked over at me. He turned his head toward the bar and caught the bartender's eye and raised his bottle. The bartender nodded. The bartender came over with the bottle, no glass, and put the beer on the table.

"That's eighty cents, sir."

Georgie handed him a dollar bill and waved away the change.

"I saw you getting on in San Francisco but you didn't see me. You walked the cars, looking. You scanned every face in every seat. You were looking for him."

"Or you."

He looked over then.

"You figured I'd be here?"

"I was hoping."

"Why did you think I would be here now?"

I shrugged.

"Thought you might have figured it out."

"It's been going on for six years. You let those years pass and seven more women get killed while I try and figure it out?"

I didn't know how to answer. Georgie took a short pull on his beer. The cigarette had burned out in the ashtray but he didn't seem to notice.

"What's the story with you, Ryan?"

"What do you mean, Georgie?"

He grimaced.

"Nobody calls me that anymore. I go by my middle name. Michael. Mike."

There was another short pause.

"When I first met you back in '39 you were a man. A young man, sure, but a man. I was a kid. Now..."He pointed to his face and then ran a hand through his hair."And you..."He jerked his chin at me.

"You look the same as the day I met you."

I sat for several seconds.

"I can't explain it, Mike."

"Can't or won't."

"Can't. All I can say is that it wouldn't have taken six years if I could have helped it."

"Right."

"What have you been doing?"

He looked at me showing a hint of a smile.

"What? The last twenty-four years? I got married and had two kids. Two girls, Pauline's the oldest..."He looked over and shrugged."...and Rachel. Pauline will be thirteen in a month and Rachel's seven. Good girls, but I was working long hours at the paper to keep the bills paid. It was easier to try and ignore this."

"What happened?"

"We bought a TV. Set me back two bills but Jeanie had to have it."

I waited. Georgie/Mike stared down at the table.

"The news was on...never cared much for the news. Get enough of it at work but we were waiting for *Gunsmoke*. And they interviewed the father of a girl who had been killed. About three blocks from where Pauline died. I knew it was connected. She was seventeen years old. The father cried on TV. So, I started looking."

We sat for a second.

"Still took a while."

He looked over.

"I have a wife and two kids. And a job. I couldn't just quit and spend all my time following this."

He continued to look at me.

"What about you?"

I told him the story of the train stop in Pittsburgh.

"You had him alone in the streets and you let him walk away?"

I nodded.

"Not again."

I flushed.

"He didn't kill anybody that night."

"Not fucking again."

It came out in a hiss laced with contempt.

"What's your point, Georgie?"

"What's my point? What's my fucking point? You kill him! You put him down like a snarling, foaming cur and you empty the pistol and then you kick him until your shoe's slick and wet with the gore, until the last foul exhale drifts across his swollen tongue.

"Or you wear them…and the tears spilled for them, and every single minute they didn't get to feel the sun or the rain or their lover's lips—"

I stood up and walked to the door of the bar car.

"Yeah. You walk away, Ryan. But the bodies are piling, so step high, lad, step high."

I stood at the door of the bar car for several seconds then turned back and took my seat again. We didn't speak for several minutes.

"What's the plan?"

"McKillops had a repair job just outside of Fort Collins and it finished up yesterday. He'll get on in Denver and I'm pretty sure he'll be hunting in Chicago. We follow him when he gets off the train and find a place to kill him. Then we walk back to the train and go home."

He pointed down to a briefcase near his foot that I hadn't noticed.

"I've got what I need in there."

164

"You don't look like a briefcase kind of guy."

"Couldn't just tuck it in my belt."

"Guess not. You want to leave it in my cabin?"

"What, you don't think I could afford my own berth? I'm just not willing to leave it there when I'm not in the room. He's not getting another chance just because my berth got robbed."

He put the bottle to his mouth and finished the last of the beer.

"I'm going to go lie down. We're ten hours out of Denver and it will be another eighteen hours to Chicago from there. I'm going to need some sleep."

He leaned over, grabbed the briefcase, and untangled himself from the barstool. His foot caught in the lower rung and he almost fell but caught himself on the edge of the table. It hadn't occurred to me until then that he might have been drinking for a while.

"You okay?"

He gave me a stone-hard grin.

"Don't worry about me. That's the last drop until we're done."

I nodded and watched him walk away. He looked okay.

I wasn't going to be able to sleep for a while.

* * *

I didn't recognize him when he first came into the bar car. It was partly because he was alone and I would have expected there to be security around him but it was also because I was familiar with the photographs from the '70s and '80s, during and after his impeachment when the lines from his nose to the corners of his mouth had deepened and his hair had receded to a distinct widow's peak and his skin was sallow and slack and speckled with thin broken blood vessels. When the smile looked forced and the bags started to pooch beneath his eyes like tiny packets of recrimination and self-loathing. This dark-haired man was tanned, confident, and had an easy full smile. But when he spoke the graveled rumble left no doubt.

"Is this stool taken, my friend?"

165

"No, sir."

He looked at me closely.

"You recognize me?"

"Yes sir."

"Hmmm, not that many do. And not the ones your age. Thank Christ."

I nodded.

"You a Republican, son?"

I shook my head.

"Not to worry. You will be. No such thing as an old Democrat."

He settled on the stool.

"Where's the bartender? I need a drink."

The bartender had been ducked below the bar stocking shelves and now came across to take Nixon's order. I don't think he recognized him.

"Sir?"

"I'll have a Rolling Rock, son. You got Rolling Rock?"

"We do, sir."

"Splendid. I'll have a Rolling Rock."

The bartender brought a bottle and glass but Nixon waved away the glass and took a long swallow from the bottle.

"Aaaahh, that's good."

"You're not worried about being seen drinking in public, sir?"

He gave me a searching look.

"Why? Who's watching?"

"The press?"

"Those fuckers? They don't give a shit. Goldwater got his ass kicked like we all knew he would. There's a whole new crew of whipping boys. I'm just another New York lawyer."

He took another pull on the bottle almost emptying it.

"Nobody gives a good goddamn about Richard Nixon, son, and that's just the way I like it."

"So, you're done with politics, sir?"

He shrugged.

"Hard to say. There's talk that I should run in '68 but I don't know."

He finished his beer and he signaled for another.

"It's a tough life, politics. Not for everybody. Not sure I'm cut out for it. What do you do, son?"

"I'm a ballplayer, sir."

His face brightened.

"Pro ball? Who do you play for, son?"

"Montreal, sir."

He made a puzzled face.

"The Royals left three or four years ago, what league do you play in?"

Shit. Nixon knew the history of Montreal baseball better than I did.

"Lower minors, sir. Class B-ball. Got a ways to go."

He reached out and patted my shoulder.

"Don't give up. That's the only sure path to defeat. Giving up."

He was quiet for a second.

"You worried about the draft, son?"

"Yes sir."

It seemed like the answer he was looking for.

"Goddamn Vietnam. We've lost too many young men there already. It's a lost war but nobody's figured it out yet. Or maybe they have but they're just not sure how to get out. And drafting young men to go there and get killed is a mistake. That would sure as hell be a different story if I had beat Kennedy."

"If you had won this time would you have pulled out?"

Nixon waved his hand.

"We weren't winning this time. Barry's not a bad guy but he's the last of the oldtimers still fighting Roosevelt. Nobody gives a shit anymore, that fight's lost. You can't win an election these days being anti-union and anti-welfare and anti-commie. I feel bad for him though. It's a she-bitch when you lose. Every cocksucker with a pen and a byline piles on, tells the world what an asshole you are and how they knew it all along. I had guys writing shit about me while my ass was still moist from where they had been licking it."

He looked over and grinned.

" Kind of nice to see somebody else lose for a change, though."

He shook his head.

"You don't want to leave the house. Your friends pity you, your enemies piss on you and you're entertainment for everybody else. In '60 I didn't leave the house for six days, didn't step out onto the porch. Slept, ate, and watched TV. Just about threw up every time I thought about the debate. You see it?"

I shook my head.

"Sweaty Dick. I'll show them a sweaty dick. Then '62—it was almost worse. I had been a pube hair from the Oval Office and now I couldn't beat fucking Pat Brown for Governor of California. I lost by two and a half times as many votes in California than I had lost in the entire country. State full of homos and dope smokers. The only saving grace was I could head east and nobody really knew what the hell had happened in California. And then that asshole Hiss goes on Smith's show and tells the world that I'm dead in the water, a lame duck. A fucking Commie convicted felon goes on national television and tells the country that I'm through."

He was getting redder and louder but then he sat back and smiled.

"But it backfired on that asshole. The public knows better. Smith is done. Hiss is done. And I'm still standing."

He pointed at my 7-Up.

"Another, son?"

Nixon was offering to buy me a drink. Couldn't figure out what was most likely to send me to hell, refusing or accepting. I nodded and Nixon caught the bartender's attention then pointed at my bottle and his.

"So, what are you doing now, sir?"

"Lawyering. In New York."

"Court cases?"

He chuckled.

"No court cases for me —wouldn't know what to do in front of a jury. The only thing I know is civil litigation and wills and it's been twenty years since I did any of that. They make me senior partner, drop my name in at the front of all the other senior partners and then trot me out for big prospective clients. I tell stories about politics and drop a bunch of names and they go away impressed."

"So, if they ask, will you run in two years?"

He stopped talking for a few seconds and rolled his beer around on the table.

"Probably not, son. I think I've had my shot. Not a bad idea to get out while I'm ahead."

We sat for a few seconds before he spoke again.

"You think I should?"

He didn't look away from the bottle when he asked. Nixon was asking me if I thought he should run for president in 1968.

"Hard to say, sir."

He looked up then.

"You don't think I would make a good president, son?"

"I'm not saying that, sir, it's just that it's going to be a tough time and you've already been through a couple of..."

He stared at me until I trailed off.

"You don't think I would make a good president do you, young man? We're sitting at a table together sharing drinks that I bought and you can't bring yourself to throw me a fucking bone."

He pushed back from the table and straightened up on his stool.

"What's the matter, don't I look the part? Not movie star handsome enough for you? Not smooth-talking enough? Wouldn't look good throwing out the first ball in the season opener?"

He slammed his open hand on the table.

" This is not a job for movie stars or baseball players or fucking PT boat captains. This is a job for pragmatic men who can make tough decisions and shed their tears in private where nobody sees or knows. Men who see the big picture and know that small ideals sometimes have to be sacrificed to reach the larger objective. Not fucking romantics who talk about the 'common man' but spent their childhoods being chauffeured to tennis lessons."

He slammed his hand again.

"The fucking 'common man.' I know the common man. I was one. They drink too much, fight too much and if you leave your wife at the bar to use the shitter they'll be on her before you put the seat down. Don't talk to me about 'the common man'. This is a country built by great men for great men. We could tell the story of this country with one hundred biographies, Henry Ford, George Washington, George S Patton…all the rest is the senseless scurrying of ants and roaches. And don't you forget it, son."

He stood up from his stool.

"You go ahead and vote for Bobby in 1968. Another one of Daddy's projects. Another fucking east coast mama's boy with a predilection for commies and cocksucking. And don't come crying to me when it all falls down around your feet."

He spun away and stormed out of the bar car. The conversation had turned so quickly that I hadn't had time to figure out where it was headed. I looked around. It was just me and the bartender and he stood looking at me then shrugged and went back to wiping down the bar. I went back to my berth to grab a few hours of sleep.

* * *

I was more tired than I thought and didn't wake up until the train stopped in Denver. I came out of sleep hard, dragging myself up from the deep, not sure where I was, and with muscles that felt slack and useless. It took me a second to remember that I was on a train and then a few more to remember why. The train had stopped and this was Denver.

I had fallen asleep with my clothes on and I stood at the end of the bed trying to slap some of the wrinkles out of my shirt and pants before stepping out into the hallway. Mike was leaning against the wall next to my door.

"I thought I was going to have to wake you."

He looked me up and down.

"You look like shit."

I looked down. He was right.

"Doesn't matter. You don't need to look good for this job."

"Have you seen him?"

He's found a spot on the boarding platform and it looks like he's settled in there. He's a cautious man. I think he'll watch the train until it's almost ready to pull out and then get on. He'll be looking for any kind of unusual activity and if he sees it he'll be in the wind."

"How did you spot him?"

"Are you kidding me? He's his old man all over again. Maybe a little shorter, carrying a little more weight, better dressed for sure, but he's his old man."

"Do you think he spotted you?"

He looked at me.

"I've been following these fuckers for twenty-five years—they don't spot me."

He nodded his chin at me.

"You, on the other hand, he's seen before. You're going to have to stay out of sight. If he sees you he's never going to believe it's a coincidence."

"I'll stay away from his car."

"You'll stay in your berth."

I made a face.

"It's eighteen hours to Chicago. I'm not spending the entire time in my berth."

He looked at me and shook his head.

"It's too strange. I forget how young you are. "

He rubbed his hand across his face and I noticed then the dark rings under his eyes and the thin red lines breaking the whites.

"So, you might be bored staying in your berth. And because you might be bored you should be able to wander around the train. And if McKillops sees you and gets spooked and more women die because we lose him, then so be it. At least you weren't bored."

He looked at me and I reddened.

"Fine."

He nodded.

"Good. I'll keep an eye on him. If we stay on schedule, it'll be almost dark when we get into Chicago. We have a nine-hour layover and I'm sure he'll be hunting. Once it's dark we won't have to worry about you being recognized although…"

He looked at me.

"What?"

"Do you have a hat?"

"Yeah, there's a ball cap in my bag."

"Wear it. Tucked low. No sense in making it easy for him."

I nodded.

"Okay. Don't leave for anything. I'll bring you food. "

He started to turn away.

"What was your impression of him when you met him?"

I shrugged.

"Tough, confident, smart, cold, hollow. Why?"

"Yeah. That's what I see too. He doesn't carry himself like a guy on the edges. He acts like a guy who's in charge and used to it."

"Unleashing his potential, I guess."

Mike shrugged.

"I guess."

* * *

I must have fallen asleep again because when I woke the train was stopped and I had no memory of it slowing down. It was full daylight and looking out the window I could see the sun was still high in the sky and we were surrounded by farmlands. I sat for several minutes, thinking that the train would start back up any second but it didn't. I put my cheek against the window and looked as far up and down the tracks as I could but couldn't see any reason to be stopped. I went to the door and pressed my ear up against it but couldn't hear anything in the hallway either. I opened the door a crack and stuck my head out. It was empty but I could hear the low murmur of voices coming from the car to my right, another berth car. I stepped out and walked to the end of my car. I could see a passenger talking loudly to a porter although with the door between us I couldn't make out what he was saying. But he wasn't happy. I opened the door and stepped through into the next car. The porter looked my way over the passenger's shoulder but the passenger kept talking loudly as if he hadn't noticed.

"How much longer will we be stuck here? I have evening meetings in Chicago and I'm already going to be late, every minute we sit here is making me later."

The porter replied much more softly.

"I'm sorry sir, track damage. We expect to be moving again soon but we have to be sure that the track is repaired."

I stood awkwardly not sure where to go next. It seemed odd to turn and go back the way I had come, as if I had only come this far to see who was talking, which was true but not a truth I wanted to acknowledge. I slipped by the two men as if I was just out for a stroll. The next car was a smoking car and McKillops sat in a window seat with a newspaper folded in his lap, staring out the window. He wasn't smoking but several men around him were and a thin veil of smoke hovered just below the cabin ceiling. I spotted him as soon as I entered the car but had a moment's hesitation while I decided whether to keep walking or turn back. I spun on my heel and caught a last glimpse of McKillop turning away from the window to look in the direction from which I had come. I hurried past the two men still talking and ducked into my room. I sat on the edge of my bed sorting out whether he had spotted me—by the time he would have seen me in the doorway my back would have been turned or almost turned. There was a chance he would have seen a profile. There was a light tap at the door and I had an irrational moment where I thought that McKillops knew where my cabin was and was waiting outside the door but when I opened it Mike slipped in with a tray of food.

"I thought you were probably getting hungry. There's some track damage. We're probably going to get started in the next few minutes."

I wanted to say nothing, act like I had stayed put and hadn't jeopardized our plans for McKillops, but I couldn't.

"I know. I saw McKillops."

He looked at me.

"You saw McKillops?"

"Two cars over in the smoking car."

"I know where he fucking is—why do you?"

"I went out to see why the train had stopped."

He looked down at the floor for a long minute, his hands clutched tight at his sides. And then spoke without looking up.

"Are you going to be distracted by every stray shiny object flapping by in the wind, Ryan? Do I have to tie you to a post like a puppy that chases scrap paper and distant sounds?"

He still hadn't looked up. I shook my head. I'm not sure he saw it.

"Did he see you?"

"I turned back right away. He wouldn't have seen more than the back of my head. Maybe a profile."

He grimaced.

"But he watched a man walk away from a car he had just entered. So, he knows a man walked into the car, looked around, and then turned immediately back the way he had come."

"There are a thousand reasons somebody would do that."

He looked away again, his thin face taut and angry. It was a few seconds before he spoke.

"Ryan, do you know what we are up against here? McKillops is extremely bright. He's been bred and raised for this. He's probably killed a dozen women and he plans to just keep killing. His nose is always in the air. He doesn't ignore anything. Right now he's sitting in his seat wondering who might have walked through that door, seen him, and then turned away because they didn't want to be recognized. He's sorting out how many people there are like that in the world and then trying to sort out the probability that one of them just walked through that door. If the probability is small enough his plans won't change. But if it's not, we've lost him. He'll stay on the train through Chicago, get off in New York and that will be that. But, what is sure is that he is going to be more alert, more cautious than he was already. He's already better at this than either of us. The only chance we have is that we know about him and he doesn't know about us. If we lose that advantage we might as well just blow our own brains out. Do you understand?"

I nodded.

He put the food down on the side table.

"Eat up. I'll be back for the tray."

He slipped back out the door.

I'll give him credit—he managed not to tell me to stay in my room.

* * *

Mike didn't come back for the tray and I didn't see him again until the train stopped in Chicago. I was on the edge of my bed trying to figure out when I should give up and go looking for him when there was a light tap at the door. I opened it and Mike slipped in. He looked more tired than he had ten hours earlier. My guess was that he hadn't slept in close to forty-eight hours.

"He's watching me."

"Watching you—he doesn't even know you exist."

"I think you got him sniffing and then I walked by his seat one too many times. For the last six hours every time I got up to come see you he was watching and got up with me. I don't think he knows about you, he's just watching me. The last time I just walked up three or four cars and then turned and came back. He was about eight steps behind me the whole way. When I turned around to go back to my seat he wouldn't move. Took up most of the aisle and I had to squeeze by him. When I got back to my seat he just stood in the aisle looking down at me. I asked him what he wanted but he didn't answer, just stood staring down at me. He must have stood there for a minute or two and then just raised his finger. A warning. And then went back to his seat."

"How did you get down here now?"

"He followed me until I stepped off the train but he doesn't want off the train until its full dark. He watched me until I went into the terminal. And then he watched for several more minutes before going back to his seat.

Then I doubled back and got on at the door near your berth."

"So, what do we do now?"

"Get your stuff together and meet me in the terminal by the South exit. I expect McKillops is going to leave by the north exit—that takes him out onto Adam and he can head east across the bridge and down to the docks. That seems to be where he does most of his work."

"Is there any chance we'll miss him?"

Mike shook his head.

"There's no way out except through the terminal unless he's willing to go over the fence. But it could be a couple of hours—hard to say what his schedule is going to be. And it's always possible we've spooked him bad and he'll just stay on the train."

We stood for a second.

"But I don't think so. He's tasting it. I think he's going."

"So, that's it. We just wait there until McKillops comes out?"

He looked over at me.

"What? You're hoping for some kind of secret agent master plan? He'll come out. We'll follow him until we find a place to come up behind him and shoot him."

I stared at him until he shrugged.

"Keep it simple stupid. Let's go. When you leave the berth turn right and get off at the first exit. Move straight across the platform to the terminal entrance right there."

He pointed out the window and I could see the glow of the inside of the terminal through the frosted glass of the double doors.

"Don't look around. Just go straight to the door. He will be able to see you from his seat for the last few steps if he's looking straight up the tracks. I don't expect he will be but don't give him a chance to see you face on. Once you're in the terminal I have to get back to my berth and get my stuff. I'll meet you by the South exit. South. Got it?"

I nodded. He motioned with his chin at the door.

"Okay. Get going."

I ducked out the door into the empty hallway. I let out a long breath. I realized I had been expecting McKillops to be there. I turned right and stepped down off the train at the exit between the cars. There was a porter there having a smoke and he nodded at me as I stepped down.

"Will you be coming back aboard, sir?"

"I hope so."

He smiled like I had made a joke.

I hurried across the platform moving faster than I intended but not able to slow down. I didn't look around, just pulled the door open and stepped into the noise and the warmth of the terminal. It felt good to be inside the door. I turned left and up the stairs to the North concourse then headed down to the south end of the building. There were a lot of people milling around but it was a big building and there was only the one set of stairs up from the North concourse tracks. There didn't seem to be much chance we would miss him. I took a spot against the wall beside the exit. Mike showed up ten minutes later with a knapsack over his shoulder.

"Do you think he saw you?"

"We're going to have a long boring night if he did."

We stood for less than an hour. He came up the stairs empty-handed and wearing a long gray trenchcoat, maybe overdressed for the weather, but he could have been coming in from someplace colder. At the top of the stairs he turned right and walked towards where we were standing.

"Shit. He's going to cross the Jackson Street bridge. Split up. Go."

Mike moved to his left and towards the south concourse stairs and I moved right towards the newspaper stands. I kept my back to McKillops looking at magazines on the rack then chanced a quick peek over my right shoulder and I could see McKillops scanning the crowd as he walked quickly towards the door but he was already by me and moving fast. I looked over my left shoulder at Mike and he motioned for me to follow McKillops. I stood for a second staring and he motioned again, waving hard. Apparently he had a plan I wasn't aware of.

By the time I stepped out the door onto Jackson, McKillops was about two hundred feet down the street. But the sidewalk wasn't crowded so I could stay well back and still keep him in sight. This was the third time I had followed a McKillops and I didn't feel like I was getting any better at it. I looked back and saw Mike about two hundred feet behind me. He crossed over to the other side of the street as I watched.

I expected McKillops to just keep walking towards the river but he turned left at the first corner and I had to hurry to make sure he didn't get out of sight. I stood at the edge of the intersection as if I was planning to cross and took a casual glance to my left. I didn't see him at first but then, across the street, he moved into a pool of light from a streetlamp, walking north with long sure strides. There was no sign he was worried about being followed. I stayed on the west side of the street and followed him north. We walked about four blocks and I kept about one hundred feet between us. I had no idea where Mike was. I hadn't seen him since we had turned north and I was just hoping he was around and keeping tabs. He had the gun.

We walked north for several blocks, the taller office buildings giving way to short, squat warehouses, empty railyard, and fewer more irregularly spaced street lamps. McKillops took a quick look over his left shoulder for traffic and then stepped into the street, crossing diagonally to my side of the street. It was late and the only traffic was a couple of cabs and a darkened out-of-service city bus. I pulled my cap tighter over my forehead but he didn't pay me any attention.

My first thought was to cross over to the side McKillops had come from but that seemed even more likely to attract attention so I just kept walking but now I was only fifty or sixty feet behind him. He seemed unaware of me and I slowed my pace to increase the distance between us. McKillops turned left at the next street without hesitation. He knew where he was going. Within a block or two we had left the warehouses behind and the street was narrower and gloomier with few street lights and most of them broken and dark and then the sidewalk ended and we walked on the street, pulling in close against the buildings for the few vehicles that passed. What little light there was leaked from around the frayed window drapes and open doorways of small makeshift bars. They looked like they had been built as storefront offices or maybe, railyard shacks for the gandy dancers in the early days of the trains but now they were in the final stages of decay before they fell over in a pile of wood and brick or were knocked down to be replaced by something shiny and gleaming. The low murmur of voices drifted from open doors, occasionally raised in anger but usually desultory and indistinct. There was no music coming from any of the bars although I saw a jukebox pushed against the wall of one when I looked in but it was dark and the plate that protected the coinbox had been forced off and the twisted, mangled metal lay on the floor where it had been dropped. I could see several people in the bar but all sitting at tables by themselves except for a couple, the man asleep his head resting on one arm flung across the table and the woman staring straight ahead out the doorway where I passed. But she didn't see me.

The lights from the bars flickered like the last few working bulbs on a string of tired Christmas lights still hanging in April. Most of the three- and four-story apartment buildings propping up the bars were dark and damaged, windows broken, front doors missing or hanging drunkenly by a single hinge. A man stepped out of the doorway of one of the buildings and my breath caught in my throat. He was short and spare, buried in a peacoat too large for him, older than middle-aged with graying hair shaved close to the skull and small buried eyes like nail heads hammered once too often and his right hand stayed in the pocket of his coat, but he just looked at me for a second and then melted back into the darkened doorway. Ahead of me McKillops turned left again down a narrow side street. He was moving more quickly. He was on the hunting grounds and searching. I looked around for Mike but still no sign. I hesitated for a second…I had no weapon, no way to stop McKillops except with my bare hands and I wasn't confident I was up to it. But I couldn't turn around now. McKillops was set to kill somebody tonight, I had no doubt. He wasn't a man out for a walk. He was eager and anxious and even from far away I had been able to sense the excitement and anticipation in the way he moved.

I followed again, stepping past the corner as if I was going to continue on but when I looked down the street I couldn't see McKillops. The street was dark and I could see little although towards the end of the street there was a single light bulb glowing above an open door. Another bar. Too low-rent for the street I was on. Hard to imagine. It was the last stop before your room with its single bed, soiled blanket, unshaded bulb, and broken twelve-inch black and white. What came after that? If your body was strong, the black stinking hole beneath the railroad tracks where you broke the empty bottles and licked the sticky residue and your tongue became thick and scarred because you didn't worry about the shards. And they found you when they followed the stink and rumor and carried you away to be buried with a name or not. But I couldn't see McKillops. Not him. I stopped and listened but there was nothing. I stood for a second uncertain of what to do next and then stepped down the side street

I should have kept a step or two out in the street but I wasn't thinking and so I stepped by a doorway and he had me before I could move. His arm clamped tight around my neck and I felt the blade, tight and sharp against my side. He had cut my breath off completely and pulled me off balance so that I had little leverage to struggle. He loosened his hold a little and I dragged a thin stream of air down into my lungs. His mouth was up against my ear and I could feel his breath slow and warm on the side of my face.

"Don't move, my friend or I'll have to use the cutter. You understand?"

I nodded.

"I had you tagged as a bad order from day one and I should have done something about you that first time. But it's been a long time since then. I thought I was rid of you. What are you doing down here on the 'can't and never will' side of town, sonny?

I had nothing to say. Denial wasn't going to work and I had nothing else.

"Are you working alone? There was another fella on the train that gave me a bit of a start. Were the two of you working together?"

I shook my head. I wasn't sure I would be able to speak.

"That seems unlikely."

I shook my head again.

"What's the point of denying it? Two guys independently tracking me? How likely is that? What's his name, sonny? Things will go easier if you tell me."

I shook my head a third time. I wasn't sure if I was still denying that I

180

knew Mike or if I was saying I wasn't going to tell. His voice in my ear changed then, got lower and huskier.

"What did you think you were doing, boy? Saving somebody? There's no saving them. They're mine. And you never had a chance from day one. We're a different breed, boy. The rabbit and the wolf and the best that the rabbit can do is get out of the way."

His voice got even lower.

"And now it's done. I'll take care of your friend when I see him again."

He pulled back hard and my wind closed off completely and I tried to reach behind me to get at his face but felt a hot burn as the knife slid into my side and then his head came apart. His arm was still hooked around my neck as he fell and though his grip loosened, my balance was already precarious and the weight pulled me down. I looked up from the ground. Mike was standing about eight feet away with the gun in his hand trailing a thin wisp of smoke. I lay with my head and upper body on McKillops and my legs spread out on the pavement. I shook off his arm still draped around my neck and started to scramble to my feet but the pain in my side kept me on one knee.

"C'mon Ryan we have to go."

"I don't know how fast I can move."

"Jesus Christ, we gotta get moving. What's wrong?"

"He stuck me pretty good."

"What?"

"He stabbed me."

"What? I didn't even see a knife."

I put my hand to my side and it came away wet. He stared at the blood on my hand then shook his head.

"We have to get back to the train. Can you walk if I help?"

I nodded and took his arm to get to my feet. The vertigo hit me hard and I would have fallen if Mike hadn't caught me.

"Whoa, boy. Hang on. Put your arm around my shoulder, we'll look like a couple of late-night drunks. We've got about twenty blocks to cover back to Union Station. Can you make it?"

I nodded, although the end of the block looked a long way away. We stuck to the side streets, but kept heading south. We stopped under a single street lamp on a deserted street near the edge of the warehouse district and Mike had a look at my side.

"Jesus Christ, that looks bad. It's still bleeding pretty hard. Shit, we have to do something."

Mike took off his jacket and stripped his belt from his pants. He folded the jacket into eighths and then pressed it against the wound.

"Hold that."

I was leaning against a warehouse wall and I pressed the jacket against my side. He wrapped the belt around my waist and started to cinch it tight. I gasped.

"Other side."

"Shit. Right."

He moved to the other side and cinched it on the uninjured side but the pain caused by the pressure still made me lightheaded. He stepped back to look at me.

"Jesus Christ, you're a mess."

He was looking at my face not my side. I touched my hair and felt the hard bits that had been McKillops's skull and the soft bits that had been brain and tissue. I pawed at them, frantically wiping what I could off my head onto the ground but smearing a bunch and matting it into my hair.

"Fuck. Fuck. That's gross. Give me something to wipe it off."

Mike looked around for anything to wipe me down but there was nothing in the small circle of light from the streetlamp. I felt something cold and slick above my eye and wiped away a glob of tissue that had slid off the top of my head.

"We're going to have to clean you up somehow. You can't get on the train like this. It's not just the shit in your hair."

He pointed down at my side – the folded jacket looked odd enough but beneath it blood had soaked into the right side of my pants from the waist almost to the knee.

"We've got to figure something out – there's no way we're getting aboard with you looking like this. What are we going to do?"

"McKillop's coat."

"What?"

"McKillop's wore a long coat."

"Fuck, right. Wait here."

I watched him run down the street and then I slid down the wall and nodded off. I don't remember much after that, bits and pieces. Mike had to wake me when he got back and I remember struggling into McKillops's coat once we got close to Union Station. And thinking that every block was the last block but it never was. Until the last one. And then waiting outside the station entrance while Mike went in and bought me a hat—I had lost my ballcap somewhere along the way. Probably when McKillops grabbed me. He ended up buying one of those floppy full-brimmed sunhats that would hide the mess in my hair better than a ball cap. The walk from the entrance of the station to my berth was a long one. I wasn't able to drape myself over Mike—it would have looked too strange. I had to walk it myself, although Mike caught me a couple of times when I swayed and I did stumble into a guy going down the stairs to the door leading onto the platform. He cursed but didn't look at me, just pushed by. I almost went down but Mike steadied me and we made it to my berth. I woke up to a porter banging on my door.

"Sir, we're in Montreal. It's time to debark the train. Are you alright?"

"I'm fine. I'll be right out."

My voice caught when I first started to speak and then when I managed to speak it was weak and raspy.

"Are you sure, sir?"

"I'm fine."

It was a little stronger.

I sat up and the pain burst in my side. I wasn't wearing a shirt, although Mike must have changed me into fresh pants. The wound was covered in a thick white bandage taped heavily around all of the edges. I could see a couple of specks of red that had worked through but it looked like the bleeding had stopped. There was a shirt at the foot of my bed next to my packed bag and a note.

THIS SHOULD BE THE LAST TIME.

It hurt but I crumpled the note, shrugged into my shirt, grabbed my bag with my good arm, and slipped out the door of my berth. The porter was still standing in the hallway and he looked at me hard but I just nodded and smiled then moved down to the end of the car and stepped off the train. We were playing the Mets in six hours. I didn't think I was going to be ready.

Chapter Seventeen

My side felt like somebody had packed burning charcoal briquets under the gauze and I could barely stay on my feet. I dropped my bag just inside the door and tottered to the bathroom, shrugged out of my shirt, and had to pinch off a scream. I was going to have to go slower. Blood had soaked through the bandage and the skin around the edges was red and inflamed. I shook a couple of Tylenol out of the bottle and looked at them in my hand before shaking out a couple more and swallowing the four of them. I tried peeling away one side of the thick wad of gauze but the blood and seepage clung to the wound. I went into my room and let myself down gingerly onto the bed to rest for a minute.

The phone woke me but it took me a few seconds to remember where I was and by the time I picked it up all I got was the dial tone and a sharp reminder that I had been stabbed in a dark Chicago alley in 1966. I looked over at the clock beside my bed. Fuck, only forty minutes until game time. I called a cab, inched into a clean shirt and suit jacket but by the time I had managed that, the cab was there and there was no time for clean pants. The first rush of adrenalin when I woke up had convinced me I was feeling better but now slumped in the back of the cab I was drained and tired, my side ached and now I felt flushed and the beginnings of a headache. And wasn't sure what I was doing—I could barely put on a shirt, I surely wasn't going to be able to swing a bat or crouch for a hot shot down the third baseline.

The clubhouse was empty when I got there except for the trainer and his assistant setting the lockers up with fresh towels. Frankie nodded but then went back to work without speaking. I stood in front of my locker for a

185

second trying to decide what to do and then went out into the hallway and right to the dugout, still in my street clothes. Most of the guys were on the field warming up but McKay was sprawled out on the bench talking with one of the coaches. He saw me first and stood up.

"Well, well, well. The golden boy has arrived. Nice of you to drop by, Spencer."

Then he noticed the street clothes and his face darkened.

"What the fuck! Get your uni on, jackoff, we got a game to play."

He stood blocking the way and I would have pushed past him but I wasn't sure I could get by without twisting in a way that might drop me to my knees.

"Let me by, McKay."

"No civvies in the dugout, asshole. You wanna be here get into a uni. Or fuck off."

"I've got to talk to the skipper."

"Baldy's busy. With ballplayers."

I sighed and looked over at the coach but he was staring out at the field. I'm not sure what would have happened if Balducci hadn't spotted me. He broke off talking to the third base umpire and came over to the rail.

"What's up, Ryan? It's ten minutes to game time and you're in the starting lineup. Get suited up."

"I don't think I can go, skipper."

"Shit. Do you believe this asshole?"

Balducci spoke without looking away from me.

Shut up, MacKay. Go take some balls at first."

"Yeah. Right."

McKay turned away and slumped back onto the bench. Balducci came around the rail and down into the dugout and walked past me.

"My office, Spencer."

He stopped for a second at the door and looked back at the bench coach.

"I put the lineup card in already. Scratch Spencer and get Jimmi in there. I may not be here for the opening pitch. Make sure the right guys end up on the field."

I followed him down the hall and into the clubhouse and then through to his office. He slumped into his chair behind the desk and I stood in the doorway. He waved his hand at the chair across from the desk.

"Sit down, Ryan."

I moved into the room and folded gingerly into the chair. He noticed.

"What's going on? What happened?"

I put my hand to my side then took it away and shook my head.

"I'm cramping up. I'm not sure what it is but I don't think I can go today." I had no idea how to explain a stab wound. This seemed like the best idea. Balducci looked at me for several long seconds.

"A cramp? Do you need Frank to look at you?"

"No, I get these once in a while, I should be okay by tomorrow morning."

He looked at me for a long time again and then waved his hand for me to leave. I pushed myself out of the chair and tried to disguise the pain that blanketed my left side. His voice stopped me at the door.

"Spencer?"

"Skipper?"

"Do you like baseball?"

"Sir?"

"It's a silly game. I know that. I've tried to explain it to people who haven't grown up around it and when I hear myself describe the game I sound like a moron. The rules must have been put together by a drunk eight-year-old. But I love this game. I'm a fifty-five-year-old man twenty-five years past having a flat stomach—"

His hand moved unconsciously across the front of his jersey.

"...and I show up every day and step into a ball uniform and walk out of the tunnel and onto the field. And I am fucking excited. Something new is going to happen and I am going to be in the middle of it. And I will do anything to be a part of this. When they tell me I'm not good enough to manage, I'll coach. And when they tell me I'm not good enough to coach, I'll scout. And when they tell me I'm not good enough to scout, I'll sweep up the sunflower shells and scrub the tobacco juice off the concrete steps. I will do anything they ask me to do for whatever crappy paycheque they want to give me just so that I get to be around the ballfield."

He didn't talk for a second but I knew he wasn't done.

"And every asshole out there feels the same way I do. So, McKay makes me sick. He's a punk and a douchebag. But he's one of mine. When I see the look on his face as he comes out of the tunnel I know we're the same. He would give his left nut to play this game. And when he's fat and forty and throwing eighty without much movement, he'll be drunk in the morning in Sioux Falls Idaho, downing a handful of Tylenol and a liter of coke so the hangover doesn't hit him quite as hard in the sixth inning of a Saturday afternoon game. And most days, nineteen-year-olds heading to where he's been will be lighting him up like a July fourth firecracker, rattling stained hardballs around a shabby A-ball park…but once in a while, his arm will be loose and limber and he'll hit his spots and for an inning or two, nobody will be able to touch him. And maybe it's just luck. Maybe he hits a run of players that aren't even good enough for A-ball or they swing and miss a ball that they would drill ninety-nine times out of a hundred but for a few batters it's like his best days, when the ball was humming and hopping and his arm felt like a bullwhip and his legs and hips released like a tendon and bone tripwire. And that will be enough to get him through a thousand mornings when he knows he's an asshole playing a fool's game headed to a grave that nobody visits."

He was quiet for a second.

"Maybe this game ain't for you, son."

I stood for a second longer without speaking. He grimaced.

"Be ready to pinch-hit if I need you."

It took me two innings to get into my uniform and I was drenched as I walked through the clubhouse, down the tunnel, and into the dugout. Their leadoff hitter in the third inning was stepping into the batter's box and our guys were in the field. I took a spot at the end of the bench but nobody looked at me and nobody sat near me.

The inning was almost over before Balducci came out and took his spot leaning on the rail next to the steps leading out of the dugout.

* * *

We were tied at three going into te top half of the eighth. Our starter had been replaced in the sixth and our long reliever's spot was scheduled to be the fourth guy up in the eighth. Ramirez smacked a double cff the wall to get us going. Jimi moved him over to third with a groundout to the right side of the field.

"You're up after Hiltz, Spencer."

I stood up and moved in beside him against the rail.

"I don't think I can do it, Skip."

He just kept looking out at the field but I saw the skin tighten around his mouth.

"Cramps? Fucking cramps, Spencer? You get out there and swing that fucking bat or you'll be playing in fucking Nashville before the end of the week. I don't care what they say upstairs."

I stood for a second looking at the side of his face but he just kept staring out at the field.

I stood in the on-deck circle leaning on my bat. I was just going to have to watch pitches. No matter what. If he grooved three straight down the middle I was just going to have to watch them and head back to the bench. I couldn't think of any alternative. And maybe I could work him for a walk. The pitcher was Jamie Wright, a compact leftie who I hadn't faced before but who could hit ninety-five mph on the gun and had a mean cutter that broke in on righties. The first pitch was the fastball and it caught the outside corner just above my knee. Even if I had been healthy I wouldn't have chased it—if he could make that pitch three times in a row he was going to sit me down. The next pitch he tried to hit the same spot but was a little further outside, didn't catch a piece of the plate but the ump gave it to him anyway. I stepped out to adjust my glove and when I stepped back in and tapped the far side of the plate like I always did, it sent a sheet of pain up my left side and I held my right hand up to step back out. The umpire moved to the side, waved his arms, and looked at me. He was a fit-looking Black guy of around forty whose name I couldn't remember but he had umped a half dozen of our games.

"What's going on, Spencer?"

I shook my head.

"Nothing. I just wasn't comfortable."

"Quit fucking around."

He waved me back in and I almost tapped the plate again but remembered at the last second. The next pitch was the cutter but it was way inside. He tried the heater on the outside corner once more and then again but strayed further and further away from the plate and the count was full.

The next pitch was over the heart of the plate and I couldn't stop myself. It's amazing how habit and training will kick in despite your conscious intentions. I had stepped up knowing that there was no way I was swinging at anything but this was like breathing. I had spent my life feasting on pitches this. It was a simple reaction I couldn't stop. I hit the ball hard and clean and it still triggered the pleasure spots in my brain. Just before the follow-through ripped apart the wound, separating the fragile cell bridges that had begun to build across the gap and sending waves of electrical impulses that smothered everything but the sensation of pain. I took a step or two down the first baseline but on the second step my leg gave out and I went to one knee. For a moment things went gray and I thought I would pass out but then my vision cleared and I saw the first baseman turning back towards the plate with his shoulders slumped and the first base ump waving his arm in the 'touch em all' circle. But then he stopped in mid-wave as he saw me go down. He started to take a step forward but I pushed myself off the ground with both hands, causing another stab of pain. My vision had narrowed to a few feet on each side of the first baseline and I moved slowly down the line, at first walking and then managing to pick up to a trot. I stumbled as I made the turn around first and the first baseman reached out to steady me.

"You alright, buddy?"

It sounded like it was being whispered down a tunnel. I shook him off and slowly circled the bases keeping my eyes focused on the bag directly in front of me until I had to make my next turn. The last thirty feet to home plate seemed to take several minutes but I made it and then stopped just the other side of the plate to gather myself again. My vision had started to widen and I could hear the crowd shouting which I hadn't noticed while I was circling the bag. It was warm and wet on my right side. I had another moment where I thought I might go down but was able to recover and walked slowly back to the dugout. Balducci met me at the top of the dugout steps.

"That was a helluva piece of—"

He stopped.

"Are you alright, Spencer?"

He didn't wait for an answer looking over his shoulder at the trainer.

"Frank. Get Ryan back into the trainer's room and figure out what the fuck is going on. I think he's going to pass out."

I made it down the tunnel to the trainer's table but just. I looked down at my side as I made my way down the tunnel and there was a large patch of red, spreading as I watched. I struggled up onto the table and lay back. Frank started to speak but then saw the growing stain on my side.

"What the fuck? What the hell happened to you, Ryan?"

I shook my head but he was already talking to his assistant trainer.

"Give me a hand here, Russ."

He turned back to me.

"Ryan, can you get your shirt off?

He was already working the buttons.

"Can you shrug out of it if I pull on the arm?"

Together we got the jersey off and he slid it out from beneath my back without me having to sit up. He looked at the large blood-soaked bandage covering the wound. He turned to the assistant trainer who was standing wide-eyed in the door of the training room.

"Russ, get me a pair of scissors, a towel, a bowl of hot soapy water, a bottle of the saline solution and, one hundred and fifty milligrams of 0.25% Marcaine."

"We're going to have to see what's under there, Ryan. What happened?"

I shook my head. He started to answer but Russ was back with the supplies. Frank washed his hands carefully and then started on the bandage. It took a while, at least ten minutes and it hurt but not as bad as I expected. Frank worked without speaking, soaking the bandage in saline solution and then cutting and gently pulling away pieces as the scab softened. When he had all the old bandage away he paused for a second and then wiped it down with the towel

"Shit. It's still bleeding pretty good. Russ, get me some of that non-stick gauze and the disinfectant."

He tapped out the syringe and injected the wound area. Russ was back in a couple of seconds.

"For fuck's sake, Russ, I'm going to need an applicator for the disinfectant." I could feel the area numbing.

"I'm going to do a little feeling around here, Ryan. It could cause a little twinge even with the Marcaine."

But I didn't feel anything. Russ was back quickly and Frank spread the disinfectant across the wound, covered it in the gauze and taped the sides down. He stood back then.

"You've got to get to the hospital, Ryan. I can't treat that kind of wound. You're cut deep. I'm pretty sure right through to the body cavity. I didn't want to disturb the wound too much but I think there's a gap in the abdominal wall. You need stitches, lots of them. Internal and external. How do you want to do this? We could call an ambulance but if we do, this is a story. We'll have reporters following us to the hospital and there will no way around it. You're going to have to answer questions about how this happened. Or we can drive you there and try and keep this under wraps. I've got you patched up for now but you can't leave it like this. So?"

I pushed myself up to a sitting position.

"Pass me my jersey. We'll drive."

He nodded.

"Russ, let the skipper know we've taken Ryan to the hospital."

He hesitated, looking over at me.

"Nothing urgent. He doesn't need to worry. I'll fill him in when I get back. You keep your mouth shut. You aren't sure what the problem is. Got it?"

Russ nodded.

"Okay, let's go, Ryan. Can you walk on your own?"

"Sure."

We made it to the car without incident. The game was still going so there was no crowd outside the door and Frank was parked nearby. It was a fifteen-minute drive to the hospital but I must have slept because it seemed like I had just settled into the passenger seat and we were there. He started to pull into the parking area but I stopped him.

"Just pull up in front of Emergency and let me out."

"Are you sure, Ryan?"

I nodded.

"Let me take it from here. You're going to have enough to explain. For now, just say that I said I needed to go to the hospital and you drove me there but you don't know what the problem was."

"I won't lie to Baldy."

"That's fine, Frank, but don't tell him more than you have to."

"There's not much to tell except that somehow you got stabbed."

I pushed the door open and swung my legs out onto the asphalt. My head spun and I rested for a second before pushing myself to my feet. I had to grab onto the car to keep from falling but was able to steady myself in a couple of seconds and leaned down into the door to look at Frank.

"Thanks, buddy. I owe you."

"Ryan?"

"It's a long story, Frank. I'll tell you when I can."

He looked at me for a second.

"Yeah. Right. Get in there before you pass out."

I stood up and pushed the car door closed. I turned and walked slowly through the front doors and into the hospital foyer. When I turned back Frank had already pulled away. There were only a half dozen people in the emergency room and I shuffled over to the check-in window.

It didn't take long to see a doctor. He didn't seem that much older than me. And he kept calling me Mr. Spencer.

"So, how did this happen Mr. Spencer?"

"I was stabbed."

"Yes, I can see that. What were the circumstances?"

"I got held up in old Montreal early this morning. They wanted my wallet and I guess I was too slow and one of the guys stabbed me."

"That was more than twenty hours ago, Mr. Spencer. What took you so long to decide to come in and see us?"

"I didn't think it was as bad as it was."

He raised an eyebrow.

"You didn't think it was very serious?"

"I didn't say it wasn't serious. Just not as serious as it is."

"Well, I'm glad you have come to understand the seriousness of this injury. This is a deep penetrating abdominal injury but I don't see any signs of peritonitis or diffuse abdominal tenderness. We will have to debride the wound and do some extensive stitching. Then, with rest, you should recover with little or no evidence that you had ever been injured. Except for a scar."

He smiled as if he had made a joke. I didn't think I had heard one.

"Have you called the police?"

"Excuse me?"

"Have you called the police about the robbery?"

"Uh, no."

You get robbed and stabbed and you didn't call the police, Mr. Spencer?"

He motioned for me to follow him without waiting for my answer. We stepped into a room two doors down from emergency with an examination table, a side tray with several surgical instruments, and a sink. The doctor whose name I had already forgotten introduced me to a young nurse.

"Jenny will get you prepped for the debriding and stitching. So, once again, Mr. Spencer, why did you not call the police?"

He was starting to bug me.

"I guess I never thought about it. Cops never catch these kinds of crimes. And I was so messed up I just went home and slept."

"Except, of course, for hitting the home run that put the Expos ahead in tonight's game."

He smiled.

"I'm a fan, Mr. Spencer. "

"Yeah, plus that. I'm a ballplayer and they would make this into a big story and—"

He raised his hand.

"I understand, Mr. Spencer, mum's the word."

He turned to the nurse.

"Jenny, prep Mr. Spencer for stitching. He's probably going to need about seventy stitches. And it's been almost twenty-four hours so you will have to do some debriding."

"Yes, Doctor."

I'm not exactly sure what debriding is but even with the additional local, it was fifteen minutes of no fun. Jenny didn't speak at all except to get me to shift positions. The doctor took almost an hour stitching me up after Jenny was through and although there was the occasional twinge it was nothing like what Nurse Jenny had put me through.

"Okay, that's it, Mr. Spencer."

I had started to doze on the table despite the tugging and occasional twinge. He stood up and stripped off his surgical gloves and tossed them in the garbage.

"How are you feeling?"

I looked down at my side. It looked like a family of spiders had got caught in a skin avalanche.

"Pretty good. Tired."

"Do you want to arrange for somebody to come get you?"

"No. I'll just call a cab."

"It would be better if somebody came for you and spent some time with you. The local is going to wear off and this will be very painful. And you are going to be weak and tired. There must be somebody you can call."

"It's one o'clock in the morning, Doc—I'm not going to call anybody at this time. I'll take a cab home and call a friend in the morning to come over."

The truth was I couldn't think of anybody to call. Jimmy's wife and Nick were the only people that came to mind. How sad was that?

"So, this person that you will call in the morning would be upset if you called them tonight?"

"I don't know about upset but I don't want to wake them. I'm sure they wouldn't mind but I would just feel bad because…"

I let it trail off.

"I'll call them in the morning."

"As you wish. Jenny, call Mr. Spencer a cab. What is your address, Mr. Spencer?"

I gave it to her and she left the room.

He wrote several notes on what must have been my file, then stood up and looked at me for several seconds before speaking.

"Mr. Spencer, if it is important to you that people believe your story about what happened, then you might want to spend more time on it. Have a good night and good luck this season."

He turned and left the room. I didn't think to thank him until he was gone. I waited for a few minutes, not sure what I was supposed to do. I finally stuck my head out of the door but there was nobody in the hallway so I walked the few steps down the hall to the door of the emergency room. There were only three people scattered around the room, a tired-looking young woman with what must have been her son, who looked three or four years old, and a middle-aged woman watching the muted TV bracketed in the corner of the room. I walked across to the admittance window.

"Excuse me, I think the nurse was going to call me a cab. I was just—"

It will be about five or ten minutes, Mr. Spencer. Just grab a seat. He will pull right up front."

The reporters arrived before the cab. It was probably the nurse but it could have been the receptionist. I was pretty sure it wasn't the doctor. And I guess it could have been one of the people that had been in the emergency room when I had arrived. To the receptionist's credit, she didn't let them into the waiting room, although one guy pretended to be sick and managed to get next to me. My taxi showed up as soon as he sat down but he followed me and I still had to get by the three reporters standing outside the emergency room.

"Can you tell us why you're here, Ryan?"…"Why aren't you being treated by team doctors and trainers?"…"We heard it was a knife wound, Ryan, is that right?"…"Will it keep you out of tomorrow night's game?"

I didn't answer, just walked by them to the cab and slipped into the backseat.

"Bonjour, Monsieur Spencer."

I nodded and gave my address but I could see it already posted on his meter. Right. The nurse had probably already given it to him. Shit, there were probably going to be reporters at my apartment. But they weren't. Either it wasn't the nurse or the receptionist or this wasn't a big enough deal to stake out my apartment at 1:30 AM.

The weakness hit me in a wave as I got out of the cab and I staggered before catching myself. I slumped against the elevator wall on the ride up and when I was standing in front of my door I fumbled with the key, dropping it twice before getting into my apartment. I went down the hall to my room in the dark, crawled onto the bed without undressing, and woke up three hours later so sore I could barely move. I started to sit up and the pain made me cry out. I lay still for a few moments while the pain subsided and then gingerly worked my legs off the side of the bed and pushed myself upright. I stopped several times to manage the pain but eventually managed to get both feet on the ground and sit hunched over the edge of the bed. The pain and nausea almost dropped me backwards onto the bed but the thought of the Tylenol in the bathroom got me on my feet. In the dim early morning light I bumped up against a shoe I must have kicked off the night before and stumbled slightly. The pain rippled up my side and I stood still with my eyes closed until I had it back under control. In the bathroom, I took a handful of Tylenol and then went back to bed. That makes it sound easy. It wasn't.

When I woke up again it was light and I wasn't feeling much better. I had a little easier time sitting up although maybe I was just getting used to it. I grabbed a few more Tylenol, called a cab, and managed to get one arm into my jacket but couldn't do anything but sling the other sleeve over my shoulder. The cab was at the curb when I came out of the lobby and I almost passed out leaning down to get in. The cabbie looked at me in the rearview mirror but didn't say anything.

"Levesque Stadium"

He nodded, pulled away from the curb and idled at the first light, looking at me several times in the rearview before speaking.

"You a ballplayer?"

His accent was thick. Not French. Maybe Jamaica, Trinidad, something Caribbean.

I nodded.

"You sick?"

I shook my head.

"You look sick."

"I'm fine."

"You say so."

We didn't speak the rest of the way. The guard at the player parking gate stopped the cab but recognized me in the back seat and waved the cab through. The cabbie pulled up outside the player's entrance and watched as I struggled to get the door open. He twisted in his seat, watching me try and figure out a way to pull my way out of the car without causing screaming pain.

"Want some help?"

I nodded.

"What do you want me to do?"

"I'm not sure."

He looked at me for a second then got out and came around to where I was sitting with my feet resting on the asphalt. He looked at me for a second.

"You pull up and I'll push you from behind."

He came around the car and opened the door behind me. I couldn't twist to see him but I could feel him sliding along the bench seat, then both hands on my lower back.

"Okay, pull."

I gripped the door frame with my good hand and pulled and he pushed me to my feet from behind. It hurt but it wasn't too bad.

He crawled back out and came around the car.

"Twenty-two bucks."

"You charging extra for the help?"

He grinned and shook his head.

"Nah, man, but I left the meter running."

"My wallet's in my back pocket—take two twenties."

"You trust me?"

He grinned again.

"Just two."

"Whacha gonna do about it?"

He took out my wallet and pulled two twenties from the sheaf of bills.

"Just kiddin, man. You ask for Nile if you need a ride again."

He went back around to the driver's side of the car and slid in. He honked on his way out.

The training room was empty except for Russ putting out towels and Balducci in his office on the phone. He waved me to a chair and then watched me ease myself into it.

"Yeah, he's here, Frank. I'll talk to you later."

He hit the end call button and lay the phone on his desk.

"What the hell's going on Ryan?"

"Not much to it, Skip. I was out late two nights ago and got stopped by a guy who asked for my wallet. I guess I wasn't quick enough and he stuck me."

"That's a fucked up story."

"What do you mean?"

"Who gets stabbed in a back alley, stumbles home, sleeps it off then comes to the ballpark to play? It's fucked up. No cops. No hospital until last night. Don't tell a soul about it. You're hiding something, Ryan."

"I was embarrassed."

"Embarrassed?"

"I was pretty drunk."

"Pretty drunk? Half this team spends most of their evenings pretty drunk. That doesn't even make the needle quiver on the embarrassment meter. Sorry, Spencer, I don't buy it."

I ducked my head and mumbled something.

"What? What was that, Spencer?"

"It wasn't a guy."

He shook his head, confused.

"Not a guy?"

"It was a girl."

He leaned back in his chair."

"You got held up by a girl?"

He started to grin.

"I hope it was a big girl. A big, hairy girl."

I shook my head.

"Not so big."

He was grinning wide now.

"You got held up and stabbed by a little bitty girl? Wait till the news guys get ahold of this."

"I was hoping we could keep it out of the news."

"Are you kidding, Ryan? They've been calling me all morning. The only reason they aren't camped outside your apartment is because I told them if anybody showed up at your place they weren't welcome in the clubhouse and that we would let them have a session with you as soon as you were well enough."

He looked at me.

"How about today?"

"There's no way around it?"

"Not a chance, Ryan. They'll follow you around until they get this one—it's too juicy. But you don't want to tell that fucking little girl story. Go with your first story that it was a guy and if the cops end up picking up a girl just say that there must have been two of them."

He looked at his watch.

"Look, there's another eight hours until game time. Let's get them down here and get it over with before the guys start coming in. You up for it?"

I nodded. Miserably.

It wasn't so bad. A couple of the TV guys looked skeptical and the woman from La Presse looked completely incredulous but most of them focused on the fact that I had hit the winning home run with a gaping wound in my side. I was a hero.

But that was pretty much it. TSN and ESPN picked up the story and it got some national attention, 'rising young star runs into late-night trouble,' kind of stuff and I heard there were a couple of inquiries to our media people but it all got handled and disappeared back beneath the waves after a day.

The team sent me home for two weeks. They played three more games at home losing them all and then headed out on a ten-day road trip without me. Balducci told me to stay home and mend up but I think he was just happy to have an excuse not to have me around. But the team lost the last seven in a row and came back to town forty-six and forty-six and in third place. We were still in it because, except for the Mets, nobody in our division was very good. New York had opened up a twelve-game lead on us but the Phillies were only two games ahead and the Cubs were a game and a half back. The wildcard spot was wide open and despite the fact that we hadn't been able to get on a consistent run we were still in the hunt. Jimmy had played terribly on the road, he was in a two for twenty-seven slump by the end of the trip and they were desperate enough to call a kid up from double AA for the last game. He went oh for five, made two errors in a nine to seven loss and was back down before I had a chance to meet him.

I spent most of my time sleeping and reading old newspapers online and at the library. There were still reports in the archives of girls turning up dead, stabbed, through the late sixties and early seventies. I made a list of seventy-three different women who had been killed between 1967 and 1973 who would have been likely targets for a guy like McKillops. Young women from big cities who had been killed by unknown assailants in places not too far from railroad terminals. The number of women killed was much higher than that but most of them didn't fit the profile. It was usually husbands or boyfriends and they would use a gun or their fists. So, seventy-three women died even though we had taken McKillops off the street. He was an aberration among aberrations. He was an outlier but the problem with a world of seven billion people was that it was full of outliers.

Outliers were a statistical certainty. And like all outliers, human outliers had a disproportionate impact on the curve, on the curve of time, on the curve of human joy and misery, on the curve of terror and transcendence. And so seventy-three women had the steady slow accumulation of rich human silt laid down by pedestrian acts of kindness and indifference, by a steadying hand on a swaying bus or a spray of slush on a crowded March street interrupted by a final moment so full of horror and disdain that all other moments were rendered meaningless. They died finally able to imagine that so little time can be filled with so much pain and fear.

And I saw her again. She had been standing across the street looking up at my window. There was no doubt it was her, the woman from the library and the coffee shop and the ballparks. I took the stairs two and three at a time but she was gone, disappeared around the corner and down into the Metro or into one of the hundred shops within a three-block radius or into a nearby car. I rode the elevator back up to my apartment, my side a little sore but not bad considering how hard I had run.

* * *

"Spencer?"

I had just arrived and hadn't had time to start dressing and already the manager stood in the doorway calling across the dressing room. A few guys looked up but most just kept getting ready to play, taping up their ankles, working on bats or gloves, a couple just sitting in front of their lockers, eyes closed, headphones shutting out the noise of the room. Jimmy was one of the ones who watched as I got up and walked across the room. I looked at him and he stared back without expression. I nodded and shrugged but he just looked at me. By the time I got to the office door Baldy was already back behind his desk. He waved his hand at the chair but then stopped me.

"Shut the door."

I turned back and closed the door behind me. A couple of guys looked up then—closed-door meetings usually meant bad news.

"How are you feeling?"

"Fine. I'm feeling good."

"One hundred percent?"

"Close. Ninety-eight. I feel a twinge once in a while when I stretch for a ball or swing big and miss."

"Do you think you're ready to play every day?"

"Sure. Yeah. I don't see that should be a problem. I feel strong and I just keep feeling better."

He nodded.

"Good. We're going to let Munoz go and I want to be sure you're ready to carry the water the rest of the way."

"Let him go, why?"

"He's making four and a half million and he can only fill in at first and third. He's not hitting and even part-time we can't be getting that kind of production from first or third. And his glove's turned to shit. When he's not hitting, his fielding suffers and he's not hitting. And I don't think it's going to get better—he's thirty-three and he's just not turning the way he used to. There's guys that he just can't get around on—on his best day. If Mueller or Centrillo throw cheese, it's a foul into the right-field stands. And when he does get around, the pop's gone. Everything's dying on the track. We just can't afford to have that kind of guy taking up space on the bench. We're going to call up Garcia from Nashville, he can play everywhere but catcher if we need him. He doesn't have much punch but he's fast and an upgrade in the field at almost every position. We'll be able to spell Nick and Freddie every five or six games. But I don't want him to play much at third because he's going to hurt us at the plate if you're out. He's going to hurt us at the plate when he replaces Nick too but he's got more range and a better arm so he'll make some of that up in the field. But at third, I'm not sure he's much quicker than you and his glove may not be quite as good."

"Are you kidding? Nick's a better fielder than me."

"Nick's a genius. He knows where to be on every batter on every pitch and he doesn't waste any motion...but he's thirty-three years old and he's a two-hundred-and-fifteen-pound pound white man playing shortstop—it's like putting a defensive tackle in the saddle for the Kentucky Derby. He's a

Saint Bernard racing greyhounds."

He mumbled something I didn't hear.

"What?"

"I said that I just wish that some of the fucking greyhounds could speak English."

I couldn't help looking over my shoulder to where Jimmy was sitting in front of his locker. He was still in his jockstrap. He had been sanding the handle of his bat but had stopped when Balducci had called my name. It looked like he hadn't moved except to swivel his head since I had stepped into the manager's office. He watched us both through the window without changing expression. I turned back to Balducci.

"When are you going to do it, skip?"

"After the game tonight. No sense making him pack up right here in front of everybody."

"I'm not going to be very popular."

He snorted.

"Are you kidding me?"

He was right. Nothing would change.

"Is that it?"

"That's it. Don't get injured."

I nodded.

"And for crissake stop getting stabbed."

I didn't look at Jimmy when I left Balducci's office. I could tell a lot more eyes were watching me as I walked back to my locker. I'm sure a bunch of guys were hoping I had been sent down for rehab but when they saw me keep dressing they lost interest. I stripped off my shirt and slipped on a skintight polyester T-shirt. I put my hand under the shirt and ran it across the thick, raised scar tissue. The skin felt numb and like it only barely belonged to me but the ache was gone. I looked over at Nick's locker and he was watching me. He nodded his head towards the manager's office and raised his eyebrows.

"He just wanted to make sure I was ready to go."

"Behind closed doors?"

I shrugged and started to say something but Nick was looking over my shoulder to where Jimmy Munoz was standing in his jockstrap still holding his bat.

Jimmy didn't speak for a minute then reddened a little and started to turn away but then turned back.

"What did Ballsie want?"

"He just wanted to know how I felt. If I was okay."

He looked at me.

"Nothing about me?"

I didn't know what to say. There was no way out. So, I just didn't say anything. He continued to look at me before finally nodding. He turned and walked back to his locker. The whole room had gone quiet.

* * *

The Mets were in town and they were young and good. They had the best young catcher in the league in Travis Arsenault—he wasn't Johnny Bench or Mike Piazza at the plate but he would hit around .300 most years with fifteen or twenty home runs and ninety RBIs. The big knock on Travis was that he was only good for thirty or forty walks a year. Behind the plate, he was quick, mobile, with the best arm in the National League. And he was tough and called a great game. Even at twenty-six years old he seemed to have a gift for pitch selection. There wasn't a pitcher on the team whose numbers weren't better when Travis was behind the plate. And they had the best young starting rotation in the league—Zach Ryder, Noah Gilgard, Mike Fuller, and Felistes Camaria—all four under twenty-eight years old and only Gilgard couldn't hit ninety-five mile per hour on the gun. And Gilgard's control was phenomenal—he was twenty-six years old and had been pitching full-time in the majors for four years. In his first couple of years, his control had been pretty good—giving up 2.5 walks every nine innings but in the last two years, he had cut those numbers in half, and in one hundred and fifty innings so far this season, he had given up eleven walks, two of them intentional. And his strikeouts had gone up from five to seven every nine innings. He didn't throw any harder, just smarter. The other guys could just straight out throw the hell out of the ball—they were all punching out eight to ten hitters a game. Camaria occasionally ticked one hundred miles per hour and had pitched an eight-inning rain-shortened shutout earlier in the year and struck out fifteen. They were no fun.

We were up against Ryder tonight. He was tall and whippet-thin. Most pitchers had the big butt and legs but Wheeler had the broad shoulders and narrow waist and thin legs of a swimmer. There was worry around the league that the lack of a strong foundation meant he was going to have arm trouble but none of that stuff made any sense to me. And watching him warm up, he didn't look like he was suffering. Balducci had given us the word on him and there didn't seem to be many weaknesses. In his first two years in the league, he had trouble on the outside of the plate, either missing away and walking batters or coming into the heart of the plate and giving up home runs but that wasn't a problem anymore. He could hit ninety-five when he needed it but mostly kept his fastball between ninety-one and ninety-four and worked the corners. His out pitch was the curveball. He threw it in the mid-'70s but it looked harder coming out of his hand and it broke as big as anybody's in the league. I had seen film of guys leaning back to avoid getting hit by a ball that ended up missing outside. He had an OK changeup that he didn't throw much. But it could be effective if he spotted it once in a while.

Tonight he was on and it was the third inning before we got a hit off him. Hiltz led off the third and squibbed one off the end of the bat between first and third…three feet either way and he would have been out. McKay was up next and he took a couple of vicious cuts that didn't come close and then watched one cut the heart out of the plate. He stomped back from the plate and fired his bat at the barrel but it caromed off the lip, banged off the concrete wall and fell into the corner. Nobody looked away from the field. Danny Lopez tapped weakly back to the mound and the inning was over. It looked like it was going to be a long afternoon. And McKay was struggling. He walked the first hitter of the game but Giannos picked him off stealing then gave up a triple to the Met's second baseman before getting the last two batters in the inning. He got the first two batters in the third, but loaded the bases on a double and two walks before Arsenault hit one to the warning track. So, the game was still tied at zero but it felt like we should be down at least a couple of runs. I struck out against Cambria leading off the second inning but I had hit a scorcher that had curled just outside the foul pole on his first pitch and then looked at a ball that was an inch off the outer corner of the plate that the ump had rung me up on. I turned and walked back to the dugout without looking at the guy—Ballsie had done all the shouting for me and got tossed from the game.

I wasn't a guess hitter preferring to see it and hit it but Cambia had started me with the curveball in the first inning and I knew he liked to mix it up so I was pretty sure he wouldn't come back with the yakker...especially after I had hit the first one so hard. So, I was waiting on the fastball. And he threw me the fucking change. I was so far in front of the pitch that it probably looked like I could have reloaded and still got a piece of the pitch. I was pretty sure I heard Arseneault snicker but when I looked back he was looking out at his pitcher and his face was serious and composed. The ump was looking at me and grinning, though. I gave him the chin jerk, like, what are you smirking about but he just shrugged and kept smiling. That's why I wasn't a guess hitter, guess wrong and you look like a jackass. I waited on the next pitch and he must have still been feeling good about the last pitch because he made a little mistake, starting the curveball too far inside and without the usual snap. I could see the rotation and knew it was a fatty. It hung like USDA prime and I pounded it like Sly Stallone. I didn't need to watch it. The season more than half over and there was still nobody at home plate when I got there. Except for Arseneault. I couldn't resist.

"Anything funny now, Travis?"

"He looked at me for a second before answering.

"Yeah, how lonely it is around here, asshole."

That hurt a little.

We held the lead for a couple more innings but McKay flirted with danger in every one and finally, in the sixth they got to us for five runs and that was it. We weren't coming back against Cambria from four runs down. I grounded out in the sixth and got hit by a pitch in the ninth. He had too much control to do that by accident and I knew it was payback for the dinger in the fourth. Toner was up next in the ninth and got three wasted pitches in a row and then swung from the heels at a high fastball that was a foot outside the strike zone and popped it up to second. The second baseman fumbled the catch but Toner hadn't left the batter's box, and so he was able to pick up the ball and throw Toner out at first. I ran past him as he stood ripping off his batting gloves halfway down the first baseline.

"Way to hustle, Toner."

"Fuck you."

"And nice at bat. Way to work the count."

He came at me then. He was a big man and quick and he got a good shot in and another before I went down. He was on me then, pounding at my head and neck but I was able to keep my arms up and fend most of them off. The umps had to pull him off me. My team watched from our dugout and their guys watched from theirs. Toner was red-faced and shouting when the umps got him up but my ears were ringing from the first shot and I couldn't make out what he was yelling about. Three of the umpires led him away and guided him down into our dugout. He would periodically look back over his shoulder and yell something at me but I couldn't hear what he was saying. The home plate ump stood with me while Toner was led away.

"What did you do, boy? I've never seen a team just stand by and watch like that."

I shrugged but didn't answer.

"Yeah, well, something's going to have to give. I've never seen the like."

He looked over to our dugout and it was empty.

"Go on, boy. It should be OK now."

I was suddenly too tired to move. I stood there between home plate and first base and had an almost overwhelming desire to just lay down where I was and close my eyes for a little bit.

"You alright, son?"

My eyes had closed and I opened them again and looked at the ump, a medium height wiry man who had seemed younger with his mask on. Now

I could see the white strands in his tight-cropped hair and the lines around his mouth and eyes. I nodded.

"I'll be fine. I just need a minute."

I looked up in the stands. The fans had stuck around to see the tussle but now were trailing out of the ballpark—it reminded me of a time-lapse video of cytoplasmic streaming that I had seen in biology class. They seemed to move as a unit—individuals but unconsciously organized. As I watched they drifted and gathered like metal filings drawn by a hidden magnet, narrowing to a thin concentrated stream at each of the exit tunnels, leaving a few scattered spectators who for one reason or another were able to resist the pull of the crowd, and stood looking out at the field. At me and the umpire or the pool-felt green of the outfield and the dull red of the infield or the far scoreboard that was still updating scores. She stood about ten or fifteen rows back and it was clear she was watching me. I had seen her in Philadelphia, and then in San Francisco, and Los Angeles and now here in Montreal. I walked towards the rail separating the field from the stands but as soon as I started she gathered up her things and walked away. Not hurrying but moving quickly enough that I knew that even if I scrambled over the rail and chased her she would be into a tunnel and gone before I could catch her. By the time I reached the rail she was at the top of her section and disappeared into the nearest tunnel without looking back. The umpire had followed me over and now he put his hand on my shoulder.

"You sure you're alright?"

"I'm good. I'm fine."

The paralyzing fatigue had dissipated and I felt okay again. I walked away from him towards our dugout but took a look back when I reached the top of the dugout stairs. He was still standing where I had left him watching me and I waved my hand and shouted across the field.

"Thanks."

He raised his hand.

"Keep your chin up, son."

I felt my throat and chest tighten. A small kindness from a stranger.

Smitty was waiting at the door as I got to the dugout.

"Skip wants to see you in his office."

I nodded. Toner was coming out of the office when I got there and he shouldered by me without looking at me but bumped me hard enough that I hit the wall. I caught my balance and went into the office.

"Sit down, Ryan."

"I hope this is going to be a short one. I'm not up for a heart-to-heart."

"Sit the fuck down, Spencer."

I sat down. It was still warm.

"What the fuck was that about?"

"You saw it. I had a few words to say that he didn't like and so he jumped me."

"I didn't see fuck-all. The camera swung away to the fucking winners celebrating and by the time it came back to you two assholes, you were on the ground covering up like a little girl."

"You would prefer I got my licks in, skipper?"

He slammed his hand on the table.

"I don't know what the fuck I would prefer, Spencer. All I know is that this team is coming apart and you're the reason why and I can't figure a way out. But opening your fucking mouth and then not being able to back it up sure ain't the way to go."

"You saw it. If he runs out that flyball we've got men on first and second and we're still alive. And if he's not such a cementhead, he lays off that pitch and we're still men on first and second with a shot to win that game."

"You believe that?"

"What?"

"That we have a shot to win the game if Toner gets on base? The way Cambria was throwing."

"No. But you know that's not the point. You play the game the right way. Every time. Whatever the score. You take that fucking pitch and you trot down to first. And if you can't do that you at least run out that ball. For fuck's sake, skipper, you run out the ball."

We sat there for several seconds and then he waved his hand at the door like he was almost too tired to lift it off the desk.

"Get the fuck out, Spencer."

I got up.

"And send Jimmy in."

I looked at him over my shoulder. He had his head in his hands and he spoke without looking up

"Yeah. It's a fucking great job, kid."

I stood there for a second and he spoke again but he never looked up.

"Just fucking tell Jimmy to come in."

I told him. Jimmy had been dressed for several minutes and waiting and he stood up right away and walked into Balducci's office. They talked for a few minutes and then they shook hands. I sat by my locker and watched as Jimmy cleared his out and left. There weren't many players left. Before he left Jimmy spoke quietly with Guitterez and they hugged. He looked okay.

* * *

She was waiting outside the player's exit when I came out, leaning against the wall behind the door so I didn't see her right away but as the door swung shut behind me I caught a glimpse of color out of the corner of my eye and turned quickly, startled. She was wearing the same bulky wool sweater that fell almost to her hips over new jeans and sneakers even though it was midsummer and warm. She didn't speak.

"What do you want?"

She still didn't answer. It was weird. Not scary weird, there was nothing threatening about her. In fact, she seemed scared and nervous, ready to flit away like a small bird. She brushed a strand of hair away from her eye but I don't think she knew she was doing it.

"You've been following me around. What do you want?"

Still nothing. I looked at her for a second more but she just stared back.

"Fine."

I turned and started walking across the service alley to my car but then she stopped me.

"Wait."

I stopped and turned around. She hadn't moved from the wall.

"You were injured? What happened?"

"You've read the stories. I was out late and I got stabbed."

"Let me see."

"What?"

"Let me see where you were stabbed."

I'm not sure why but I pulled up the right side of my shirt. The scar was about ten centimeters long, red, and bunched like a homemade rope. There had been too long between injury and suturing to do a really tidy job and so it looked like a large worm had burrowed just beneath the skin and started working its way around my abdomen.

"How did that happen?"

"I told you, I was stabbed."

"When? Where?"

"You read the story. It was late, a side street off Denis."

She looked at me for a long time.

"You take the trains. Why?"

"I won't fly."

Usually, people want to know why I won't fly but she didn't ask.

"What happens on the trains?"

"What?"

"What happens when you ride the trains?"

"What do you mean?"

She looked at me without speaking.

"Nothing happens. It's a train ride. It's long and it's boring."

We stood looking at each other until she pushed herself off the wall and walked away to her right—there was a rented Toyota parked illegally by the loading dock. It was my turn to call after her but she didn't turn around. She got in her car and drove past me still standing there but didn't turn her head to look at me.

Chapter Eighteen

I didn't see her again during that homestand. We got hot after losing to the Mets and won nine of the last ten games on the homestand and headed out on the road with a record of fifty-five and forty-eight. Everybody started hitting, even Nick…and the pitching stayed solid. I played every game at third, batted a little over .400 with seven home runs and sixteen RBIs over that ten-game stretch. Nobody was very happy about Jimmy getting cut, especially the Latinos, but when you're winning nobody makes waves.

* * *

He shook me awake. He looked a lot older. His hairline hadn't changed but his cheeks were sunken and hollow and lines splintered under and around his eyes. The corners of his small mouth pulled down harder at the corners than I remembered and his eyes were dark and clouded.

"Hey, Ryan."

"What's up, Georgie. Sorry. Mike."

He smiled and shook his head.

"Naw, Georgie's fine. I never hear it anymore. Don't mind much these days."

I nodded and he spoke again.

"We're not done, Ryan."

"I figured as much."

"You're not surprised."

"I read the newspapers. Somebody's still out there."

"Yeah. It's the brother."

"You're sure?"

He shrugged.

"No question. He likes to go back and visit his killing spots."

"You've seen him?"

He nodded.

"It took me a few years to catch on but I started spotting stories about the bodies again…"

"What year are we?"

He didn't even blink.

"1977."

I nodded.

"So, I started reading the papers again and the bodies were popping up but I just convinced myself that was how it is, you know? There's always going to be guys out there doing this shit. But I knew better. The stories were too on the nose."

I nodded.

"So, I just stopped reading the papers. Then Jeannie got sick."

From the look on his face, I could tell it hadn't ended well.

"Sorry, Georgie."

He shrugged.

"What can you do. Breast cancer. We thought she was okay but you know how it goes. Two years pretending she was cured and then it came back. Eight months after that she was dead. Pauline was seventeen and Rachel was eleven and I just hunkered down, tried to give them some kind of home."

I nodded.

"Pauline got out as quick as she could, headed south, too many ghosts at the dinner table. Rachel's seventeen and she'll be leaving after this year for Boston College. She's a soccer player. A good one."

"So, what happened?"

He looked down at his hands. They were small and fine-boned but nicked and worn.

"I saw the fucker."

"When?"

"Last summer."

I waited.

"Pauline came back to visit. Second time since she left home. Rachel and I were seeing her off."

He looked at me and nodded.

"Yeah. Train station. She likes to see the country. So, I'm sitting on the benches, the girls are walking around checking out some of the shops. Mostly just a chance to talk without their old man listening in. And he comes up the escalator. I thought it was him...back from the dead. My first thought was to duck my head so he doesn't see me but then he looks at me and right by and I can see it's not him. Not just because he doesn't recognize me but there was something missing in his face and the way he moved. Wearier, weaker, not the same kind of ferocity. It could have been age but it wasn't. Our guy would have burned right until the last fucking breath but this guy's banked."

"Still a dentist?"

Georgie shook his head.

"Our guy was the dentist."

"What?"

"Yeah. Remember we were trying to sort out why our guy stopped to see his brother...well, he wasn't stopping to see him. He was changing places with him. So, Dr. McKillops leaves his twin brother behind—I don't know if he actually treated patients and fucked our guy's wife but he was the front."

"How do you know this?"

"Once I see him in the train station I start checking around a little. This guy's back in the old neighborhood. Not the same place, but the same area. And when I track the funeral records down it's not the down-on-his-luck brother that gets waked and buried, it's the dentist. And the business gets shut down and the wife moves with her two boys out west, Albuquerque area I think. Family there. Not hard to put the story together after that. Dentist can't just up and hit the rails without explanation but nobody will even pay attention if the other brother disappears for a few days."

"You think the wife knew?"

"Hard to imagine that I can see the difference and she couldn't but I don't know for sure."

"Doesn't mean he's killing people. Or that he even knew his brother was killing women."

Georgie looked at him.

"You think I'm stupid, college boy?"

I flushed.

"No. I'm just talking, trying to sort things through in my head..."

I stopped.

"Sorry."

He nodded.

"So, I start following him when I can get away for a while. Rachel had a week-long school trip and she went to visit her sister a couple of times and I watched him. And occasionally I would make up a story and go away for the weekend. Most times McKillops just stays at this dump he rents in a shitty little neighborhood down by the river—a place called the Devil's Pocket. He's drunk most of the time and he doesn't seem to do much except drink, with an occasional trip to the church. I'm guessing his brother must have left him something because he doesn't even do the odd jobs anymore and he seems to have enough to keep himself in booze and the rent paid."

"But...?"

"But twice he takes a train trip."

I leaned forward.

"You saw him?"

Georgie shook his head.

"Not kill anybody. But he goes back to places that he's killed before. It's fucking weird. Both times he goes to one of the spots. The exact spot as near as I can tell from the news stories. And he just stands there. Just stands with his eyes closed. And I don't mean for a minute or two. He gets there just at dusk and he stands without moving until dawn."

"He stands there all night?"

"Both times I followed him that's what he did."

"And he just stands there?"

"He fell down a couple of times one of the nights. Couldn't tell if he was drunk or just tired."

"What happened after he fell?"

"He got up."

I looked at him and he shrugged.

"What can I say?"

"Doesn't anybody question him standing there all night?"

"These spots are a little out of the way. Not a whole lot of traffic after dark. The first time, a cop car did pull up and talk to him and he pretended to walk away but as soon as the cop left he was back."

"Anything else"

"When he leaves he takes a stone."

"A stone?"

"Yeah. And it doesn't look like just any stone. He'll pick one up and roll it around in his fingers, have a good look at it and then toss it away. Eventually, he finds what he's looking for and puts it in his pocket."

"Trophy."

"That's what I figure."

"Now what?"

"He's on the train."

I straightened up.

"He's on the train?"

He put his hand on my arm.

"Relax, he's four cars up. And he's not his brother or his father. He's not watching. And he doesn't know us."

That was true—he had never seen either of us. Well, as long as Georgie was careful he hadn't seen either of us.

"Do you think he's hunting?"

Georgie shrugged.

"Hard to say. I haven't seen a weapon but he had a carry-on that could have held something."

"So...?"

"Same as last time—we follow him when he leaves the train and we kill him."

"Do we know where he's going?"

"If he's hunting, no. Could be Chicago, Denver, Sacramento, even Lincoln—we stop at all those. If he's reminiscing, then it's Reno. A waitress was killed there eight weeks ago. It's the only killing at any of our stops that matches up. She was knifed in a neighborhood about half a mile from the train station."

"How are we going to do this? We're more than two days out of Reno and then it's another twelve hours from there to San Francisco."

"We'll both need to be awake at every stop because we may have to move quick but we have lots of stretches with several hours between stops so we can get sleep—have you booked a berth?

I nodded.

"Yeah, I get both—a seat and a berth. I don't like being trapped in my berth for three days."

"Must be nice, deep pockets."

I flushed.

"The team pays."

"Even better. You tired?"

"No, I'm good."

"I'm beat."

I pulled the key out of my pocket and handed it to him.

"Next car over. Berth three eleven."

"We're three hours out of Chicago. I don't think he's headed there but you never know so wake me about fifteen minutes before we're pulling in."

I nodded.

"McKillops is four cars up. He'll be facing you as you come in the car on the left side of the aisle. You won't have any trouble recognizing him but don't spook him."

I stood looking in at McKillops through the window of the door leading into his car. At first glance, he was a replica of his brother. Even though the last time I had seen his brother was ten years earlier the resemblance was startling. His eyes were closed and his head lolled back against the window. The roll and rumble of the train rocked his head occasionally but not enough to wake him. He didn't open his eyes when I pushed open the door between cars. His brother would never have let anybody enter the car without his being aware and now that I had a chance to really look at him I could see differences. He looked a little bigger but softer. His face was puffy although ten years might have done that to his brother as well. Mostly, the air of electric alertness was missing. Everything about him seemed a little sloppier, a little duller, tempered at a lesser heat.

I found the bar car several cars down from McKillops. It was full and there was music playing and people talking loudly. I started to turn away and head back to my seat but noticed a woman getting up from a booth in the corner. I watched to see if she was leaving or just getting another drink but she went through the door leading to the next car and I went to the booth to sit down and had already started to slide in when I realized there was still a guy in the booth, tucked into the far corner where I hadn't been able to see him. I stopped and started to stand back up.

"I'm sorry, man, I didn't see you there…I thought the booth was empty. I'll just—"

"Sit down. Sit down. The little lady's headed to bed and I was just going to have another drink or two but wasn't sure I wanted to drink alone."

I hadn't been looking for company and wasn't sure I wanted any but it was the only seat and I was already in it. I settled back down and reached across the table.

"Hi, Ryan Spencer. Pleased to meet you."

He shook my hand.

"Nice to meet you, Ryan."

There was a short pause.

"Oh yeah. Right. Me."

He giggled and I could tell he had probably already had several although there was only one bottle in front of him. He paused for a second.

"My name's Hugh. Hugh Thompson."

219

"Nice to meet you, Hugh."

"So, where you headed, Ryan?"

He was older than me but not middle-aged, maybe thirty or thirty-five.

"I'm a ballplayer. Just got signed to play out west."

He leaned forward eagerly.

"No shit? A ballplayer. The Dodgers? The Giants?"

I laughed.

"Nothing so lofty, A ball in Salinas."

I had taken the time to put a little story together. His face dropped a little and he settled back in his seat.

"A-Ball. Shit. I could have played A-ball."

I paused a beat then laughed.

"Yeah, you probably could."

He leaned forward again.

"Just kidding. No offense, man. I'm sure it's good baseball. Some of those guys make it to the majors, eh?

It ended up being a question.

"I hope so."

He paused a beat looking at me then grinned.

"Right. Sure. I get it. I'm sure you've got a shot."

He took a long pull on the beer in front of him and it was empty when he put it down.

"You want one?"

"Here let me get it. I'm trespassing on your booth."

"Fuck no, man. This one's on me. What do you want."

"Just a soft drink. Sprite or 7-Up."

"Soda? You're not going to be any fun.'

He grinned and tapped my shoulder.

"Just fuckin' kidding, man. 7-Up it is."

He came back carrying two beers for himself and a Sprite for me. He almost spilled one of the beers setting them down on the table but I managed to grab it before it tipped all the way over.

"Nice hands, Ryan."

220

He slid back into the booth.

"But I was a pretty good ballplayer, man. Played all through high school and that was some pretty good ball in Florida. Our school was more about the football but we still had a pretty good baseball team."

"What position did you play?"

"Second base. Quick hands, feet, and bat. Had some scouts show up in my senior year. They liked what they saw. This guy from the Reds said they were thinking of drafting me but then I decided to join the Army so everybody backed off. No sense wasting a draft pick on a guy that was going to fight a war. And I just thought it was more important to defend my country than pick up a big paycheck playing a kids game."

He looked at me and raised his hands.

"No offense."

I smiled and shook my head.

"None taken. So, you were in Vietnam."

He nodded and took a long drink from the first bottle.

"Yep. The tradition in our house. My daddy was in the big one. In the Navy, not the Army but still…"

He took another drink and put the bottle down in front of him. I wasn't sure what to say but he looked at me, waiting

"What was it like?"

He laughed a short bark.

"What was it like?"

He wrapped his hands around the bottle but didn't lift it to his mouth.

"What was it like?"

That second time he wasn't looking at me. He was looking through me, remembering.

"It was like some kind of evil carnival, man. You paid your money and you took your chances. Everybody wore a clown mask, big red grinning lips hiding tiny sharp teeth and a slippery tongue. And bodies flying off the merry-go-round like sweat off a chain-gang mutt."

I nodded. We sat without speaking for several seconds before he started up again.

221

"There didn't seem to be rules over there. It was a complete fucking clusterfuck. Guys were dying but you never saw a fucking thing. Just out on patrol and you'd hear the thing go off and then the fucking screaming and shouting and we'd try and stop the bleeding and sometimes we could and sometimes we couldn't. And you never knew what hit you. And you never knew who was on your side. We'd be on patrol and see the old men and the women with their little kids and babies in the fields. And just past them one of our guys would get chucked, body bits flying like confetti at a wedding and they wouldn't even turn to look, just keep working. Like they knew exactly what was coming."

He shook his head.

"I was there eight months and I saw half my unit shipped out – either in bags or bandages. It fucked you up, man. It always felt like a matter of time."

He stopped for a bit then and I finished off my soft drink. I was about to stand up when he started again.

"You heard of My Lai?"

I nodded.

"What do you know?"

"I don't remember many of the details. It was a massacre in a Vietnamese village. Carried out by American soldiers. I forget the officer's name, Caffey? I'm not sure how many Vietnamese were killed—"

"Calley. More than five hundred."

I looked at him.

"I didn't know it was that many."

He nodded.

"Yeah. More than five hundred."

We sat quietly for a second.

"I was there."

I looked up but he was looking down at the table now.

"In the village?"

He nodded without looking up.

"It was fucked up, man. We were told to move in and kill everything that moves, that they were all Viet Cong."

It was like he was talking to himself now.

"It started slow. The guys were just pulling people from the fields and going from hut to hut rounding people up. Just getting everybody into small groups, old men and women and little kids. And they weren't saying much, just doing what they were told. A couple of the women were crying and some of the kids too but not too bad. It seemed orderly. A routine shakedown. And then somebody started shooting. Not sure who. Automatic fire. I didn't hear anybody give an order. And then the screaming started and people were running and it was target practice. Guys were just shooting everything that was moving and not wearing a uniform."

He looked up then and stared at me for a second before shaking his head.

"Not me. I didn't do anything at first. You're too shocked. It's loud and people are shouting and screaming and bodies are hitting the ground and bullets are everywhere and it takes a second to figure out what the fuck is going on. I almost started shooting too because your first thought when the shooting starts and bodies are falling is that we were receiving fire, that we were under attack. A bunch of us moved away, looking for cover, not shooting but too fucked up to figure out what was going on. I ended up standing with two other guys and we're watching the shooting and realized that we aren't under fire, that it's our guys doing all the shooting. And I know it sounds bad but you had to be there. It was fucking pandemonium. I bet half the guys thought they were under attack and the other half thought they were killing VC. That they may have been women and old men but they knew where the tripwires were buried and they were keeping body counts."

He looked at me again.

"'Cause that's the way it was. You never knew who was on your side. It felt like nobody was on your side except the guys in your dugout."

He played with the second beer and then took a short drink.

"But this was too much. Once we realized that there was no incoming fire......

He paused then started again.

Even if they were with the Cong we shouldn't just be killing them. Not like this. At that point, we saw that five or six of our guys, Charlie Company guys, had found eleven or twelve villagers in a bunker and they were trying to figure out how to get them out. I waved for the two guys I was with to come with me and we walked down towards our guys. I must have lost my automatic rifle in the confusion because I remember all I had was a sidearm. But, both the guys I was with had their rifles. The Charlie Company guys didn't even notice us until we were almost on top of them and then they looked up startled, almost guilty like.

I said to the one guy who looked like he was in charge "What are you boys doing?" and he says to me "We're trying to figure out how to get them out of the bunker." And I say to him, "How were you thinking you would do that?" And he says, "A grenade." I said, "Like fuck, you will." And I turn to my two guys and said "I'm going down to get those people out. You cover these assholes and if they raise a finger to stop me, you shoot them." One of the two guys had a radioset and I said "Call in for a gunship, we're going to get these people out of here." Those boys weren't very happy. And I understand. To them, these were the enemy and we were going to let them get free to bury more mines and dig more tunnels but this shooting them down like pigs in the yard just wasn't right. So, I walked down to that bunker—and let me tell you that was one long fucking walk. I kept waiting for the shooting to start and I didn't know if my guys would be willing to shoot back. But those boys didn't start shooting and I was able to get those people to come out—mostly women, a couple of old guys, and three little kids. And me and my two guys stood guard on them for forty-five minutes until the gunship showed up and we loaded them on board, and those boys stood there looking at us with hard eyes for the whole time. I have no doubt if we hadn't been there they would have been dead."

He looked down at his beer.

"Might have saved some American boys' lives if they had died but killing them there just wasn't right."

I thought his eyes might be damp when he looked up but they weren't – they were hard and bright. But then they clouded over. I hadn't noticed the woman walk up to the table. It was the same woman I had seen leave just before I sat down. Hugh spoke first.

"What do you want?"

"Are you going to stay here all night, Billy?"

"Go back to fucking bed, Penny."

She looked down at me then and I could see she was drunk.

"So, is he telling you stories? Telling his war stories?"

She was looking at me but talking to him.

"You know who he is? Did he tell you who he is?"

He stood up and took her by the arm.

"It's okay, hon. Let's go. We've had enough for one night."

But she kept speaking even as he turned her away.

"He's Billy Calley. William Calley. Look it up."

She had to look over her shoulder to shout it at me and other people in the bar car looked around at the commotion. He ignored everything but her, though. He had one hand on her arm and the other around her shoulders and he moved her towards the door and he didn't look back as he led her through the doors, sliding open the bar car door with the hand that had been on her arm but keeping the other around her shoulders. I stood up and went to the door to watch them walk down the hall. I'm not sure why. Maybe worried that he was angry and might hurt her…but it didn't look like it. Her head had fallen on his shoulder and they walked away looking like any youngish couple on a long trip, bored and tired but still a little in love.

* * *

It had been light for an hour and we were almost in Chicago before I remembered that I was supposed to wake Georgie. I knocked lightly and heard rustling in the room and he came to the door quickly. The train was already slowing.

"I said fifteen minutes."

"I know. I forgot."

He looked at me, expressionless.

"Forgot?"

I thought about telling him about my conversation in the bar car but I decided to let it drop. I shrugged.

"We're not playing, Ryan. You know that, right? This isn't a game. If we fuck this up somebody ends up covered in her own blood. You get that, right?"

He had been slipping into his shoes and tying them up while he talked and now he looked up.

I didn't say anything and he kept looking at me.

"I get it."

He closed the door and pushed past me in the narrow hall and I followed him. He spoke without looking back at me.

"Get off at this door coming up. There is a bank of doors leading into the station, just keep an eye out for McKillop getting off the train. He's six cars up, so there are only a couple of the train doors that you have to watch. If you see him, you follow him. I'll catch up with you. I'm going to watch from inside the train. He may surprise us and leave from another door and I want to have an eye on him. If he doesn't get off the train stay by the doors, I'll signal you if he's settled back in and is staying on the train. Don't get back on the train until you get the signal from me. "

It was an hour stopover and McKillops never showed. I was still standing by the doors when the last announcement to board the train came over the loudspeakers. I stood, uncertain what to do when Georgie came to the door and waved me back in. I jogged over and stepped back up into the train.

"He hasn't moved since the train stopped."

The train doors closed and it started rumbling forward.

"Cut it a little close, didn't you?"

"Had to be sure he wasn't leaving."

"You could have given me some kind of heads-up."

"Wanted to see how well you could follow instructions."

"How did I do?"

"You got a little twitchy there at the end."

We stood in the narrow space between the cars, swaying as the train sped up.

"What now?"

"Like I said, I think it's Reno but we've got three stops between here and Reno and we'll run the same game at every stop. You outside, me inside. We've got another eighteen hours until Denver. Why don't you get some sleep."

"I'm not tired."

I was but he was starting to piss me off. He gave a small smile but didn't say anything. I turned and pushed through the doors and headed towards the bar car. Georgie followed me. I really want to lie down. The table I had been sitting at earlier had three young guys sprawled across the bench seats but the booth behind them was empty and I slid in. Georgie slid in across from me.

"What's bugging you?"

I shook my head.

"Look. I've been following these fuckers for a long time. I know what I'm doing."

"I've been here too."

"Bullshit, Ryan. I won't pretend to know what the hell is going on but how old were you when this started?"

I didn't answer.

"Yeah. I don't know exactly how old—twenty-one? Twenty-two? But it doesn't matter. The main thing is that you're the same age now that you were when this started. Not me. I'm fifty-two fucking years old and I've been living with this for forty-three years. It used to be every night I would wake up with Pauly's bloody body hanging in the dark in front of me. And it would feel real. As real as the dark and the sound of breathing next to me in the bed and the sweat on my face and the kids in the other room. And now it's maybe once a month. You think that makes me feel better?"

He turned and looked at the window. He stared for a long while then shook his head. It looked like he was going to shout but he didn't. When he spoke, it was softly.

"No. I don't feel better. It scares the shit out of me. It's getting away from me. There was a time when it burned so fucking hot that I was afraid it would burn me down. That maybe I thought I was the forge but I was really the fuel. Now, there's times I think I could forget. I could just walk away and it would be somebody else's problem."

I nodded.

"Don't fucking nod, Ryan. You don't know what the fuck I'm talking about. This is just another warm-up for you. You feel like you're still waiting to figure out what you're going to be. You don't know yet that this is it. That you're being who you're going to be. If this one gets away from you it'll just be a disappointment. For me, this is it. There's more behind me than in front of me. Way more. This my story. This is who I am. And it could still end badly. And if I don't get this right, Ryan, there's no starting over, there's no new project, there's no do-over. There's just more girls like Pauly."

He looked back at me.

"Just fucking do what I tell you, Ryan."

I nodded but didn't move. He stared down at his hands for several seconds and his face relaxed a little.

"Are you going to sleep?"

I nodded again.

"Okay. I'll come get you after eight hours. I'm going to need to sleep again too."

I looked at him without speaking and he looked back and then waved his hand wearily.

"Go on, Ryan. I'm getting tired already."

I thought I might have trouble falling asleep but I didn't and Georgie's knock pulled me from deep. I fumbled at the door before getting it open. Georgie looked as tired as I had ever seen him look. His eyes were red-rimmed and his shoulders curled in on his chest. He was not a big guy but usually it was like his frame was too small for the energy it had to contain, like he was vibrating at a higher frequency than most people. But not now. Now he looked like he was leaking air, like he was losing the battle to keep his skin stretched tight. He pushed past me.

"I just checked in on McKillop. He's reading. He's got no place to go, but check in on him every hour or so…just don't let him see you. If he's half as good as his father or brother he could be on to us."

Georgie tried pushing the door closed behind him and I had to step forward so he could get it to close tight. I stood there for a second trying to decide where to go. The door opened behind me.

"Fifteen minutes before we get in, Ryan?"

"Sure."

The door closed behind me again. I didn't feel like the bar car again. It looked like I was going to spend the next eight or nine hours staring out a train window.

McKillop's got up from his seat once to use the washroom but other than that slept or stared out the window for the entire time. When we were fifteen minutes out of Denver, I knocked on the berth door. Georgie looked better but not a lot better when he opened the door. He already had his shoes on so he slipped out of the door and closed it behind him.

"Okay. Same deal. When we get in, you take the doors. The station at Denver's not as big as Chicago so it should be harder to miss him if he decides to move. I don't think he's going to, I think we're headed for Reno but stay sharp. Stay until I signal you to get back on the train. If he moves, follow him. Don't worry about me, I'll be behind you."

The train slowed as it entered the city limits and it took several minutes to labor through the city and into the station. I got off the train and took up my spot next to the doors into the station.

I wasn't standing there for more than a few seconds when McKillop got off the train. I wasn't sure there had even been time for Georgie to get down to McKillop's car. McKillop looked smaller walking across the platform than he had in the seat. His head was hunched down between his shoulders and his eyes stayed on the ground rather than up and scanning the platform. His steps were short and plodding, like his torso was too heavy for his legs. He almost brushed against me as he went past but he never looked up or gave any sign that he noticed I was standing there. I scanned the doors of the train for Georgie but didn't see him. I stood for several seconds watching the door of the train where McKillop had stepped down but Georgie didn't show. I couldn't wait any longer and turned back to the Denver train station. The doors led to a small lobby and two hallways at either end of the lobby led into the main hall of the station. McKillops wasn't in the lobby. I stood for a moment but the crowd coming in through the doors was growing and I moved with them into the left-hand hallway. Shit. I couldn't see McKillops in the group of people moving through the hallway into the main hall. I was looking above the crowd trying to spot McKillop's head and almost bumped into a middle-aged woman who had stopped to adjust her baggage. She looked at me startled and I mumbled an apology. Several people stood at the entrance to the main hall trying to get their bearings. I pushed through them and started across the polished granite floor scanning the crowd left and right. There were a lot of people in the hall, too many to pick out McKillops. I was going to lose him in the first minutes after he left the train. And this wasn't Reno. He was hunting again.

I stood in the middle of the high ceilinged hall forcing my eyes to trace a grid back and forth across the hall. There was a bank of doors running along the front of the station and people were streaming in and out of the revolving doors. If McKillops had headed straight for those doors he would be out in the street and gone by now. Maybe he would be waiting for a cab. I started across the floor still looking left and right across the crowd. I saw him then, almost at the exit, set in the north-east wall of the station. He stood out for a moment because he was alone and moving without urgency. As he reached the door he stuck out his arm, pushed down in the handle to swing the door open, and step through. I looked around for Georgie but still didn't see him. I followed and pushed open the door expecting that he would be gone again, disappeared into the street crowd, but the door exited onto a narrow dark pathway that led to a busy downtown street about one hundred yards away and I could just make out the shift and shadow of McKillops trudging down the alleyway. After the bright lights of the station, I could barely see but didn't want to wait until my eyes adjusted to the dark. The path was rough cobble and my foot caught. I almost went down, stumbling and scraping as I caught my balance and knocked hard against a wooden garbage rack. The noise echoed back to me but the dim shape ahead of me didn't slow or turn. He was almost at the street now so I could see him more clearly in the light bleeding in between the buildings lining the pathway. He turned right without hesitating and I hurried after him.

He wasn't difficult to follow and he didn't seem to be trying to avoid being seen. The street we were on was a rundown one-way commercial street and McKillops and I moved from island to island of light under the widely spaced street lamps. I passed an all-night laundromat with a young woman folding towels on a table against the back wall but she didn't look out. There was a clock on the back wall and I saw that it was just after two AM. A couple of taxis drifted by and a police car—I felt the cop looking me over but I kept watching McKillop slump his way south. I hung back but I didn't want to end up too far away if he made a sudden move. That's what I expected, that the shuffling figure one hundred yards ahead of me would make a surprise move and I would have to stay with him. But he just continued to move slowly along Eighth for several blocks until we got to a street called Lawrence where McKillops turned left.

He wasn't moving quickly but he seemed to know where he was going. I stopped at the corner to look back the way I had come but there was nobody else on the street. If Georgie was around he was keeping out of sight. We walked for several blocks along Lawrence, past rundown body shops and fenced-in car and truck rental outlets before the street started to become more residential with old red-brick homes wedged in next to four-and five- story low rises. We walked for a couple more minutes before he stopped suddenly. I stepped back off the sidewalk and out of the light. He had stopped in front of a rambling ranch-style house with blue siding and a blue awning stretching across the front of the house. He stopped and turned a full circle but didn't look up the street towards me. He stood for a second then turned his head to the left to look at the blue house. He was standing directly under a streetlight so I could see every movement he made. I had stepped back into the shadows so I was almost certain McKillop hadn't seen me. I didn't notice Georgie until he tapped me. I started so hard I almost lost my balance and he grabbed my elbow to steady me. He leaned into my ear.

"What's he doing?"

I looked at him without answering

Georgie looked at me blankly then whispered again.

"What do you think he's doing?"

I leaned close.

"Where the hell have you been?"

Georgie's face shifted slightly, a small smile, and pointed with his thumb back across his shoulder to the street running parallel to Lawrence but one block back towards the way we had come. We turned back to McKillop but he still hadn't moved from the spot where he had stopped. He looked around for several more seconds and then seemed to recognize something and moved forward past the house and stepped off the sidewalk toward a big maple separating the house from an empty lot. Georgie started moving forward.

"He's going in."

I grabbed his arm. He turned to look at me and I held up my hand and then one finger. Wait one minute. We couldn't see him very well under the tree but enough to know that he was standing beside the tree without moving. Georgie whispered in my ear.

"He's scouting the place."

I shook my head and held up my finger again.

We waited for a second and McKillops came out from under the tree pulling up his zipper and started walking again. Georgie looked over at me and shrugged. I hadn't seen him look sheepish in a long while. We only walked a little more than a block before McKillops started to slow but now he didn't look uncertain at all. He knew where he was. He moved slowly past an old grey two-story place with flaking paint on the siding and a dirty smudged white door in the center of the building. McKillops slipped past the edge of the house and we lost sight of him. Georgie broke into a run and I followed him our feet echoing loudly up the street. We almost ran into him once we got to the corner of the house. There was a narrow band of grass maybe ten meters wide between the gray house and the 60's style bungalow next door. The side lawn was canopied by three large maples so that the area was shaded from the streetlights. We had been expecting him to be moving but McKillops was kneeling under the last tree looking through the chain-link fence at a parking lot. He didn't turn towards us. We stopped when we saw him but we were only about ten feet from where he was kneeling. Georgie put his hand on my arm as if to hold me back. I wasn't moving.

"She died just over there."

His voice was low but it carried easily to where we were. I still don't know if he knew we were there and was talking to us.

"Just over the fence there. You can see the spot. They cleaned up the blood. Or maybe the rain and snow did that."

He didn't speak for a moment.

"There was a lot of blood. There was always a lot of blood."

I felt Georgie shift beside me and then he stepped forward in two quick strides placed the barrel behind McKillops's ear and pulled the trigger. The blast was deafening, reverberating back and forth between the walls of the two houses. McKillops pitched forward into the fence so that his body slumped awkwardly with his face and shoulders up against the chainlink but his lower torso and legs stretched out on the ground under the tree. Georgie turned away and walked out from under the trees and onto the sidewalk.

"Come on, Ryan, we have to get going."

His voice was calm. I couldn't move for a second, looking at McKillops's body tossed up against the fence, a crumpled mound of cloth and flesh.

"Come on, Ryan."

His voice was a little more urgent. A light came on in the house to my left and that got me moving. I stepped out beside him and we walked up the street the way we had come until we reached the next block and then turned right. We heard distant police sirens when we were about halfway back to the train station. We zigzagged our way back towards the train station coming out on Eighth Street about two blocks from the path where I had started trailing McKillop. We didn't speak until then.

"I should probably dump the gun."

I hadn't even thought about it.

"Probably."

He pulled it out and looked at it and then put it back into the loose pocket of the canvas jacket he was wearing. It pulled down heavy on that side. He looked at me and shrugged.

"They aren't coming back to me on this." He shrugged. "And guns aren't cheap."

I didn't say anything. We walked the last two blocks to the station without speaking again. It was a little past four AM and the main hall of the station was almost empty. It was only a little over two hours since I had looked in the laundromat window. Our train wasn't due to leave for another three hours. Our steps echoed as we walked across the hall to the doors leading to the platforms.

"What now?"

"I'll take the train on to Reno and then catch something heading back the other way."

"You want the berth?"

He looked over at me.

"I could sleep."

I nodded.

"You get a few hours. I don't think I'm ready to sleep just yet anyway."

We stepped out the doors onto our platform. Georgie looked over at me again.

"Had to be done."

I nodded.

"He just didn't seem very scary. Not like his brother."

"I guess they come in all shapes and sizes."

I nodded and passed him the key to my berth. He slept until midday and then I slept until Reno. He was already gone by the time I was dressed and out on the Reno platform. The train pulled into San Francisco just after seven AM the next morning—I missed the first two games of the West Coast road trip and we lost them both.

Chapter Nineteen

We got hot through August and won twenty-two of twenty-seven games and headed into September with a record of seventy-seven wins and fifty-five losses, a game behind the first-place Phillies who had been in a tailspin since late July and tied with the Mets for the wildcard spot. For the next road trip I rented a car and drove cross country from the coast. I just couldn't take another long train trip.

But things were as bad as ever in the clubhouse and on the field. The first game of September, Cincinnati was in town and I came to the plate in the first inning with two men on and one out and the first pitch almost took my head off. I got up and dusted myself off and looked out at the pitcher, a Dominican named Mendoza, and he smirked back at me but didn't say anything. I looked at him for a long time until he finally stepped off the mound and put his hands on his hips waiting for me. I waited another second and then went to step back into the batter's box and but the catcher stepped up from behind the plate and put his hand on my chest.

"Did you just shit stare my pitcher?"

I looked at him.

"Are you kidding me?"

"Listen, Spencer, if my boy wants to throw at you you'll just take it and step back in the box like the little bitch you are. And if you don't like that then let's get started right now."

The ump spoke up.

"Get down behind the plate, Churowski. Back in the box, Spencer. Let's go."

The catcher didn't move for a second.

"Let's go, Churowski. Enough fuckin' around."

He turned then and crouched down behind the plate and the next one was behind my head. Your first instinct is to pull back. Everybody's is. That's why the pitch behind the head is the one that gets things started. It's the one where you end up in the dirt because you pull back but realize that you've just stepped onto the tracks and the train's on time. So, you let everything go and hope gravity can do what a million years of evolution and a disproportionate share of fast-twitch fibers can't. You let go of all control of your body except, you hope, your sphincter and you imagine that a small white sphere—with Rawlings in cursive cupped in the gentle hollow of red stitching and the signature of Allan H Selig perfectly reproduced so that when you grip the ball to throw a ninety-five mile per hour two-seamer, Bud's name appears between your index and middle fingers and the stitches offset so the seams can be pulled tight and snug so the ball flies straight and true if released in just the right way but rises or dips or flutters unpredictably if thrown in a way that allows the raised stitches to disrupt the air and create forces that are applied unevenly to the surface—will miss. And it did.

Well, not completely. I felt it kiss off my helmet just above where the brim met the body of the helmet. It was enough to alter its trajectory so that the ball clipped off the edge of Churowski's glove and rolled to the backstop. Churowski turned to chase the ball , which gave me time to get up and start walking towards the mound. The ump called out to me but I'm not sure what he said. I think because I didn't rush the mound Mendoza wasn't ready. He didn't even raise his hands. It would be easy—I imagined the shot. It would hit him flush, just above the mandible. Fighters will tell you that you should never aim for a spot on a guy's body, you should always be aiming for a spot six to eight inches past the contact point. I imagined the bone giving way under my knuckles. He'd fall like water from a bucket and Cincinnati would pour from their dugout. But it was too late, I wasn't really even angry anymore. That had always been a problem for me, staying angry. I stood in front of him and we stared at each other. He spoke first.

"What do you want, Spencer?"

I shrugged.

"You could have killed me."

He smirked.

"It ain't a game for punks."

"You threw behind my head."

I felt a hand on my arm.

"What the fuck are you doing, Spencer?"

It was Churowski. The crowd had let out a roar early on but I had thought it was just in response to the play, me dropping to the dirt and then heading out to the mound but it had been in response to the entire Cincinnati team leaving the bench and Churowski dashing out to the mound. Cincinnati now stood in a ring around me with Churowski leading the way. Rushing the mound didn't usually end in a calm chat and the players weren't sure what to do. I ignored him.

"You threw behind my head, Mendoza. It could have killed me. You're okay with that?"

Churowski grabbed my arm again.

"I'm who you talk to, frat boy. You leave my pitchers alone."

I shook him off without looking at him but felt his hand tighten again around my arm.

"Everything okay here, Ryan?"

Nick had pushed his way through the circle of players around me.

"Fine, Nick."

"Let go, Churowski."

"What are you gonna do about it, Fagen?"

"Two things Churowski. I'll kick your ass here before any of your guys can even move. And then we will be taking a piece out of you every time you come to the plate. And I mean every time. I don't care if it's extra innings for the pennant and the bases are loaded, if you come up to the plate we are going to hurt you. Every fucking time."

"Your guys won't do it. Nobody like's this asshole."

"They'll do it if I tell them to. And I will tell them to."

Nick turned to me.

"You done, Ryan?"

I looked at the faces around me and then back at Mendoza.

"I'm good."

"Okay." He turned and started back towards the dugout. The Reds moved out of the way and I followed him. We took a few steps and then he stopped and leaned in.

"Where are you going?"

I looked back at the cluster of Reds players still standing around Mendoza and Churowski.

"What? Do you want to—"

"He hit you, dummy, you're on first."

I flushed.

"Oh, yeah."

I started jogging down to first. The umpire called after me.

"Where are you going, Spencer?"

"He hit me, I'm taking first."

"There was no contact. Clean miss."

"Are you kidding me, Jerry?"

"It's ball two, Spencer, get back in the box."

I went over and picked my batting helmet up from where it had fallen in the dirt. I ran my finger over the scar just above the brim where the ball had scraped off a line of paint. The helmet was grey under the blue paint.

"Get in the fucking box, Spencer."

I put the helmet back in and pressed it down snug against my head. I started to step into the box but noticed that Mendoza had stepped off the mound and was looking over towards our dugout. Nick had come back up the stairs and taken a couple of steps towards the mound. The stands were still buzzing but he talked loud and his voice carried across the field.

"I'm coming back up the middle, Mendoza. Every time. I doubt if I can hit you but I'm going to be trying. And don't get on base because if you get anywhere near second base, you'll be eating the tag. You'll be sucking dinner through a straw for a month."

I watched as he turned and went back into the dugout. McKay was standing and Nick shouldered past knocking him hard against the rail. I flew out moving the runner over to third and nobody looked at me when I got back to the dugout except Balducci who met me for a fist bump by the stairs and Nick who nodded from his spot on the bench.

The rest of the game was uneventful except that Mendoza walked in the seventh and the lead-off hitter tried to move him over with a bunt along the third-base line that I barehanded and whipped to second. It was the second baseman's play but Nick took the bag and Hiltz had to bail out. Mendoza stopped halfway down the baseline and turned around. Nick stood at second base staring after him as he walked back to the dugout.

* * *

I hadn't seen her on the road trip or our first two series at home but she was at the first Dodgers game. The Dodgers were in town for four games to end our twelve-game home stand. We had a couple of short road trips over the last part of the season and then we were finishing up the season with a four-game series against the Mets. The way things were going, it might matter. The Phillies and the Mets were playing good ball too and we couldn't seem to gain much ground. Philly had won seven of their last eight and were two games up and the Mets had kept pace and we were still tied for the wildcard.

She sat three rows back behind the visiting team dugout. I tipped my batting helmet before my first at bat and she nodded. The catcher for the Dodgers was a veteran, Gary Wallace, good glove, no bat although he had found a little power just as his catching skills had started to drop off. He was just good enough to play on a bad team. He looked over into the stands then back at me.

"Didn't know you were a horndog, Spencer."

I didn't say anything and he shrugged.

"Just trying to be friendly. Thought you might enjoy the conversation. Word is nobody on your team will talk to you."

He slipped the mask over his head and settled into his crouch.

"I've heard there's not a fucking guy on the team talks to you."

I had stepped into the box and was staring out at the mound. The Dodgers pitcher was a young guy named Ross Stirling. He had an inconsistent fastball, decent curve, and an improving change-up. The book on him was that he could hit ninety-five or ninety-six on the gun some days and other days he had trouble cracking ninety.

"How do you piss off every fucking guy on your team? I know there's guys that don't like me but I can find a few that do."

Stirling went into his wind-up and the ball crackled, catching the corner low and outside and exploding through the strike zone. It looked like Stirling had his good stuff today. I stepped out of the box and rearranged my hitting gloves before stepping back in.

"I heard you guys had a bench-clearing brawl? Except your bench didn't clear. Is that right? I've never heard that shit before."

Stirling was going into his windup but I held up my hand for time. The ump stepped out waving his arms to call off the pitch. I looked at the ump.

"Can he do this?"

"Do what?"

"Talk. Talk and not stop talking?"

"Nothing in the rulebook says he can't."

"Really?"

He shook his head.

"There should be."

"Yeah. Well, there ain't. Play Ball."

"I'm just making a little friendly conversation, Spencer. I thought you would appreciate the company. "

I was expecting the fastball again but he threw the change-up. This was the second time I had faced him and his change-up was much better than the last time – it looked more like his fastball. I couldn't tell until right at the end that it wasn't his fastball. The windup and the arm slot all looked like fastball, it was only as he released the ball that I could see he didn't have his fingers in quite the same spot on the ball. I started the weight shift a little early but managed to delay starting my hands the fraction of a second I needed so that I wasn't way out in front of the pitch when I connected. Holding back on the hands meant I couldn't release my hips the way I wanted to but I still got good wood on the ball and stroked a clean single up the middle. Their first baseman was another veteran, Blaine Jepson, who couldn't move very well anymore but had a quick bat and a great glove.

"Nice piece of hitting, Spencer."

I looked at him and he shrugged.

"Hey, what can I say, I appreciate good hitting. And we're twenty-two games out of a wildcard spot, you hitting a clean single is the least of our problems."

He moved to the bag and leaned out ready to take the pickoff throw.

"Hey, word is your guys hate you—what the fuck's going on? Bench-clearing brawl and your guys don't leave the bench? Except Fagan."

Stirling came over to the bag and I had to go in head first and just beat the tag. He was right-handed. If he had been left-handed he would have had me. I looked up from the ground.

"Are all you guys like this?"

"Like what?"

"Chatty."

Jepson smiled.

"Yeah, that Wallace, he's a fucking talker alright. He's one of the only guys that doesn't want his own room on the road. But he's got his own room because nobody can stand it. He never stops."

I stood up and dusted off and took two strides off the base and one sideways shuffle step so that I was seven or eight feet off the bag.

"Who's the hottie?"

"What?"

The woman in the stands that you nodded at. She's looking over here all the time."

I looked over but she was watching Stirling. By the time I looked back Jepson had the ball. He stepped off the bag and gently laid the tag on my

241

shoulder. He looked a little sheepish

"I wasn't lying, she did look over a couple of times."

I put my head down to hide the flush of embarrassment as I ran back to the dugout. The voice came from high in the stands behind third.

"Get your head out of your ass, Spencer!"

There was a short wash of laughter from the crowd.

Nobody looked at me or spoke in the dugout although Jaquet who had been waiting to hit fired his bat angrily into the bat bin.

I came up again in the fourth and we were down one-nothing. Stirling had walked a couple and given up the hit to me and one to Hiltz, a bloop single over second. He had his A stuff. Actually, he was pitching better than I had seen on any of the tape. His fastball was at the high end of ninety-five to ninety-six but his change-up was freezing guys. He had figured out a way to disguise it better than he ever could before. Even his curve, which was usually mediocre, seemed to have a little more bend. I stepped into the box.

"That can't have helped any with the boys. What the hell were you thinking? It was like watching one of those Discovery Channel movies where the baby emu is down by the water drinking and the crocodile is cruising in towards the shore and the only one that doesn't fucking see it is the fucking defenceless little emu. You're shouting at the fucking screen – "Run little emu, Run. But no, the emu keeps drinking and the crocodile comes out of the water like a thrown rod at Indy and all that's left is hooves and…"

I was ready for the change-up this time and Stirling left it up and over the plate and I got all of it. I thought there was a chance it was getting out of the stadium but the wind was blowing in and it ended up in the second deck. Jepson didn't say anything when I rounded first. Wallace was on one knee a few feet back of home plate adjusting the straps on his shin guard when I got there.

"An emu's a bird."

He didn't look up.

"Fuck you."

Balducci was at the top of the steps when I got to the dugout. The rest of the team didn't look at me. Even Hiltz who had been on first and scored in front of me had found a spot on the bench.

We won going away. I hit a double and knocked a couple more runs in during the sixth. The dark-haired woman left her seat in the sixth inning and didn't come back. I was the last out in the ninth. I struck out against one of their mop-up guys on a weak curve that I should never have chased. Wallace didn't say a word to me after the fourth inning.

She was waiting in the parking lot again. It was dark and I didn't notice her until I was almost at my car. She had parked beside it and was leaning against her driver's side door. I'm not sure I would have noticed her at all if her shoe hadn't scraped against the asphalt as she shifted her weight.

"I need to talk to you."

"About what?"

"About my grandfather."

"What about your grandfather?"

"How did you really get that knife wound in your side?"

"I told you."

"It doesn't make sense."

"What doesn't make sense?"

"You've never been seen out on the town in Montreal. You're a famous baseball player but nobody remembers seeing you that night even though you say you were out all night. A young woman stole a professional athlete's wallet and stabbed him in the side without him being able to stop her, slow her down or provide a description of anybody? You don't go to the hospital until many hours later and the doctor who treated you doesn't believe you and says that the timing doesn't match up. Shall I keep going?"

"It doesn't matter. It happened the way I said it happened and that's the end of it. And why do you care? What is the obsession? You've been following me around for months now. Why does this matter?"

She didn't speak for several seconds.

"Fine. You've got your secrets and I've got mine. It's been a pleasure meeting you, Miss…."

"Do you want to get a coffee?"

"All of this just so we can have a coffee? I'm flattered and all but..."

"I've got a story you should hear and then you can decide if you want to tell me your story."

I paused and then nodded.

"Okay."

"Okay then."

"You want to drive with me?"

"I'd rather take my own car. I'll follow you. Where are we going?"

"There's a little place near my apartment. We can park in my parking garage and walk over."

She nodded.

"I know the way—don't worry about losing me. Just don't leave without me."

She was already idling in front of the garage door when I got there. I couldn't figure out how she had arrived ahead of me, but she had.

We didn't talk much on the short walk to the diner—she walked fast with her head up and looking straight ahead. It was like I wasn't there.

"So, are you from Montreal?"

She didn't look over.

"No."

There was a short silence.

"Okay then, that's one city...there can't be that many more. New York?"

"No."

"Fair enough. Scranton?"

She started to speak but I interrupted.

"And to be fair, I think Scranton should include Wilkes-Barre so if you say no to Scranton you're also saying no to Wilkes-Barre. OK?"

"She looked over then.

"Stockton. Stockton, California."

"You like it there?"

She looked over at me again.

"Like it? It's the tenth most dangerous city in the country, it has the third highest illiteracy rate in the US, the fattest people in the nation, just became the largest city to ever file for bankruptcy and the biggest annual event is the asparagus festival. No. I don't like it."

I looked her up and down.

"You're not doing your part...pulling your weight, so to speak."

"Really? You're more likely to get violently assaulted in Stockton than almost any city in the US, only seventeen percent of the population has a college degree, it just declared Chapter nine and you think that the 'fat people' story is my main take-home message?"

"Well, there was the asparagus thing. That didn't sound like so much fun."

There was another short pause.

"C'mon, it's kind of strange that a city full of fat people would celebrate the asparagus."

She didn't look over but I could see her jaw working.

"What are they doing with asparagus? Deep frying them in beer batter? Using them to scoop ice cream from five-gallon tubs? Trading them even up for Skittles? "

She didn't speak again until we got to the diner. Me neither.

It was just after midnight so there were a few people scattered around but there were several empty tables and a couple of empty booths and we slid into one. The place would start to fill up around three or four AM as people drifted in from the clubs. I waved off the menu but then realized I was hungry and ordered a burger and fries with a coke. She ordered a coffee.

We didn't speak while we waited for the drinks to arrive. The waitress settled the woman's cup in front of her gently but it was too full and some spilled onto the table. She came back with a cloth but the young woman had already wiped it away with a napkin. I sat looking at her after the waitress left. She stared down at the soggy beige napkin on the table for a long while.

"My grandfather thinks he knows you."

"What's your name?"

"What?"

"I said, what's your name?"

She blushed then.

"I'm sorry. Amy Robbins."

"Hi, Amy. I'm Ryan Spencer."

She smiled a little.

"Okay then. Your grandfather says he knows me. What's his name?"

She looked across the table at me for a long moment.

"George. Georgie Abbott."

I looked at her and she just stared back, waiting. She had been waiting for this and she was watching every muscle in my face, I think, trying to get a sign. I finally spoke.

"I thought he preferred Mike."

She didn't answer. I waited but she didn't speak.

"How's he doing?"

She shook her head.

"Not well. Emphysema. He's on oxygen twenty-four hours a day. He's got a few months. Maybe a few weeks."

I thought of the dark, scrap dog thin, cool fire man I remembered from a few weeks ago and it was hard to imagine.

"I'm sorry to hear that."

"So you do know him?"

I nodded my head.

"How?"

"We've shared a train."

She shook her head and the mass of dark curls fell in front of her face and then away again.

"No, how is it possible?"

"What do you mean?"

"My grandfather's been sick for years. He came to California in '97 and he hasn't been well enough to travel much since. How could you have shared a train with him? You would have been four or five years old."

The waitress showed up then with my burger and took away the coke to refill it. We sat silently until she returned with the drink. Amy waved away more coffee.

"It's a long story."

"Georgie told me the story. I don't believe it."

"What did he tell you?"

She told me the story then. McKillop's murdering Georgie's sister, Georgie meeting me on the train the first time, and then each time after that. Georgie killing Mckillops the elder and then killing both McKillops juniors. At the end of the story, I nodded.

"That sounds about right."

She looked at me for a long second and then stood up banging the table hard with her legs and tipping her coffee cup so that it spilled across the table. There wasn't enough left in the cup to make it across to me.

"Fuck you."

She was angry. Her face had reddened and she was breathing hard.

"Fuck you. This is bullshit. You and Georgie planned this out. I don't know why he wants to do this but this is bullshit."

"No, Amy…"

"Fuck you. Shut up. This is absolute bullshit."

People were looking at us. The waitress had been wiping down the long counter in front of the grill and she was standing now with the cloth in her hand watching us.

"Sit down, Amy, ther—"

Her face started to twist and she managed one more "fuck you" before walking away and out the door. I stood up and the waitress came quickly around the counter. I stopped and searched around in my pocket, pulled out a twenty from a crumpled wad of bills, and tossed it on the table. She didn't change expression but she stopped at the corner of the counter. I turned and followed Amy out the door. I had expected her to be down the street, maybe out of sight but she was just to the left of the door leaning against the wall and crying.

"Amy?"

"Fuck off. This is bullshit."

"Amy. It's not. He's not lying to you."

She looked at me and her face was wet and her eyes were red.

"Ryan, either this is a cruel trick or he's delusional. And you are too. I don't know which I'm hoping for. Either he's mean or crazy. I guess I'm hoping crazy."

I lifted the edge of my shirt just above the scar.

"What about this?"

"You were stabbed by a Montreal hooker."

"You heard yourself. It doesn't make sense. I don't go out at night. And I don't get jacked by little ladies of the night. And then stabbed. This was McKillops. This was McKillops in 1966, twenty-one years before I was born, he slid a knife into my side."

She reached out and touched the ragged raised scar tissue and the touch felt cool but distant.

"What was it like?" She spoke low so that I could hardly hear her.

I hadn't thought about it much in the few weeks since it had happened. I hadn't wanted to.

"It's nothing. It passes like a breeze. It was barely there and now it's gone again. If Georgie doesn't blow McKillop's brains out he sinks that knife all the way and the only difference between that and this is that I'm dead. For me, everything turns on that bullet and that blade and your grandfather but it's nothing. It could have gone the other way. It's just chance it didn't. That moment happened as easy as spilling your coffee, buying a token on the subway, and stepping into the street without looking. It's just another thing that happens. It's hard to explain. It was just another thing."

We stood for a moment.

"Georgie wants to see you."

I nodded.

"He's mad I didn't talk to you sooner."

I smiled.

"He's a cantankerous bastard."

"You don't know the half of it."

"How long do I have?"

"The sooner, the better. I think he's just waiting on you."

I nodded.

"We're done on the West Coast for the season. The season's done in two weeks and even if we make the playoffs there should be a day off in there. Have I got two weeks?"

She hesitated but then nodded.

"I think so."

"Okay, give me the two weeks."

She nodded.

"Do you believe us, Amy?"

She looked at me for a long time then shrugged.

"Just come talk to Georgie. "

We didn't talk on the way back to her car. We stood by her door for a second still not speaking.

"You don't have to go home now."

She looked at me and I flushed.

"No, I've got a couch you could use."

She grinned.

"Quite the gentleman."

I reddened further.

"Right. I could take the couch. You could have the bed."

She put her hand on my arm.

"I'm just kidding, Ryan. I'm not far. But thanks for the offer."

She got into her car backed it out and drove away. But she looked over as she pulled away. And she smiled.

Chapter Twenty

The buzzer rang early the next morning and when I hit the intercom it was Amy.

"I need to speak to you."

I buzzed her in and waited at my door watching for the elevator. She looked the wrong way when she first stepped off the elevator. She had changed clothes since the night before but she looked tired, like maybe she hadn't slept. Despite that, she looked great.

"Hey, Amy."

She turned and saw me standing in the doorway and gave a small tired smile.

"Hey, Ryan."

"Come on in."

I turned to walk back into my apartment but she held up her hand.

"No time, Ryan."

I turned back.

"He's got worse, a lot worse. You don't have two weeks. I'm not sure you've got one week. I'm flying out in ninety minutes. I just thought I should let you know."

"What happened?"

She shrugged.

"It's hard to tell with this disease. Things can happen quickly near the end. He's gone way downhill. Mom says it's almost over. I've got to get home."

"I don't fly."

"I know."

"If I left today?"

"How long does it take?"

"About three days."

"Maybe. No guarantees."

I looked at her.

"You want to come?"

"On the train?"

I nodded.

"What's going to happen?"

"I don't know. Maybe nothing."

"I can be in Stockton by tomorrow morning if I fly."

I nodded.

"I could miss him if I don't get back for three days."

I nodded again.

She shook her head then.

"No. I can't. I can't take the chance."

"Okay."

She looked at me.

"You're going to come."

I nodded.

"Okay. I'll see you in Stockton."

She turned and hit the button on the elevator and the doors slid open right away. She started to get on but then stopped and stepped back out.

"Oh. Do you know where to go?"

"Shit. No. What's the address?"

She pressed her knee against the elevator door and it rattled back and forth against her leg while she wrote out the address in Stockton. I walked the few steps to the elevator and took the scrap of paper from her and she got onto the elevator and the doors slid shut.

* * *

"What the fuck do you mean you're going to be gone for a few days?"

I was standing in Balducci's office again. Things never seemed to go well here.

"It's a family matter, skipper. An emergency. I have to go."

"Emergency? A fucking emergency? Is your son trapped down a well? Has your brother taken seventeen hostages inside a lab that does research on biological warfare? Is your mother dying of gonorrhea and you're the only one with the right blood type to give her a life-saving transfusion. Because those are the three options. If one of those three things has happened, then you can go with my blessing. Otherwise, we're in a pennant race, you're our third baseman and you're not going anywhere."

"It's a personal matter, sir. I'm afraid I can't tell you the details but it's unavoidable. I can't not go."

He stepped out from behind his desk and came around to stand in front of me. He was almost pleading when he spoke again.

"Listen, Ryan, you can't do this. If you do this, you're fucked. Walking out on the team with two weeks left in the season while we're in the middle of a tight pennant race? It's career suicide. If you think things are bad now, it's going to get much worse. Give this another thought, kid. Don't make this mistake."

"I've got no choice, sir. I have to go."

"You've always got choices, Ryan. Stop making the wrong ones. This is it. This is the moment where you turn things around and make the right decision. You stay here and you help your team win a pennant. And then you go home and you take care of any family issues you need to take care of. But here and now, you do the right thing."

He was begging.

"I'm sorry, skipper. I've got to go."

I turned and walked out of his office into the locker room and I heard him following me. It was ninety minutes until game time and the room was full. I walked to the door and Balducci shouted behind me.

"Okay, everybody. Say goodbye to Spencer. Spencer's got family issues and has to leave for a few days. Everybody wave goodbye to fucking Spencer."

I could feel eyes turning to me. The only one that didn't look over was Nick. He just kept taping up his bat. I stepped into the hall and I could hear a rumble of conversation behind me but it was muffled and indistinguishable.

* * *

I didn't fall asleep until somewhere past Chicago. It was almost thirty hours to Chicago but I couldn't sleep. When I woke up he was in the seat beside me.

"No berth, Ryan?"

"I've got a berth, Georgie. I just couldn't sleep. And then I did."

"We should talk."

I waited.

"Not here. I've got my granddaughter with me. She's asleep a couple of cars back. Come on back, there's a couple of empty seats near ours."

He didn't look good. He was even thinner than he had been when I saw him last. The lines were cut in deep furrows under his cheekbones and from the corners of his mouth to his chin and nested in webs beneath his eyes. His hair had been black with a hint of gray when I had seen him last but now it was white. And the electricity was almost gone. It was down to a faint crackle. He moved slowly when he stood and he moved slowly when he walked—he was seventy-one or seventy-two years old and he looked every day of it. I followed his rounded shoulders through two cars.

She was asleep, curled in the corner of the window seat. He stopped for a second to look down at her then gestured to the seat behind her.

"Nobody's sitting in those seats. We can talk there."

That was the first I noticed the troubles he was having breathing. The walk through the train had winded him.

"How long were you waiting for me to wake?"

"About an hour."

"You left your granddaughter sleeping alone for an hour, Georgie?"

"Don't try and tell me my business, Ryan. We're way past that."

We sat for a second.

"What's wrong with you?"

"Emphysema. Thought it was cancer at first. I smoked for a long time. I figured I had the lung cancer."

He shook his head.

"Emphysema. Not sure which is worse. Cancer kills you quicker. The way I hear it, it might be a mercy."

"What caused it?"

"Same shit. Smoking. Getting old. Inhaling ink. All the same shit, it's just that everybody talks about cancer. Don't say much about emphysema."

"What's the cure?"

He laughed and coughed then spoke once he had recovered.

"New lungs. Got any?"

He waved his hand then.

"Enough about me, we've got to talk."

He started to cough again and pulled a handkerchief from his pocket to his mouth. He was an old man. When he was done he started to speak again but was interrupted.

"Are you okay, Daddo?"

She had her face pressed up against the narrow gap between the two seats. He leaned into the space and spoke to her.

"I'm fine, girl. You go back to sleep."

"Who are you talking to?"

An old friend, little girl. An old, old friend. You go back to sleep."

It's too squishy here, Daddo, I can't sleep."

"Would she be better in my berth, Georgie?"

He looked at me and then leaned back into the space.

"Come around here, girl, and meet my friend."

I heard her rustling around in the seat in front and then she was standing beside our seats. She had looked younger asleep in the seat. I had thought she was five or six but she was probably eight or nine...or maybe she was tall for her age. And it was her.

"Amy, meet my friend Ryan.

I stuck out my hand and she took it. I could see the hint of the beautiful woman she was going to be but her face was soft and guileless, lacking the sharply defined edges that would arrive over the next ten or twelve years. It was her but just the beginning of her.

"Nice to meet you, Amy."

She nodded and ducked her head. The burnished rosewood barrette holding her bangs back had come undone while she slept and her curls fell across her face. She brushed at them and felt the barrette hanging and tangled in her hair and pulled it out and refastened it so that it pulled her hair back from her face.

"Ryan's offered to let you sleep in his cabin. Do you think you could sleep if you had a bed to lie down on?"

She nodded.

"I'm tired, Daddo, I just can't sleep anymore in the seat."

I handed him the key.

"It's one car back."

He got to his feet and she took his hand.

"Just walk slow, Daddo, we don't have to hurry."

It was almost half an hour before he returned and when he did his breathing was even more labored.

"Beautiful girl, Georgie."

He waved his hand.

"She's her mother all over again. Hard to tell when you just meet her but too smart for her years and a tongue like a serrated blade—she's going to make some lucky man miserable someday."

"Why's she with you?"

"She flew up a couple of weeks ago, just to visit her granddad and I promised her a train ride home. I'm supposed to fly home next week but I think her mother's going to try and get me to stay. Might be the best idea."

He was only able to say a couple of words at a time without panting. I stopped asking questions and he rested for a few minutes until his wind came back a little bit.

"I fucked up."

"What do you mean?"

"Denver. I fucked up."

I waited.

"That McKillops twin never killed anybody."

I stared at him waiting but he didn't continue. I tried to speak but nothing came out. I closed my mouth and then tried again.

"You know that for sure?"

"Pretty sure."

"How?"

"He kept a diary."

"How do you know?"

He sat for a minute without speaking.

"I couldn't let it go. I kept watching the papers and girls were still dying."

"Girls are always dying. What? You thought killing the McKillops was going to fix that?"

He shook his head.

"No. They were dying in the same places and the same way. Always near the tracks and with a knife. We had got rid of all the McKillops but it looked like it was still going."

I shook my head.

"This is messed up, Georgie. None of this makes sense."

"I know. So, it takes me a few years but I figure out that things are still happening. The first couple of years I just try and write it off but after a while, there's just too many. Something's going on."

So, I figure I'll start with people who know the McKillops boys. By the way, the one that died in Denver was Dan. The other guy was Phillip. At first, it's tough even finding anybody who remembers Dan. It's been four or five years since he died and people barely noticed him when he was alive. But it turns out he had a woman friend. I don't know if she was a girlfriend, like that. But they were friends."

I nodded.

"This takes me another four or five years, Ryan. I'm doing these searches when I can, on vacations, on weekends. The girls are grown and gone so I've got more time but it's still bits and pieces. And I'm working on both

256

of them, Phillip and Dan. And I'm focusing more on Phillip, the dentist, because I think he's the kingpin. But I get nothing on Phillip. He's just too fucking smart. His wife knew something was going on—how could she not—but she's not talking. It can only hurt her. But I find a bartender in the old neighborhood that remembers Dan. And he remembers a girl who used to drink with our Danny once in a while. He couldn't remember her name but remembered that she's a dishwasher at a diner just off Lombard Street. So, I find the place and go in for coffee. The first day there's a guy washing the dishes, must have been seventy-five years old, hands cracked and bleeding from the soap and the water. He comes out to grab a pan of dishes to take back to the dish pit and I ask him about the woman. He says it must be Shelagh and she works the evening shift.

"So, I come back that evening and I pick a table where I can see into the kitchen and I can see her in the back spraying down the dishes and feeding the steam washer. When it gets quiet I see her pull a pack of cigarettes from her coat and go out the backdoor. I go around the back and she's leaning against the wall smoking. She was a little nervous to see me at first—the diner backs onto an alley that hardly anybody uses so she wasn't expecting company. But when I bring up Dan she tears up right away. Telling me what a good man he was. A lost soul but a good man. Of course, I'm thinking 'Good man. Yeah, right.' But she sees what I'm thinking right away. She says to me "You think Danny was like his brother, his brother, Phillip." I haven't even mentioned the brother. I didn't even know she knew the brother existed. But when I push her on Phillip she won't say anything more but she offers that she's got a book I should read. Danny's diary. She said she would meet me the next day with the diary but I can't let it go so I wait until she's done her shift at one AM and her place is only a short walk.

"The apartment's small, pretty shabby, a bedroom, a sitting room, and the kitchen. She keeps the book in a locked drawer beside her bed. I thought she might not want to part with the book, that it was some kind of keepsake, a memory she would want to hang onto, a worn thread tying her to a younger time, maybe a better time. But she can't give it to me fast enough. And she doesn't want it back. She just couldn't throw it out. She knew it had a story that somebody would want to hear and she was waiting for that person and now I had shown up and she could pass it along. She didn't even really want an explanation. She unlocked the drawer and handed me the book without looking at it and then waited for me to leave. I started to explain but she shook her head. "It's okay, I don't need to know. I don't want to know. It's time for somebody else to read it." And I left with the book. That was it."

"What was in the book, Georgie?"

He shook his head.

"You should read it."

"You've got it with you?"

He nodded and gestured to the rack above our heads.

"It's in my overnight bag, the side pocket."

It wasn't what I expected. I thought it would be a regular diary with a clasp or a lock or something. Or at least a book with hard black covers. But it was a school notebook with the stapled binding and corners that were dogeared and starting to split and separate. I sat down with it in my lap and looked over and Georgie and he just nodded. I flipped open the front cover. Danny had ripped out a few of the front pages. My guess was that it had been a school notebook, his or somebody else's, that had only used the first few pages for class notes and he had ripped those notes out and started his diary.

The first entry was December 12, 1940.

> Phillip and Father went out tonight. I won't be going anymore. I didn't do well the last time. I know that Father's disappointed and Phillip thinks I'm a sissy but I can't do it. It's the noises. They make noises.
>
> April 5, 1941.
>
> Phillip and Father left. They don't even tell me anymore. I saw them leave though. They've bought new coats. Long coats. I'm not sure how long they will be gone.
>
> April 9, 1941.
>
> They're back. I can hear them laughing and drinking downstairs.

They came in very late, after I was asleep, but they were loud and woke me up. They have a fire going in the oil drum out back. It's hard to see what they're burning but I think it's clothing.

August 10, 1941

Phillip and Father argued tonight. I think Phillip did one on his own. They argued for a long time and then Father hit Phillip. Things were quiet after that.

September 14, 1941

Father left and didn't bring Phillip. Phillip's in an ugly mood. He found Father's liquor and he's been drinking. I'm going to stay in my room. I think Father didn't bring him because of what happened last month.

September 22, 1941

Father's still not back. He's never been gone this long. We're almost out of food. I don't know what to do.

October 15, 1941

Father's dead. They found him in San Francisco.

Feb 3, 1942

We joined the Army. Phillip said it's this or starve. We're only sixteen but Phillip faked the papers and he said that we're big enough that nobody will care. Phillip says that they feed you breakfast, lunch, and supper in the Army.

Then there was a ten-year gap between entries.

June 16. 1952

Phillip said he wants my help. I'm not sure what he means but he's meeting me at Mackie's tonight to talk. I don't think I can do it.

June 19, 1952

It's not what I thought. He doesn't want me with him. He just wants me to take his place while he's gone. I won't see any patients but he wants me to show up at work every day. Wearing his clothes. He introduced me to his wife, Jenny. She's very pretty. He told her that I'll be staying there while he's gone. I don't think she was happy but she didn't say anything.

July 17, 1952

Phillip was gone for four days. She tried to talk to me about where he goes but I left the room.

There were one or two entries a year after that all referencing trips for Phillip while Dan took his place. But the notes started to change in the early 1960s

February 24, 1963

Phillip told Jenny what he does when he's away. She asked him about it as soon as he came in the house and he ignored her but she kept asking. He didn't speak to her at all for the longest time. I was standing at the door waiting for him to drive me home. And then finally he started talking. He told her everything. The way he follows them, making sure he makes just enough noise that they start to get nervous, and then when he thinks they've been afraid long enough he steps out. He says that they're relieved at first because he looks respectable. He says that they think a well-cut suit and an expensive hat means that he won't hurt them. And then he hurts them. He told her everything. What the knife looks like, what it feels like in his hand, how it feels when the blade enters and how it feels when he pulls it out, how he covers their mouth so they can't scream, and how strong they can be for a few moments but it never lasts. He didn't talk about the sounds they make but I remember those. And when he was done talking he drove me home.

August 11, 1963

Phillip is coming to pick me up. I don't want to go.

April 5, 1964

Phillip is coming.

April 9, 1964

Phillip talks to me. I don't know how to tell him that I don't want to know. He told me where. Where he first spotted her and then how far he followed her and then where he grabbed her and killed her. He told me everything. I asked him if she had been to an abortionist, like the girls that father found. He says that Father was weak and deluded. That Father needed permission to do this thing but that he, Phillip, asks permission of nobody. That most men are unable, unwilling to make this long step into the dark and so they never reach their full potential. Phillip says that when he takes the life of one girl, he gives life to another. I wish he wouldn't tell me.

November 17, 1964

Phillip is coming.

November 21, 1964

Phillip was in Detroit. He spotted her in a park off sixth street near the river and followed her west past 12th Street. She was looking behind her for the last two blocks but he was able to stay out of sight. She had crossed a parking lot near W. Lafayette Boulevard and he stepped out of the shadows. She had relaxed a little when she saw his suit and smile but then she had spotted the blade in his hand.

June 9, 1965

Phillip is coming.

June 16. 1965

Phillip was in San Diego. He saw her near Second and Island and followed her for several blocks east until she had cut across a parking lot towards Market. He caught up just as she had started into the parking lot.

December 23, 1965

Phillip is coming.

December 24, 1965

There were three men at the house when I got there with Phillip. One was older, about Phillip's age and the other two were younger, maybe brothers. They talked for several hours in the kitchen before leaving. I stayed in the sitting room. I could hear their voices but not what they were saying. It was almost dark when we left and I drove them to the train station but nobody spoke. Usually, I just let Phillip out and then leave but this time I let them all out and then parked the car and came back to watch what they did. I hurried because I thought I might miss them but they were huddled talking near the door to one of the platforms. I stood outside the main entrance to the station looking in occasionally – it was a mild night a little above freezing. Phillip and the three men stood together talking for about half an hour then split up, going to three different platforms. Only the two younger men stayed together.

December 29, 1965

I thought that with his new friends Phillip wouldn't tell me the stories but he does. St. Louis. East from the train station to a park near Biddle Street. She was so afraid she hardly struggled.

April 5, 1966

Phillip came to get me. The three men are here again. Nobody talks to me.

April 13, 1966

I must be a witness. That is my place. I am a witness for these women. My brother and his friends are evil, misguided men, doing wrong in God's eyes. Of this, I am almost certain. New Orleans. He caught her in a park just north of Johnson and St. Philip.

June 16, 1966

Phillip is coming.

June 18

Boston. He followed her for more than a mile into South Boston and she died in a church parking lot off of E Fifth Street

October 11, 1966

There was a fourth man this time. Even younger than the other two, maybe twenty, twenty-one years old.

October 16, 1966

Indianapolis. She ran. East. He caught her in an alley near Hoyt and Spruce. I won't forget.

January 2, 1967

Phillip is coming.

January 9, 1967

Kansas City. He guessed she would head south out of the train station but she hadn't and he thought he had lost her. But she had stopped at a payphone and when he circled the station he picked up her trail again. He pulled her into a small wooded area near West Nickel and River Blvd.

April 13, 1967

Phillip is coming. I can't do this anymore.

April 17, 1967

Phillip found me. He was very angry. He hasn't hit me since we were teenagers. He is stronger than I remember. There was Phillip and four men again. I've been here for four days. Jenny never leaves her room.

April 19, 1967

Charlotte. A wooded backyard near Woodside and Duncan.

July 7, 1967

Phillip is coming. I'm not sure how long I can continue. I want to run. But he's been everywhere. He knows every hiding place. Every park and vacant lot and deserted culvert.

July 17, 1967

Phillip has never been gone for this long. The phone rang several times over the last two days but I don't answer. Jenny doesn't answer either. She stays in her room. I hear her at night making food but I stay in my room. I don't think she likes me.

July 19, 1967

I have been going to Phillip's office but people are showing up to have work done. I hide in the back until they stop ringing the bell. I won't be going back. Phillip should have been back at least five days ago.

July 24, 1967

The police came to the door today. They said they found a body in Chicago and they were pretty sure it was Phillip. I went with them to the station. His face was swollen and discolored and part of his head was missing but it was him. Was I sure? Yes, I was sure. His hands were like my father's but unlike them—unmarked and white but big-knuckled and strong. My father had the same hands but scarred and stained by hard, dirty work and shameful deeds. I cried for my brother. He was the evil in a graceless world but he was my twin and we were the same man in so many ways.

There was an eighteen-month gap before his next entry.

December 10, 1969

I thought when Phillip died it was over but I was wrong. I can't forget the girls. I remember all of them. They shouldn't be forgotten. I will start in Las Vegas, the night we were together... the last night together.

December 18, 1969

I wasn't sure I would be able to find the place but I did. We followed her to a neighborhood near the river and Father thought we waited too long, that she was home. But she kept going down to a spot by the river. A short path from the road along the river led to the shoreline and we followed her to a spot where she stood looking over the river. She called out when she heard our footsteps and my father answered. His voice was even and friendly and soothed her so that Phillip could get close and sink the blade. She made a noise before my father's hand fell across her mouth. Without hope. A mouse in the shadow of a hawk. I never touched the blade at my waist and stumbled back up the path to the Parkway and stood in the gloom of the trees at the edge of the woods until I heard them walking up the path. I walked behind them all the way to the station. They didn't speak a word.

I stand at the edge of the river. The Parkway had been widened and there was more traffic and fewer trees between the road and the river but it still seems much the same. I pray for her. I pray through the night. That she was more than the last sounds she made. That she was more than my father and brother had made her. More than we had made her.

I looked up from the book.

"He didn't kill anybody."

Georgie nodded. He waited for me to say more but I didn't. He nodded again.

"The other guys are still going?"

He nodded.

"Are you sure?"

He nodded again.

"The bodies are coming as fast as ever. Faster. They may be recruiting."

"What do we do?"

He shook his head.

"I don't know. I'm going to talk to Phillip's wife again. Now that I have the twin's diary maybe she'll talk to me."

"When?"

He stared at me for a second and I noticed for the first time that one of his eyes had a milky area that covered part of the lens of his eye. His head dropped then and he looked down at his hands.

"I don't know."

He looked back up.

"I'm getting tired."

We sat for a few minutes without speaking.

"What about Danny?"

"What about him?"

"You killed him. And he wasn't what you thought he was. How are you doing with that?"

Georgie shrugged.

"Not bad."

He didn't speak for a couple more seconds.

"Not because he let this happen."

He looked up.

"He did let it happen. If he had said something, if he hadn't been too afraid or too timid or just too fucked up to know better, there would be a lot of girls still alive today. But that's not why I don't care."

I thought he was gathering his thoughts and I waited for him to keep talking but I realized after a bit that he had finished, that he didn't have more to say.

"Why don't you care?"

He looked over at me, like he was surprised to hear my voice, like he had forgotten I was there. Then he smiled.

"Oh. Why? Because my back hurts. And if I walk a block I have to stop and sit for ten minutes. And I don't see so well out of one eye. And pizza tastes like cardboard, and a cold beer makes me shit soft, and when a woman smiles at me it's because I remind her of her grandfather, and most of my friends are gone and the ones that aren't, are bent and curled like a used twist tie, and every time I piss it's barely worth the trouble to stand."

I thought he was done again but then he spoke more quietly.

"Everything fades and wanes. Including the stain of sins committed. The only thing that doesn't get blurred and less distinct is the distance between what you are and what you were."

We sat for a second more.

"You'll learn."

He didn't speak for several seconds. Then,

"So, I don't much care about Dan McKillops. Poor fucker."

There wasn't much left to read in Dan McKillops's diary. A half dozen more entries describing trips he had taken. And then an entry that he was going to Denver. I stood and stuffed the notebook back into the side pocket of Georgie's carry-all and he nodded his head in thanks when I sat back down.

"What now?"

"I don't know. I guess I'll visit the wife and see if she'll talk to me. It's not as if I'm going to the cops with it."

"Why not?"

He shrugged.

"It's a fucked-up story. The best I can hope is they think I'm a nut job with a diary I wrote myself and a story that doesn't make sense. At worst, they'll think it was me."

"And what can the wife tell you?"

"Maybe she'll know some names. Have heard some names when they were talking? I don't know. Anything that will help me track down the four guys."

"And then what?"

He took a while to answer.

"What should I do? "

I shrugged.

"It hasn't been enough? There's still more? This has been my life since I was nine years old and it's not done yet? That all the moments of my life, my first time with a woman, the birth of my children, the backyard BBQs, the ball games, the Christmas concerts in middle school, have been in the shadow of McKillops and his sons. That, I've carried the weight every single step, knowing that every moment of respite, every pause to hold my children or love my wife may have come at far too high a cost and that the path to heaven is dark and lonely, narrow and treacherous and when you slip in the last few steps you fall as far as there is to fall. And it's all the worse because you saw the gates, and the muted glow beyond and you did your best but it wasn't enough."

He stopped and took a big breath and when he exhaled he was done. I thought.

"I don't know. If I get the names…if I get a name and I can still walk, I'll find them. And I'll kill them."

"Daddo?"

We hadn't heard her come up the aisle.

"Kill who?"

Her hair was tousled and falling across her eyes and I could see where the pillow or blankets had bunched against her face and left lines. Georgie reached out to her and she slid by me and into his lap, curling into him with her head under his chin.

"Kill who?"

"Never mind, girl. Did you sleep good?"

She nodded without speaking.

"Why would you want to kill somebody, Daddo?"

"I wouldn't, little girl. Mr. Spencer and I were just telling stories. Let yourself wake up and stop thinking so much."

She nodded.

"Okay, Daddo."

He looked at me.

"You should sleep now, Ryan."

"What about you Georgie? You could use a few hours."

He shook his head.

"I don't sleep much these days. An hour here, an hour there. And I have to stay with this one. "

He nodded down at Amy.

"She'll be full awake soon and once she is she'll want to talk and I should be there for that."

"Okay then. I will sleep for a while. I'll stop by in a few hours to see how you're doing."

But I couldn't sleep.

* * *

My father sat at a table with a woman I didn't recognize. She was young and pretty and when she laughed it sounded like delicate chimes stirred by an unexpected breeze. And she laughed often at things my father said but I couldn't hear. She touched him on the arms and hands and once she reached up to wipe a thin line of beer foam from his upper lip. It was shockingly intimate.

I had seen him as soon as I had entered the bar car. He looked exactly as I remembered—thick dark hair, too long for a military man but excused because he was a flyboy, a square Hollywood jaw, and a face that even in repose looked like it wanted to smile, laugh lines etching at the corners of his eyes. His eyes stayed on me for a moment when I came in the bar car, puzzled, that maybe he should know me but unsure and then dismissing it, looking away. I found a seat at the bar where I could sit, watch the room and take the chance to study him. He sat alone at first with a beer in front of him. The woman arrived a half-hour after me, the tables and bar full, and Dad, alone at a table for four, offered her a chair.

It was difficult to watch. In the early awkward moments, there were seconds when neither spoke and they looked away out the window or around the room, unprepared to look at each other without speaking but unwilling or unable to leave. I prayed for my father to speak to her, a short sentence, and then stand, turn away and leave the room but he didn't and the words started to come more easily. I couldn't hear them but they spoke more often and smiled around and between the words and their eyes held even when they were no longer speaking. She touched him now, just for a moment, as she spoke, as if she was unaware that she was touching him, as if it was the natural thing, the right thing to do. The first time my own hand jerked away involuntarily like I had been scalded or slapped.

She ordered a drink and drank it quickly, something in a short glass, clear with ice and lime, and when she was done my father ordered her another and himself another beer. She finished hers before my father had taken more than a few sips and he ordered for her again. Dad spoke more than the woman and she laughed often and easily at the things he said and when she wasn't laughing her lips pursed in a way that suggested a kiss. And then she reached up and wiped his mouth and her fore and middle finger rested for a moment on his lower lip, lingering like wasps on a ripened berry.

They talked and laughed and drank for several hours and I didn't leave, I couldn't leave. Dad had four beers but she had many drinks and when she stood to use the ladies room the train pitched and she stumbled and Dad rose quickly to catch her and she fell so that her hips and breasts were pressed up hard against him and they stood like that for what seemed like many seconds before she stepped away and steadied herself. Dad watched as she walked away and he was watching when she returned. They had one more drink after that and I prayed that when she left my father would stay in his seat but I knew better and when she stood to go he stood with her. They stopped at the bar and Dad settled the bill and when the train pitched again the woman grabbed my father's arm and then she kept it there so that when they left the bar car she held his arm.

I knew I should return to my berth, that it was wrong to follow but I had to see the end. They walked through several cars and I followed until they came to a door and she stopped. She pulled a key from her purse and opened the door. She had let go of my father's arm to unlock the door but now she took it again and started to back into the room pulling gently on his sleeve but he didn't move from where he stood. I looked at his face and he was smiling but shaking his head. She stepped back into the hallway and stood on her tiptoes to whisper in his ear and he smiled and shook his head again, gently pulling her hand from his sleeve. He leaned over and kissed her forehead and my Dad walked away down the hallway. The woman watched him until he was several cars back and then went into her room and closed the door. I returned to my room and slept for fourteen hours.

When I woke up 1997 was a long time ago and we were ten minutes from Stockton. I flipped the sheets and blanket flat on the bed so I could lay my suitcase out and when I did something small and brown fell onto the floor—a barrette. I picked it up and stuffed it into my pants pocket.

It turned out that the address Amy had given me was actually a little town outside of Stockton called Lodi. Like the Creedence song. There were a lot of cars outside the house when I got there and as I pulled up a couple was getting out of a Subaru van holding a casserole dish. It wasn't a good sign. I watched as the couple walked up the sidewalk to the address I had on the crumpled slip of paper beside me in the cab. The driver looked back at me.

"It's twenty-seven bucks, pal."

"Give me a second. You can keep the meter running."

He shrugged.

A woman of about fifty answered the door. There was no question it was Georgie's daughter, even from where I was sitting. Same lean build, narrow face, and dark hair. I was pretty sure this was the younger daughter, Rachel.

The couple stepped into the house and the door shut behind them. I leaned over the seat.

"How much do I owe you?

"Still twenty-seven bucks, pal."

I handed him forty over the seat.

"Keep it."

"Thanks, friend."

I got out of the cab and stood looking at the house as the taxi pulled away. The door opened again and Amy stood in the doorway. She was wearing black jeans and a red sweater that fell almost to her knees.

"Ryan?"

"Yeah."

"I thought it was you. Are you coming in?"

"Georgie died?"

I saw her head nod from where I stood.

"Two nights ago. Less than a day after I got back."

I hadn't moved from where I stood and now she walked down the pathway from the house leaving the door open behind her.

"How was it?"

She shrugged.

"As good as we could have hoped. Emphysema's a tough way to go."

"Did he know I was coming?"

"Yeah, he knew. He just couldn't hang on any longer."

"I'm sorry."

She nodded.

"Come on inside. It's just the neighbors and some friends. You must be hungry…you can get something to eat."

"Do you mind? Could we just go for a walk? I don't think I'm up for a bunch of people."

"Sure."

She started up the street and I followed her.

"How was the trip?"

"Good."

I wasn't sure if she was expecting more but she didn't push. We walked without talking for a bit.

"Ryan, I'm not sure what happened in Montreal. I'm feeling a bit silly for having followed you there and telling you Georgie's stories. He was an old man and he had stories. I feel like you were just trying to make me feel better, feel not so crazy. I'm glad you've come but I never should have pushed so hard."

"It's all true, Amy."

She slowed down but didn't look over.

"How can it be, Ryan? It's crazy. He's been chasing killers for seventy years and you've been helping him? You seem like a nice guy Ryan but how can I take this seriously. Either it's a joke that you and Georgie dreamed up or you're as deluded as he is. Was."

"I can't explain it, Amy, but it's no joke. All I can tell you is that Georgie spent his life tracking down the bad guys. And I helped him once in a while."

She shook her head.

"Stop it, Ryan."

"It's true."

"That's enough, Ryan. Stop saying it's true."

I didn't answer. We had walked around the block. She was angry at me and when she spoke the words were hard and short.

"Do you want to come in?"

"I probably shouldn't."

She didn't answer.

"I'll need a cab back to the train station."

She nodded.

"I'll call. Do you want to wait inside?"

"I'm good here. It's a nice night."

She started across the street to the pathway and I called after her.

"Did he leave anything for me, Amy? A message? A note? Anything?"

She stopped in the middle of the street but didn't turn around. She stood for several seconds before answering.

"No."

Then she kept walking into the house. I stood for a few minutes alone. It was late afternoon but the street was quiet. After a few minutes, the door opened. I was expecting Amy but it was her mother. She stood in the doorway and motioned to me so I walked across the street to the end of the path just close enough so I wouldn't have to shout.

"It's OK Mrs. Robbins, Amy's calling me a cab."

"Hello, Mr. Spencer. She says you've come from Montreal. By train."

"Yes ma'am."

"And that you were a friend of my father's?"

I nodded.

"How is it that a young man like you was a friend of my father's."

"It's a long story, ma'am. He was a fan and we used to chat online."

"He was not a fan and he didn't chat online. Would you like to come in?"

"That's alright, ma'am, I'll just wait out here for the cab."

"You'll be waiting a long time. I wouldn't let Amy call a cab for a man who had traveled from Montreal by train to visit my father. So, you come in and have a plate or I'll bring one out here to you."

"I'll come in, ma'am."

She smiled.

"Good choice."

There were about twenty people in the house, most holding paper plates with food but none of them was Amy.

"There's food in the kitchen, Mr. Spencer. Just grab a plate."

"Thanks, Mrs. Robbins."

"Call me, Rachel. And it's Abbott. Amy's father and I divorced a long while back."

"Yes, ma'am. "

"Can I call you Ryan?"

I flushed.

"Of course, ma'am. I wasn't thinking…I just…sure, Ryan's fine."

There was ham and baked beans and coleslaw and I realized I was hungry. I filled a plate and went into the living room. Amy had come back into the room. She came over when she saw me.

"I'm sorry. That was rude."

I shook my head.

"It's okay. It's a hard time. And I'm making it harder."

She shrugged. We stood awkwardly.

"Why did you call him Daddo?"

"What?"

"Daddo? Where does it come from?"

"How do you know that name? Did he tell you about it?"

"No, I heard you…"

I stopped myself.

"When would you have heard me? I haven't called him that since I was a child. Once I got older he didn't like it. He wanted Georgie."

I stared at the floor for a long while and then began to speak.

"I met you on the train. You were a little girl and he was old. He already had emphysema and he was an old man…older than his years. You called him Daddo. He was coming from out east to stay with you and your mother."

She was staring at me now and shaking her head.

"No. No…"

"You met me on the train. You slept in my berth while me and Georgie talked. About the McKillops twins and the new guys, the guys who are still out there. "

"No, no…that man was older, bigger…"

I shook my head.

"No. It was me. You overheard us talking and you heard Georgie say he was going to kill them and you asked who he was going to kill. Not worried or upset, just matter-of-fact…who was he going to kill. He put you off and you forgot about it then."

She was shaking her head with her hand covering her mouth. A couple of people in the room were looking over.

"Maybe we should talk outside."

She nodded and we didn't talk again until we were outside. I still had my plate in my hand and I set it down on the stoop. She had regained her composure.

274

"I don't know what your game is Ryan but this is a story my grandfather must have told you and now you're using it on me."

"Using it for what, Amy?"

"I don't know but I'm sure I'll find out."

"You followed me around out here and in Pittsburgh and in Philadelphia and then came all the way to Montreal because you believed your grandfather's story. What's changed?"

"My grandfather was a persuasive man. He was a sad and tired and haunted man and he carried his days like a bag of stones and when he said he loved me, he spoke it like a broken promise. He told me a crazy story as he was dying and I wanted to believe him. I wanted to believe that he was a brave and crippled man who had been belittled by time and a losing battle against the worst of us. I wanted to believe that he had turned his face into a cold wind and walked for a lifetime in search of lost and frightened souls. And that a lifetime of that will leave you spent and worn, but still a man."

She paused.

"But the truth is, he was an old and bitter man telling stories that gave his life more weight than it could bear."

"You're wrong. And I think you know you're wrong. Nobody could know your grandfather and think he was an insubstantial man. He shouldered every load and though he may have stumbled, he never fell."

We walked in silence for two blocks.

"Was that his last train ride?"

"When?"

"In 1997, the trip from Boston to here that you took with him? Was that his last train ride?"

She shook her head and turned to look at me.

"No. He took a trip home the next summer. I wanted to go but he wouldn't let me. Said he was going to visit friends and I would get in the way. I remember crying for the two days before he left and the whole next day after he left. He had never not wanted me with him before."

"He was going to see Phillip's widow. Try and find out who the other men were. That's why he couldn't bring you."

Amy didn't answer.

"How long was he gone?"

"I don't remember exactly. Ten days? Two weeks?"

"Do you remember what he was like when he got back?"

Her head came around quickly.

"Why?"

I looked over.

"He was different, wasn't he?"

She looked away again.

"He was different. It was like he could stand a little taller, walk a little further. He didn't sleep as much. And he made mom take him to the library for a few weeks. Said he was doing some kind of little research project."

"Phillip's widow had something."

"That wasn't his last trip."

It was my turn to look over at her.

"He took another trip?"

She nodded.

"It was about six months after he got back from Boston. I remember because he called a cab right after Mom left for work. Usually, Mom drove him everywhere but not that day. And he left a note for Mom inside a sealed envelope. I never did find out what it said but I remember Mom crying when she read it. Then she got straight in the car and went to the train station. She had to bring me because there was nobody to look after me and she went to every platform looking for him but he had planned it pretty well. We didn't find him."

I nodded, thinking of the car I had rented rather than taking the train.

"How was he when he got back?"

"Quiet. Smaller. He didn't joke as much. It wasn't long after that he told me to stop calling him Daddo."

We walked another block in silence.

"Ryan?"

I looked over.

"What happened on that second trip?"

I looked at her for a long while before speaking.

"He got one. He got one of the men."

"He was an old man. How could he?"

"He was a tough old man, you're Daddo. But I bet he was expecting some help. And he ended up having to do it on his own."

We had done a large circle and were almost back at Amy's mother's house.

"He did leave something."

I nodded.

"What was it?"

"An envelope for you."

"What was in it?"

She flushed.

"Just a list. A list of names. Six names. The name at the top had a line through it."

"That's it?"

"Not another word. No message."

"Can I have it?"

She nodded.

Many of the people had already left the house when we got back. Amy went into the back room to get the list from her purse. Amy's mother was in the kitchen.

"Ma'am, do you mind if I phone a cab?"

"Let me do it, Ryan. You go ahead and say goodbye to Amy."

We stood at the door waiting together. I had the envelope in my hand but hadn't bothered looking at the list inside. I was certain I wouldn't recognize the names.

"Who are the names on the list?"

I looked over at her.

"You know who they are."

"How did he get them?"

"At least one from Phillip's widow. The rest I don't know. Maybe the widow. Maybe from the first guy."

"What are you going to do?"

"I don't know."

"Can you do it?"

"I don't know."

We didn't talk again until the cab pulled up. I took the rosewood barrette out of my pocket then and held it out to her. She looked at it for a long time before taking it from me. She hugged me and I could feel her shaking against me. She pulled back and her face was wet.

"You okay?"

She smiled.

"Why didn't you give it to me sooner?"

"I'm not sure. It seemed like a trick or something."

She nodded

"Thanks."

The cab honked and I grabbed my bag from the stoop.

"Keep in touch, Amy."

She nodded. I went back to Montreal.

* * *

I stepped off the train in Chicago and he was there.

I had fallen asleep just past Denver and slept hard. I hadn't thought about it much when I awoke because nothing really seemed different. I had just stepped out onto the platform to stretch my legs, we were only stopping for fifteen minutes. We were parked on one of the middle tracks and I would have had to go down the stairs and underneath the tracks and through the tunnel to the lobby of the station and it was too far. It was late, after midnight, and there was only one other train, two tracks over getting ready to pull out. He came up out of the stairwell leading to the tunnel and into the artificial light of the platform. He stopped at the top of the stairs to set his bag down and pull out the handle so he could roll it. He paused then. I think to rest because he had had to carry the bag up the stairs. He looked out of place, out of time. He had found a fedora that I had never seen before but taken it off and his hair had grown too long and it fell across

278

his forehead in thin white strands. His shoulders were slumped and curled under a long worn coat and he stood for several seconds staring at the ground then reached inside his coat and felt around for something in the breast pocket, just checking to be sure whatever it was, was still there. Then he turned and dragged his suitcase over the concrete towards the waiting train. A porter, a balding, red-haired man, came to one of the open doors of the train and stood watching as Georgie walked stiffly across the platform. It seemed to take forever to walk from the top of the stairs to the train and Georgie never looked up from the ground. When he got to the door he started to step up into the train but lost his balance and the porter had to grab his arm and steady him before helping him up on. From where I stood it didn't seem that Georgie even looked at or spoke to the porter. I almost called out. But for what? He had a train to catch. And we had a list. I put my hand inside my jacket and fingered it to be sure that it was still there.

Chapter Twenty-One

I had showed up at the park on Monday at one PM and nobody spoke to me. We had lost five of seven while I was gone and were two games out of the wildcard spot with five to play. The players never did but none of the coaches or Baldy had a word to say. I wasn't in the lineup that night and we lost five to one but didn't lose any ground because the Mets lost to Cincy. We loaded the bases in the ninth and Baldy pinch-hit with a kid just up from AAA who hit into a double-play. I was the first one into the tunnel and got to my locker before the rest of the team made it to the room. There was a note pinned to my locker. The team was quiet entering the room. Balducci came in last but didn't even look at the players, just walked into his office and slammed the door behind him. Nobody looked my way except Nick who slumped into his stall looked over at me standing by my locker and nodded. He had been on first when the kid had grounded out and had gone into the second baseman hard trying to break up the DP. The second baseman had made a bad throw but the first baseman had been able to dig it out of the dirt and make the play. The way Nick winced when he took off his jersey he must have banged up his ribs.

I was standing at my locker looking at the note. It just said UPSTAIRS. I knew what it meant. The GM wanted to see me. I hadn't spoken to Mr. McCarthy since spring training. He hardly ever came in the locker room and when he did it was to speak to Balducci. I changed quickly, no need to shower, and left the locker room. There was an elevator from just outside the lockers that led to the offices high in the stadium behind the owner's box but you needed an electronic pass card to get to the top floors. The elevator doors were open and I stepped in and hit the button for the top floor but nothing lit up. The doors slid closed and I stood in the mirrored compartment staring at the unlit buttons. I pressed the 'Open Doors' button and the doors slid open to reveal the same empty hallway running under the stadium. I waited for a second and they slid closed again.

"Mr. Spencer?"

The voice came from a grill above the buttons.

"Yes?"

It felt strange speaking inside an empty elevator.

"That's fine. I'm just making sure it was you. Come right up."

The elevator started with a subtle jerk and almost soundlessly began to glide upwards. The elevator slid to a smooth stop and the doors opened. I stepped out into a long hallway with several doors along the right side of the hallway and a large set of double doors at the end of the hallway. I walked down and let myself into the small anteroom where McCarthy's executive assistant sat guarding the entrance to his office. She barely looked up when I came in the door.

"Have a seat, Mr. Spencer. Mr. McCarthy will be with you in a second."

He left me waiting for twenty minutes. When Judy led me into his office McCarthy was on the phone and he waved to the chair in front of his desk and then mouthed 'Thank you' to Judy before she left. He talked for another ten minutes before putting the phone down. He didn't speak for several seconds just looking at me across his desk. I looked back.

"Baldy wants to send you down."

I shrugged but didn't speak.

"He thinks you're a cancer, that you don't care, that you're a dilettante and that he'll lose the team and the team will lose if you stay."

I tried to imagine Balducci using the word "dilettante" but the picture wouldn't form.

"What's funny, Spencer?"

I shook my head and he made a face.

"This is the kind of shit he's talking about, Ryan. I tell you you're hurting the team and you smile at some joke only you heard."

"No joke, Mr. McCarthy."

He stared at me a second before starting again.

"He wants you off the field, out of the clubhouse, out of the city. What do you think about that?"

"Hard to blame him, sir."

"So, why did you do it, Ryan?"

"Personal matter, Mr. McCarthy. All I can say is that I had to do it, there were no alternatives."

He slammed his hand on the desk.

"Enough with the mystery, Spencer. What's going on? A woman? Drugs? A man?"

I shook my head.

"It's a personal matter, sir. All I can assure you is that it couldn't be avoided but I'm back and ready to play."

He paused for several seconds.

"Okay, Ryan. We've got four games left to make up three games in the standings and I don't think we're doing it without your bat in the lineup. Just don't fucking embarrass me. Now, get the fuck out."

* * *

The lineup card was posted where it was always posted, just outside Balducci's office, and my name was on it. But I could see that the page had been balled up and then somebody had tried to smooth it out. Garcia's name had been there first but then scratched out and replaced by mine. Just two words. In pencil. Fuckin' Spencer. He had me batting ninth...behind the pitcher.

I was late and the room was almost full but nobody looked at me although it felt like their eyes were on me as soon as I turned away to my locker. Fagan was already at his locker taping up. He looked over and gave a small smile.

"You're back in the lineup."

"Yeah. Prodigal son. When's the feast?"

"Just be careful he doesn't feast on your ass, Spencer."

"Why aren't you in the lineup?"

"Ribs. I'm having trouble getting around on the ball. I'll be okay in the field if they need me."

I nodded.

I found a spot to stretch and nobody came near me and then moved in to the lineup to take batting practice. I was fourth in line and it took about fifteen minutes to get to the plate. I kicked at the dirt with my foot creating a little depression that suited me and then looked out to the mound. Charlie was standing behind the screen with a ball in his hand but not looking ready to throw. He had his head down looking at the ground in front of the basket of baseballs. I stood for several seconds the bat cocked but he never looked up and finally I stepped out. He was one of the few guys that had talked to me most of the season although even he had stopped looking at me in the last week.

"Choo-Choo? You okay?"

He didn't look up from the ground as if he hadn't heard me. One of the hard-core fans shouted from just behind the dugout.

"Throw the fuckin' ball, Choo-Choo." And there was a thin ripple of laughter from the stands. I looked back at the guys waiting to bat—Toner was next in line and he just stared at me without blinking. I looked back out at the mound and Charlie was still staring at the ground. I walked out to the mound.

"What's up?"

He looked up then and his face was miserable.

"Sorry, Spencer. Skip's orders."

"Baldy told you not to throw to me?"

He looked back down and nodded.

"Sorry."

I reached out and patted his shoulder.

"No problem, Chooch, what can you do?"

He nodded again but didn't look up.

I walked back to the dugout where Balducci was standing in the door to the runway. He never came out until just before game time but he was standing there now and he stared at me as I put my bat back in the rack and sat on the bench, then he turned and went back up the hallway to his office.

It was the same during the infield warm-up. We had pre-game drills, just getting a feel for the ball but also working cuts to the first,, second, and third basemen, and playing some quick toss around the infield but today nothing came to third base. No throws, no cutoffs, no ground balls. A couple of the Mets had been standing on the top step of the dugout waiting their turn in the field but the word must have got out and within a few minutes there were fifteen or twenty New York Mets standing along their rail watching the pre-game drill happening around me. You could see them half turning to say a few words to a teammate but not wanting to look completely away. I stood crouched and ready for the first few minutes and then straight, watching the ball moving around the infield with my arms at my side for the next few and then finally I walked off the field to the dugout while they finished. I tried to keep my face expressionless but I knew that I was red and flushed. Balducci was in the doorway to the tunnel again.

My first at bat was in the second inning and I stroked a single over second base knocking in Hiltz. I rounded first base hard and then jogged back to the bag when the centerfielder made a clean throw into the second baseman.

"What the fuck was going on there, Spencer, you get caught in a three-way with Balducci's mom and dad?"

He was the Mets regular first baseman but I couldn't remember his name. I shrugged.

"You know, ups and downs."

"Up and downs? Are you kidding me? That was cold. Fucking ice-cold. I've never seen anything like it."

I didn't have an answer. Fanteaux was pitching for us and he was on. He threw a three- hitter, I went four for four with a walk, a triple, a home-run and four runs batted in and we won nine to one. Nobody was at home plate after my home run other than the catcher and the umpire. At least that hadn't changed. We were two games back of the wildcard with three to go.

I should have guessed there would be questions after the game. We were in a pennant race so the attention was heating up and word had got out about what had happened at the pre-game. It was the first question when I got out the door. It came from a female reporter from *La Presse*.

"Ryan, what happened in the warmup today? It looked like the players and coaches were snubbing you."

"We've just won a game nine to one on a three-hitter and you want to talk about stuff that happened in the pre-game?"

"It looked like a deliberate attempt to embarrass you. And you batted ninth behind the pitcher. What's going on? Does it have anything to do with the games you missed in the last week?"

This came from an SI stringer.

I started to answer but McKay banged through the door behind me and they moved towards him.

"Randy, can you explain what happened to Ryan Spencer before today's game?"

He was a tall man and he looked over the reporters at me.

"Yeah, that's what we do to shitbags and cocksuckers."

He pushed his way through the crowd. A few reporters followed him but the rest turned and looked at me. There was a short silent pause.

"That McKay. What a kidder." This from a long-time columnist with the *Gazette*. There was a low murmur of laughter among the reporters.

"Care to comment, Ryan?"

I shook my head and worked my way through the pack to my car.

* * *

The next night, the Mets had their ace on the mound. Enrico Sanchez threw in the high nineties, had a cruel curve that could freeze you if you didn't recognize it and he was comfortable working the inside of the plate. And he was a big man. Six foot four inches and two hundred and sixty pounds with a fierce scowl and a reputation for never backing off from a charging batter. To make matters worse it was a cold September night in Montreal only a few degrees above freezing and the bat was going to sting. I was batting ninth again and his first pitch to me in the third inning I took to the gap for a double. He came off the mound to get the ball from the second baseman after the ball had been thrown back in. He didn't look at me but it was clear he was talking to me.

"Every time you get a hit I'm going to plunk you."

He didn't have much of an accent but he had a hard time with 'plunk.'

"What?"

"Don't get any more hits. It's easy."

I started to answer but he had already taken the ball and headed back towards the mound. He hit me hard on the hip in the fifth. I couldn't feel my leg above the knee for a few seconds and I almost fell getting down to first. I didn't even look over. I stroked a clean single with two out in the seventh to knock in Tuquet and take a two-one lead. The Mets tied it up in the eight and brought in their closer in the ninth. Gorritz threw a little harder than Sanchez and put one behind my head, another that caromed off my bat for a strike as I tried to get out of the way and a third that caught me high on the bicep. That pushed Giannos to second and he scored on a single by Danny Lopez and we won in the ninth. I was still trying to get feeling in my arm when he crossed the plate. I hadn't made an out in nine straight at bats and we were one game out of a wildcard spot.

It took me longer than usual to leave the clubhouse—I stood under the water for a long time because the heat felt good and it took me a while to dress because my hip and arm were both tender. Just as I was leaving Nick came back from the parking lot—he grabbed me by the arm and pulled me away from the door.

"You might want to go out another way—it's a shit storm out there."

"What do you mean? What's happened?"

Nick looked at me.

"They fucked up your car."

"Who fucked up my car? What do you mean?"

"McKay. His boys. It had to be."

"What did they do? What did those fuckers do?"

"Look, it's probably best…"

I pushed by him and out into the parking lot. The reporters were still there but not gathered around the door like they usually were. They were around my car. I couldn't see much because there were so many people around it but I could see enough to know that it had been spray painted. The reporters didn't notice me until I was almost to the car and then one of them looked over and nudged another and it wasn't long until they were all looking at me. They moved away from the car like oil from soap and then I could see what they had written. SHITBAG on the side that I could see in large, sloppy white letters. I walked around the car and they had written COCKSUC along the side but then had run out of space and had to add the KER along the front of the hood. Nobody spoke for a long time as I stood staring at the car then,

"Who do you think did this, Ryan?"

I looked across the car at the speaker. A short tousled haired guy whose name I couldn't remember.

"I don't know. You have any ideas?"

He looked away.

"Do you think this was done by somebody on the team?"

I couldn't see who had asked. I started to answer and then stopped.

"Is this a prank?"

It was a woman from a local radio station. This time I answered.

"Yeah, it's going to cost me a thousand bucks to avoid driving around town covered in shitbag and cocksucker. I love a good gag."

Nick had come out and was standing by the door watching. I got in my car and drove away.

* * *

The next morning I left the car still covered in paint in the player's parking lot—with no other cars in the lot it was hard to miss. The clubhouse was empty, not even the clubhouse attendants or Frankie had showed up yet. My arm and hip were stiff and sore and I fired up the whirlpool and let it heat up while I stripped down. It felt good. I had been soaking for about thirty minutes when I heard the door from the tunnel open. I kept my eyes closed even when I heard the door to the training room open. He walked in and stood for several seconds before speaking.

"Get that fucking car out of the parking lot and cleaned up, Spencer."

"Sorry, skipper. You want that car cleaned up you're going to have to do it. It's kind of grown on me."

"You fucking heard me, Spencer, get that car off the lot."

"Or what, skip? You've shot your wad. Batting me ninth is all you've got left. You don't like the car, you do something about it."

He slammed the door when he left. Hard.

It took another fifteen minutes for McCarthy to show up. I heard him pull a chair up to the whirlpool but still didn't open my eyes. The arm and hip were loosening up.

"Ryan?"

"Hey, Mr. McCarthy."

"Ryan, why are you doing this?"

"What's that, Mr. McCarthy?"

"The car, you can't leave it painted up like that in the parking lot."

"I needed to get to the ballpark, Mr. McCarthy and that's how I get to the park."

"You could have cleaned it up first, Ryan."

"I didn't mess it up, Mr. McCarthy. You don't like it, you clean it up. Otherwise, I'll be driving it like that until the season's done."

Neither of us spoke for several minutes and then I heard him leave. Frankie showed up twenty minutes later.

"Get out, Spencer, we need the tub."

"Sorry, Frankie, I'm looking at another hour or two."

"The fuck you are, Spencer. I got guys need the tub. Get the fuck out."

I opened one eye to look at him.

"You've got another tub, Frankie, use it. I'm using this one for another while yet."

"We need both tubs. Don't make me go to the skipper."

I laughed.

"Mr. McCarthy just left, Frankie, you might want to start there—me and the skipper have an understanding."

I closed my eye again and listened to Frankie storm out.

I spent another ninety minutes in the tub and when I got out I barely had any stiffness in either the hip or arm. I knew they would get sore again but it might be enough to get through the game.

It was a blowout. The Mets started a guy that had only pitched twenty-three innings in the majors and he was fine for an inning or two but then Toner blasted one and the plate umpire stiffed him on a couple of ball/strikes and he fell apart. By the time they got him out of the game it was six-zero and the bases were loaded. Walford followed with a double and Riley Cooper who was filling in for Nick hit a home run and it was eleven-zero after three. They scratched a few runs back in the seventh and eighth but we won fourteen-four. I went two for two with three walks—I hadn't made an out in fourteen straight at bats. It was a quiet room for a team that had just tied for the wildcard spot with one game left.

A few reporters were around my car when I got to it but most of them were gathered around Walford by the door—he had gone three for four with two home runs and six RBIs.

"What do you think your chances are?"

It was the same kid who had asked me who I thought had done the paint job the night before. I leaned on the hood and looked across the car at him.

"Not bad. Pretty good."

He nodded at the car.

"You going to get this fixed up?"

"Not yet. I'm okay with it. It kind of grows on you."

He chuckled and we stood there for a second.

"Why do they hate you so much?"

It was weird to hear it out loud. I continued to look at him across the car and then finally I shook my head.

"I don't know. I really don't know."

I opened the driver's side door and started to lean in and he spoke but I didn't catch it. I stood back up.

"What did you say?"

"I said, you're only three off the record."

"What record?"

"Most consecutive plate appearances without making an out."

"That's a real record?"

"I guess so. Earl Averill held it. And a guy names Piggy Ward from the early days but really it's about Earl Averill."

"I've heard of him."

"Good player. Hall-of-Famer. Played on a shitty team in Cleveland for most of his career."

We stood there for a second longer without speaking.

"Well, thanks for letting me know."

"Yeah. Good luck with the record."

The phone was ringing when I got home.

"Ryan?"

"What's up, Amy?"

There was quiet at the other end of the line for several seconds.

"I'm sorry. I shouldn't have called."

"I saw him on the way home."

"What?"

"I saw him. He didn't look good. Tired and old."

"Did you talk?"

"No. He didn't see me. I just watched him get on the train. He almost fell."

She was quiet for a second.

"That was his last trip. He was okay for a year or so, tired but still working on something. He spent most days at the library when he could get Mom to drive him there but then he started getting worse. And then one day he stopped going to the library, came home, got in bed and hardly got out. He lasted another nine years but he was barely there. He didn't even read the papers after that. He used to always read the papers. Papers from all over the country but not at the end. He just waited. Until the last six months when he started talking. Not to Mom. Just to me. "

She was quiet on her end. I wasn't sure what to say.

290

CHAPTER TWENTY-ONE

"He told you everything?"

"I doubt that. He told me about the McKillops, and the girls, and his sister and you. And at the end, he gave me the list. The names and the addresses. It's funny I didn't really believe him until that night in the diner. And then when I got home it faded again. It seemed foolish. And I didn't really believe until I saw you again. And then you went back to Montreal and I had to call you again."

"It's true, Amy."

"I know. What are you going to do?"

"I don't know. I'll decide when the season's over."

"It could last another month."

"It could."

"But who knows w—"

"I'll decide at the end of the season."

She was quiet.

"I shouldn't have called you."

I didn't answer.

"Goodbye, Ryan."

"Yeah."

I listened to the dial tone for a second then hung up. The list was in the drawer beside my bed. I didn't need to pull it out, I knew the six names by heart.

But I did anyway.

And their addresses. There had been a short story on the top name on the list, the name with the line through it. He had been an executive for IBM, divorced with custody of two daughters, and living in suburban Detroit with a new girlfriend. He had been shot in a home invasion while his girlfriend was out and his two daughters were spending the weekend with their mother. There was a picture with the story, a headshot from the announcement of his VP promotion. He looked pleasant, nice even. Three of the others had moved since Georgie had written the list but it wasn't hard to track them from the old address to their new address. They were all still alive. Three had been married but two were divorced. The other two looked like they had always been single, always one initial for the home phone, no wedding or birth announcements or mention of wives or children. I had crossed out the old addresses and printed in the new ones. My printing was smaller and more cramped than the precise almost calligraphic loops and lines that Georgie had used. It was my list now.

* * *

I dove but couldn't get a glove on the ball and it dropped just inside the foul line and skidded into the leftfield corner. I had been playing off the line expecting him to pull and he had gone the other way. The ball rattled around in the corner for a couple of seconds and by the time Tuquet had fired it back into the infield, their leadoff guy was standing at third barely puffing. It would have been a double for most guys but it was a standup triple for the Mets centerfielder—he could scamper. The next batter went the other way and grounded into a fielder's choice—Hiltz took the sure out at first and the runner scored. McKay got the next two batters swinging at big curveballs but we were down one to zero. He was pitching on three days' rest. It had been Stolz's turn in the rotation but McKay was pitching.

The Mets had their number one guy going too, Jason Daniels, but they hadn't had to change their rotation. Daniels was a huge man— six foot five and two hundred and thirty pounds who had been drafted number two out of Cal State Fullerton after playing for the US team in the Pan Am games. He had a great fastball, topping out at ninety-six miles per hour that he threw about half the time, a hard change, a big sweeping curve and a tight slider all of which he could throw for strikes. His first full season in the league he had won seventeen games and now six years in he was one of the top three pitchers in the league and if he could stay healthy a first-ballot Hall-of-Famer. This year he was headed for the Cy Young—he had already won twenty-three games and lost only seven, his ERA was under two and if he managed to get three strikeouts against us he would have three hundred in under two hundred and fifty innings. Balducci still had me batting ninth so I didn't get to the plate until there were two outs in the third inning and his first pitch sent me sprawling in the dirt.

I lay there for a second looking out at the mound but he ignored me, just taking the toss from the catcher and removing his glove to rub at the ball with both hands. I turned to look up at the ump from the ground.

"No warning?"

He shrugged.

"Sure. Stay alert."

I stood up and took my time dusting myself off then stepped back in. The next pitch was meant to catch the inside of the plate but drifted too far inside and I had to lean away. I looked back at the ump again. He spoke without taking his mask off or looking at me.

"You look back at me one more time and every fucking pitch from here on is a strike, Spencer."

The next pitch was outside but he called it a strike. I started to turn but stopped myself. Daniels tried for the same spot again. I was waiting on it and took the ball into right field for a single but then Garcia hit a hard liner back to the mound and the Mets were out of the inning.

McKay didn't have his good stuff and he was pitching with men on base in every inning and gave up runs in the second and third. In the fourth, he loaded the bases with none out but I stabbed a hard liner, then stepped on the bag to double the runner off third. The runner on second had taken off thinking that the ball was getting through I started to snap the ball to second but saw that Cooper, who was filling for Hiltz, hadn't moved to the bag soon enough. If I had thrown the ball would have been into centerfield. I double clutched and then finally made the throw as Cooper realized his mistake and started for the bag but the runner made it back in time. Cooper tossed the ball back to McKay and he swiped at it angrily but didn't catch the ball clean and it squirted out of his glove towards the gap between second and third. Nick chased it down but the runner at second had taken off as soon as he had seen the ball roll away. Nick had to twist and throw off balance while falling and the ball sailed so that I had to leap way above the bag to bring it down and stop the ball from rolling to the stands. The runner at first had started for second, thought better of it but then realized that Cooper was standing watching and not covering the bag and trotted in standing up.

Nick had tried to scramble to his feet to cover second but there wasn't time. I held onto the ball. McKay stepped off the mound and gestured angrily for the ball. I tossed it his way and then moved back to my spot on the infield. McKay stepped up onto the mound to set himself to go into his windup and stood there for a long time looking in at Giannos. I could see his jaw muscles working from where I was standing. He finally took his foot off the rubber and stepped away from the mound. Giannos stood up behind home plate and the umpire stepped out waving his arms. McKay paced around the mound a couple of times staring at the ground and then looked over to where I was standing. He took two steps over in my direction

"We should have had that third out, you fucker."

I just stared back.

"All you had to do was make the throw to second and we're out of the inning, asshole."

He was talking loud enough that every player in the infield could hear.

"You're a team-killer, Spencer. You've been a team-killer since you showed up at spring training."

I was too surprised to reply. I had figured he was angry at Cooper or himself. Nick spoke first. He walked up close to McKay and spoke just loud enough that I could hear.

"Shut up, McKay, you're making an ass of yourself."

McKay didn't even look at him, he just kept glaring at me.

"Fuck off, Fagan."

Nick took a step closer.

"Ryan made a great play on that ball and if your boy hadn't been scratching his ass we would have had the third out. And if you hadn't been such a careless asshole we'd have men at first and second with the force in play instead of men at second and third and having to make the tough out."

McKay still didn't look at him, staring at me. But when he spoke it was to Nick.

"Don't think we haven't heard the stories, Fagan. Spencer your new boy? What is it they say? Don't shit where you eat?"

294

Nick stepped back as if slapped and then started forward. I moved so that I was between them.

"Don't do it, Nick. He's an asshole. It's not worth it."

That seemed to break the spell and Cooper and Giannos and Toner headed for the three of us. Giannos got there first.

"What the fuck is going on here? Have you guys lost you're fucking minds? You're going to get into it here in front of sixty thousand people?"

Giannos stuck out his hand.

"Give me the ball, McKay. Give me the fucking ball."

McKay turned to him red-faced and angry.

"Fuck off, Giannos, this f—"

Giannos grabbed the ball out of his hand and held it up in his face.

"You're going to take this ball and you're going to throw three strikes to the next batter as hard as you can fucking throw them and then you're going to head for the showers and we're going to get somebody else out here to finish off the job. And if you don't do that, I'm going to shove this ball so far up your ass you're going to be coughing red stitching for a month."

That caught McKay's attention.

"I'm not coming out of the ball game."

Giannos spoke a little more softly.

"You've got three pitches left in you, Randy, and then you're done. You know you haven't got your stuff today. It's bullshit luck that things are only as bad as they are. So, get us this last guy, get us out of here just three runs down and let us work our way back into the game."

McKay looked at him for a long time then grabbed the ball out of his hand and walked up on the mound. Giannos looked at the rest of us, "On your toes, boys." Then turned and headed back to the plate. The rest of us drifted into position. McKay threw one pitch, their rookie shortstop got almost all of it, and pushed Garcia to the deepest part of the park where he caught the ball at the wall. I watched Giannos coming off the field—he and Balducci exchanged glances at the top of the stairs and Giannos shook his head. Balducci looked over at his pitching coach and tapped his left arm. Stolz got up in the bullpen.

Stolz pitched well for us, hitting the corners and forcing the Mets to put the ball in play. He gave up a double in the fifth and a single in the sixth but didn't allow anybody past second. Daniels had put nine down in order after my single and I came up again in the bottom of the sixth with two out and nobody on and still down three-zero. He surprised me by starting off with a pitch low and away that just clipped the corner for a strike. The next one was a little further away and low but the ump gave it to him. I didn't look at him but I did look at the plate for several seconds before stepping out to adjust my glove.

"You got a problem, Spencer?"

I didn't answer. I fouled off the next couple of pitches and then he came way inside leaving the count at one and two. He tried to go away with the next pitch but left it up and over the plate and I put it four hundred and twenty feet into the rightfield stands to make it three-one. The crowd went crazy but there was nobody at the plate when I rounded third and nobody standing in the dugout when I got to the top of the stairs. Balducci didn't look at me. Nick caught my eye and nodded.

"Nice swing, Ryan"

It didn't seem to faze Daniels—he struck out on three pitches. Stolz started to fade in the seventh, giving up a walk and a single with one out but rather than bring in Minton, our closer, Balducci pitched Blee Fanteaux, one of our starters. I guess he figured this was our last hurrah, no sense holding him back for games we might not play. It worked. Fanteaux got the next two batters on strikes and the runners didn't move off their bags. Daniels started coming apart in our half of the seventh, loading the bases with one out but then getting Toner to hit into a double-play on a hard smash to short. Fanteaux set the Mets down in order in the eighth and Daniels put the first two batters on base, hitting Cooper and walking Akins who pinch-hit for Fanteaux. I was up next and they brought in their closer. Daniels kept looking in at me as he argued with the manager to let him keep the ball but he lost the argument and they brought in Dean Grover. He was a veteran who could still throw low nineties but his out pitch was a forkball that he could get up around eighty-eight or eighty-nine that dropped like water of a cliff just before the plate. He had blown one of forty-nine save opportunities and that one had been back in May. I took the first fastball off the plate to right and made the score three-two. Garcia walked, Walford and Nick grounded out, Toner stroked a single into short leftfield, I had to hold up at third and Tuquet popped out to end the inning. Minton came in in the ninth. It was the first time he had come into a game all season without the lead. It was a one-two-three inning with all the balls coming to me, a sharp grounder that was an easy play at first, a pop-up to the right of the pitcher's mound that Giannos called for me to take, and a foul into our dugout. Nobody went to the rail to catch me and I toppled over onto the concrete. McKay smirked at me when I stood up. With the ball in my glove. Nobody else would look at me.

Giannos hit the first pitch from Grover into the gap for a double and the Mets get a couple of guys up in the bullpen. Cooper took two forkballs for strikes and then swung at a neck-high fastball and missed by a foot. Now Balducci has to pinch hit for Minton, his best relief pitcher, or let a guy who hasn't swung a bat in anger all season hit for himself. Minton steps in and gets four fastballs. He misses the first two completely, gets a little piece of the third, and misses the fourth pitch by two feet. He looked almost as bad as Cooper. Grover spends a lot of time between pitches three and four, shaking his head about the fact that Minton got wood on his fastball. After they get Minton, Grover, the pitching coach, and the catcher huddle at the mound for several minutes before the ump strolls out to break it up.

I know what the discussion is about—first base is open and I've been on base seventeen straight times without making an out. But I'm the winning run. If I score their season is over. And the next guys up are Garcia, Walford, and Fagan, all guys who can hit. They're going to pitch to me. But carefully. I'm not going to see anything good. But I know that when Grover wastes a pitch he wastes high and away and he's going to waste this one and he throws me a chin-high fastball out over the plate and I swing through it. There's no doubt about it. Grover doesn't turn, his shoulders just slump. The centerfielder turns but he's the only one.

The noise is physical. It seems to make the air waver. I stumble a little going around first and I see Giannos jumping up and down between second and third, thrusting his arms in the air, looking into the dugout, and then back at me, and then he's hugging the third base coach as he rounds third base and the team has poured out towards the plate and Giannos steps onto the plate and then disappears into the crowd of waiting players. I step on second base and I can see that the second baseman is trying to hide tears, his hat pulled lower over his eyes as he starts to walk past me to his dugout. I look back and Giannos has come out of the crowd of players and stepped out in front of home plate, they aren't moving away from the plate like they have all season.

I slow down between second and third, waiting for them to drift away from home plate like they always have. But they don't. They're waiting for me. The third base coach is holding out his fist for a bump but I ignore him. I stop on top of third base and look in at the players. I can see Toner's grinning face above the crowd and Tuquet standing to the side but shouting something and waving, and Balducci's white hair flashing as the player's mill about.

I shake my head at them. I don't think they get it at first. They've forgotten who I am, who they've been. The crowd is still deafening. I know they're shouting at me to keep coming but I can't hear them over the crowd and I stay where I am. The third base coach grabs my arm and tries to pull me along, thinking I'm stunned or frozen by emotion but I shake him off hard. I wave for them to move away from the plate, with both hands like those guys that direct planes. The crowd is confused because I'm not leaving thirdd base, beginning to wonder if they had missed something but the ump behind second base has whirled his hand around his head—'touch em all'. The third base umpire steps in and leans into my ear.

"What are you doing, son?"

But I ignore him. And the team doesn't move, it continues to stand there, waiting. But they've stopped jumping and shouting, they're just standing watching me perched on third base. And then the crowd quiets. It happens in a wave starting with the seats behind our dugout and then spreading out from there and it takes several seconds, maybe ten or twenty, for it to spread across the stadium. For a second it is completely silent and then a voice from the bleachers shouts "You da man, Spencer." There's a burst of laughter but then the crowd quiets again. I shake my head at my team.

"Not a fucking chance. Not now."

I wasn't talking loudly but they could hear me.

"Fuck you. You think this is how it goes? That this is about you? The team? Not a fucking chance. You dug the fucking hole. Six by fucking six. And if I had been willing to step in and lie down you would have buried me. Buried me deep and buried me cold. But now I'm your boy. Now, I'm your guy."

I shook my head again.

"No way. You get the fuck off that plate and let me walk in alone like I have every time this season. This is about me."

Nobody moved from the plate for a second and then Balducci stepped out from the crowd to the front of the plate.

"C'mon son, run it in. It's water under the bridge. Everybody makes mistakes. We're in the playoffs."

I looked over to the dugout. Nick was sitting in his usual spot. He wasn't watching, he had his elbows on his knees looking at something down between his feet, but he seemed to sense that I was looking and looked up at me. He made a small grimace and shook his head and then looked back down. I stepped off the bag and walked straight over to the rail, vaulted it, and ducked into the tunnel. I could hear the crowd noise building, the game was tied and I had made an out on my eighteenth at bat. You and me, Earl.

* * *

The Expos lost in the thirteenth when Nick got caught stealing with the tying run on third and two out. I didn't shower. Just collected my stuff and drove home. And headed out on the road with my list.

299

Acknowledgements

Thanks to Shawn and all the folks at Level Best for your hard work on *Long Train Home.* Thanks to Phil Spitzer for seeing something in the book. And to Jack David of ECW for encouraging words at a time when I needed them. Thanks also to Michel Lalonde for letting me know that it was OK to 'write more'. Most of all to my wife for understanding that Saturday mornings were all mine…and for everything else.

About the Author

Jeff Houlahan was born in Calgary, Alberta and grew up on a series of military bases in Canada and Germany before settling in Ottawa, Canada.He has been a waiter, a security guard (there is nothing less hip than being a nineteen-year-old security guard in full uniform at a midnight showing of *The Rocky Horror Picture Show*), a bartender, made pool liners (a much tougher job than it sounds), delivered mail on Parliament Hill and played guitar in a punk band called The Rainkings.

Along the way, Jeff had a short post-doctoral stint with James Brown, one of the great ecologists of the last 50 years, and the third most famous person with that name. But, for folks with a literary bent, Jim's greatest claim to fame is that he was Barbara Kingsolver's M. Sc. supervisor at The University of Arizona. Barbara received her degree sometime between 1983 and 1985 and published *The Bean Trees* in 1988, so there is a chance that book was in the works while she was studying with Jim.

Today, Jeff lives with his wife Kim in Saint John, New Brunswick and is an ecologist and conservation biologist at the University of New Brunswick. All along he's been writing – short stories, songs, and, over the last dozen years, novels.

www.ingramcontent.com/pod-product-compliance
Lightning Source LLC
Chambersburg PA
CBHW021503110726
47899CB00001BA/277